Libraries of Stevens County
www.thelosc.org
509-233-3016

The Sea House

A Novel

ELISABETH GIFFORD

St. Martin's Press New York

This is a work of fiction. All of the characters, organizations, and events portrayed in this novel are either products of the author's imagination or are used fictitiously.

Extract from 1809 letter to the Editor, *The Times* reprinted with thanks to *The Times*/NI Syndication.

Map by Jamie Whyte

www.stmartins.com

Library of Congress Cataloging-in-Publication Data

Gifford, Elisabeth.
  [Secrets of the sea house.]
  The sea house: a novel / Elisabeth Gifford. — First U.S. Edition.
    p. cm.
  Originally published as: Secrets of the sea house, Rearsby, Leicester ; WF Howes Ltd, 2013.
  ISBN 978-1-250-04334-4 (hardcover)
  ISBN 978-1-4668-4140-6 (e-book)
1. Secrets—Fiction. 2. Bones—Fiction. 3. Mermaids—Fiction. 4. Hebrides (Scotland)—Fiction. I. Title.
  PR6107.I37S43 2014
  823'.92—dc23

2013045689

St. Martin's Press books may be purchased for educational, business, or promotional use. For information on bulk purchases, please contact Macmillan Corporate and Premium Sales Department at 1-800-221-7945, extension 5442, or write specialmarkets@macmillan.com.

First published in Great Britain under the title *Secrets of the Sea House* by Corvus, an imprint of Atlantic Books Ltd.

First U.S. Edition: April 2014

10 9 8 7 6 5 4 3 2 1

To Josh, Hugh, Kirsty and George

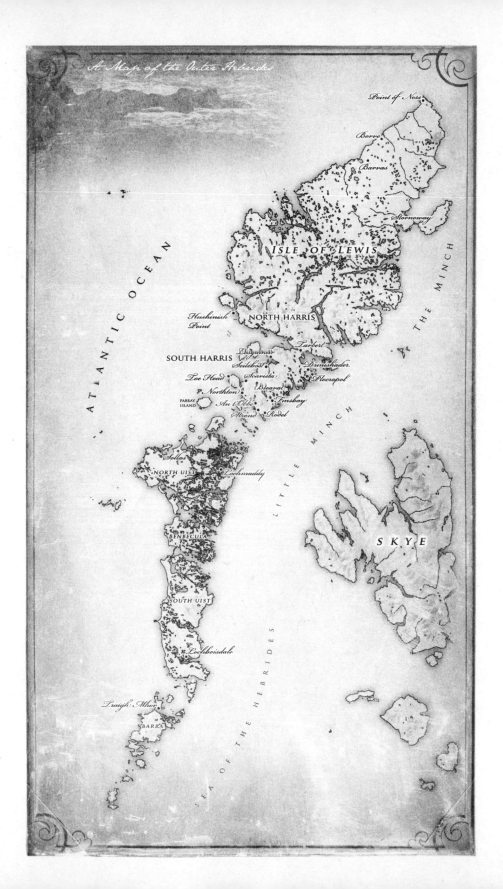

My grandmother's grandmother was a seal woman. She cast off her seal skin, fell in love with a fisherman, had his child, and then she left them. Sooner or later, seal people always go back to the sea.

At least, that's the story that Mum used to tell me.

'But is it true?' I wanted to know.

'It's as true as you and me, Ruthie,' she said. 'There're plenty of people up in the islands that come from the seal people.'

And later I used to think, Of course, that's what must have happened. That's why she left me. She couldn't resist going back to the water, because she was a Selkie.

For a long time, I liked to think that. Because it meant she might come back one day, and then I could go home.

PART ONE

CHAPTER 1

Ruth, 1992

I don't think I had ever felt so piled with gifts as I did that first night we slept in the Sea House, or so excited. I was ready to get up and carry on with the painting there and then. It was completely dark, no slur of city light. I pressed the little light on the alarm. Two a.m.

I curled up closer to Michael's long back. He was so solid in the darkness; his presence filled the room like a comfort. When I first met Michael, I thought he was too tall and elongated, a species I didn't recognise. Then I realised that he was just how he should be, a sapling in a wood, his pale brown hair the colour of winter leaves. And right now, he was exhausted, completely dead to the world.

It had taken months of back-breaking and filthy work to get the old place scraped down to a blank canvas, and then we'd had to start the long haul of repairs ready for us to move in. The truth was that our bedroom and the half-finished kitchen were still the only inhabitable bits, but you could see from the proportions of the Georgian rooms with their elegant windows and carved fireplaces that one day the house was going to be beautiful.

I turned over again, far too awake for two in the morning, and also incredibly thirsty, probably because of the dubious cava from the Tarbert Co-op. I didn't want to get a drink from the bedroom sink: we'd just cleared a dead bird from the tank feeding the upstairs taps.

It was icy when I slid outside the bedcovers. The fire in the bedroom grate had gone out. I went down the stairs as quietly as I could, feeling with my hands along the cold plaster where it was too dark to see.

Down in the kitchen, I filled a mug from the tap, and drank the water as I stared out at the dark shapes of the hills. A glassy moon clear in the black sky. The room was flooded with monochrome shadows, but then the kitchen looked at its best in the dark. You could almost imagine that the humped shape in the corner was a new Aga rather than a builder's old trestle covered with a cloth, a tiny Belling hot-plate and washing-up bowl on top.

Next to the window, the moonlight showed the pale squares of my noticeboard with its To Do lists for every room; snippets of cloth and paint cards; pictures of ideal rooms torn from magazines; a collage of how the Sea House was going to be – one day. I loved sitting at the rickety kitchen table updating the lists, adding and crossing off, enjoying the delicious feeling of our forever home finally rising up from the rather disgusting ruin we'd bought in the dead of winter.

I'd first seen the house by torchlight, running the pale light over the boarded-up windows, the walls cracked and streaked with green damp. We had to force the back door to get in. The air was thick with vegetal rot. Piles of filthy fleeces stacked up in the wreck of a kitchen. Crumbling dirt and debris everywhere. The air had felt so cold it sucked the heat from my face and hands.

I was ready to turn round and go back to London.

'But don't look at the mess,' Michael said. 'Think of it freshly painted, curtains at the kitchen windows, a nice big pine table here.'

Now, with the outside more or less weatherproofed, the rats evicted and the holes in the roof remedied, the debris swept away, and after hours and hours of plastering and painting, we were finally in – and it was possible to imagine that one day, instead of a chilly building site, the Sea House would feel like a real home.

And always the next thought, the one that seemed impossible. When the house was completely ready, we'd come in through the front door, and I'd be holding a small, warm weight, a little sleeping face in a nest of soft shawls. Our child.

I avoided glancing down to the bottom of the noticeboard and the scruffy wad of bills still to be paid. Felt the niggle of worry stir in my stomach.

I tipped the mug up and put it on the draining board – carefully, as the sink was a bit loose from the wall, propped up with some wood offcuts. The flagstones were freezing and starting to make my feet hurt. My shoulders felt pinched by the cold.

There was hardly any moonlight as I crossed the hall to go back upstairs. The new floorboards felt unpleasantly gritty under my bare feet and a freezing draught was coming up from the missing skirting board, bringing with it a clayey odour. I shivered and made for a pool of moonlight on the lower banisters. I put my hand out to take the newel post and felt the cold of the gloss paint under my palm.

That's when I saw it: a quick blur of movement like a tiny wing caught from the corner of my eye. I saw a hand descending on the newel post just after mine.

I froze. A sudden, painful pricking of blood in my feet, the smell of clay sharp in my nostrils, every instinct primed to get out of there. She was so close, so palpably present, I thought she would appear in front of me. I couldn't breathe. My heart was gabbling so hard I thought it was going to give out.

And then she was gone. The air relaxed.

I ran up those stairs, the door to our room half ajar just as I had left it. I got back into bed with a thump and lay close to Michael. He murmured but didn't wake.

I stared into the dark. What on earth had just happened? Some delay in the messages from my eye to my brain. Some silly trick of the mind half roused from sleep had sent me into a stupid panic. Eventually my heart slowed to normal and I'd almost talked myself down, was almost drifting off when I woke up once more, very alert. I opened my eyes onto the darkness. Then why had it felt so intensely real, as if someone else was there in the hallway, standing beside me so closely that for a moment I wasn't sure who I was?

The fear was beginning to seep back in. I felt sick from fatigue, but there was nothing I could do; I stayed alert and awake, listening out to the minute sounds of a silent house, all my senses still primed.

I could hear the waves breaking along the shore like soft breaths. I got up and wrapped a blanket from the chair round my shoulders, went to the window and lifted the wax blind. The moon was completely round in the blackness. There were bright lines of its phosphorescence along the waves, continuously moving through the darkness and then disappearing.

I watched them for a while. After that I felt calmer. Eventually, I got some sleep.

When Michael came in with two mugs of coffee next morning, the sun was already strong through the blinds.

'The wood's being delivered this morning,' he said, picking out a T-shirt and giving it a sniff. He worked his arms into it. 'We might have a floor in the sea room today.'

He sat on the bed, making the mattress bounce, and pulled on his grubby jeans from the day before. I had to cradle my coffee so that it didn't spill on the new duvet. It had an oily bitter smell. I wondered if the jar of Nescafé had gone stale. I put the coffee to one side on the orange box that was covered in a new tea towel for elegance.

'Donny's coming to help pull up the rest of the old boards. Although we're going to dig a channel in the earth underneath to lay a cable first.'

'I'll come down and help,' I said.

'I thought you were going to finish your drawings.'

He leaned over and bashed my chin with a quick kiss. His long, slim arms looked different, the muscles and veins more prominent. He'd worked so hard to get us out of the caravan. He'd hated the little bed that didn't let him stretch out, but I'd got to quite like living in the shelter of the dunes, right next to the deserted beaches and the wide Atlantic rollers that towered up like molten glass in the blue winter air. I was glad that the Sea House was almost as close to the water, just the other side of the dunes, where the green machair broke into sandy waves of undulating silver marram grass. And then the beginning of the wide, flat beaches.

Michael stood up, stretched his long torso and combed his hands through his curly hair. I think the thing that made me fall in love with Michael was the way he stooped to listen to me because he was so tall, as if he really wanted to hear what I was saying; and he was so kind and willowy, his mop of wiry, fair hair like a medieval angel in a picture. He pulled on a jumper, then his grimy overalls. He smiled, slapped his legs, ready to get started.

'So, Donny'll be here in half an hour.'

'I'm getting up. It's just, I didn't sleep well.'

'Yeah, I know. I'm constantly thinking about the next thing to do, seeing us open, the first guests rolling up. And I still can't believe we live in this house, in this fantastic place.'

I could hear him whistling as he went downstairs.

I got the fire going again in the grate and had a horrible cold wash in the sink in the corner of the bedroom. I pulled on my jeans and a flannel shirt, feeling guilty that it was Michael who was doing all the back-breaking work, while I got to sit in the only good room and draw lizards. The book was on reptile neurology and I'd just started the last chapter: 'The Brain and Nervous System of *Podarcis erhardii*, commonly known as Erhard's Wall Lizard'. Michael had got used to sleeping in a room with the dry aquarium and its lizard family, and the faint acrid smell of waxy chrysalises that collected at the bottom of the tank.

I lifted the insulation wadding and looked through the side of the lizard tank to see how they were getting on; immediately, a flick of a tail and a scuttle; the two lizards flashed into a different position and then froze. The thing about lizards is you can never tame them. They have a very small, very ancient brain that operates on one principle: survival. They spend their whole lives on high alert, listening out for danger, scanning their surroundings with their lizard eyes, their toe pads picking up every vibration in the earth, ready to send back one message to the brain cortex: flee, flee now. They don't consider, or think; they simply reach a certain overload in feedback criteria and then run. They are sleek little bundles of vigilant self-preservation with an evolutionary strategy so effective, you can find a lizard brain tucked inside every developed species.

I pushed back the sleeve of my jumper and carefully lowered my hand into the glass tank. There was a flicker and they both scuttled to the other end in a flurry of sand and tiny sideways straggle legs. But there was nowhere else for them to go. I slowly moved my hand towards the corner; another quick scuffle, and my hand closed round one of them. I could feel the little whip of muscle working inside my palm and the scratching of its back legs.

I held the chloroform bottle against my chest with the top of my arm and unscrewed the top. Then I covered the opening with a wad of cotton wool and tipped it over with my free hand. I held the damp cotton over the struggling lizard. Waited till it stopped. I put the lid back on the bottle, and sat down at the desk. The lizard was lying across the piece of card, its arms and legs something between a minute plucked chicken and a cartoon frog in its anthropomorphic arms-up pose. I picked up the scalpel and started to slit along the belly skin, ready to map out the nerves.

I realised that the banging and splintering from downstairs had stopped. I have an amazing ability to sit through noise and not notice it once I begin to work, but the sudden silence was unsettling. Not even the sound of digging. Something's come up, I thought, and went downstairs with my arms folded. I only hoped it wasn't more problems. Michael's father had lent us enough to get the manse ready to take our first bed and breakfasters, but we needed to be open as soon as possible if we were to keep up the payments.

I made my way down through the hallway, crossing my arms across my chest against the chill. Down in the sea room, every one of the square sash windows was filled with views of the Atlantic so that the place always felt more sea than room. Michael and Donny were standing thigh deep among the floor joists, looking at something. When Michael saw me coming in he didn't look pleased.

'What is it?' I asked. 'Just tell me the worst. Is it dry rot?'

Donny looked upset and serious. Michael was white under his summer tan and the grime from ripping up the old wood. It was freezing in there. There was a fusty smell of rot and damp.

'I don't want you to look,' he said. 'You won't like it.'

'What is it? Oh God, not another rat.'

I walked round the edge of the walls where there were still some floorboards down and then lowered myself into the floor space between the joists. The floor was damp and sandy and littered with dirt and debris. Michael and Donny were standing one each side of a small dark-brown box, or rather a little metal trunk that was rusted away in places. It had evidently just been dug up from the sandy soil.

The lid was open.

I squeezed next to Michael so that he had to hold on to the joist behind him.

'Don't,' he said.

I squatted down and looked inside. The earth smelled very sour and close there. I could see a jumble of tiny bones mixed in with a nest of disintegrating woollen material. There was some kind of symmetry to them; a tiny round skull, like a rabbit or a cat. The bones had a yellowish tinge, scoured clean by beetles and other organisms that had got into the trunk as it rusted, probably over many years. I wondered why someone had buried a cat under the house. Then I tipped my head sideways, frowned.

This was no family pet or small animal. No, this was the skull of a human baby, but everything so tiny that it must have been born either very underweight, or premature. My eyes traced along the arm bone and then down the bones of one of the legs.

Something was wrong. Where was the other leg? I shuffled closer, and noted the strange thickness of the single leg bone, the long central indentation along its length, and then I realised that it wasn't so much that any of the bones were missing but that both legs had been fused into one solid mass, the feet barely there and oddly splayed out like tiny appendages.

My heart missed a beat. I couldn't believe what I was looking at.

CHAPTER 2

Ruth

The same day we found the remains under our house, the police arrived from Tarbert. They parked several cars on the grass in front, churning the green turf with muddy tyre tracks.

As I watched them through the kitchen window, for a moment I was there again, a child standing alone beside the canal, watching from my hiding place behind the police van while they worked to bring something up from under the water. I felt dizzy, my breath short as I saw the muddied body rising up from the water again.

A wave of nausea made me grip the back of the kitchen chair. I dipped my head and concentrated on breathing. After a while, I straightened and looked around the kitchen.

Michael went out to see them and I left him to it. I focussed on sorting out the mess in hand, clearing away the breakfast things, but I couldn't stop shivering.

I felt a hand on my shoulder and jumped.

'You going to be okay?' Michael said.

'It's just cold in here with them going in and out of the front door all the time.'

'I'll ask them not to leave it open.'

For the rest of the morning, Michael kept shooting worried, sideways glances in my direction each time he came in.

Michael knows about my past of course. It was always out in the open. On the first day we met, I told him: I was brought up in a children's home. After Mum died. After she drowned herself.

He knows, and he doesn't know. So many things I'll never tell him about those years. Things I don't even tell myself any more.

I pulled on an old jumper that Michael had left hanging behind the kitchen door and clutched a mug of tea in my frozen hands. I could hear them tramping in and out, their voices calling, doors slamming.

I went out into the hallway and saw the tracks of brown mud being brought in by the police, staining the new hall floorboards before we'd had a chance to seal them clean with layers of varnish. Sounds of them digging deeper under the floor coming from the sea room. Trembling with anger, I went back into the kitchen and closed the door.

'I'm afraid it will be at least two more days before Forensics arrive from Inverness,' said Sergeant MacAllister, coming into the kitchen where Michael and I were holed up together eating lunch, pretending to live a normal life. 'Perhaps it would be better if you moved out for a few days, until we can take the remains away.'

The caravan felt damp and unused when we went back. It smelled like the inside of an old biscuit tin. And it was freezing in there, even with the paraffin heater on. Every surface I touched leached the heat from my skin.

The day was now wasted. I sloshed formaldehyde into the prepared lizard's tray and slid it into the bottom of the tiny caravan fridge.

'I can't believe we're being driven out of our own home by that thing,' I said to Michael as we lay in the cramped bed.

'They'll take it away soon, and given time, we'll forget it was ever there.'

He sounded so certain and so confident. We huddled together, waiting to feel warm, waiting for sleep.

The next day, high winds came in. I woke up to the stale smell of the caravan. The memory of the rusting trunk and the bones inside like the remains of a small animal made me feel too nauseous to eat any of the porridge that Michael had made.

Michael went back to the house to carry on papering the upstairs bedroom, and so he was there when the call came in from the police about the forensic team who were supposed to be coming over from the mainland. I heard the wind slam the caravan door against the van. He came in looking gloomy, his hair wet and blown about by the squally rain.

'Ferry's being held up in Uig for the weekend.' He sat down at the tiny caravan table, the water running off his yellow sailing jacket. 'We're not going to be back in the house any time soon I'm afraid, love.'

'You're dripping on the paper,' I said, irritated that nothing was going right. 'This is going to set us back weeks. Could jeopardise us opening in time for next season, and starting to pay off the loan.'

I glanced up; saw Michael's face anxious and white.

'Well, there's nothing we can do till they take the … you know… the remains away.' He sighed. He turned a drawing of the lizard's nervous system round and looked at it. 'How's it going? This looks beautiful, like the veins of a leaf.'

'At least when these are finished we'll get paid.'

'I'd better get on too. We're out of woodchip and we need more paint. Donny and I are going to drive up to the store in Tarbert.'

I kissed his cold, wet cheek and dabbed at the sploshes he'd left on the table.

For the next hour, I worked solidly on the illustration, absorbed in minutely delineating the nerve pathways and intricate blood vessels that lay ready to flood the lizard's muscles with blood at the first semaphoring of danger.

All the while, the wind thumped vengefully on the side of the van. I could feel the compressions of air like waves of dizziness, the vibrations travelling through the table. As I took up the scalpel and started to open the tiny muscles in the lizard's forearm, a vicious blow thudded into the van; I jumped and sliced into my thumb, dropped the knife and swore.

I found a plaster, struggled with the sticky adhesive.

For a moment I caught a whiff of Mum's talcy smell as she had unwound a strip of plasters; a memory of how she'd leaned over to wash my gouged knee, the lilt of her voice as she took out the playground grit. She was telling me about the island siths, the scattered boulders left by ancient glaciers that changed at dusk into funny, stupid creatures. The crinkly orange plaster neatly fastened to my skin, the wound clean and smelling of Germolene, she had bent over and kissed my head, told me I was her *mo ghaol.*

Mum came from the islands, though she brought me up in London. I grew up in a block of council flats with long brick balconies that smelled of bleach and stairwells that smelled of wee.

She never told me which island she came from exactly.

I snapped the first-aid tin shut with my good hand and manhandled it back into the little cupboard. I sat back down in front of the drawings but the rain had come in like buckets of grit being poured over the roof. It was impossible to concentrate.

I sat watching the flattened marram grass through the blurred window. Then I took a fresh piece of paper and began to sketch out another anatomical drawing, from what I could remember of that poor child in its makeshift, rusty coffin. I stared at what I'd drawn, at the bony appendage where legs should have been. I thought about the child's mother. Wondered if it was she who had dug down into the earth beneath our house, covered the little trunk over, nailed down the boards.

As I sat tapping my pencil on the Formica table, it occurred to me that I knew someone I could ask about such an odd foetal mutation. I gave a little laugh not to have thought of it before. After I'd rooted around for the number of my old anatomy professor in London, I decided to go back over to the Sea House where our new phone was sitting on a chair in the hallway. I hesitated for a moment, knowing that Michael and Donny weren't there, but roundly scolding myself for being so weak-minded, I wrapped up in a huge oilskin jacket of Michael's and walked over to the house – or rather I was bodily driven there by the strength of the wind.

I closed the Sea House door behind me, glad to be out of the rain, and hung the dripping oilskin over the banister. I was ready to feel purposeful about calling Professor Carter. I turned round to get the phone, my eyes glancing back over the cold space of the hallway. The same tightening in the air. The anxiety seeping in again, creeping through the systems of my body; my heart was starting to hammer; my hands felt clammy and slippery. Once more, I was overwhelmed by an urgent and unpleasant instinct to get right out of there.

But this time, I wasn't going to let her get to me. I pulled the phone number out of my pocket, picked up the receiver and started to dial.

I waited in the empty hallway for someone to answer, tensing the muscles in the back of my neck against the cold air on my skin. Against her. I knew it was a she. And I understood something else – this child was no newborn. She was older, knowing.

And I wanted her gone. I listened to the phone ringing somewhere in London, and felt a flood of relief as I heard Professor Carter's sensible voice answer.

We talked for quite a long time. He said that he'd heard of such a condition, but it was very rare. He promised to get some information together and send it in the post.

'Don't forget, Ruth,' he said, 'any time you can make Christmas dinner again. We miss you.'

I put the phone down and let myself out of the front door.

Speaking with him on the phone had left me feeling a bit homesick for the professor and his wife. That first Christmas at university, when the halls of residence cleared and everyone went home, they had rounded up all the strays with nowhere to go. It was the best Christmas I'd had for years, even though it was shadowed by an odd resentment, a memory of the broken train sets and scraggy-haired Sindy dolls wrapped up in Christmas paper and left in a giant scrum in the dining-room hall of the home. No idea who sent those parcels.

But then if I hadn't hated the children's home so completely, I would never have spent so much time hanging out in the local library.

You don't want to live with twenty-nine teenage girls like me. It took a while to learn how to fit in. I got steel rings from Woolworths; I showed them I could give as good as I got when cornered in a fight. I cut my hair off, got workmen's steel-capped boots and a black Crombie coat – skinhead gear.

Where do you go when you've no real home to go to? Hours and hours walking around the city, my hands bright red with cold. Where do you go when you're the sort of person people can overlook, forget about – the sort of person anything can happen to, and no one cares?

One afternoon, in a freezing November fog, I'd walked off the streets into the marble halls of a London library, the quiet air spiced with the smell of old books, and everything else just fell away

I liked the reference section best. Running my hand along the smooth spines, I'd take a book out at random. A whole world of things I hadn't known. That's how I got the grades to read Biology at university.

Year Zero. University. You could be anyone. I lost the monkey boots and the steel rings; and it seemed like I finally lost the fug that they said we home kids always carried on our clothes in school. I turned up on freshers' day in a crowd of endless new faces, wearing my brand-new jeans and a coat bought with my grant money.

The campus libraries were modern, made of white concrete and glass, and full of people who might be just like me, or perhaps I could be like them. It was all to invent, to create, and no one was more hard-working than me.

In my second term, I met Michael in a laundromat. He carried my washing and his washing back to the halls of residence. I thought he was mad, and I thought he was handsome – in a woolly jumper way, like one of the lecturers; and so clean and gentle. I watched him manhandling both bags. He had such a polite, soft voice – posh even.

He had the gift of caring; it radiated off him like a warmth. First bite at the apple of happiness when I kissed Michael.

The day we got married, there were no family guests on my side of the church. We filled it with friends from university. Professor Carter and his wife came.

My hands were beginning to lose their chill as I walked across the grass back to the caravan. The air actually felt warmer outside the house, and soft and damp now that the rain had passed over. In the distance, I noticed a tiny van approaching along the coast road. Squinting at it, I was relieved to make out a police van. The ferry must have managed to sail from Uig after all. They'd be coming to take away the remains.

'One thing I know from rummaging around in boxes of bones in the zoology department, that child must have died at least a hundred years ago,' I said to Michael as we sat in the Sea House kitchen once more.

'Ruth, it's gone. I think we should stop talking about it now,' Michael said through a mouthful of toast.

'I don't know how you can say that. How can you stand it, not knowing exactly what happened here?'

He got up and started running water in the washing-up bowl. 'I grew up in a house that was a priory in medieval times. An archaeologist friend told my dad once that there were probably dead monks buried in our garden. But if there were, they never bothered us. Ruth, it's pointless thinking about something that's over.'

I sat on at the table, dabbing my finger in a pool of honey till Michael took the plate away.

I went over to dry the dishes. I stacked them on the trestle table, looking out through the kitchen window towards the little white church. Dougal, the minister, had parked his car outside.

We bought the Sea House from the church board. It had been the church manse originally, until it became too expensive to heat and they built a nice pebbledash bungalow for the minister down in Tarbert. So its official address was the Manse, but the few people who lived in the sparse and scattered village of Scarista always called it the Sea House, *Tigh na Mara*. It stood away from the other houses, at the edge of the miles of empty, undulating grasslands that were surrounded by a half circle of hills. It was so close to the sea that sand from the dunes blew into the hallway.

Wherever you stood in the house, you heard the soft breaths of the waves. The view from the front of the house showed water so turquoise and sand so white that it looked like a holiday poster for the Bahamas – except with ragged sheep wandering the beach instead of people in swimsuits.

Ideal for a holiday business – until now.

'I think I might walk over and ask Dougal some questions. There must be records of who lived here once.'

Michael sighed.

I walked up to the church past the walled-in graveyard. The fancier headstones, now toppling at crazy angles, had been placed importantly on the top of a rise in the grass. At the base lay the poorer stones, little more than dug-up rocks, and with no inscriptions. There were also newer, sharp-cut headstones, standing in municipal rows down near the road – and plenty of room to bury a baby properly under the turf of the churchyard.

The church was empty, silent. Michael liked to go along to the Gaelic services; he said he found them meditative, calming even, but sitting through the foreign sounds of their psalm singing created a mounting pressure in my chest that made me want to stand up and protest. Having lived on Harris now for a few months, I was starting to get a fair idea of why Mum might have hidden herself away in London, coming as she did from this strict religious community that locked up the children's swings on Sundays and had no concept of an unmarried mother other than in biblical terms. It made me feel irritable and argumentative every time I met poor old Dougal the vicar.

I found Dougal in the vestry. He was standing on a chair, emptying out a large cupboard in the wall. As always, he wore a black suit, his white hair and pink face made even brighter above the white vicar's collar. His elderly skin had a surprising smoothness to it, as if it was washed clean and back to innocence each morning by the island rain.

'Ah, Ruth, there's you,' he said, getting down carefully from his chair. 'What can I help you with? And I wanted to tell you how sorry I am for all your trouble with the manse. We had no idea.'

'Thanks, Dougal, but actually that's why I've come to see you. I was wondering if there might be some old records in the church, some information about the people who used to live in our house, say about a century ago?'

'Sergeant MacAllister was asking me just the same thing and so I'm here to get the old ledgers out. This cupboard can't have been emptied properly for years. You could give me a hand.'

He balanced his solid frame on the rickety chair again and began passing things down. I took a pile of floppy green hymn books, a stack of missionary society pamphlets in thick Victorian print, armfuls of parchment-coloured ledgers. 'I think that's everything,' he said, leaning further into the cupboard. 'Although…' I heard something heavy falling onto wooden board. He pulled out a small bundle wrapped in a cloth and banged off the dust. He handed it down to me and stretched his arm to the back of the cupboard again.

He stepped down and placed a small metal lion on the table. It was a kind of paperweight, the dull greenish yellow of old brass. It needed a good shine with metal polish.

The bundle was wrapped in brown velvet. The cloth felt old and silky and gave off the smoky odour of mildew as I folded it back. Inside was a notebook marbled with blues and reds, and a square glass bottle with a line of dried ink. There was also an old-fashioned ink pen, nothing more than a wand of mother-of-pearl with a nib; faint layers of light glowed as I turned it.

'This looks like a minister's notebook for sermons,' said Dougal as he flicked through the pages, 'but there's no name.' He passed me the book. I scanned the insides of the covers.

'There's a date though, look,' I said, pointing to the corner of a page, '1860.'

He pulled a ledger from the pile on the table. The faded black ink of the entries had sunk into the paper with a yellow bleed. He counted back until he came to 1860.

'There you are: the Reverend Alexander Ferguson, minister in Scarista in 1860.'

'So these must have belonged to him.' The edges of the mother-of-pearl pen were fluted for decoration. It seemed rather pretty for a man.

Dougal was still frowning as he continued to scan the ledger. 'According to this, he was in sole charge of the parish at just twenty-six. Not an easy task for a man so young. And I see Ferguson wasn't a married minister, so the child couldn't have been his.'

'We can't rule him out just because he wasn't married,' I said. Then, noticing how embarrassed Dougal looked, I quickly added, 'Who else was living in the house at that time?'

He hunted through the pile of ledgers and found a slim accounts book for the manse farm. He spread it out to show a list of staff and their wages for September 1860: Margaret Kintail, Moira Gillies, Effie MacAllister, several male farmhands.

'Maybe Ferguson never knew what was buried beneath his floor,' I said, thinking aloud. 'Perhaps the baby was the child of one of these men and one of the maids. But why on earth would they choose to bury it under the floorboards of the manse study?'

I started making some notes from the ledger on the back of an old parish newsletter.

'Dougal, would you mind if I took Alexander's notebook with me to read? I'll bring it back.'

'I'm sure Sergeant MacAllister isn't going to be interested in a book of sermons, and I can always look at it later. In fact, why don't you take the writing set back to the house? After all, it must have belonged there once, and I know you young people like these old things.'

Part of me hesitated – a vague fear of making too many connections back to the past. Decided I was being silly.

'That's really kind,' I told him. 'We've nearly finished restoring the fireplace in the sea room, and these would look wonderful on the mantelpiece.'

Dougal came outside with me and we stood in the wind looking over the graveyard. He looked worried. It felt like there was something more he wanted to say.

'I was sorry to hear about your mother, Ruth,' said Dougal. 'You were very young to lose her, and in such sad circumstances.'

Taken aback that he should suddenly refer to her like that, I realised there must have been some conversation between him and Michael.

'Oh well,' I said. 'Thanks.'

'And it must have been so very hard for you, with your father never being around.'

I shrugged. 'Actually, Dougal, I prefer not to talk about all that.'

'I wanted to let you know, Ruth, that once the remains are returned to the island, we will be holding a proper burial for the baby.'

I nodded, and we stood in silence for a while, watching the frantic drama of the breakers. The sea was mountainous with navy blue waves, the spray blowing off like fine white hair streaming in the wind.

'And I was thinking,' he said, 'I could be holding a house blessing for you if you would like me to. It might help you to feel more settled, after all that has happened.'

'How do you mean, a house blessing?'

'When people move in to a new house, I often come over and pray in each room to bless it. A fresh start.'

'I don't mean to be rude, Dougal, but that's not really my sort of thing. But thank you anyway.'

He smiled and nodded, and we shook hands.

I walked away, half tempted to turn back and say, Yes, come over right away and do your house-blessing thing, but it smacked too much of superstition and magic and holy water, and I was still angry with myself for letting my stupid nervousness taint how I felt about the Sea House. No, if there was an unquiet spirit in our house, the only way to lay it to rest was to find out exactly what had happened to that child.

A few days later, I heard something land on the floor in the hallway and ran down to get the post. Professor Carter had sent a wad of photocopied pictures and articles. I took them back to bed, passing them over to Michael as I read through them.

'There's a condition called Mermaid Syndrome then?'

I nodded. 'The correct name is Sirenomelia.' I showed him a grainy photo of a large specimen jar containing a baby floating in preserving fluid, its round face placid, eyes closed in sleep. The torso was extended to a tapering sleeve of flesh twisted slightly to one side. At the end were two malformed tiny flipper feet. It wasn't pretty. He pulled a face.

'So this is how the mermaid baby would have looked?'

I nodded.

'Grief! Poor thing.'

The article explained that the child had been born with a large vein missing from its lower body. The mother's blood supply to the legs had probably been so poor *in utero* that the infant's legs had simply failed to develop. The child had no kidneys and several other organs were underdeveloped. It would have been able to live for only a few hours before it passed away from its fatal mutations.

I read on and found that the condition was often linked to poor health in the mother: some illness, or exposure to a toxic chemical, perhaps poor nutrition. There was no incidence — and here I leaned forward and felt my heart beating too hard — no record of the condition being hereditary. No child had ever survived to pass on the gene. It was an extremely rare condition, each case a new mutation that died out almost as soon as it was born.

The relief I felt on reading that made me realise that I had actually been wondering if there was some kind of link between my mother's wild sea people stories and the child under our house. I picked up the picture of the baby floating in the jar, and shivered.

We finally heard from the police about the post-mortem findings. The report showed that the baby had died of natural causes, just as Professor Carter had anticipated, and since it had happened such a long time ago, the coroner had recommended that the case be closed.

But I was more determined than ever to find out who'd been involved. Who had taken the decision to take up the floorboards, dig down into the compacted earth?

It would have taken such a lot of effort to do that. And why leave the child under our house when there was a whole island out there where a child could be tucked away in a quiet grave?

The old-fashioned cursive handwriting and dense theology made Alexander Ferguson's book of sermons hard going. Each sermon was transcribed into a wall of impenetrable Gaelic. I realised with a pang that Mum would have been able to read all that. I could only remember tiny snatches of her Gaelic. I remembered '*mo ghaol*', 'dear one', and a few other words she used to say when she was angry – words that she told me not to repeat – but that was it.

I was pleased to discover the occasional journal entry in English: nature observations; notes on Alexander's daily life. Here the writing was looser, snippets of comments and reflections where you could almost hear Alexander's voice. I flicked through the book to see if I could find more, the thin breath of the paper fanning my wrist. I realised that a couple of the pages were a loose insert. I carefully took them out.

The thicker piece of paper seemed to be a letter, copied out from *The Times* newspaper. Even in Ferguson's time, the article would have been some fifty years old. I read on, blinked, then read it through again. A schoolmaster in Reay was reporting a sighting of a mermaid. I gave a half laugh, and turned the page over. On the back was a list of three further sightings with names and dates.

The second piece of paper was thin enough to act as tracing paper. Opening it out, I found some rather fine anatomical drawings. I turned the paper round, held it closer. The upper body of each one was human, but the lower part tapered to the bone structure of assorted sea mammals. It was as if someone had tried combining two skeletal systems to create the mythical form of a merman. I could see they didn't really make sense at the join. I shook my head. Why on earth was Ferguson inventing mermaid skeletons?

When I showed the letter to Michael, he whistled. I called up Dougal on the phone.

'Oh yes,' he said, seemingly unfazed. 'There were a lot of mermaid sightings in the old days. Not so much now, of course, now that we know better. But you know, don't you, that there is the grave of a mermaid, down in Benbecula, in Father Mac's parish?'

'Really?'

'Oh yes.'

'But it can't have been a real mermaid. What on earth did they see to make them think that? Dougal, what do you think it was that the schoolmaster in Reay actually saw?'

'That, we may never know. But evidently our Reverend Ferguson was asking the same questions.'

I put the phone down feeling a bit shaken. I'd always accepted that Mum's tales of sea people were some kind of old fairy story – nice, but nothing significant. But now I was beginning to wonder. Suddenly, I felt a lot less smug about being able to explain the baby skeleton. Frowning, I went back to Alexander's notebook and began to read through the journal entries with close attention.

CHAPTER 3

Alexander Ferguson, 1860

As soon as I heard the news from my servant girl, I hurried to Benbecula, but with the tides being difficult and the journey through the
Uist isles long, I arrived too late. The wake was already finishing, the
crofters almost all dispersed to their homes, and the minister refused
my request to have the coffin dug up and opened, so that I might make
an examination of the body. I thus made a further arduous journey,
returning across the estuary to enlist the help of the harbour sheriff
in Lochmaddy but he refused to go above the minister, and made it
quite clear that he looked upon my request to disinter the mermaid
– if such she be – with great suspicion.

The hour was growing late, and on the islands darkness is complete
unless there is a moon, so I found lodgings at the harbour inn. While
my dinner was being prepared, I took the opportunity to walk out
and enquire among the fishermen if there were any among them who
had seen the mermaid while she was still alive, or had had occasion to
see her body before it was buried. By their frowns and puzzled faces
they implied that my poor Gaelic was causing them great difficulty
in understanding my questions, but as they turned away, I saw some
of the men cross themselves. They understood me perfectly well. As
soon as they decently could, each one of them turned his back and
resumed stacking his ropes and creels. The water in the harbour beyond
them was unusually still, a great sheet of red glass in the setting sun

and I noted that there was a second black inn and customs house perfectly inverted in the water. Eventually, the silence grew long and I had no choice but to return to the inn's bare little dining room and wait for my supper.

I found the landlady, however, a devoted gossip, and kindly disposed to help me improve my Gaelic. During the course of my dinner she settled herself at the far end of the table. 'It was the MacKinnons who found the poor lady, lying dead on the shore. And I heard that Eilidh MacKinnon touched her with her own hand, just as I am touching this plate now.'

I slept between somewhat damp and musty sheets that night but I slept most contentedly. The landlady had given me directions to find the aforementioned persons, and my feelings may well be imagined as I lay in the dark and anticipated speaking with the very people who had seen and even touched this as yet scientifically unrecorded creature.

I was awake with the first light and composed a letter to the Dean of Science at the university in Edinburgh, requesting him to order an exhumation. I assured him that there were eyewitnesses who could attest to the existence of this half-fish, half-human specimen, and though I could not lay claim to complete certainty in the matter, it was my belief that the creature might hold the key to some previously undiscovered branch of the evolutionary chain.

This was an opportunity such as may not come twice in a man's life, I assured him, and I urged the Dean to kindly dispatch his reply with every haste.

I left the letter with the landlady, along with an entire shilling to deliver it to the mail boat, and rode out towards the sea the happiest man in Scotland.

Of course, at that time I was not to know that the Dean's reply would be most discouraging. He refused to order the raising of the mermaid's coffin and wrote that I was too ready to give credence to 'the fanciful tales of fairies and legends held by the aboriginal peoples of the Western Islands in their state of ignorance'. He suggested, now that my health was improving, I should consider making arrangements to return to a parish nearer to Edinburgh, where I could study once more alongside men of science and reason, and so continue perhaps with my classification of molluscs and crustaceans from the coast of Fife.

By late afternoon I had arrived back at the western seaboard of Benbecula. After enquiring at some of the black houses – which a visitor may easily mistake for a pile of stones, since they are surely some of the least civilised habitations in Europe – I was able to locate the whereabouts of the women mentioned by the landlady. I rode out to Traigh Mhor and left my horse grazing while I walked across a vast plain of wet sand that mirrored the wide brightness of the sky, to where two black figures were stooping to fill their buckets with periwinkles.

Once they understood my request, the women were very anxious to share their story. They asked for no coin. They appeared to be simple women of good character, deeply affected by the encounter. The details were as follows.

On the morning of June the sixteenth, 1860, Kate MacKinnon, and her mother, Eilidh MacKinnon, were gathering periwinkles and other seaware from the shores of the island of Benbecula on the Atlantic seaboard, when they were astonished to see a woman, visible only from the waist up, gliding along a little way out to sea, her lower portion hidden under the water. She swam in closer, whereupon a huge tail could be seen wavering beneath the sea's surface. The creature remained with them a good hour, travelling up and down the shore as the women worked. Since the creature had a cheerful face and called out to them in a kindly voice, they called back to her, although they were unable to understand her language. They were sorry to see her swim away and not return.

The following morning, after a great storm, the two women returned to their work on the shore and were grieved indeed to discover the mermaid lying dead on the white sands. She was of small, adult size, her face clearly a human face, and with long black hair. The skin of her naked body, however, was unlike that of any man or woman living, being smooth and '*sleekit*' as the skin of a seal. She did not have legs, but in their place, a tail covered in a thin, loose skin. One of the women told me that she had touched the tail, which felt as smooth as a fish, but without any fish-like scales.

I made my way back to Harris by boat and horseback, feeling increasingly feverish and cold, and once again fell prey to doubts: how could it be that I, a man of science and education, was willing to entertain a belief in mermaids? And yet, I remonstrated with myself, are we not, as scientists, called to consider the evidence? Could it not be possible that these persistent rumours and sightings were reports of some undiscovered link in the transmutation of species, the type of link that had been recently predicted by Mr Darwin? Might there be, visiting these very shores, a creature as fantastical as any newly uncovered, ancient fossil – but which was not yet extinct?

I returned to the manse very late, the house a black shape against the dark sky. I was glad to see a lamp still lit in the hallway. After so many hours of mental speculation beneath the host of white coals in the night sky, it seemed to me that I had taken fever less from the cold than from attempting to encompass the whole of Creation within my own small brain. Dizzy and aching, I fell rather than alighted from my horse and was heartily glad to see the maid come out carrying a lantern.

I was gratified to see that she had waited up for my arrival though it was not many hours till morning. In spite of an inauspicious start, my faith in her was beginning to pay off, evidenced by her daily progress towards civilisation and thoughtfulness.

I also noted with a sigh, as she helped me unbutton my wet great-coat – my fingers too numb and cold to achieve this small task myself – that many were the days when I would wish to see the evidence of such progress in myself.

As I pulled off my boots and left them to steam in front of the fire, I was forced to admit that there were personal reasons for my determination to discover any truth behind such rumours of sea people. For when I was a child, my dearest grandmother taught me not only her native Gaelic but also the stories braided into that tongue. My mother expressly forbade such superstition, but many were the evenings when the old lady held me spellbound with the old tales while the Aberdeen mists came in round the house and the ships' horns boomed down in the harbour. She insisted my own black hair was dark and *sleekit* because all Selkie children are born covered with such hair, though, she said, it falls away quickly from the rest of the body.

As I grew older, I dismissed my grandmother's stories as the innocent ramblings of the uneducated. But now, living in the islands, where the stories of the sea people seemed to be but yesterday's news, I felt compelled to follow through with my enquiries – only trusting that in seeking out the truth of the matter, I would not thus destroy my own reputation, or indeed, my own peace of mind.

CHAPTER 4

Moira, 1860

The first day I came to the house of Reverend Ferguson, he looked down at my bare feet and said, 'We must get you some boots, Moira, my dear.'

So he sent off to Glasgow and they came in a brown paper parcel, and they fitted me well longways, but they never did fit me for width. So he wrote off again to the shop that sent them, asking if they had any wider boots, but they replied that it was my feet that was wrong, not their boots, since feet didn't ought to have been so wide in a woman.

The Reverend stuffed them with wet paper to make the leather stretch a little, but even so they were still sore to my feet. When not serving at the table, I pulled loose those laces and always kicked them off whenever I went out on the grass.

I knew I had good feet. Where I come from, forty miles away from here out in the Atlantic, everyone had good strong feet. My father, he had powerful big ankles, standing steady on the cliff face as he tucked the gannets under his belt like a fat skirt. Uisdean and me, we used to lie on the turf, put our heads in the wind and peer over the clifftop and watch the sea boiling a thousand feet away below us – almost as far away as the sky above. And there, down on the crags, my father, standing steady as he eased the bamboo pole along, slipped the noose over the guga's neck. A tug on the rope to Finlay to say he was climbing up, and we watched him as he made his careful, easy way, back up the cliff face.

When they cleared us off the island, my father said we would not go to Canada with the others. So the factor of Lord Marstone promised us a home, on his own big island. 'John,' he told my father, 'I have long valued you as a tenant. I will make sure that your new home will be far more suitable than this place. You will have a shop you can walk to.'

So we had a village shop ten miles away, and no road, and no money to buy bread and tea. He put us away on the Minch side of his big island, where the sour soil poisoned the crops and rotted the potatoes in the little bits of bog between the rocks. And we soon found out that our improvements in circumstances was a hovel that had killed all those who lived in it before us. There never was such a badly built, cobbled together pile of stones, more tumbling down than standing.

The coughing disease was in the walls. That's why it was empty. I watched them all die, my dear ones. I got tired of the long walk across the island to where the soil is soft enough to bury a coffin. The factor came and burned the house down when he thought we was all gone. He did not see me watching him from up on the cairn as he fired the roof.

After, the world forgot I was ever there. There was talk of a witch haunting the marshes up on Bleaval, of ghostly fires set on the bog waters. Though I was then but a girl of sixteen, I was fast, you see, at snapping a rabbit's neck and could lay a fire in a hollow to cook it quick as you like. I was glad they didn't come near, glad they was afeared of me, because I was getting strong, and I had my reasons for getting stronger. When I had all my strength, then I would find that place where that landlord lived, and while he lay quiet in his bed, I would slit his throat, to pay me for the family he stole, to pay me for myself. For it sometimes seems to me that I must have died and live on only in the empty houses of our village.

But now, I work in the Reverend's house. He it was who found me half starved in a winter ditch and brought me here and gave me boots and taught me the English. It was a great shock and hard on a body's pride to see in his mirror what he had been seeing all along, and, I have to confess, a disappointment when I did realise it was me. My hair had got matted and wide like a dirty sheep's fleece, and my face was dark and lined with the peat smoke. But the Reverend saw I could be cleaned up, and he got me a dress and other things from Mrs Macleod, who came and instructed me in the ways of his fancy kitchen and made sure I didn't kill him off with my cooking. But I am fast to learn, and soon it was me that was showing her how to manage the flue on the stove.

And now I would die for this good man. I set the fires before he wakes and I make the *brose* in the morning for his breakfast. I wash his white shirts, and I strip the milk cow's udder in the byre so well that she gives enough milk to make curd cheese. And when he frets and sighs in his library over his books and his notes, because he cannot see the sea lady with his own eyes, and because he can find no one new to tell him more stories of sea ladies and seal men, then I make up stories for him, about sea ladies visiting our island. He writes them down in English, in beautiful curled letters like the flight of the kittiwakes over the sea.

I do not tell him my true stories because they are too sore for me to speak. The telling of such things raises up a great sadness in me and then I do feel again that I am but a ghost in this place. Then I must climb to the top of Toe Head and try and see our island, and imagine that I see it there, a blue smudge of cloud on the far horizon just before it tips over the edge of the world.

And my mind will not stop itself from going back to all our pain. And I think then on how our end was slow coming, but it fell upon us hard, when the dogs began to bark in the night, because they could smell the rot in the potatoes before it got to our noses, like something burned and then wetly rotting. So we must loan money from Lord Marstone to buy our flour to eat, and when we cannot pay it back, then he has his opportunity to turn us out of our village and clear the island for his fat, white sheep.

His Lordship said he would transport only our essentials. But it was hard to see what was to be essential for our new lives; not the barrels for salting the birds over winter, not the table that my grandfather made. But my father trusted to the landlord's promises of a steady future, a cottage with some land on the big island – so long as we signed on the paper, never to come home.

The cattle and as many sheep as they could catch were all loaded in another boat that stood low in the water. We never did see any money for our beasts. The landlord claimed it as forfeit to pay for the evacuation. And still my father hoped for our new future, trusted.

My father was a proud man. He was the bard in our village, and he remembered all the old stories and told them in a deep voice that made everyone come near and listen. But when he saw the hovel the landlord's factor led us to, then he understood what we had become in the eyes of the world. No man, not even my father, could wrest a living from that sour soil. He considered us lower than the beasts, Lord Marstone. He left us to die one by one, and slowly, so that we could grasp how truly we did not matter in this world.

Now I must find a way to show that man his grave error. I shall show him my strength, how I do stand here on God's earth, and the last thing he will see shall be the glint of my knife. I will make him understand that I cannot be denied and I shall crush the life from his old windpipe. Or perhaps the knife is a better plan.

I do not know yet how this plan shall come about, except that since it is now me that looks after his Reverend, I must return here after to care for him, and so it must be done in secret. It has taken me several days to dry out his clothes and get rid of his fever but thanks be, he is now up and about and worrying at his books again.

And while I am skinning a rabbit, which I got by my own means, though the Reverend does not notice, the Reverend himself comes into the kitchen as I am thinking my plans and says, 'Dear little Moira. How few troubles you have in your head, always so patient with your lot in life. Humming your little tunes.' And he goes off sighing about his sermons and his mermaids. And I am smiling so very much because I have seen his beautiful face once more, which is as handsome as God ever intended for mankind, created on a day when He was feeling well disposed to our race. He is so young, my Reverend, with his hair as black and glossy as the little Kerry cow, and his eyes that do startle you, as blue as the sea between here and Taransay.

My English is not perfect enough yet to say things well to the Reverend, but then his own Gaelic is not so much better – and much worse than he believes – so I am not so very sure that he writes down the stories just as I am telling him. But it does not matter if he writes this or that down a little incorrect, since lately, I am but making my stories up – now that I have used all the old ones.

CHAPTER 5

Alexander

Dear Alexander,

I received your letter and read it with growing amazement. I myself have a mind open to the many and endless possibilities in God's Creation, and hold that following the example of Mr Darwin, we must bravely face the evidence before our eyes — and yet a mermaid!

My dear Alexander, you know how difficult it is of late to be taken as seriously as those career scientists Huxley and Lyell; the Reverend palaeontologist who dabbles in fossils is now all too easily overlooked as a mere amateur — an epithet that makes me boil with rage since I would attest that a certain moral strength proves the theologian a rigorous scientist committed to the necessary minutiae of detail. Many were the happy days we spent assiduously examining the variety of forms of molluscs and cetaceans along the east coast, and I had the highest of hopes that your continued studies in your new parish in the outer isles would bring further discoveries, but little did I expect a proposed treatise upon the divergent linkage between fish and man, and never did I anticipate a study of the mermaid. And though it makes my heart quicken with some romantic hope that such a thing could be true, and though I have every confidence in your judgment and integrity, I urge you to present this to no one else until you have some evidence.

It is chiefly your own reputation that I fear for at present. You must be aware of how such credence in fairy tales could quickly do great damage to your standing among your peers. If you must in all conscience follow this enquiry, then do so in private, nay in secret. And should you find proof, then my friend, on that day blaze forth and astonish the world.

I was so intrigued by your letter that I took myself to the university library and searched for any book or pamphlet that might refer to the condition we term mermaids or mermen. The librarian brought to my attention an intriguing article in The Times newspaper of 1809. With some misgivings I enclose a transcription for your interest.

Fanny and I find ourselves extremely snug in the house that accompanies my new tenure as curate of All Souls parish in a very pleasant suburb of Edinburgh, where I can continue to pursue my study of river flukes around the Firth, alongside Carfax and McGreevy in the science faculty.

My dear friend, you must know that you have left behind more than one broken heart here in Edinburgh and it is a cross you are given to bear, that in spite of your will to cast off all worldly impediments, the females of our species do find themselves much taken by your person. If you should meet a young lady of your rank who might please your heart, then I can greatly commend to you the state of matrimony. Our molluscs and our mermaids may well intrigue, but they do not have the kind heart or the warm dry cheek of a small wife sitting behind a tray of tea and unconscionably delicious cakes and scones. I am, I regret, as a result, a greater man than when we last met, and become shockingly lazy about getting out into the fields and along the shores to follow my research.

I await your response with great interest.
Your devoted friend,
Matthew

I unfolded a hand-copied transcript of a letter published in *The Times* newspaper, dated the 8th of September 1809.

Dear Sir,

It has taken me some years to find the courage to report an incident that I witnessed while working as a schoolmaster in the village of Reay. Though I anticipate considerable censure, I will relate the incident exactly as it occurred.

In the month of August, 1797, in the course of walking along the nearby sands of the Pentland Firth, being a fine warm day in summer, my attention was arrested by the appearance of a figure resembling an unclothed human female, sitting upon a rock some hundred feet out to sea, and apparently in the action of combing out its hair, which flowed around its shoulders and was of a light brown colour.

The rock upon which the creature was seated was entirely cut off from land by a deep gully where the surf pounded against the rocks in a manner that prevented any human from reaching the rock without loss of life. The creature however sat in possession of its rocky seat, with no concern for the surf dashing around the rock's slopes. Clearly, this could be no human creature, and yet its upper portion was an exact replica of a human figure, with a human face and perfectly proportioned arms. Before I could examine the long tail, the sea person saw me and slid swiftly into the surf around the rock, submerged and then reappeared some yards distant where it made haste to propel itself away until it could be seen no more.

I have kept this sighting to myself for some twelve years. As a schoolmaster and a person of some standing in the community, it did not behove me to put myself in a position of ridicule before those I was called upon to instruct. But now I have the leisure of my closing days to reflect upon what I saw that day and the conviction has never dimmed that I have looked upon one of the race we term mermaids.

I have thus decided, that it is fitting that I make report of my observations. If the above narrative can in any degree serve towards establishing the existence of phenomena hitherto almost incredible to naturalists, or to remove the scepticism of others, who are ready to dispute everything which they cannot fully comprehend, then you are welcome to it.

From, dear Sir, your most obliged and most humble servant,
William Munroe

When Moira came in with a plate of fried eggs, scorched at the edges but the dryness of the yolks an improvement on previous breakfasts, she found me with the letter in my hand, staring out of the window towards the sea, in a stupor of amazement.

'Come here, Moira,' I told her. 'Look at what this says,' and I spread out the neat copperplate of the transcript on the white cloth.

She considered it for a while and nodded her head sagaciously, but she seemed to be admiring the general beauty of the note, rather than to be at all engaged with the content.

'Oh, but Moira,' I said, 'I expect there are words you do not understand yet in English. Look, let me explain for example, "phenomena", it means unexpected things that occur, which are natural and which we cannot yet explain; or then "scepticism"…'

I glanced up at her and saw that her cheeks were burning red. She never likes to be put in the wrong, our little Moira. Her cap was skewed from the exertions of breakfast, and she has begun to take on a faint kippered smell of peat smoke now that she sleeps in the bothy with old Mrs Kintail, since it has been made clear to me that in spite of my charitable intentions, it is not entirely seemly for a single man to have a young single female sleeping on the settle of his kitchen each night, even though the likelihood of the evils implied in such a supposition makes me smile.

'I do understand English words,' said Moira. 'I understand English words very well, except for the ones I do not need to use or have never heard of before, and then I work them out very well, thank you.'

Then it was my turn to blush. How clumsy it was of me to embarrass the poor girl so. I had seen Moira pull books from my shelves as she dusted them, open them and gaze at their pages. It had never occurred to me that she could not read them.

'Why don't I read this aloud, since I am so fond of my own voice and rather love to have an audience, if you can spare me some of your time?'

'Well, I suppose I can wait a while,' she said, and she listened haughtily while I read out Munroe's letter, and by the end of it she was transfixed, her eyes shining.

'I wish I had seen her,' she cried. 'I wish with all my heart.'

'Why, so do I, Moira,' I told her.

'How I wish I were one of the sea people. Perhaps then they would show themselves to me.'

'Well,' I told her with a smile and a shake of my head, 'I am one of the sea people, a Selkie, if my grandmother is to be believed, and so far no sea people have shown themselves to me.'

This made Moira sit down on the tapestry chair and stare at me with wide-open mouth.

'And you have never, never breathed a word of this to me,' she cried. 'A Reverend Minister who is descended from the *sliochd nan ron*. How can it be that you have never said this, while I prattle on and on with my sea stories, trying to amaze you, and all the while you were holding on to your secret?'

'It is really no great matter,' I told her, trying to lead her back to some composure. 'It was a fancy of my father's mother who grew up on Uist. She would hold forth to all and sundry that her distant ancestor was truly one of the sea people who become men on the land.

Sadly, the truth is that this fancy of hers has been an embarrassment to the family. My own mother forbade me to speak of it, and indeed I forgot about it until I took the parish here, whereupon it has rather come back to haunt me.

'But I tell you this in confidence, dear Moira, knowing that I can entrust my reputation to you. It would not do one bit for the minister to be seen to believe in fairy stories, or to announce himself half fish, you do see, so it must be a secret between us, and indeed I can only conclude that my grandmother was mistaken, since if I am of the sea people, then at no point have they chosen to make themselves known to me, in spite of me living but moments from the shore. I can thus only conclude that I am not of their people, or such a distant and minor branch of the Harris Selkies that they do not deign to know me, any more than Lord Marstone at Avenbuidhe Castle has seen fit to come calling.'

Moira, who had been laughing at my silliness, now stopped and looked serious.

'You do not want to let that man across your threshold, sir,' she said. 'No good will ever come of any word with the Marstone family.' She cleared the porridge bowl onto her tray. Resting the tray on one hip, she pushed back her red hair. She is a pale girl at the best of times, and her freckles seem to float on milk, but now she was gone grey and ill looking.

'It were best he never came here,' she told me, and went off to her kitchen.

I had already said the devotional offices before breakfast in the quietness of the church where the high windows frame the blue-glass sea with colours as true as any stained glass window. I was somewhat distracted by the insistent rasp of a corncrake in the silverweed banks near the graveyard, but I returned from my prayers feeling in better communion

with our Lord. I had learned that it was best to do one's devotions before one of Moira's breakfasts, since the burn of internal indigestion and the memory of fried eggs did little to aid divine contemplation.

I went in to my study to send off some letters; one to the library in Edinburgh, enquiring whether they might hold any similar letters or accounts from national or local newspapers, and to further request a possible reading list on the history of these islands and the legends of seal folk, or mermaids, as the phenomena seem to be variously known in the area. I also wrote to a bookshop that I use in Edinburgh, requesting that they send an early reader and alphabet primer, something that would not prove too offensive to the adult reader.

I then replied to Matthew, to thank him for his advice and his kindness in procuring *The Times* article, and to send hearty good wishes to his wife, whom I have met and found a solid and sensible girl although failing to see her through Matthew's rosy-tinted spectacles. It was she who gave me the rather girlish pen on my desk, a white pearl, with a crystal bottle for the ink. 'That you may remember to write to us,' Fanny said.

Then I must attend to my parishioners, though they were but small in number.

It was a walk of an hour or so to Northton village. The island was almost treeless, except for the bushes and stunted pines existing in sheltered gullies and folds, and the entire stretch of land between Scarista and my destination lay spread out like a map. Across the fertile grasslands between the hill slopes and the sea dunes, only ruined walls remained of once numerous bothies, now looking like villages of thick-walled sheep fanks. One felt a lingering nostalgia in the midst of such beautiful emptiness, for the history of a people now gone from that place.

I had packed the small communion cup and plate, along with wafers and a phial of communion wine, to take down to a certain old lady in Northton village too feeble to come to the church. Fearing for her health, she was anxious to take of the Lord's supper before she passed away – though I soon learned that she had been waiting for this event for a good many years.

While I was seated by her peat fire and forcing myself to take a cup of the smoky black brew so as not to offend – in spite of the horror of watching her lick her thumb and rub it round the cup to make sure of its cleanliness before filling and then offering it to me – she told me of a most interesting fact.

I had remarked that it being such a fine day, I might walk out further to the end of Toe Head.

'Then you'll see the ruins of Ruariah Mhor's village,' she told me. 'A bad man if ever there was one.'

It would seem that Big Rory was, in truth, a small man, but large in evil deeds. Desiring to add the lower village to his sheep run, he was one of the first lairds to order the people off the land and fire the roofs of the houses. Forced to move out onto the poor soil of the headland where the constant Atlantic winds burned the crops and blew sheep clean off the hillsides in winter, the people had no choice but to leave for Canada.

'Aye, but he got his comeuppance,' she told me. 'He was out on the headland one day, and he saw something in the sea that so frighted him that he then left the islands and never returned. And 'twas divine Providence that sent the monster to judge him of his sins, Reverend. If ye walk out that way awhile, beyond the ruins of the chapel, then you'll see the walls of the poor houses those people built there still.'

I had wanted to examine the remains of the ancient church, built in the time of the first saints who sailed there from Ireland in their coracles, and so decided to walk on and also see the site of the old laird's village.

My efforts were rewarded by a day without equal, a cloudless blue sky as vast as the sparkling sea, the bright green sward spread out above the white beaches, the wet sand streaked with the reflection of the heavens; though, by the time I reached the ruins, a veil of grey cloud had pulled itself across half the sky and was threatening to cover it entirely.

I was aware of being unable to resist constantly glancing out at the sea, ostensibly to spot a seal or something larger, but always with a shiver that something stranger might appear. Once or twice I was startled by a break in the sea surface, a disturbance and a glimpse of black, but surmised a rock covered in seaweed occasionally uncovered by the surface of the water.

On finding the ruined chapel, and the sad, abandoned walls of roofless huts — now no more than a series of tumbled stone walls — I sat down on the water's rocky outcrops and gave myself over to gazing out to sea.

Across the great expanse of water were the dusky legends of hills, and the blue peaks of the Uist mountains. The stretches of Skye to my left showed a paler lilac, and further away still, the mountains of Argyll made a low ridge of cloud, the sky above them massed with huge, grey-blue formations. The whole view before my eyes seemed made entirely of air and water, the very land become without substance. Gradually, the sun became covered in clouds and the water turned as opaque as the land.

As I watched, I began to discern a tip of shiny black denseness making its way through the water, just level with the sea's surface. Behind was a ridge of black and the tips of two more black triangular shapes in decreasing size. I understood with a quickening heart that I was witnessing my first sighting of a great basking shark. I stood up and hurriedly climbed down the rocks as close to the water as I could, soaking the leather of my boots, holding my breath.

The thrill of sighting so great a beast left me exalted throughout the returning walk. I made a further discovery on retracing the dune path, a species of tiny blue snails in flat whorls, striped faintly with white. It was a species particular to that headland, as small and delicate as a lady's earrings.

Kneeling in the marram grass and engrossed in this discovery, I failed to hear the sound of a horse's hooves until the animal was almost upon me. I managed to jump aside from the path in great haste, narrowly escaping injury. It was true that I had been concealed by my crouching down and by a dip in the dune land, but I wondered at who might be so inconsiderate as to ride recklessly along uneven ground. I saw a white pony, compact and stocky, of the type native to the islands, and upon its back a woman of small stature riding side-saddle. She did not seem to be dressed in riding clothes, but wore a thin blue dress that one might see in the drawing rooms of Edinburgh, and yet she rode well, as if experienced in the handling of horses.

She did not cast a glance backwards, and I doubt that she even saw me. She headed at great speed across the open land towards the long white beaches of Scarista and I watched her grow smaller and smaller beneath the hugeness of the sky as she attempted to come near the deep blue shadows of the North Harris mountains.

I had never seen the woman before, and was very surprised not to have heard of her, as on an island of so few people a lady of such consequence would surely have been the occasion of much talk. I was also greatly surprised that Moira, who seems to have an ear for all the local gossip, had never mentioned her arrival.

I walked back quite looking forward to sharing my news with Moira.

CHAPTER 6

Ruth

Passing the open door of the sea room early one morning, I caught a glint from the mantelpiece. A square of moonlight was framing the collection of little objects from Dougal, and throwing an almost perfect shadow of the crystal ink bottle on the wall.

It was seven in the morning and still dark.

As I stood there in the doorway, I felt an odd prickle of apprehension, as if the house were still held by the night's shadows, a slippage in time where the darkness might hold a room strewn with Alexander Ferguson's papers and books, or perhaps hide the house we first walked into, the rank debris and crumbling brown plaster of a building left empty and decaying for ten years.

My feet were frozen in the draught, so I hurried into the kitchen. Through the window, frost sparkled on the grass as if it was midnight. I switched on the light, made a coffee and got a biscuit.

The biscuit tasted odd: I wondered if the damp was making things stale. The coffee was too harsh and turned my stomach. I tipped it away and got some water.

I was sitting at the table, rewriting the To Do lists, rubbing my feet together inside woolly walking socks to generate some heat, and enjoying a certain neatness to my handwriting, when I realised that I'd stopped thinking about the papers in front of me. I sat with the pen poised, motionless. Some pretty impossible things were adding themselves up in my head.

Granted, I'd missed the last few months, but then I often did, if I wasn't eating properly or I got really tired, and granted, I'd found my clothes tighter than I liked recently; but now I was feeling nauseous all the time, light-headed when I got up in the morning.

I sat with both hands on my belly for ages, shivering with excitement, horrified that this should be happening. We weren't nearly ready for this. It was too soon.

Dr Lawson confirmed that I was about fifteen weeks pregnant. Michael was over the moon. A week or so later, we got a letter from the maternity clinic in Stornoway hospital to go up for a check-up and an ultrasound scan.

The letter said that we would be able to see our baby in considerable detail. I felt a weird tingle in my fingers, like something uncanny was happening. So far, the baby had been an idea, a thought growing out of some place in the heart, but still just an idea, like Christianity or world peace – beautiful but far off; but in the clinic in Stornoway, they had already worked out that we were talking flesh and blood and bones.

I lay on a trolley, holding onto Michael's hand, as we stared at the monitor. The nurse squeezed some gel on my stomach. She began to push her strange phone with its long cord across my skin, moving this way and that to get a signal. On the screen there was nothing but whorls of static, a transmission of a storm happening far out to sea. Then something gave a pulse. We saw a curved backbone flicker, like a tail swimming in a blizzard of pixels. It vanished. The nurse went back, and began to hunt out the baby's body parts, naming them for us.

'Nice spine. That's a healthy baby you have there.' She beamed like we'd passed her exam. I realised with a pang that she didn't always say that, and felt that little worry switch click on – the one you can't ever switch off again.

Michael was looking stunned. The nurse gave him a print-out while I wiped off my stomach with some of the blue paper and pulled my dress down. We huddled together over the tiny photo. It felt like we were holding something secret, something forbidden – shadows of a future self, caught on film.

'I think that's the face,' Michael said, tilting his head.

'It could be a hip.' I turned it round. 'So that little white blur there could be an arm.'

'It's waving at us,' said Michael.

It was an hour back to Harris, crossing the Barvas moors along an unlit single track. Michael drove slowly, perched forward over the wheel, concentrating on the stretch of tarmac that appeared in the headlights, disappeared behind us in the growing dark. He puffed out his cheeks and made a sound as if we'd just come through something.

'Aren't you pleased?' I asked him.

'Blown away. Can't wait to get back and phone Mum and Dad, tell them we've got a photo of the baby.'

I thought of my six pictures of Mum in an envelope: no matter what I told them, her expression would never change. No photos at all of Dad – whoever he was. If the baby took after him, we'd never know; he'd never know.

The light was almost gone, the lochs on the black moor glimmering like pale glass. Michael suddenly swerved. The sheep loved to sit on the dry tarmac once the sunlight went; they never remembered about the cars.

'Careful,' I told him, louder than I meant to be.

Michael reached out his hand and squeezed mine. He had to let go to steer round another sheep. I saw two red eyes glinting in the headlights, the jaws chewing cud.

'Sorry, Ruth. Didn't think. Going on about ringing my folks.

'Of course you must ring them. No need to be sorry. Just the way it is. I lose people. Probably leave this baby in a pushchair somewhere, go home and forget it. People do that, you know.'

'Ruth, you'll be a great mum.'

I shrugged and turned my head to look out of the dark window. The moor carried on slipping past, the light refusing to entirely leave the sky where the horizon held it. I got out the grainy photograph. Tried to make out the shape of a baby in the glow from the headlights.

I thought then of the child that had been tucked away to sleep under our house, the inadequate blood supply starving its bones of nutrition, the half-formed legs. How did you know? How did you know what a child needed?

'I don't know if I can do this.'

'Hey, you're not doing this alone, you know. I'm going to be there.'

'You'd better be.' And that was enough, as if my foot had touched bottom, and I felt that fierce determination to swim up, reach the air. This child forming under my skin was going to thrive, and it would never doubt, even for a moment, how much it was loved.

It made me wonder, but hadn't she felt that about me?

How could she do it, let herself slip away into the dark water? Couldn't she understand that when a mother takes her own life, she reaches out a hand to take her child with her? That cold, white hand reaching up from the water, willing me to slip away with her.

I shut my eyes, blinked those years away. Whatever it took, I was going to be there for this child.

It was dark when we let ourselves into the house. And, oh my, how sorry the kitchen looked in the bald light of one bulb dangling from the ceiling. The black glass of the windows still had no curtains to pull over them. The sink was still hanging away from the wall, propped up by bits of wood torn off a builder's pallet. I let my eyes travel around the unplastered walls that sifted brick dust down onto the food. I thought around the rest of the house; every room a list of jobs; several rooms habitable only in theory.

I slumped at the table, too tired and too cold to take my coat off.

'This house is like living in a documentary about slum conditions.'

Michael looked hunted. He started making cocoa on the Belling, mixing the powder into a pan of milk.

'We were going to have everything so organised, do it all properly, and now… Michael, I don't think this house wants us here.'

'Oh come on, Ruth.'

I watched some splashes landing on the table as Michael plonked the mugs down. He sat down heavily. He held out some kitchen roll. I blew my nose.

'We're never going to be open in time for the holiday season are we?' I said through sniffs.

'Doesn't look that way. But we'll have to start making the repayments on the loan in September, whatever happens.'

We stared at the table, trying to make the impossible add up.

'Perhaps we should give up. Michael, perhaps we should just go back to London.'

He shook his head. He looked white and defiant.

'Listen, Ruth, I got a letter from Jamie this morning.'

I wondered why he'd changed the subject. 'And?'

'You know how he's been working his way round the world, looking for the most beautiful place on the planet. I told him, it's right here. Well, he's back in Edinburgh now, and he wants to come and stay.'

Michael and his brother were close, only two years apart, Jamie a darker, slightly shorter version of Michael.

'Of course. How long for?'

'Here's the thing. Why don't we ask him to stay a while, help us work on the house? We could get this place fixed in half the time. What d'you think?' He reached across the table and held my hand.

'Jamie's great. It'll be fun with him around,' I said. Michael squeezed my fingers, looked relieved.

'And he wants to bring his girlfriend.'

'His girlfriend?'

'Yes. He met her on a beach, in California. She was living in a sort of tent commune. Protesting about something. And she's, er, called Leaf.'

Two new lists: things we needed for our guests' room; things we'd need for the baby. It was all happening so fast.

I don't think I'd ever wanted something so much as that baby, or felt so ill prepared; a vague anxiety, like an emptiness or vertigo. I wondered if there were some books I could get, books that told you what you were supposed to actually do with a baby once it arrived. I decided to try the little shop by the harbour.

If there was something vital that had been damaged in the years after I'd lost Mum, then I was determined to make up for it, fill in the gaps. Whatever it took.

I found myself standing by the shelves of groceries in the store in Tarbert. I looked at the wire basket in my hands, looked at the magazines on the rack. I couldn't remember coming into the shop. No idea what I was buying.

I pretended to read the captions on *Woman's Weekly*, clutching the wire handle, trying to work out what I needed to put in the basket, breathing in the smell of damp cardboard, the smell of branny earth in a sack of potatoes. I dug the wire handle into my hand. Everyone needed bread didn't they? I picked up a loaf of bread, soft inside the plastic bag, the slices of bread giving way and parting under my fingers.

I came out of the shop feeling uneasy. It had been a long while since something like that had happened. In the first year at uni, it used to happen quite a lot. In those months when I started deciding who I was going to be, sometimes the world would stop; I'd be halfway down a street and suddenly sort of wake up, unable to remember why I was there or what I was doing – odd little moments, when who I was completely faded away.

In the haberdasher's I managed to find a box of knitting patterns for impossibly tiny jackets and cardigans. Pages of instructions and numbers, a dense code that bore no relation to my clumsy knit-one-pearl-one.

The clouds were curdling to lilac as I got off the bus and walked up to the Sea House. The low light raised shadows across the hillsides, revealing the corrugations of old potato beds, vast expanses of swirling rigs and ditches that must have taken hundreds of hands to dig out. Now, there were only a handful of crofters and their houses left across the empty machair grassland. I wondered just what had occurred to make the people leave such a beautiful place.

Up in the field near the road I saw Mrs MacKay walking back towards her house carrying a bucket. She had a woollen scarf tying down her white perm, a face that was as unlined as new soap. She waved me over.

'Come away in now, Ruth, why don't you and we'll make ourselves a cup of tea?'

Mrs MacKay's kitchen smelled damply of baking and washing drying over the Rayburn. There was a lamb in a wire pen next to the stove. Neat and white as a shorn poodle, it bleated indignantly, showing a trembling pink tongue.

'What happened to this one?' I said, putting my hand on its woolly head. The lamb butted it off and moved away to the back of the pen.

'He arrived very early in the season, and his mother must have been a gimmer, a first-time mum. The new mums can forget they have a baby and wander off.' She shook her head. 'Jonny'll go up on the hill later and see if he can find her. She might recognise the lamb and take it back.'

Mr MacKay appeared at the back door. Whether sorting the peat bricks or digging black tangles of seaweed into the potato beds, he always wore an immaculate blue boiler suit.

Mrs MacKay took a plate of her baking through to their deeply quiet and rather bleak sitting room. We sat drinking our tea in silence under the framed Bible verse, 'Thou God seest me'. I decided this was a good chance to ask Mrs MacKay if she had any old family memories of the Sea House from Ferguson's time, perhaps some gossip or memory passed down from her grandmother.

'Oh yes, well, after your troubles, I expect you will want to know.' She shook her head, very apologetic. 'I can tell you about this minister and the minister before him, but we don't know anything about your Reverend Ferguson. Our parents were from Lewis, you see. They only moved down here after the Great War.'

'Aye, and that was only because the landlord up at the castle was forced to let crofters back on his land by a government commission. When the government realised they couldn't send the sheep to fight in their wars,' said Mr MacKay.

On the way back home, I passed Mrs MacDonald's croft house. Next to it was a blue corrugated iron shed with a large hand-painted sign over the door: '*Oifis a' Phuist*' – Post Office. I called in on the pretext of buying one of the tins of soup or beans spaced out at lonely intervals along the shelves.

Mrs MacDonald spent a lot of time looking out through the window for customers and the minute she saw one approaching she'd come bustling into the shed wearing a coat and the dignified expression of the village post mistress. She knew everything there was to know about the comings and goings in Scarista, but when it came to the manse a century back, even she drew a complete blank.

I walked back to the house puzzling how everyone in the sparse village seemed to be a relatively recent incomer, their croft tenancy going back fifty years at the most. There'd been a complete break in the village's timeline.

It was proving difficult to find out any more information – and part of me was almost glad. I was nervous about what I might turn up, but the remains of that woollen blanket round the child had left me feeling that someone must have tried to care for her.

Michael came out to meet me, hands in his back pockets, the old jaunty lollop to his stride as he came down the path to take the shopping.

'Dougal came by. He dropped something off for you.'

On the kitchen trestle table were some thick sheets of paper covered with a familiar cursive in even, flowing lines. The black ink was rusted by time and a dusty, grey border ran along the top sheet, as if the papers had been left sticking out from a book or folder. There was a title: 'The Story of Ishbel and the Seal Man'.

'Dougal was looking through some other papers in the vestry and came across these, something else written by Ferguson, and – you'll like this – he said it isn't a sermon this time; it's a story about a Selkie. Looks like our Reverend Ferguson had seal people in his family – just like you.'

'Really? You're joking.'

'And he says there's a dedication, there at the top of it, to a Miss Marstone.'

'That name sounds familiar. Wasn't it the Marstones who owned the castle back then, over at Avenbuidhe? I wonder if there are any photos of her in the library? And I'm guessing that our Miss Marstone was rather pretty.'

CHAPTER 7

Moira

Every third Sunday, the offices at church are said in English and that is the day when those who consider themselves as good as the gentry bestir themselves to come and worship. So every Sunday the farm workers from the manse's glebe are all there, seated in the back row in what passes as their Sunday best, caps on their knees and the women in their bonnets. I sit alongside Maggie Kintail, and if ever there was a lady of quality that came to our church out here on the machair, then I do believe she would be far outshone by the glory of Maggie Kintail.

Maggie Kintail is seventy-nine and as thin and sprightly as an old chicken. She has worked for the tacksmen's wives for near seventy years and over that time has received many presents of gaudy, cheap trinkets and jewellery from those women, since this is what pleases Maggie most. The gaudier the piece the better in Maggie's eyes, even if it cost but two pence, and Maggie Kintail does wear all of them, all of the time, be she milking the cow or manuring the rigs with rotten seaweed. No circumstance can dim the glory of Maggie, and no one has a more cheerful disposition, since you can hear Maggie singing away, the old songs and the *puirt a beul* mouth tunes, long before you catch sight of her bent low over her work.

Time was when this big church was full of the many families roundabouts, but since they have all been cleared away, the church has an empty feel, even when every last soul is out of bed and here at Sunday matins.

So even though the church is all but empty, we of the manse farm do sit politely towards the back of the church. Those poor cottars left as squatters on the land, hoping for daily work and even daily pay as the tacksmen see fit, sometimes creep in and sit behind us. Mr Stewart, His Lordship's bailiff and tacksman, and his wife and bairns in their Glasgow hats and suits and boots, they process down almost to the front and arrange themselves along the pew – though never directly at the front, beneath where the very word of God is spoken from the pulpit, since even they would not presume.

No, that row is reserved for the Marstone family. And we will have to wait a long time, most likely until the Second Coming till we see him in the Lord's house. His wife and his daughter do not live here in the islands. They prefer to stay in London. The story is that Lady Marstone took one look at the grandest castle in these parts and declared it smaller than her father's stables. She stayed a few years, then took herself away home and was never seen here again. I cannot say that I blame her for her desertion.

So, here we all are in our places, waiting for the Reverend to come in his white robe and satin stole, and the door creaks open and a woman I have never seen before walks in – a woman in a fancy gown – and she walks down to the front of the church and sits herself in the Marstones' pew.

Everyone is trying not to move their heads and show how they are staring, but every eye is on that woman. Maggie Kintail is standing up, gawking, hopping from foot to foot to get a better look, most likely for the fashions she can copy. I pull her hard back down on the seat.

Maggie's behind makes a thump on the wooden pew and the woman turns her head. I see a face before me that would fair make you gasp. She has the full cheeks of an apple and a smooth forehead with yellow hair all piled up under a small blue hat. And she has the large eyes and the smiling lips that make you unsure if you might be jealous or in love. I could not tell her age but she was very young, perhaps still a girl.

Then the door creaked open again and I heard the rustle of the Reverend's robes as he walked down to the front and we all stood up in respect. I saw her dark blue dress, so smoothed and fitted round her form that I was puzzling how exactly you cut up the pieces of cloth to make them sit so close to a person.

If the Reverend felt curious about this stranger then he did not show it, other than a flicker of his eyes to where the besom sat proud as you like in her little hat. He gave a sermon of great fire and conviction, which did concern striving and casting off of sins to better run the race – though I did find it hard to follow since my own mind was running all over the place as to who she was. I found myself hoping that she was not staying in these parts for very long, since I reckoned that she could only be a guest of Lord Marstone. And yes, I thought, it is surely she who is the stranger lady on the horse, and she who near killed the Reverend.

After the service, she spoke with the Reverend at the back of the church, he laughing and with a great deal to say to her, and then he asked us to come and all greet her. 'I'd like you to meet the workers on the glebe farm,' he told her. 'And you must report to your father that they are the most admirable workers, trustworthy and diligent and very clean.'

Maggie Kintail stepped forward and gave her a deep curtsy. 'Honoured, Your Ladyship,' she said in English. Then I saw it was expected that I step forward and curtsy to her also and my heart began to pound and I thought I might faint away on the spot.

How could I not have understood? She was the very daughter of him. She was a Marstone. And now the Reverend was wanting me to curtsy and shake her little gloved hand. It was Lord Marstone as was the owner of the Reverend's church, and His lands the church was built on; the glebe farm that put bread on Reverend Alexander's table was in His gift. I had not chose to think upon it, but the truth of my situation was that it was himself, the Lord Marstone, I was working for and beholden to.

I don't recall how it went, but I was leaving the church and I must have shaken that besom's hand and done my curtsy because next thing I knew I was walking back down the path past the gravestones. Maggie Kintail was going on about did you see the feather in her hat, but my dress was soaked through under the arms, and I was chilled and shaking and I badly wanted to lie down in the box bed and draw the curtain in front of me in the smoky little house I live in now with Maggie, because nothing and no one can get away from being owned by the Marstones, and God lets it all happen, even in his church.

But I had the Sunday lunch to get served up, and so I went and did that. But by the end I had got into such a sweat and lather with the shock of it all that even Maggie did tell me that I stank and I had to wash my clothes and put on my old worn dress while my good one dried.

I was sad for the next few days because that day did recall to me all that I had lost in the twelve months since we were put from the island. I saw myself, running out as the mists poured off the hills and the sky was coming through blue, picking grass to feed Bessie before I milked her, and taking the pail home for breakfast where my father led the prayers and we all bowed our heads.

Then I did see my dear ones, my mother and father and my brothers and sister, lying sick in their beds in that hovel they moved us to, where the rain washed into the mud of the wall and then the stones collapsed. How I tried to get food from nothing, and how I did never change my clothes for six weeks but got wet through in the rain then let them dry on me, again and again, till they chaffed my skin sore. One by one, I found their bodies, cold in the bed, and must watch the men come to carry them on the long walk to the graveyard. I got more and more chill, till they was all gone and I was there, up on the hill, watching Marstone's men fire the thatch of our house – them no doubt thinking that I was inside.

So it was for several days after that Sunday that I was too tired to speak a word, and the Reverend said, 'Moira, why do we not hear you prattling on as you do usually?' And then, but sadly now, 'Moira, we must as Christians learn to forgive the past.'

One morning, after the breakfast was cleared away, I was called back in to be spoken to, in the Reverend's study where he writes his sermons. I was ready for my scolding, since I knew I had been distracted of late, and my cooking not as good as it usually was, but I found him looking most cheerful and pleased with himself.

Callum the post had brought a big parcel for the Reverend early that morning, and the brown paper was all over the floor. The Reverend said that he had sent off for something from Glasgow, and there were some items for me. So I went over to his desk, and there was some blue cloth and some green flowered cloth all folded neatly and smelling new, like cotton freshly ironed. He said I could make myself two new dresses, since time had worn the old ones, and perhaps the green would make a Sunday frock.

It was a shock to me, that he should have thought of that, and tears welled up in my eyes, which I rubbed away, and he said, 'Oh, don't you like them, Moira?' and I told him it was just his kindness that was making me weep.

So then he said, all gruff and cross, 'Come, come now. Let's have none of that. We have much work to do.' And he showed me a primer for the ABC, and some books such as children read in school, and he did say that they were for me. I was not sure how to teach myself to read them, but he said, 'We shall have a lesson every day, until you know all your letters, and then on the day that you can read, I promise you that I will let you borrow any book you wish from my own library. I would particularly recommend those devotional books written by my mentor in the theology faculty, although the fiction of Miss Austen can be very amusing.'

It was all that I could do to stop myself from throwing my arms round that good man, but instead I gave a stiff curtsy, and thanked him very politely for all his kindness, and then took myself back to the cottage and wept like a fool until my eyes were big and swollen and no doubt red. I had to bathe them in cold stream water and pretend that I had caught a cold while I finished my work.

Her Ladyship was not at church that next Sunday. The Reverend had a message saying she was indisposed with a chill, no doubt, I thought, from riding everywhere in all weathers on that horse of hers. And I thought, she is a Marstone after all: it is not likely we shall be seeing her in the church again. This thought made me feel almost happy.

And then the Thursday afternoon, when I went in for my reading lesson, after helping rake in the hay from the upper field, I heard voices in the drawing room and knocked, wondering who the Reverend had visiting with him in there, since he usually would say, so I would know to set a tray and boil water. And when I walked in to ask if he wanted tea, there she was, sat in her slim blue dress with the hems all spread round her feet, smiling like a cat. And he said to me, 'Oh, Moira, please could you fetch us tea, and if you have it, some of your delicious cloutie cake?'

So I closed the door on what I had just seen, herself sitting in there in the drawing room, and went off to the kitchen where I crashed about and set a tray, doing as much damage to the crockery as I could without breaking anything. I got the big polished wood tray and set it with a lace cloth and two cups and saucers and two little plates. On each one I put a slice of cloutie dumpling, one thick for him and one dainty slice for her. And then I leaned over the dainty slice and spat on it. Not so much that you would notice, but still it was a terrible thing to do. I watched myself spread the butter on top and boil the water for the tea and pour it in the silver teapot and set it on the tray, and then I picked it up.

It was a bad thing I was doing, but it soothed the raging in my breast and I felt a great calm, of something assuaged, as I carried the tray in and set it down on the little table. I poured out the tea slowly and then handed them each their slice and watched as she put it to her mouth.

'Moira,' said the Reverend, making me jump, 'Katriona wishes to learn Gaelic, and she has asked me to be her teacher. Would you recommend me now?' He turned to her. 'You see, I am teaching my maid to read,' he said, without a thought for how I might feel about her knowing how I was too ignorant to read.

I mumbled something in Gaelic, that I knew even the Reverend would not comprehend, and they both stared at me. Then she laughed.

'Oh, but I shall soon understand what everyone is saying here,' she trilled. 'You see, Alexander, that is why I must learn to speak the native tongue. All the people say to me when I address them is, "No English, lady; no English, lady." It is most vexing. I thought more people here would know English.'

The Reverend said nothing, but he knew as well as I did that everyone has at least some English, and the young ones who have been to the new board school have very good English. It is simply that the people here do not want to speak to anyone from the house of Marstone.

I went back to my kitchen exhausted, repentant already of the thing I had just done, but also glad of it: a little way towards our settling of accounts. And I thought of all I had vowed to do, and all the miles between here and the castle of Lord Marstone, and with me with no pony and trap, but must get there in my pinching boots or bare feet. Then there were the reasons I must give so they would let me in, and so much to be planned before I could go in and settle my accounts with himself.

At Avenbuidhe Castle, they only use maids from Glasgow, who come for a year or so, and then go away from the homesickness. Girls from the islands are never taken on, being too reeking of peat smoke and lisping with Gaelic. How could I then get myself a place there to work and find my opportunity? Must I go by night and creep in a window? And as for the knife, which one would I take? It would leave Alexander a knife short for the cooking. And then who was to care for him after I was gone?

I was so very tired, so very empty and exhausted. I went back in to collect the tea things in a stupor, and when she told me my cake was very good, I felt nothing, even with all my plans going around my mind.

'So,' she was saying to the Reverend, 'will you write down your lovely seal story for me? It sounds so intriguing. How I wish we had such a lovely legend in my family. I would love to be descended from a Selkie.'

And after that, I have to confess, I did smash a china cup in the kitchen. And it did happen to be the one she had been drinking from. That she should waltz into the house, and in five minutes get my Reverend to give up his great secret, that he has trusted only me to keep for him. And that she should get to read the story before I have even heard it. And I did promise myself that I would learn to read by the end of the week so that I could find the Selkie story on his desk and read it before she ever got to set her eyes on it.

After she left, I solemnly told the Reverend I would pay for a new cup from my wages, but he said, 'Oh no matter, no matter,' and he went off to his study no doubt to write his grandmother's tale out for her, and he quite forgot about my reading lesson, which was a pity since I had planned to surprise him greatly by how far I had come in the reader about the doings of a hen and a rat and in how fast I could now string the letters together into words.

It was some few weeks later, and after I had found all there was to know of that hen and that rat, that I went in early to set the fire and I found a paper on his desk, neatly written out, a note to Dear Miss Marstone. I took the lion paperweight off it as it was in need of a little polish, and that's when I noticed the title on the paper: 'The Story of Ishbel and the Seal Man'. Well, the beady eyes of the little brass lion were watching me, but I placed him back on the desk and picked up the paper. I sat down in the Reverend's big chair and then I began to read, although much of it took me more than one try before I got the sense of the words.

I was glad I had worked so very hard at my letters then, for I read it all, and I saw them before me, that woman and her seal man. I saw how she lived in a place so very like my own home. I knew as I read it that I could know her life better than Miss Marstone ever could, and better even than the Reverend, my Alexander, who is, it is true, even the descendant of a Selkie.

CHAPTER 8

Alexander

Dear Miss Marstone,

I offer below my attempts to transcribe the story of the Selkie, as told to me by my late grandmother. I cannot say, in all honesty, if some details are precisely as she recounted them to me. It may be that the intervening years have allowed elements of my own imaginings to creep in. Likewise, in the retelling, I suspect that over generations, the clarity of the story may owe as much to dramatic invention as to the recalling of facts. I offer it therefore as a curio that may amuse, and not as an historical account that should be taken with any seriousness.

I remain your humble servant,
Reverend Alexander Ferguson

The Story of Ishbel and the Seal Man

Ishbel McOdrum was a plain girl but strong. She had a long beak of a nose and above her lip, a faint line of hair was visible, suggesting in thirty years' time a notable moustache. She had long, capable hands and her feet were as big as a man's.

Since she was covered from wrist to ankle in brown woollen skirts and shawls, no one knew that Ishbel McOdrum was in possession of a tiny waist, and since her hair was habitually covered by a red scarf, tied securely round her shoulders to keep out the weather, no one was aware of the long chestnut tresses that flowed down her back.

Everyone on the island knew that Ishbel was as strong as any crofter. She could lift a creel of sea kelp heavy as a wet sheep and carry it from the glistening rocks to the croft without faltering once. If you were to look down upon the green sweep of the hillside, there you would see Ishbel, carrying over the baskets of seaweed from the shore to build up the sandy machair soil, or moving up and down the long rigs of potato beds, breaking her back with the heavy work of the digging.

Ishbel's father was a widower and frail. Both her sisters were married and gone so he was glad to have her remain with him as the seasons went by. In winter when the gales blew in from hundreds of miles across the Atlantic, gathering strength as they came, to beat upon the squat stone house, Ishbel would sing under the booming wind, carding wool or working the distaff to spin woollen thread.

With the return of the sun came the white terns from the Arctic and Ishbel and her father would resume once more the arduous summer struggle to lay down enough food for the following winter.

Several summers and several winters went by in this way. Ishbel's father died and was buried in the little cemetery by the sea. A further two years went by but still no husband was found for Ishbel; no husband came sailing into the cove in a small fishing boat; no husband jumped over its side and ran towards her as she stood in front of a sapphire sea and watched the gannets diving out of the sky, leaving nothing but plumes of spray.

And after the sun had set, throwing vermilion light across the wide sea, and faded quietly into grey and black night, then only the wind watched the steady stars with Ishbel McOdrum as she stepped out after a silent supper to listen to the waves.

The truth was that most people forgot that Ishbel might once have been married. She came to be counted as a man for the work she could do in one day; how many peat blocks she could cut with the curved spade; how many turfs she could throw up on the bank, stacking them to dry like rows of black hymn books stood up on the grass. So it was a great surprise to everyone when just at that age when most women know they will have no more children, or will never have children, Ishbel married and had a son.

Ishbel did not win her husband easily and she knew in her heart that she would have to struggle to keep him.

The first time she saw him was for a few brief minutes. He was some way out in the sea, beyond the Island of Scarp, floating half out of the water. Beneath the clear blue skin of the sea she espied his long fish-like tail, moving tremulously with the ebb of the water. His smooth chest was devoid of garments, his hair black and long. Ishbel's heart began to hammer with a multitude of emotions. She had never thought to see one of the sea people with her own eyes, and she was full of disbelief and wonder. They watched each other with equal amounts of curiosity and she kept very still, afraid to break the spell, longing for him to come in closer so that she might see him better.

Suddenly, he began to propel himself towards her. Ishbel gave a scream of terror and with a flash of his long tail the Selkie immediately rolled and submerged. He reappeared twenty yards further out and began to swim away until the far islands hid him from her view.

Ishbel got no work done that day. She climbed to the top of Hushinish Point and cast her gaze around the half circle of the horizon, but she could see nothing clearly in the bright haze. She followed the line of the shore on foot, but saw only sleeping seals lying on the smaller islands, their forms blended against the rocks. Perhaps she saw him there. She could not tell.

Then she saw a man's face rising up from the shining waters, but as the long grey profile turned and rolled in the sea, she surmised that it was nothing more than an old seal that snorted water from its nostrils. It melted away beneath the water.

She returned to her home pondering many things. She knew from the old stories that she had seen a Selkie, a creature half man and half seal by blood, *from a race of beings that appeared but rarely in the islands, being descended from royalty – from the time when the King of Norway's children were turned into seals by their stepmother and forced to live in the northern seas.*

That night, a tremendous storm rose up from the Atlantic and tore at the grass roof of the cottage. Ishbel could hear the screams of the wind through the walls even though they were four feet thick. She was tormented at the thought of the seal man alone on the mountainous surf of the storm.

As soon as first light broke, Ishbel made her way down to the shore. The storm had worn itself out. Torn kelp lay along the beach like sodden brown rags. Jellyfish lay as sightless eyes. Dead birds slept on the white sand.

Then Ishbel saw the long fish tail of a Selkie, being lifted up and down by the low surf. Summoning all her courage, she waded in and pulled the empty skin ashore, finding it smooth and brown, the stiff skin heavy and oily with water. Ishbel looked up and down the beach for signs of the Selkie man himself, and with a leap of her stomach she saw him lying prostrate on the sand, his feet and legs half hidden behind a rock.

She ran across the beach, her feet sinking into the soft, white sand, and sick with grief because she thought she would find him dead. Placing a hand on his neck, she found that he was breathing still, but he was as cold as the Atlantic water.

Even in his human form, Ishbel could see that he was from a race of Selkies. His skin was smooth as seal skin and his eyes unnaturally long at the edges. His cheekbones were high and sloping and his black hair was as straight as seaweed in the water's tide.

Ishbel raised him up in her arms. Staggering under his weight, she began to carry him to her croft. The seawater was lit by the early sun. The sky showed a bruised red over the agate mountains as the small figure carried her burden home across the sands.

In the croft, Ishbel laid the Selkie man on the bed that was built into the thick wall and lined with warm blankets. She built up a good fire in the hearth in the middle of the floor, and then, summoning all her courage, she peeled off the remains of his wet and slimy seal skin. She tended to his wounds and after wrapping him in every blanket she possessed, she held his head up to sip hot water and whisky.

The Selkie man awoke, gazing into the face of Ishbel McOdrum. She had removed her customary scarf and her long hair fell down over the skin of his chest. He took a strand of her hair between his fingers and raised it up so that it shone in the firelight like kelp on the water.

Ishbel nursed him for a week. She had never seen such a face and found his small, happy features most pleasing. His dark eyes were liquid and deep, and so very like the eyes of the seals that appeared in the bay.

Ishbel hid his Selkie skins. She rolled them up, even though they were stiff and heavy with oil. She hid them away at the back of the old stone barn built by her father in the high summer pastures.

Without his seal skins the Selkie was a man, and the first man to be aware that Ishbel was a woman. He had an uncanny way of sensing her feelings and was most courteous. She christened him Finlay and tried to teach him the names of things in Gaelic.

Ishbel hid him for another week but as he grew stronger and able to walk again, it was impossible to prevent him from going outside and down to the ocean. She fetched some of her father's clothes for him. The woollen trousers fell in folds around his ankles and had to be cut short. He did not like the rough wool and scratched his arms and pulled a face, but he tolerated the garments in order to go down to his sea.

The Selkie man made straight for the shore and sat down near the hissing surf. Ishbel wondered that he could be friends with something that had all but killed him a few weeks before. The ocean around him was out to entice that morning with twenty shades of blue and green, but he sat and gazed far beyond, where the sea dipped over the curve of the earth, beyond where the boldest fishing boat had ever travelled — to a place where Ishbel could never follow him.

But he could not go back there. Ishbel had hidden away his Selkie skin and she meant to keep it hidden away.

Ishbel was not cruel to keep him. She knew then that the Selkie man loved her. He would sing her songs in a strange piercing voice that Ishbel knew were for her, and yet day after day he made his way back to the shore and sang quietly, sadly, to the sea. Ishbel would find him cold and stiff in the wind, and must pull him gently back to the croft.

The priest from St Columba's chapel came to see Ishbel, dismayed to learn that she was sharing a house with a man not her husband. Ishbel recounted that he was a fisherman who had all but drowned and she had given him shelter. She said that they wished to be married.

Everyone was happy for Ishbel. After the wedding they danced to the pipes out on the machair grass and ate mutton and drank the uisg a bhaig.

After a year of marriage, Ishbel McOdrum gave birth to a baby boy. He came into the world covered in smooth black hair like a tiny otter. Ishbel feared that the midwife would be afraid of such a child but the woman said he was a healthy infant and the hair would fall away. She had seen such a thing before.

As soon as he could walk, the boy was drawn towards water. Any jug of water in the house would be spilled and paddled in while her back was turned. He found every spring within a mile of their croft. But it was the sea that drew him most. He would stand at the small window after dark, watching the silver curves roll up the shore. If Ishbel did not bolt the door, he would disappear during the night and run down to play by the dark sea. Sometimes Ishbel could not find him. Then she must wake her husband who would find the child within minutes, by some instinct he shared with the boy.

It was good that Ishbel was a strong woman. On the days that her husband was mesmerised by the sea, no work was done by his hand. It was Ishbel who must see to the potato beds, fetch the sheep down, get water and prepare a meal. But she was used to hard work and simply waited until she could draw him back to her, warm him in her arms and restore him to the world.

Without warning, after four years of happiness together, he was gone. Yet his boat remained pulled up on the beach, so he could not be out at sea — at least not in the way of men.

He returned some days later, recounting that he had been up where the sheep were pastured in summer. Relieved to have him home once more, she did not reflect on how he had been walking up by the barn where she had hidden his Selkie skins, neatly folded in a wooden box.

The last months of winter were long and difficult. The wind roared into the bay, scouring the dried-out pastures. The cottage was blasted from all sides and seemed to rock as if tossing on the ocean. The ropes that held down the turf roof creaked in the storm. Ishbel would not let the child outside without holding onto him, so strongly did she feel the power of the gale trying to blow him down to the shore. The dark closed in early and stayed until late.

Ishbel's husband lay in the box bed sleeping or staring into the smoky air. Sometimes he would sit close to the turf embers, rocking to and fro and singing his unearthly songs in a language that only his son could understand. Or he would carve from bone, tiny figures of seals and porpoises that he gave to the boy.

To Ishbel it was a scene of contentment. They had never been as close or as tender with each other. She held him secure by the ropes of her love, steadying him on course as he pushed through the waters of his past life, through his old memories, to stay with her.

She did not know that he had already found the seal skin hidden in the box. She did not know that it called to him each evening.

He did not want to wear the skins again. He did not want to leave. At night he would cover his ears with the blanket and sleep fitfully.

When spring came, he returned to the high pastures, thinking to mend the tears in his Selkie skin, out of a sense of thrift; but the Selkie skin was his own skin, and once it lay in his hand, the urge to wear it again became irresistible. He thought of floating on the water in his old life and found that he was drifting on the sea. He was no longer a man but a Selkie and he could not turn back.

His son heard his father's cries from across the water and called out to Ishbel to hurry. She ran down to the shore and plunged into the waves with her arms held out and called and called for him to come back, but his eerie cries of farewell echoed across the bay. Then the small figure swam out towards the horizon, until they could see him no more.

Ishbel comforted her son. She told him to be brave, for his father might not return: the Selkie curse was strong and hard to break.

'But he will return,' said her son. 'He cried out in a seal voice that one day he will return with my Selkie skin and take me out to sea with him.'

When she heard this, her heart went cold. With great haste, she gathered together her belongings in a blanket and they set off on a stony track to the middle of the island. She built with her own hands from the unforgiving stones a small house, and thus she stayed hidden away and landlocked. And in time her son married and became father to five sons of the McOdrum name.

When Ishbel was very old and her chestnut hair turned thin and silver, she began to long to go back to her cottage by the shore once more. So she walked home along the stony paths and found the roof timbers of her home broken and gaping. White sand had blown across the floor. The box bed in the wall was strewn with debris where once there had been blankets. She brushed the boards clean and lay down in the space where they had lain together, wrapping herself in the blanket that she wore as a cape.

She stayed in her cottage listening to the sea until her time came to go beneath the soft machair grass, where the dead may look out on the shining sea and feel the spray rising up over Hushinish Point. And on the night that she died, whales beached themselves on the shore and scores of seals were seen gathering together in the bay. When the morning came, they were gone.

CHAPTER 9

Ruth

There was a tremendous noise going on through the night, the sheep calling out in the dark, some bleats deep and glottal, some new and tentative.

'It's because it's lambing season,' said Michael, who was brought up near a farm. 'It's the mums and babies learning each other's cries.' He put the pillow over his head and went back to sleep. Around six I gave up and got dressed. It was almost light, the first signs that the days were starting to get longer.

In the half-finished sea room, I wrapped myself in a blanket, sat by the electric heater and read the story through once again. It was strange to think that Ferguson had also had a Selkie story in the family. It felt a bit like discovering a photo of some unknown relative in a dusty box in the attic.

The dawn brought pale gradations of light around the bay. I found myself staring out of the window towards Hushinish, over towards where Ishbel had waited and waited on the seashore for her seal husband. My hand was resting on my barely changed stomach. There was a flicker in my belly, wilful and fluid, like a tiny fish turning in water. I was stunned. It was the first time I'd been able to feel it moving.

One thing I knew: I could never leave my child like Mum had left me. How could she?

All through my childhood, the answer to that had been because there was something wrong with me, something lacking and unlovable – until I felt myself starting to melt away. That flash of a white hand reaching up from the oily water, calling me to let myself slip away with her.

I put the story in the drawer, banged it shut. In the kitchen, poured lentils into a pan to soak them ready for supper. Later that day, Jamie and his girlfriend would be arriving on the evening ferry.

I made up the bed in the other finished bedroom, opening the window to let the wind blow in from the machair and get rid of the oily paint smell. I hung curtains and found a reasonable-looking sheepskin rug to put by the bed. Then I tidied round the half-finished sea room, adjusting the blanket that covered the battered sofa we'd acquired through the *Stornoway Gazette*.

Walking over the new floorboards, I couldn't stop my eyes flicking over to the spot where we'd stood and looked down at the rusting trunk and the mess inside.

I picked up some books and magazines from the floor and neatened them on the bookcase shelves and promised myself that as soon as things were less busy, I'd look into finding more records dating back to that time – perhaps from the library.

It had started to rain, not a polite shower like you get in town, but bucketfuls of water thrown against the window, as if the sea had changed its usual level and was beating on the house in waves. I stood watching the streaming windows, hoping the new struts and repaired panes would hold.

And I wondered how you went about looking up a mother who said she came from the sea, a mother who had left the barest amount of real information and no records of the family she once belonged to – a family who for all I knew comprised cousins or aunts walking around somewhere in the islands.

★

The storm had blown away as suddenly as it had appeared, leaving a calm and innocent sky. The first hints of the setting sun were deepening the colours of both land and sky as we went to meet Jamie and Leaf from the ferry late that afternoon.

They rumbled down the boat's metal ramp in an old Bedford van. Jamie was driving. A blond girl was sitting next to him with her bare feet up on the dashboard.

Jamie leapt out of the van, pushing back his long fringe, and gave me a huge hug, enveloping me in his baggy checked shirt. Leaf was small and slender with pale blond hair. She was a couple of years older than Jamie, and the sun had begun carving fine lines along the delicate skin of her tanned forehead. She wore a large, striped jumper that fell away from one shoulder and pale jeans with artful rips across the thighs. Her earrings tinkled as she held me in a bony hug. Michael was already walking away, talking non-stop with Jamie.

'Wow,' I heard him say to Jamie, 'Leaf's a bit of a stunner.'

I'd made lentil lasagne as Leaf never ate meat. We lit candles and sat round the kitchen table, a jug of early machair flowers in the middle. I think that was the evening we talked about the child's remains, but it felt like something finished and historic, nothing really to do with us.

'So, how did your parents come to christen you Leaf?' Michael said, filling everyone's glass.

She laughed. 'My parents call me Audrey. Audrey Marilynne Bloomfeld. Leaf's my nickname. It's kind of nice, isn't it?'

Jamie told us a long story about how Leaf had appeared beside him with a pamphlet, the sun behind her as he lay on the beach in swimming trunks. She'd spent the next hour trying to convert him to the cause, saving a forest up along the California coast.

'In the end, it was me who was converted to the way of Jamie,' said Leaf, blowing him a kiss across the table, along with a waft of perfume that smelled of suntan oil, mixed in with a faint whiff of cigarette smoke. 'And we've even been to see the lovely house where you grew up in Chichester, Michael. I love that old house. Where did you grow up, Ruth?'

I paused, too many snapshots crowding in. I put my palm round a glass of cool water. Took a sip. Placed it back in its own damp ring on the table.

'In a children's home.'

A great way to close down a conversation.

Leaf let out a tiny gasp. 'But what happened? Your parents?'

'Never met my dad. Mum drowned.'

'I'm so sorry. That must be so hard for you.'

I shrugged. It was always tiring, explaining to people. Me ending up having to reassure them that I'm fine, really. Don't worry about it.

'Honestly. I don't think about it now. Just one of those things.'

'But don't you have any family left now?'

'I've got Michael.'

He reached over and took my hand, decisively changing the subject by telling a funny story about our neighbour Angus John. I felt my chest relax so that I could breathe again. Leaning against Michael, the fabric of his old denim shirt felt soft as peach skin against my arm. I was aware of the strength of his body when he stretched to refill our glasses.

We sat up late, drinking the wine that Jamie had brought, laying out our plans and hopes for the house and the holiday business; the little boat we were going to buy one day to do sailing trips, the walking tours up into the mountains, the wildlife-sketching holidays I'd put on. At the end of the evening, I gave out the schedules I'd drawn up for how we could share out the work and the expenses.

Eventually, we made our way up to bed, after Leaf had hugged everyone again and told us with tears in her eyes that she felt it here

– banging her chest at this point – that she was really going to be happy in this place, and asked if we made our own bread.

'Grief,' I said as we got into bed. 'If I am ever that obsessed with what I do or don't eat, please shoot me.'

Michael laughed and it felt then like we were always going to agree, lying close together, his presence solid and reassuring, the house tamed, and the dark friendly with the sounds of other people.

Later, I heard someone wake up in the night and pad across the landing. I was already asleep before they must have padded back to their room again.

CHAPTER 10

Ruth

The days were getting noticeably longer, the air smelling wetly of rain, but at night it was still very cold. Finally, we got the central heating installed and the house relaxed in the warmth. New gloss paint baking on radiators became the aroma of well-being and comfort.

And with four sets of hands working on the house, we began to see real progress over the next few weeks. The house had taken on a different mood, the rooms full of voices, the transistor radio going all day, the air sweetened with turpentine and new wood. The sea room was painted white. Hard to think it was the same room where we had stood over the rusty little trunk a few weeks before – still that annoying little flicker of the eyes each time I walked across the newly varnished floorboards. When was that going to stop?

Two more bedrooms were now completed and we'd even made a start on the kitchen; having Jamie and Leaf helping out was making such a difference. True, it was Jamie who did most of the work. Leaf had a funny way of wandering off before something was finished. The paintbrush would be left to go waxy in the paint tray. You'd find her cross-legged somewhere, reading a book and twirling the end of the blond ponytail that she swept up to one side with a scrunchie. But when she was around, Leaf was a lot of fun. I'd never really had a girlfriend before who you could talk to about almost anything.

Of course, the home had been full of girls, but it was always tense in that place; we'd circled around each other, making brittle allegiances or breaking into fights – in the bathrooms, where the sound was dulled by the tiled walls. Getting close to one of the girls was tricky; you never knew when you'd press on something that could make someone explode into bitter words and punches.

Leaf and I talked as we slapped white paint onto walls. She was outrageously open: no topic was off limits. I knew so much about her that sometimes I felt I'd grown up in that wooden house by a river in California, the music of Dylan and Beethoven coming from her dad's study, her mother furious when she found how Leaf had jumped out of the bedroom window to go to a forbidden beach party; the life of a doted-on daughter.

I told her funny stories about meeting Michael and then Jamie and their parents.

I didn't feel keen to drag on about the tedium of my own childhood.

Michael and I were working outside one morning. He was painting the front window struts in the sun, humming the tune of 'Aileen Duin', while the wind trembled the yellow irises along the streams. Bright daisies had opened across the machair turf like stars. Drifts of sea pink shivered across the turf down by the sea.

I was sanding down a cot passed on to us by Mrs MacKay. Once it was re-varnished, it was going to look good as new.

'Old Angus John says we're to give him a lift tomorrow,' said Michael. 'According to some calendar, it's time for the village to go and cut their peat bricks, and we're counted in.'

'It's nice, isn't it?' I said to Michael. 'Being part of a place. I've never really had that before.'

'Yes; but you know, home's wherever you are now,' he said.

'That's what I feel too.'

I carried on carefully sanding the cot bars, too happy to say anything, contentment settling over the morning.

The first time I met Angus John, I honestly thought he might be a bit simple. He lived alone in a ramshackle one-storey bothy at the end of the village. The roof was a hump of bleached thatch, criss-crossed with ropes that were weighted down against the Atlantic storms with a ring of dangling sea stones.

His nearest neighbours, the MacKays, were model crofters. Every day you'd see Mr MacKay sorting peats or digging seaweed into the rigs, or you'd see Mrs MacKay in her nylon overall, crossing the field in the early morning mist to milk the cow. Everything scrubbed and mended neatly. Nothing was ever wasted in that house.

Angus John had his thrifty ways too. His fences were made from rusty bedsteads and old doors, cobbled together with sections of blue fishing net. Behind the house was a whole graveyard of corroded tractor parts and an upended bath slowly sinking back into the turf.

The first day we moved into the caravan, the Sea House still not habitable, I was washing up at the sink when an arm suddenly reached up through the open window, holding a whisky bottle. 'There'll be one of those for you every day,' a voice shouted in a thick Gaelic accent. I ducked down to see who it was and saw an old man with a creased face, an unravelling jumper, a shirt buttoned up to the neck. His trousers were belted with thick rope. He gave a grim nod and left.

The whisky bottle was a funny opaque colour. I opened it and sniffed. It was filled with milk.

'Ah, that's just Angus John,' said Mrs MacDonald when I went to buy stamps and, more importantly, ask her if I should be worried about the old man who kept wandering into our caravan. 'And to think he was the cleverest in his family as a boy,' she said, looking out of the window towards his bothy. 'All his brothers and sisters, they have left the croft now for high-flying careers on the mainland, teachers and bankers, but Angus John, he came back from the war and never wanted to leave. Ah well, he's the nearest thing we have to a bard here.' She sniffed. 'He writes beautiful poems in the Gaelic, Ruth. And once, a man came from the BBC with a tape recorder so Angus John could tell his stories into it.'

Angus John's habit of walking in without knocking was our introduction to how you socialised in the islands. It turned out that it was quite in order to wander into someone's house and sit there in companionable silence while the host got on with whatever they were doing. We soon realised that what the host should be doing was preparing a snack, or *strupach,* a courtesy from the times when people would tramp miles across unmade tracks between villages – or in Angus's case, from his croft to our kitchen.

I felt bad that Angus, who seemed to have nothing, should be bringing us so much milk and crowdie cheese which was soft and grainy and slightly sour and made by Angus on top of the stove in his kitchen. But he wouldn't hear of being thanked. He had a cow, and we did not, so of course he'd bring round his extra milk. No need to make a song and dance about it.

And since we had a van and he did not, it was only natural that he should inform us when we'd be taking his calf down to Plocropol, or giving two of his sheep a lift up to the market in Stornoway. His English might sound abrupt, but the Gaelic he was translating from probably had more suggestion in the phrasing; braided into the old language were all the assumptions of a close-knit subsistence community, where sharing was a way of life.

Early the next morning, we picked up Angus John and drove across the island to where Scarista village had its peat beds. Right up to the start of summer, the east side of the island had been a place of industrial colours, of smoke-coloured mist and rusty heather, lochs black as oil, sheets of steel-grey rock slick with the wet. But now the heather was beginning to green over. We got out of the van to a wide view across the island, of silver rocks and the silver-blue of the Minch. In the distance, the blue smudges of Skye and the paler mountains of the mainland.

The peat was several feet deep, banks of it sliced down into the moor like seams of soft coal. Most of the villagers from Scarista were already cutting out the wet slabs, tossing them up the bank to where someone else caught them and stood them in small dolmens to dry out. To begin with, we were not much help, but gradually we got into the rhythm: the push of the blade into the wet soil, the catching of the slab of peat, the bending to stack it upright, the sun hot on our necks and a sea breeze coming off the sparkling Minch.

At around twelve we stopped. Mr MacDonald carried a mysterious, bundled-up sheet from his van and a huge pile of home baking made its magical appearance in the middle of the moor. Mrs MacKay got a kettle boiling and we sat down to eat, drinking mugs of peaty tea and sharing jokes in English.

Mr MacKay passed round the smallest glass in the world and we each took a nip. Leaf offered the whisky to Angus John but he waved the glass away, staring out to sea and holding on to his skinny knees like a man avoiding evil and depressed about it.

'Oh no, don't be giving the bottle to him,' Mrs MacDonald told her, leaning over to take it away. 'Angus John has taken the *curam*.'

'The *curam*?'

'It's when a man sees his ways of drink and sin are going nowhere, and gets religion,' said Donald Allan, a nephew of Mrs MacDonald's. 'It's one or the other here on the island, and I dare say when I get old and have done with my drinking, I might go that way.'

I thought of the bottles that came filled with milk each day. A lot of whisky bottles for someone that didn't drink.

'And how long is it till the baby is born now, Ruth?' said Mrs MacKay.

'Just under five months.'

'That will come round soon. You'll be wanting a name. Of course, the young people now they want modern names like Tracey and Craig. But in my day, the boys were all given their father's name, the girls too sometimes. Not always a good thing. My aunt was a Murdina, after her father Murdo. Ah, but you've never been able to find any of your relatives here on the island?'

'Nothing. Mum was a Macleod, but then so are half the people on the island.'

'It's not right,' she said, shaking her head. 'Everyone should know who their people are.' Then her face cleared. 'What you should do, Ruth, is go and see Christine MacAulay down at Northton. She traces the family trees for Americans and Canadians. Now she'd be just the one to help.'

'I'd probably be wasting her time. There's not much to go on really.'

I helped Mrs MacKay wash the plates in the stream, and then everybody got back to work.

Leaf walked a little way off and climbed up onto some rocks. For some reason, she'd decided to wear a long flowery tea dress to cut peats, and a droopy jumper rolled up to the elbows that fell off her shoulder if she tried to dig. She sat cross-legged, facing out towards the sea, and held up her face to the sun. She laid her hands palms up, one on each knee. Leaf believed in meditating every day.

As she sat in the sun, her white-blond hair lifted with the breeze, twirling and then falling. I saw the wives looking sideways at her, bemused, as they worked on. Mrs MacDonald was in front of me, her woollen skirt taking the strain over her behind as she dug the peats.

Her hair was secured under a nylon scarf, firmly tied under her chin so that the wind had no chance to mess about with the perm she had every Tuesday in Tarbert.

Only Leaf, I thought, could be entirely oblivious to the fact that everyone else was shifting and breaking into a sweat, as the sun got further round the island.

I watched as the breeze played with Leaf's hair. For some reason, I saw a picture of myself at thirteen, in a barber's shop. I'd gone in and asked him to shave it all off. The hair fell like feathers from my scalp and when I saw myself in the mirror, it looked brutal, but I was glad.

'You can have this spade now, Leaf,' I yelled.

Leaf slowly lay back onto the turf, and put her elbow across her eyes. 'Um hum, just a minute,' she said sleepily and didn't move.

Something snapped in the back of my head. I felt, at that moment, as though Leaf had stolen the life I should have had. I had the sensation of flying over the turf. I was aware that I was down low, right in her face, and her pale green eyes were wide open with surprise.

'I don't know why you think you can keep living in our house when you hardly lift a bloody finger!' I was shouting. 'How come you get to do all the fucking meditating, and we get to do all the fucking washing-up?'

She was frowning up at me in confusion, like some little kid who's been told off. I saw Jamie running up the slope towards us.

'Everything okay there?'

There was the sound of a spade slapping into the turf. A bird rose up into the sky, a lark, singing madly.

'She freeloads off you, Jamie,' I said, walking away.

'But I don't mind,' he said with a half laugh. 'If Leaf has stuff she needs to do.' He started helping her up. The bird kept on winding its song higher and I walked back to the group standing around the peats, and politely not looking.

I could feel my cheeks roasting in the sun, my head bursting. Michael shot me a baleful look, a God-not-again look, but I blanked him.

The sea breeze was starting to cool the air, and the anger was going out like the tide now, as distant and ridiculous as tiny figures gesticulating on a shoreline.

By the end of the day, Michael was beaming: we were going to be able to take our share of the peat bricks home when they were dry. Months later, when winter came round and we started to burn the peat, it would have an unexpected smell, blue and woody, tinged with something like paraffin; and I would recognise it then as the smell of the islands, the particular odour that had been there all along.

As we drove home, exhausted and grubby, I watched Leaf staring out of her window; a pang of regret for how the afternoon had gone.

Sometimes I saw her, that girl that I might have been, if things had been different. She would have been nice, good with kids, sweet even; the image of her flickered before me like a TV screen where ghostly signals waver and compete. Hard to know what was real. Surely, all I had to do was focus on her to make her clearer.

I leaned over and put my hand on Leaf's wrist.

'I'm sorry about… you know.'

'Hey, don't worry,' she said. But there was something behind her eyes. A shutter had come down.

I got out of the van that day, slamming the door hard, determined to change, to do better. In just a few months' time I'd be holding a small child.

The thing was, I had a bit of a history of losing it – each time I was sure it was the last time. Things really were going to be different now, I told myself.

They had to be.

I still hadn't understood; how there's a certain smell to a disposses-sed soul, acrid, bitter as smoke, the irrefutable odour of an angry refugee, banging on the doors of strangers, asking for money, for water, for food for the children, for recompense.

And I was so, so tired. I would have given anything to lie down and sleep for a few years, but as we went inside, I realised there was no relaxing in our home, not while the image of that infant's remains lay at the edge of every thought like an unanswered question.

CHAPTER 11

Ruth

In spite of my determination to get hold of something like facts about what had happened in our house, I got no further. I was beginning to think that too much time had gone by; we'd simply never know who that child was, why she'd been hidden away.

A fine rain set in, making everything feel cold and shut in. Morning after morning, we woke to find the house stranded in a white mist that only cleared by noon.

'I'm driving into Tarbert,' Michael yelled up the stairs one morning. 'Anyone else want to come?' We'd been cooped up inside for days. Everyone was in the van and ready to go within minutes.

We drove out along the coast road. The grey cloud let through an obscured light, sad and thin, yet the sodden ground was bright with colours; cuts of liquorice peat; purple and orange heather stems; electric-green moss. The lochs were black and brimming, stippled with reed tips like the stubble on an old man's chin.

We turned into Tarbert High Street, which is little more than a row of cottages looking out over the harbour. A group of bandit sheep shambled along in front of the van, taking their time and apparently heading for the post office. We parked in front of Parek's haberdashery store, where gruesome truncated bodies modelled blouses and corsets in the window. A yellow acetate blind was pulled down against the unlikely event that strong sunlight might damage the goods.

Leaf and I headed for the MacDonalds' grocery store. She hummed as we walked up the hill. We hadn't really spoken much in the days since the peat cutting. She was pleasant enough, but it felt a bit rusty trying to open up a conversation.

'Did you get a letter from your parents this morning?'

'Yes.' She smiled.

'How are they?'

'Just fine.'

I nodded and we turned into the grocer's shop.

Norman and Kenneth MacDonald might have looked like civil servants with their neat jumpers and ties and their blameless and studious faces, but they had their own slaughter shed out back and were the stopping post between the sheep on the hills and the chops and joints spread out on the display counter. At the back of the shop stood a large aluminium contraption. I watched it feeding the pinkish beef mash into sausage casings. The fruit and veg were expensive. I bought apples and carrots – but not the bright yellow cabbages wilting on the bottom shelf, mutated into toxic balls of sulphur.

Standing in the queue to pay, I listened to the knots of Gaelic conversation between the crofters and their wives. When we first came to the island, it had been a shock to hear everyone speaking with the breathy twang that I had always thought of as peculiar to my mum. It made her feel so near. It gave me a constant feeling that she'd left the place I'd just arrived at, only moments before. I decided to learn Gaelic and bought a Gaelic grammar from the bookshop. It turned out learning Chinese would have been easier. 'Oh, they all mean to learn Gaelic when they move here,' the lady in the bookshop said, 'but you need to grow up in a Gaelic house to speak it properly.' I had four words of Gaelic from my childhood – two of them quite unrepeatable, according to Mrs MacKay.

In that first week, I'd been sure I was going to discover more about Mum now that we were living in the islands. Walking across the moors in blinding rain with Michael, we'd sheltered in an unlikely red telephone box stranded at a junction of small tracks. I'd looked up my surname in the phone book, excited to think it could be that easy to contact a distant relative. There were pages and pages of Macleods. It was evidently the Hebridean equivalent of Smith. Impossible to phone every number and quiz them.

Now, as I waited in the grocery store queue, I felt frustrated and disappointed again, to think how impossible it had proved to find any hint of Mum's family.

And yet, somewhere in the islands there had to be people that I was related to – and no way now to find out anything about them. Mum had made sure of that when she slipped away into the silent water. There was the woman Mrs MacKay had mentioned, Christine, but I was pretty sure that would only be another dead end, another rebuttal: trying to find lost bits of your past does nothing but make old sores weep and sting.

I stopped at the haberdasher's to pick out some knitting wool for the baby-jacket pattern I'd bought last time. As I went to pay, I saw a loose skein of soft green wool that was almost the colour of Leaf's green-and-yellow-flecked eyes. In a moment of inspiration, I decided I'd knit her a gift – a scarf. I could do a scarf.

I paid for the wool then headed down to the hardware shop where Michael and Jamie had gone to buy bags of cement.

Macleod's hardware store was a wonderful barn-like shed, open to the sea air in all weathers, the pine panelling painted in odds and ends of beige and blue. There was a huge handwritten board over the door listing 'Wellies, Fish Hooks, Chicken Feed, Tweed Caps, Worm Bait, Outboard Motors, Nylon Rope, Tick Tweezers, Light Bulbs, Overalls', and everything was stacked up on roof-high metal shelving, accessed by enormous wooden stepladders.

I found Michael and Jamie in a gully of boat equipment, discussing the merits of separation pumps as if we actually had a boat that might need one. I wandered off to the middle of the shed where there was a great Edwardian dresser piled with woollen socks, hot water bottles, parish newsletters and WD40 cans. I glanced at the notices taped to its mirrored back; there was one for a ceilidh at An t'Obbe in a few weeks' time; another with the hours of the Tarbert museum.

'I didn't know there was a museum here,' I said to Johnny, the shop owner.

'It's new. Up next to the fish and chip shop. I think it's open if you want to go up and see awhile. Just knock on the door.'

I headed back up, keen to find out if there might be something about the Sea House.

Next to the smallest fish and chip shop in the world – the front room of a tiny terraced cottage where a fat fryer took up nearly all the space – was an equally small cottage. A notice covered in a plastic bag was pinned to the front door: 'Tarbert Museum, all donations to be approved by Morag MacIver.'

I pushed the door and stepped down into a whitewashed room with a stone floor. There was a motley collection of articles along one wall and a trestle table on the other side, piled up with elderly photograph albums. It felt colder inside the room than out in the misty air. I recognised a few of the old farm implements: hoes and *cas-chrom* spades, a group of rough and ready butter churns and a large stone with a hollowed-out centre – an old hand quern for grinding corn. There was also a Tilley lamp, some Victorian crockery, and several black bibles in Gaelic.

On the wall was a photograph of Avenbuidhe Castle, a small turreted and castellated building tucked into a bay below the mountains. I wondered if there were any photos of the Marstones.

The jumble of photo albums didn't look promising. I turned the pages. There were black and white photos of cottages in full sun with people milking or spinning wool outside the bothy door, and endless formal line-ups of people looking serious and stiffly wearing their plain, best clothes for communions or weddings. There were also some wonderful Victorian photos in a box, of fishermen with huge moustaches, and women in bonnets and black skirts cutting hay with scythes, but nothing that would help me.

Then, in the next picture, I saw our house. It was a very old photograph, printed on thick card and faded to a yellowed sepia, the faces and clothes of the people shining pale and silvery as moths. It showed a minister in a clerical collar, his staff assembled each side of him outside the front gate. I turned the picture over. Some indecipherable words were written on the back with the date: 1860. My heart skipped. I flipped it back over.

So I was looking at the Reverend Ferguson. A dapper young man with pale eyes and a serious expression looked back at me. He wore a high, white collar band and a watch chain across his waistcoat. He looked serious and was holding a little black bible against his chest, as if affecting gravitas. His parting was remarkably neat, his hair oiled. But the most striking thing was that even from the faded photo, it was clear that Alexander Ferguson was very personable, with the kind of small, even features that can seem almost pretty in a man.

Either side of him stood a row of farm workers, the females to the left, and it wasn't hard to guess that they all would have been in love with the Reverend in some way – even down to the old lady with the extraordinary bonnet.

I noticed that one girl was better dressed than the others, wearing a cotton frock rather than a rough skirt, more like a housemaid than a farm worker. Her hair was twisted up in a bun, frizzy wisps escaping. She looked ready to say something sharp.

On the other side, three big farm men stood bashful in front of the camera.

Was I looking at the faces of the baby's parents among that little group?

Reluctantly, I put the photo back.

It was late afternoon when I headed back to find the others. With a sinking heart, I remembered it was Leaf's turn to cook. We would be eating late then. Not, I hoped, more lentils with crunchy centres like bits of grit embedded in mush.

I scanned the high street and across to the car park by the wooden pier where the ferry docked. No one. Then I saw a row of three people sitting on the wall at the top of the harbour; in the middle, long fair hair blowing in the breeze. They were all eating chips.

And fish. They were definitely pulling bits off fried fish. I totted it up in my head. That would blow our budget for a couple of days.

I sat down on the wall. Michael handed me a newspaper parcel. I could feel the soft chips inside. Leaf beamed.

The oil was soaking through the paper, the heat rapidly leaving.

'How much did this cost?' I asked, clutching my bag in front of me like a defence.

'Oh, don't worry about that,' Leaf said, waving a chip at the sky. 'It's my treat. It won't come out of the budget thingy.'

'Thanks, Leaf,' Michael said.

'Nice one,' echoed Jamie.

'But the point is we're supposed to all put in the same, take out the same. You can't just make presents of meals, just because, because you can.'

'Hey, don't sweat the small stuff,' Jamie said. 'Leaf's cool with it. Anyway, her dad's loaded.'

Leaf looked confused and apologetic, shrugged her shoulders. 'Really, don't worry about it.'

She was daintily picking out the bits she liked. She handed the rest of her meal to Jamie, who polished it off.

I sat stabbing my chips with a wooden fork. They were almost cold.

'Did anyone get tomato sauce?'

Later, I almost wished I'd never seen that photo. I woke in the dark and pictured those pale, silvery faces, those moth-coloured clothes. There was an odd smell in the room, like the mustiness of old garments. I lay restless and alert. No hope of going back to sleep.

I decided that there was no good reason why I shouldn't go down, switch on the sensible kitchen light and make some hot milk.

But I didn't get up. I had a ridiculous, shrinking fear that if I walked through the blackness I might feel another hand brush against mine. Something claustrophobic and anxious, making it hard to breathe the dark air.

It wasn't meant to be like this.

When I was sixteen, the council put me in a bedsit. I never slept well in that bedsit – not that I ever slept soundly when I was in the children's home; I used to look forward, so much, to getting out of that place.

My bedsit was on the third floor of a tall redbrick house. Late at night, I used to sit up in bed listening to people coming in: heavy footsteps running up and down the stairs; people shouting at each other; thumps. I sat watching the door handle, hoping the lock would hold, and listening, always listening. Sometimes I'd read or study all night just so I could stay awake.

As soon as it was light, I'd pull on my clothes and get out of the building to walk around the streets. I'd watch the milkman delivering bottles, the rubbish truck arriving, then I'd walk down to the greasy spoon on the high street and order strong tea, pour in a stream of sugar and hope no one would speak to me.

I used to imagine how it must feel, to lie down in your own home and feel safe. I'd peek into back-lit rooms at dusk, and pick out the paper lampshade from Habitat; the potted palms casting shadows on white walls; all the things I'd have in my own place one day and feel safe.

I turned my pillow over and thumped it into a better position, determined that I would sleep. But it wasn't till round about four, when the room began to fill with light, that I finally let go of my vigilance and drifted off.

CHAPTER 12

Alexander

In the early hours of the morning I woke sweating from a nightmare so distasteful, I felt sullied by the very memory. I dreamed I was a large and corpulent animal without limbs, strenuously moving along the seashore in large, grub-like motions, and propelled forward by such intense animal instincts that I later blushed to recall them. I was making haste to where the females of the species waited, baying with their harsh cries.

Finding my passage barred by another male, I savaged the bull animal until the sands ran with blood. When I saw what I had done, I tried to form words to make the beast understand that I was in truth a man, trapped within the flesh of an animal, but my words came out as lowing, inarticulate noises. I had never experienced such isolation and despair.

The horror of that moment woke me. I threw back the bed sheets and stumbled in the darkness towards a faint line of dawn round the window. I pushed aside the curtain to see a landscape made of floating shadows and half-light.

I lit a candle and made my way down to my study. I began to read from St Anthony, but waking some hours later, I found the book still open at the same page. I could hear the sounds of Moira banking up the peat fires in the kitchen. She would shortly come in to lay the fire and she would not be pleased to see that I had been in my room without any heat – though I had a perfectly sturdy blanket to keep out the early morning chill, and I counted such deprivation as a beneficial discipline.

For though it made my eyes sore and weary, it was only by rising early each day that I renewed my daily hope to finally set out upon the path I so greatly desired, towards a mind and heart given wholly to God. But in spite of such vows, by close of each day all my efforts seemed to have been to undo those same resolutions. Surely, by now, I thought, after all my years of study, I might have trained myself in godly ways. And yet I saw no change in my nature, no evidence in my own heart that here was a man saved by grace – and how bitterly I saw that failure.

And now all my efforts were to publicly cast a doubtful light upon my own character. In speaking with Maggie Kintail, I realised that my family superstitions had become known to all my parishioners. And what had induced me to want to share my unseemly fables with Miss Marstone, knowing full well that she was too young to keep a confidence? It was as if she had the power to make me do things I would later regret, and I thought again of how she leaned on my arm, how her round cheek blushed with pleasure when I complimented her, and in a way that made me quite forget myself.

I had thus vowed to myself to not let this happen again. I had fasted and prayed for three days on the matter, until I was weary to the bone and in such ill humour that I did nothing but further prove my own unfitness.

And for three days Moira had been cooking her most delicious stews and banging plates of food in front of me, in spite of my express instructions to cancel all my meals.

'If the grace of our Lord will do for the likes of a wretch like me,' she scolded, 'then I don't see why you, a minister, should improve upon the Lord's grace by near starving yourself to death with holiness.'

A tap on the door and Moira came in, stepping round the

books and papers that covered my study floor. I shut my eyes so that she would think me napping, but she was too quick. A cluck of disapproval and I saw that she was planning not to speak to me to better demonstrate her displeasure, but as she stepped round the books her curiosity got the better of her and she had to ask me about a drawing in yesterday's newspaper. I had left the newspaper open at a lithographic reproduction of a fossilised creature recently uncovered in Germany – a creature half bird and half reptile.

To me, this article had been the most wonderful news, arriving at a time when I had almost felt ready to abandon my project. For, although I now had six various accounts of sightings of merpeople taken from newspapers or court statements to magistrates, I had not one scrap of concrete evidence; no bone structure to examine; no skein of hair to touch with my hand; and no clue at all as to the precise texture of a skin or hide. I had nothing but a hypothesis based on stories and distant glimpses.

This new report in *The Times*, of the London museum's latest acquisition, had set my heart racing with hope for my own studies; but Moira wrinkled her nose as she turned the page round to better follow the shape of the incredible bird reptile.

'What is it?' she asked.

'It's been christened Archaeopteryx.'

'I can see that, sir, but what sort of bird is it? It looks like the leavings of a chicken, but with nasty claws to it.'

'That,' I said, 'is exactly the creature that Mr Darwin predicted we would find one day. He postulated that there must have once been some creature with features halfway between those of a reptile and a bird – though at the time no evidence for such a creature had ever been found, and yet even as he sat writing those words, men in Bavaria were unearthing a new vein of fossil remains; within the year they had uncovered the bird-lizard.'

'And the museum paid seven hundred pounds,' said Moira, who by now had read through the article. 'You could buy Avenbuidhe Castle twice over for that! It's not even got a head.'

'But look,' I said, going to stand next to her, 'it has wings, and feathers, and yet it has these spiny claws midway down the wings to kill prey. And see, it has a tail, a long bony tail more like a lizard than a bird. These, Moira, are the bones not only of a bird, but also of a true reptile, a link between the species.'

I traced for her the outline. The faint wing feathers seemed blurred with movement, as if caught on a photographic plate; a ghostly record of a day long ended.

She shuddered. 'I'm glad that nasty thing isn't flying in the skies around here. It's bad enough having the terns dive in your hair if you disturb a nest in the dunes. I say we are well rid of it. Now, if you don't mind me pointing it out, sir, but you're white as a sheet and I'm going to fetch you your breakfast.'

Moira bustled back to the kitchen before I had the chance to tell her that I would abstain, and in truth, I was rather glad since my stomach was making sounds that agreed with her.

I sat with the newspaper across my lap, too weary to move. Darwin had had enough faith to predict this missing step in the process of transmutation, and in time the evidence had finally proved him right. But my own poor theories remained just that, nothing but faith and speculation. It seemed to me that I could make no further progress until I had settled in my own mind whether my sea creatures might be men evolved back into the sea, or some primordial type of sub-human, somewhat like the various families of higher primates.

This latter thought was harder to countenance. I pictured for a moment a creature with the face of a man, with the mind and speech of a man, but with no more of a soul than a crow or a lizard, a creature that might as readily tear you limb from limb as engage in conversation.

Such speculations left me staring out towards the seaboard, caught among my thoughts, until I ate three eggs and a large bowl of brose with cream, Moira staying to watch me spoon down every mouthful – and I was deeply touched by the care she had taken to burn nothing. Then I must go to the church to say my offices.

Standing at the lectern in the morning sun, I read aloud from the allotted passage from Hebrews:

For the word of God is quick, and powerful, and sharper than any two edged sword, piercing even to the dividing asunder of soul and spirit, of the joints and marrow, and is a discerner of the thoughts and intents of the heart.

In solitary prayer, I pondered upon the soul and the spirit of a man, how they might differ in essence, but I pictured only shreds of luminous and transparent tissue, lodged within a clumsy scaffold of mortal bones.

Occupied with many thoughts, I walked down to the beaches beneath the manse. A mile, perhaps two miles, of pure white sand, the sea coming up in rollers of transparent glass, and reassuringly devoid of any sea creatures. The air was sharp with sea minerals, the blueness of the sky and mountains startling under the sunshine. After an hour briskly walking in such great beauty, I arrived home calm and with a feeling of well-being – a mood no doubt connected not only with the glory of Creation, but also with the oat brose and fried eggs.

And it had become clear to me as I walked, that the creature I sought must surely be as human as I: every encounter with mankind seemed to stress this fellow feeling, and report a shared ability to communicate. And if one were to add in the various stories and legends, then the sea people were able to also walk on land, and even interbreed with the rest of mankind.

I thus came home quite convinced that my next path of enquiry should be to further study the adapted anatomy of those land mammals returned to the sea: the cetaceans, the Phocidae and the Sirenia.

I also determined to better serve my parishioners. I understood from Moira that several displaced families had recently arrived from a nearby island. They had been sent to live along the eastern bays where conditions were already congested and harsh. I decided to see what could be done for them. And if what I heard from Moira about their sad circumstances were true, then I would respectfully enquire of Lord Marstone why more was not being done for those chased from their homes and now seeking refuge on his land in Finsbay.

I first sat down in my study to write to Matthew, asking if I might visit again and thus spend some time in the anatomy and zoology departments of the university museum, very much cheered by the thought of once again enjoying the wise conversation of my old foraging companion in the midst of the civilised hum of Edinburgh. I was finding it a lonely situation, stranded as I was on the edge of the Atlantic, and though I was sometimes tempted to confide more than I should in Miss Marstone, I resolved that in future I must guard against such indiscretions. A good minister makes no friends and favourites, and he is always above reproach.

CHAPTER 13

Ruth

That morning I had to go into Tarbert for a check-up with the nurse. I handed her my pot of wee, then sat and waited on the plastic chair, tapping my foot and wondering why the nurses' room always had such an unpleasantly sweet smell, some chemical or disinfectant. I glanced at the posters on the wall: a diagram of the inner ear, a pregnant woman sliced in half. A list of practice staff was pinned up on a green felt board. At the bottom, a new name had been written in by hand: 'Dr Susan Montgomery – Counsellor and Clinical Psychologist'.

I wondered what sort of problems you had to have to end up going to see someone like that.

For a moment, I saw myself there, knocking on her door – and for the briefest moment I really wanted to – but even thinking about it seemed theatrical and self-important. Why would you do that? What did I think I had to say to her?

The nurse came back. She was also new to the practice. Just moved down from Stornoway, she told me, as she gently padded her hands over my stomach to feel how things were going. 'Ketone levels are fine, and no sign of puffiness here,' she said, picking up my ankle and rotating my foot as I lay on the couch.

I sat up and she strapped a velcroed sleeve round my arm and pumped up the blood pressure monitor on the trolley. I watched the flickering red figures on the screen as she waited for them to settle on a number. She took the sleeve off my arm with a ripping sound. 'Not high exactly, but we should watch that. Are you getting plenty of chances to relax?'

There were flecks of paint in my hair and under my nails from decorating walls, old paint under my nails from stripping fireplaces.

'Yes, plenty,' I said.

She was dark haired and sweet faced. Late middle-age. From where I sat, I saw that the ornate clasp on her belt had been polished and polished over time and with so much care that it had worn to a beautiful silver pebble.

'And nothing worrying you?'

'No,' I said. 'Not that I can think of.'

'You've put your name down on the ante-natal class list?'

'Yes.'

She patted my hand. 'Good girl, Ruth. You'll learn a lot that will help you.' She looked over my chart and put it back in the Manila folder. 'And I expect you're on the phone to your mother all the time now, wondering how she coped with you?'

I shook my head. The nurse looked surprised.

'Mum died. Years ago. She probably killed herself,' I heard myself blurting out.

The nurse's smile crumpled.

'You know you can ring me, any time you want to, Ruth.'

I felt a hard lump in my throat. Didn't dare speak again.

I hung my coat up. We had pegs by the front door, a luxury Jamie had recently added; usually the coats ended up clogging up the kitchen chairs or falling onto the floor. I looked around at the quiet hall space, the pale yellow walls, the smell of fresh paint in the air and wondered how I could have been so silly those times – just because it had been dark.

After supper, the boys threw Leaf and me out of the kitchen, saying it was their turn to wash up. We took mugs of tea through to the sea room, although going in there still felt a bit like happening on someone else's room. We hadn't got used to having such a civilised space: large paper lampshades like moons; white calico curtains – not yet hemmed; the pale wooden floor varnished; a red kelim rug by the sofa. Leaf leaned back in the old armchair that Angus John had rescued from its journey to the dump. She blew on her tea and looked at me over the rim of her mug.

'The check-up went okay?'

'Yes. They said it's all going really well.'

There was the lonely piping of a curlew in the distance, the breaths of the sea, the tide far out.

'You must be tired.' She looked at the bump like it was a conundrum.

'And crabby,' I said.

'Only natural you'll feel up and down, all the changes with the baby.'

I swallowed. We listened to the birds outside whistling regretfully in a minor key.

'You know, I'm sorry, Leaf, if I've been a bit off sometimes.'

She paused, got up and came and sat on the sofa alongside me. 'Ruth, all the time I've been here, you've never really told me what happened.'

'How do you mean?'

'With your mother.'

'She drowned. I told you that.'

She put her hand on my breastbone, near the base of my throat. 'Not really. You haven't really told me. You keep it all bottled up. In here.'

I moved back a little, hoping she'd take her hand away. It felt horribly intrusive.

'Well, that's the English way,' I said, making a joke of it.

Her face was hanging in front of mine, a pale moon with green eyes.

'You can always talk to me, Ruth. You should talk. Let it breathe.'

I thought, that's what friends do, they share their secrets. They give a little bit of themselves away. But I felt like I was standing too near the edge of a long drop, dizzy with vertigo. My heart was thumping. I was sure she could feel it through the chest bone. My palms were sticky.

I stood up and her hand fell away.

'Thanks anyway, for offering.' I found myself glancing at the door.

'But how do you do it? Living here, on an island, the sea all around us. Don't you ever...'

I gave a short laugh, irritated now. 'Why would that bother me, Leaf? I mean, really. I'm a bloody good swimmer. Believe me, I made sure of that. And I actually really love the sea. Don't think for a minute I'm going to let what happened to Mum – what she did – spoil that. And this child here, it's never going to be afraid of the sea either.'

She sat nodding her head, her lips compressed like someone who still has plenty to say.

'Might take my tea up to bed. I'm pretty exhausted.'

'Sure. You should get your rest.'

Michael was shaking my shoulder.

I startled awake, not sure where I was; panic and loss filled the room. I gasped.

'Ruth, you were shouting. It's okay, Ruth.'

The pillow was wet and cold; as if in my dreams she came to me again, the water from her clothes seeping into the room.

I had been crying. I turned the face of the pillow over and Michael scooped me into his arm as we settled back down to sleep; but his arm under my ribs kept me awake.

In my dream, she had been so present, so real, that I couldn't believe she wasn't still there, asleep in the next room, breathing quietly; and I wanted her to be there, so much, so much, that the pain was as new as the day she left me.

It's three days after my tenth birthday. She has a chiffon scarf tied like an Alice band to keep her long black hair out of her blue eyes. She wears a yellow dress with long sleeves and a floaty skirt. I don't know anyone with a mum as pretty as mine. We stop in Bethnal Green to buy cherries from the greengrocer and I carry the soft bag like it's a prize to the top of the bus, the dark red already soaking into the paper at one edge. The cherries are warm and feel soft as a cheek inside the paper. They taste dark red and sweet.

We sit together in the front seat and sail through the London streets, swaying round the traffic. The hot sun bathes us all over, although, after a bit, my arm against the window feels like it's burning.

Once inside the museum, it is calm and cool; the heat can't get at us in here. We walk past glass cases where old things are spread out like clues to a mystery or objects rescued from a crime scene.

We make up stories about the jewelled treasures locked inside glass cases in Ancient India, a golden comb given to a beautiful princess by the prince in the miniature painting. We think the metal bowl is the one the princess used to serve poison to avenge her prince. Mum walks on to the next case, but I can't stop staring into the peacock colours of the Indian bowl: she is happy right now, and I don't want to break it.

In Ancient Egypt, she walks along the columns of hieroglyphics and whispers funny stories about the lists of tiny figures. They look like vases with Afro wigs and long black eyes. I giggle too loudly.

We walk down polished stone stairs, through enormous halls, and reach the Eskimo and North American section. At the far end, there's a case with a leather-fringed coat spread out like birds' wings. Next

to it, lit from behind, there's a huge Eskimo parka made of something so fine it looks like a transparent angel. I want to tell this story. I run towards it but as I get there my rubber sneakers catch on the waxy floor and I stumble forward, thumping my palms against the glass. The whole case vibrates.

The museum curator comes over to us like an off-duty policeman. He tells Mum she will have to take me out if she can't control me. We walk away through the tall rooms feeling ashamed. Mum is patting her hair in place and walking fast. After that, she doesn't seem to want to hear the silly stories I make up. We are sitting on a stone bench in a corridor between Ancient Rome and Persia. I can see she has slipped away now, into her own inside story that goes around her head. Two slow tears are coming out down her cheeks, making me feel really horrible. I sit closer to her, but it makes no difference.

She smells of her Mum deodorant and there's a faint tang from the brown paper with the cherry stones screwed up in her straw shopping bag on the floor. I look down at her feet. Her cream leather sandals have a maze of papery cracks in the pretend leather. Her toenails are yellowish and curve over, and for some reason they make my stomach tight with worry. They make me think of the bodies in the glass cases in Ancient Egypt. She's leaning forward now and stays like that for a long time.

Eventually, I get really bored and go and look at the displays of black carvings, always keeping her in my sight. Then I go back and sit down. She's still crying into her hanky.

'Oh for God's sake,' she says, when I demand that we go and find a cold drink.

She stands up very fast, yanks my arm and starts for the entrance.

We are back out into the hot air of London in summer and she is cross with me now because she wants to be alone to concentrate on crying.

We have all the way back on the bus still to do, but the day is already over. I insist on the top deck again, hoping it might remind her of being happy, but as soon as we get up there, I realise it's a mistake. It is so hot on the top deck, I can't breathe. She stares ahead, tense and preoccupied, and I feel sorry for spoiling everything.

We get back to Carlisle House and go up the concrete stairs to the second floor. Doris has put her washing across the balcony walkway and we have to duck beneath it to get to our door.

Mum makes beans on toast and then sits at the kitchen table smoking while I eat my tea in front of the TV. At seven she tells me to get into my pyjamas and I watch her put on her white mac. She's got a late shift at the pub. She takes one last look in the mirror over the electric fire. She licks her finger and smoothes an eyebrow. Tuts.

'I'm just popping out,' she tells me. 'Doris is there next door, eh, *mo ghaol*?' and she pats the wall with the back of her fingers. 'You get to bed and go to sleep at nine.'

I think she kissed me. I can't remember, to tell the truth. She looked very young and pretty with the floaty blue scarf in her hair and the mac belted round her waist so that the skirt stuck out above her boots.

I kneeled up on the sofa after the door closed so I could look out of the window. I pulled up the grey net curtain and waited until she appeared down below, between the blocks of flats, heading along the concrete pavements. I saw her white mac slipping round the grey corner of Devonshire House and then she was gone. She would be walking away to the bus stop by the canals.

At nine o'clock, I turned off the TV and got into bed. It was dark outside, so I left the electric light shining like a sentry above my bed. Mum had forgotten to put a lampshade on it, and it shone through my eyelids. I saw the clock say two, but I must have gone to sleep soon after that because I woke up from a horrible dream. There was a ghost with no face in Mum's room and I couldn't get past him.

I shouted out for Mum to come. I just wanted her to stand there, bad tempered and exhausted and shout at me to stop having these bloody nightmares. I'd dreamed again of the tall man in his feather cloak, who came from a dark forest, carrying his rack of dead birds with their drooping necks and curled claws.

But Mum didn't appear in the doorway. I got up and turned on the hall light, looked up and down the hallway to check there was no ghost and then opened Mum's door. My heart was hammering so hard, making me feel worn out.

I walked over to her bed in the shadows and ran my hands over the candlewick bedspread. The bed was flat and empty. I couldn't understand why she wasn't back. Where was she? I started to cry. I went back to my room to wait for her and shut the door tight.

When I woke up in the morning, the flat was very quiet. No radio playing the hits. I went through to her room, the purple candlewick bedspread still neat and flat over her bed. There were some of her hairpins and bits of her hair trailing from them on the dressing table, a worn-down red lipstick, pots of blue and green eye cream, a bottle of Pagan scent that smelled stale when I tried it. The ashtray was full. I stirred it with a hairpin and got a cloud of its old, ashy breath. I picked up a little brown bottle with pills inside, a printed label on the front. Why had she gone to the doctor? What was wrong?

The clock ticked, making a lonely echo in the top of the dresser.

She'd never, never been this late before.

I played with my Sindy dolls, and later in the day watched telly. I made myself tomato sauce sandwiches in the kitchen. Then I spent a long time kneeling up on the sofa watching from the window to see her coming back across the scuffed grass spaces between the flats.

When it started to get dark again, I went out onto the long brick balcony and knocked on Doris's door.

Doris was very old and always wore a hairnet and the same apron dress with washed-out flowers. She looked at me with a startled, pouchy face while I told her about Mum. She said I could come in. Her house always smelled of soapsuds. I sat on the edge of a chair by a china dog that stared at me without blinking and I waited for Mum to come and get me.

Two ladies in coats came and asked me a lot of questions, wrote things down. They said I could stay with Doris, till Mum came back.

I stayed with Doris for a week. I went back to school each day, and even though Doris gave me some pennies to get fruit salad chews from Molly's sweetshop on the way home, I didn't go past the sweetshop. I took the long way round, past the road that goes down to the canals, walking slowly by the bus stop where Mum would have waited.

After a couple of days I couldn't resist going down the road to the canal, and I started walking along the canal bank, staring at the grey, opaque surface and the bits of plank or old bike coming up out of the water, like they were going to help me understand something. The weeds scratched at my knees over the tops of my socks.

On the last day I went to the canals, I had a bag of sweets with me. As I walked down between the blank wall of Sankey's factory and the wooden paling of a coal yard, eating penny chews, I saw two vans parked down by the canal at an angle, their backs to the water. There were lots of people down there, policemen – one with an Alsatian on a lead that kept barking – people in blue suits and a man who looked like those plastic divers you could put in the bath and blow down a tube to make them float. He was sitting on the edge of the bank. He pushed off and sank under the water.

No one noticed me. I expected someone to shout at me to go away, but I was able to walk right round the back of the van and watch what was happening. Someone yelled at the man with the dog, and he put the dog in the front of the van. The dog was in the seat right above where I was standing. He turned his head and pawed at the window and whined.

There were other divers. You could only see them when they came up like the bobbing heads of seals, the water was so murky – a thick grey-green with a rainbow skim of petrol at the edges of everything. They were bringing something up from the water, quite big, because it took all three of them. Someone on the bank had a sort of pulley. In the end the thing came out of the water quickly, and for a moment it hung in the air. It had a head and arms, and the water was pouring off the arms in the sunlight, a white shape dripping with wings of watery light, like an angel. And then I saw the white mac, the long white legs, the black hair tangled with weeds and a muddy blue scarf.

I think I screamed for a long time. I remember them running round the van to see what was going on, and I remember them talking to me in a shouty voice. They kept asking my name, and I told them. They kept shouting it at me, like I was deaf, 'Ruth, Ruth, listen to us. Ruth, Ruth. Tell us where you live. Can we ring your mother? Ruth, it's all right.'

They took me in the back of the van. I caught a glimpse of them carrying a black shape into the other van. The lady policeman pulled my head against her side so I couldn't see any more. They sat with me in the back, and a policeman gave me his jacket because I couldn't stop my teeth chattering. They gave me tea from a flask, spooned in three little wings of sugar from a bag. When I was drinking it, the woman said, 'There, that's better now, isn't it? You've had a nasty shock seeing something nasty like that. Where do you live? Can we phone your mum to come and get you? Where's your mum?'

I couldn't say anything. My throat wouldn't work.

The policeman gave me a little shake on one shoulder.

'Come on, love,' he said.

'She's in the van,' I told them.

I told them, because I wanted them to explain it. I wanted them to make it all right, because they were policemen.

'What do you mean? That van out there?' said the policeman who gave me the jacket.

I nodded.

I saw them look at each other. They were pulling faces, like they'd just seen something really bad, mouthing words. Then the lady with her arm round my shoulders said, 'You've had a fright, love. It's made you think bad things. That's not your mum. That's just some poor woman. Let's take you home.'

CHAPTER 14

Moira

Miss Katriona Marstone came for her lesson each week in the parlour, and every Sunday she turned out eagerly for the services and listened with showy interest to my Alexander's sermons (for this is how I think of him now, my Alexander) but she did not see what I had already seen, I who had loved Alexander from the day he took me in from the moors and saved my life – though no one else in the world cared about that. For I had seen through his smooth and boyish face, and though it made my heart grow small with fear, I had seen the narrow old man waiting under his smooth skin.

Well might a girl stand next to Alexander and long to press the fine firmness of that forearm, and well might she long to stroke the shiny smoothness of his black hair, or even note how his eyes did follow the movement of a body and for a moment feel some encouragement. In the end it would do a body no good. For the Reverend, so scrubbed clean and unsullied, his love was only for his Saviour. And though as a result he did love the whole of mankind, he would never allow himself to love just one soft sweetheart – not while that old and watchful Alexander was in charge of all his doings.

After the Sunday service, most of the congregation had melted away but the Reverend was still in church, packing away the green linen hymn books. I saw with dismay how Miss Katriona was still there too, pretending to help, but moving about to very little effect, lifting the odd hymn book into a small stack. So I did also stay and take the books from her and stack them properly along the shelf.

And still the besom wasn't leaving, but trying to get him to get into her pony and trap, saying he must come back to the castle across the bay for a small lunch and then stay for dinner. I smiled when I heard her plans, because I knew Alexander would not go. Charming as that Miss was, Alex was not easy pickings.

So when my Alexander got into her little trap with his hat on his knees and rode away with his back showing – and only the briefest word of how I could let the dinner I was roasting for him get cold and he would eat it another time – I stood with my mouth open, watching them disappear along the track, unable to understand how she had wove her spell round him so quick and got him to do her bidding with a mere smile and a small hand on his forearm. Truly that besom has her powers.

I was a long way beyond feeling any rage. I was as cold as if I were miles out in the sea, and drowning from a loss of hope. I did not know if I could carry on with the dreariness of living.

I had never for a moment thought that the Reverend would return my love. I am not without understanding of how the world is, and how I stand in his eyes, but yet I never thought I would lose him.

Now I saw that I was mistook in that. And to lose him to a Marstone, to the ones who have already stripped me of every soul I ever loved.

Only a couple of days later, I was out in the manse garden hanging the sheets to dry when I was disappointed to see Miss Marstone's pony and trap once more driving along the road between the machair and the slopes of the bens that rise up behind the manse. She looked very small, making her little way towards us along the wide grass sweeps of Scarista, and I thought, she is but a girl, even younger than me, and yet how she does plague me.

I had already been up to the burn and set the tub to boil on a fire next to it so that I could wash the blankets while the weather was fair, and I was sticky with the toil, but I left that and hurried back to the house to be ready to open the door to her – and keep an eye on what mischief she was thinking to make. I pulled my hair straight as it would go with the comb that I keeps in the kitchen, for now I pass the hall mirror often during the day and this makes me want not to go around with my hair looking like a tinker's. Then I straightened my skirt, which will always twist round to the left as I work, folded up my apron, dirty as it was from carrying in the peats, and stood behind the front door of the manse ready to open it to her and be there to serve the tea.

It wasn't her usual day for her lesson, which as everyone for twenty miles knows is of a Thursday, just as everybody knows that I do sit and sew as they do the said lesson, since otherwise they would be the scandal of the island – and it is me that has told them this must be done. I listen in to all they say, and see how she is clever in some of her ways, and yet the Reverend cannot see it. I watch them and see how, though His Reverence is the oldest and the wisest in the room, in some matters he is remarkable for how foolish he do think.

And great progress the Miss is making too with her lessons, since I opens the door to her that morning and she is greeting me in Gaelic with, 'Good morning, my dear Moira and how are your fleas?'

I do not respond in kind, though I am sore tempted, but reply my health is very good, thank you. But she is not listening of course, she is looking in the mirror to see if she is still beautiful, and my eyes, yes she still is. I am about to bundle her hat and her fancy cloak into the cupboard and I see, for just a moment, she is not smiling at that pretty face in the glass. She is looking in the mirror as if she has seen something very bad inside it and she stares for a while then turns away quickly. She puts on the little smile again, and she puts away the face I just glimpsed.

And before I can get her things hung up, she gives a quick knock and goes straight in to the Reverend and I can just see through the half-open door how she does kiss him on top of the head and laugh, and he puts down his pen from the sermon he was writing, and well might he do so since I am seeing how every holy thought he was just writing on his paper has clean dropped out of his head. He looks up at the Miss and blinks at her in a daze, and I want to run in there and say…

Well, I don't know what I should say, but instead I get together the things for her tea fast as can be done, willing the water for the tea to boil quicker, and carry it through with the cups all rattling. Then when they are served, I sit down in the corner with my sewing like I am a shadowy thing.

But she turns then, and smiles right at me, says to the Reverend, 'Now you mustn't be cross with me, because I know it is not my lesson, and I am disturbing your work, but I had a wonderful idea and I wanted to come and tell you straight away. And you must not look worried, Alexander, because I have not come to see you. I have come to see Moira, to ask her a very special favour.'

This made me look up because I was not expecting her to say any such thing, any more than I was expecting the concern for my fleas, but I was listening.

'You see, I know you are teaching me Gaelic with great pains, Alexander, and you are a very good teacher for such a dim-headed little pupil, but like me you are firstly an English speaker, and it is Moira here who has the greatest facility with the language. And since I am in a hurry to understand this place, and to speak the language like a native, I have come to ask if Moira will let me come and visit her to chat with just her. I can visit her little cottage, and we can have tea by the fire, and she can tell me all her wonderful stories about fairies and she can teach me some songs.'

Well 'she', whoever she might be, was thinking of a lot of problems with this arrangement, not least Maggie Kintail's chickens, which like to live under the bench near the fire and roam around the house laying their eggs where it pleases them; not to mention the ram that was a pet of Maggie's when it was a lamb and still tries to get back in through the door when you are not looking. I have been putting the milk in the bowl to settle to cream and found the ram in the kitchen, ready to butt me from behind. It were only that Maggie came back to catch him that he did not butt me and spill the milk all over the floor.

I could feel my cheeks hot and red at the thought of Her Ladyship coming in to see our poor ways and she turning her nose up, no doubt, and I felt shamed already, but I had to look pleased because it is her father who holds the Reverend in his gift, just as his factor do tell the cottars to move as he pleases, even to clearing them off to Cape Breton and Manitoba. So I smiled and said it would be an honour and a privilege.

But she was prattling on, hardly waiting for my permission, all stirred up and feverish. She did seem to be very strange, I thought. It seemed her gestures were mannered as if she was acting on a stage. Then she was getting up to go, and kissing me and telling me how I was her true friend. I must wait and watch while she flirts her goodbyes to the Reverend and see how he is left with his hair ruffled and on end, looking at her sideways as she lingers her fingers along his hand and flaps her eyelids at him.

It was a relief to finally shut the door on her, and have the house go quiet and calm. The Reverend was left even more pink than usual after a visit from that little witch. I heard him shuffling his papers and fussing about like he must put more order into his affairs of a sudden. Leaning on the old door I had shut on her, I saw her through the watery glass, just a little puppet thing again, riding away in her little trap since she has been forbidden of late by His Lordship to go about the county in all weathers, sitting on the horse itself. She looked small and stiff and jolted about, rattling across the track back up to the mountains and their castle at Avenbuidhe.

I stood at the window with its wavy glass and pondered as she travelled along the machair road, the wide sea bluer than the blue sky, and thought about her very strange way of behaving; how capricious the gentry are and how we must agree to whatever they please to do, whether it be to shoot their guns across the shielings where the girls are milking the cows, or turn us from our homes for their big English sheep, or come in their tweed suits and write down our stories and songs so that they may go off to London and amaze their friends with their booming voices.

I walked back to my kitchen and I was about to put the puzzle of that besom out of my mind, and then I saw. Or rather, I did not see it, but I felt it, come up from behind me like a fear. Something was very wrong for her, something was very wrong indeed for the Miss Marstone. A chill came over me that gripped my heart and I went very cold and afeared for her.

So a few days later, she was back, good as her word. Miss Marstone – *No, call me Katriona, dear Moira, now we shall be friends* – came into our little house where me and Maggie live, stooping low under the lintel and turning first the wrong way into the byre where the cow sleeps, and then after exclaiming at how clever this arrangement was, turning left up to where we do live. And oh how prettily the dishes on the rack do shine through the smoke, and how delightful to sit on these little low stools so close together round a fire so cleverly in the middle of the floor.

Though I did not ask her to join us, Maggie put off digging the potatoes and put on her bonnet and all of her bright trinkets in honour of this visit. She had the sooty kettle on the fire and the tea boiling so that it was good and dark. She spoons in three sugars and gives a cup to Her Ladyship before I can stop her – since I know that Her Ladyship drinks China tea with no milk. We insist that the Miss has the long bench by the wall and we seat ourselves on the stools.

Maggie gives us three songs in a voice which may be rustier than when she was a girl, yet still is true and very beautiful. I saw how the Miss was sat upright with her hands clasped together, not wanting Maggie to stop, and then I did see the tears running down her cheek, which made me angry that she should enjoy the songs of our sadness; as Maggie did sing about the Uists, where she lived as a girl before the factor there cleared them all away to live or die best they can.

Then Maggie gives a quick song with no words so that her mouth is playing music for a jig, and all with nonsense words from the time when the King did ban our Gaelic entirely, and the Miss is tapping her foot and saying, how clever, how clever, and why, I have never heard anyone so talented. If Maggie lived in London, Moira, I do believe she could have studied piano and trained to be a musician. But it would help me greatly if Maggie could tell me a story in Gaelic perhaps, something like the Reverend's fairy story about Selkies. I can try and follow some of the words if you will translate for me, and then I can begin my book of fairy stories, which I intend to illustrate also.

Maggie does not have perfect English but she has the gist of what the Miss is saying, and for Maggie the old tales must always be told in the tongue in which they were birthed; so before I can stop her, Maggie has closed her eyes and in her sing-song voice, she begins a long story in Gaelic that rambles on, up and down the island. I am about to translate her story of fairies under the hill, but as I watch the Miss so comfy on her bench, her eyes like a little girl waiting for her bedtime story, something in me gets red and spiteful and I begin to tell another story, whispering it to the Miss's ear, the story that I know Maggie will not tell.

'It was when Maggie was a young woman, Miss, when your father's father was still the laird here,' I tell her carefully, stopping and pausing like I am following what Maggie is saying. 'She was up in the hills here, coming back from the high shielings where they put the cows in summer. She was with her father, and they looked down on the houses that sit on the machair, those homes that were so low and so snug, with their thick thatch roofs tied down with ropes against the wind. You had never seen such a beautiful sight than the village which was Maggie's home. But as they came down the ben, they could see that the house at the end had smoke coming up from the roof – not the mist of blue peat smoke, this was black and tarry with billows of sooty smoke. And so they began to run down the hill.

'His Lordship's factor had his men in the village. All the dogs were barking and the factor's men were turning out the houses. And Maggie ran in her home and the factor's man was holding the great bowl of milk that was set for cream, and he was pouring it on the fire in the middle of the floor – and this was the fire that had never once gone out, the fire that Maggie's mother smoored each night with peat ash and a prayer for the Lord's blessing, so as it would be ready to stir up in the morning to cook some breakfast. You see, Miss, there was not a house in the village where the fire had ever gone out, any more than a heart stops beating in a body, but they took the children's milk and doused every fire with it.

'Maggie says her father tried to cut the tweed from the loom, but they put fire to the roof and it did drop on the loom. Then they chained the doors shut and Maggie's family had nothing but what they had pulled out before the firing of the roofs.

'And she saw the factor's men carrying Peigi Macuish out on a blanket because she had a new babe the night before and could not yet get up. They did leave Peigi by the ditch, though her husband begged them to let her bide another day under their roof.

'The dark was coming down and they must walk across the coffin road to the other side of the island where the ground is rock, and too hard to bury the dead. Or they must go down to Tarbert to wait for a ship to take them to Australia. Maggie's father knew that when they cleared Sollas, then the people went on a ship that had typhus, and they did have to throw their own children in the sea when they died. So Maggie's family went to the barren parts of the island and that is how they did kill themselves, trying to raise crops out of rock and marsh, till Maggie did hire herself out to the factor's wife. And now she sings in her head all day to bring back the faces around the fire – the fire where she learned her songs, before the milk they was to drink that night did splutter in the ashes. And that is the story of Maggie Kintail.'

Maggie Kintail had long finished speaking. The Miss had gone white as a sheet. Maggie had been telling her best ghost story, and so she was clucking away and saying, but it is but a tale, and best not to mind it. I translated that last part direct to Her Ladyship.

But she shook her head and said, 'I did not know how much everyone must hate me.' And she got up and would not look me in the eye, but fussed around with her dress like she did not know what to do with her person, like she was much ashamed. And she went out of the house, looking very ill, so I followed her, wishing I had not told her, but also rejoicing because I had put some of my pain in her soul, and this was what I dearly wanted. But she looked so wild with it, and so white, I began to fear for what I had done. I had never thought that she would take it so badly. And we walked up and down, and she stopped and looked over at the church, and all the broad sweep of green grass, between us and the sea, where the big Cheviot sheep from the mainland snatch, snatch, snatch at the machair grass.

'I used to dream about here,' she said, 'when I lived far away with my mother. And I blamed her that she kept me from this place, from my father. I dreamed how I would one day come back home, as a bride, and would walk up this path with all the blue sea behind me and the honey smell of hundreds of machair flowers, and I would walk to the church where the one I loved so dearly would be waiting, though I did not know then what he would look like.'

I stood next to her in silence, and wondered if it was spite on her part, that she should be telling me about how she would one day become Alexander's wife. So I said nothing but felt all the big empty wind fill my soul and blow away every last hope. You see, I thought, the gentry never care for long, because they never need to, and so they soon forget.

And she turned to me and I saw she had tears running down her face, and she said, 'But it's all spoiled now, isn't it? It's all too late now.'

I could not follow her meaning, so I said, 'Miss, you are getting ill standing out in the wind. You must get home.'

So I helped her into the trap and her hand was as cold as the seawater, and off she went back to her castle with her stiff little back and shoulders bumped about by the ruts and the ridges in the track.

CHAPTER 15

Ruth

I ordered a name plate for the house from the Barvas potter, a white disk to go by the door with the words '*Tigh na Mara*', the Sea House, painted in blue lettering and glazed firmly in place.

But while Michael was restoring the front door, he uncovered the old door plaque beneath thick layers of paint. The chemical stripper had scoured the brass clean as the day it was made and 'Scarista Manse' was engraved into the shining metal in bold letters that made my '*Tigh na Mara*' in painted script look like a suggestion.

At least the post arrived correctly addressed to the Sea House – and it was mostly bills, piles of them. We were going to be very overdrawn by the time we opened and we were going to need to make serious returns in the next year.

'If we could just get the initial money together,' I said, pushing the account books across the table, 'then we could offer guests trips to see seals and porpoises; basking sharks if they're lucky. It would make all the difference to the figures. At the Lochboisdale Inn in Uist they make a mint from London bankers who come to fish for sea trout and stuff like that.'

Michael totted up the sums again, but they still wouldn't allow for a boat.

The thing you have to understand is that the islands are not separated by the sea but connected by it. Everyone has a boat of some description, sooner or later.

That first day we sailed out on the ferry from Skye to Harris, I fell in love with the Minch. The evening was beginning to thicken and turn blue, the outline of Skye behind us nothing more than inky smudges, dark isthmuses sliding past each other as we pulled away. A low light filled the surface of the sea, glass peaks of jade rising and falling. I stared out of the ferry window, mesmerised, until a blurred reflection of the ship's interior started to assert itself over the seascape and I realised that the lights of cottages on the distant shore were in fact reflections of electric lights hanging from the canteen ceiling.

Outside, a fierce wind blew across the deck, huge layers of cloud split against an apricot sky. I pulled my coat tighter and let the wind scour the skin of my face cold and clean. Ahead, our new life, a white house in front of a wide beach, the wind bowling in from the Atlantic; I saw the children we'd have one day, those bright shapes tumbling in and out of the front door; and down on the beach, a boat ready to explore the wide plains of sea.

Hard to let go of even a small bit of that dream.

Michael fetched a beer. We stared at the closed account book as if the answer might appear on the cover.

Jamie joined us at the kitchen table. He pulled over the discarded book. Opened it and glanced at the figures with a frown, then gave up. 'Look, why don't I chip in with you guys? I've money saved from the year I did at the bank – felt more like for ever. And Dad would always come in with us, Michael. You know Dad and boats.'

The day we drove out to visit Lachlan's boat shed was one of those odd, wintery days that the island can sometimes throw up even in early summer. We headed through the middle of the island over narrow, switchback roads that turned so sharply, the van seemed to be launching into thin air.

Most islanders live over on the east side, their cottages and tin bungalows perched among stony outcrops in an unlikely landscape of grandeur and sage beauty, the sweeps of rock polished with age and running with silver burns sparking in the sun; the Minch always in sight, a vast plane of metalled, shimmering sea. Across the water were Skye and the pale outlines of the mainland mountains, everything brightening or fading beneath a sky filled with huge dramas.

We pulled up in the sparse village of Finsbay. Lachlan's house stood next to a small loch, where the wind was casting nets of ripples across the black water.

Jamie knocked and we waited. The turf of Lachlan's garden was scattered with empty mussel and limpet shells, as if the tide had risen during the night and retreated without anyone noticing. A large, flat rock piled with broken shells, like a Stone Age meal, showed where the gulls had been aiming in an effort to smash open their catches. Lachlan was suddenly at the door, shaking hands with everyone.

There was something very orderly about Lachlan: his perfectly white hair, a navy fisherman's jumper and blue jeans, the disciplined bearing of an ex-navy man.

'Come away in,' he said, showing us through to a Nissan hut long enough to house a boat under construction. A row of esoteric-looking tools lined the wall on each side, the handles polished and crafted and pale and grubby as bulbs waiting to be planted. In the centre stood the chocked-up skeleton of a boat, a giant's ribcage with a small square cabin in place of a heart, the whole thing a miraculous transformation from tree to ship.

'This one's based on a birlinn, the old rowing boats from these parts, so it's a bit bigger than you'll be wanting. But you'd do well to keep to the traditional shape for these waters. That way you'll be able to sail in even the roughest weather that the Minch can throw at you.'

Arms folded, faces rapt, Jamie and Michael followed his hand movements as he sketched out our boat in the air.

'Let's go and make a pot and you can have a look at the plans,' he said. 'Or maybe we should have something stronger to seal the deal.'

Apart from boats, Lachlan's other big interest turned out to be the history of the island. He was a proud member of the Edinburgh Historical Society. He wanted to know every last detail about the baby discovered under our floorboards and I found myself telling him what I'd found out so far.

'The next time I am over at the Historical Society's library I am going to have a good hunt and see what I can find for you, Ruth, but not before you've all come out on the *Airdasaig*, see the sort of craft you'll be getting.'

Early the next morning, Leaf and I packed a picnic. I'd sent off for some cookbooks, determined to be the sort of mum who bakes cakes and does whatever it is that mums do in the kitchen – make jam? Leaf and I had taken to reading them avidly, planning lists for what we were going to try out that week. As a result, we had an ambitious picnic; quiche and a fairly successful Victoria sponge. I also packed a bag with a sketchbook and pencils, and rooted out the old binoculars. Lachlan would leave us on remote Pabbay Island for a few hours; it was the best place to see seals at all stages in the large colony out there.

We met up with Lachlan down at An t'Obbe sound. He directed us to a wooden boat scraping up and down against the seaweed-smeared posts of the harbour jetty. It looked like a scaled-up wooden toy. Red-and-pink buoys hung in bunches from the sides like balloons. Lachlan gave us all life vests, mine just about fastening round the bump, then we set out in the blazing mid-morning sun.

The water of the sound was shallow and as clear as air. You could look down and see little white crabs stirring up minute clouds of white sand as they levitated sideways. Shoals of tiny grey fish darted through the seaweed that frilled through the surface of the water like the tops of small, ochre trees.

The drone of the engine changed and we began to pull further away from land: the sea became opaque and dark, full of shadows, unknowable.

As we got out to the first of the rocky islets, we were surprised to see dappled boulders slide into the sea with a splash; the domed heads of seals appeared out of the water behind us, their round, melancholy eyes staring at us as the boat carried on pulling away.

Out of nowhere, a cold wind got up. We were now out on the open water, every horizon nothing but sky. The boat began to skip and jump, smacking into the waves. The sea had turned dark grey, the darker shadows moving below us. I felt an odd kind of vertigo, dizzily aware of the tall miles of insubstantial water beneath us, where a body could sink down without a trace.

In front of us, a huge black cloud was cranking up and filling the sky.

'Don't you worry about that,' said Lachlan when I pointed it out. 'The worst of the weather's not going to be heading this way.' He was shouting above the noise of the engine and the slap of the boat on the water, above the little wail of Leaf singing something.

'But are you sure it's safe to carry on?' I shouted back.

'You can never be sure,' he yelled. 'But if you've brought your waterproofs, you'll be just fine in this.'

I thought again about the smallness of a body against the tonnage of the sea. The spiteful wind was whipping hair across my eyes. I felt my palms sliding wetly against the wooden seat. Something was wrong. Something was going to go wrong. I put a protective arm across my stomach.

'Michael, we need to turn back,' I yelled.

'How much further?' Michael called out to Lachlan.

'Twenty minutes and we're there.'

The water slopped over the side and soaked my arm. I couldn't believe no one else was worried. Every nerve was now on full alert, my heart skittering, my head buzzing. Every fibre in my body knew that we had to get back. No alternative.

Michael moved across the boat to sit next to me. He was stooping towards me, a thin man, donnish and reasonable, talking earnestly. It was going to be fine.

The buzzing in my head was drowning out his words. I couldn't believe he was willing to take such a risk. I heard, '… another half hour, so no point going back now…'

'Listen to me—'

I think I must have lost it then. I couldn't breathe. I felt my arms flailing, catching his face with my flying hands. Someone was screaming words. I saw Jamie stand up, moving towards us. I stopped. Looked at Michael half cowering against the open water.

No sound but the drone of the engine as all other eyes slid away from us.

Michael sat straight, holding very still. Then he got up and made his way to the cabin, went in to speak to Lachlan.

Lachlan threw the motor into a higher gear and the boat turned. No one was speaking; Jamie was looking out to sea and whistling.

The twenty minutes that it took us to get back to An t'Obbe were unbearable. I willed the boat back to land, cold and sticky with sweat, exhausted.

I was so very glad to scramble out. The solid, unmoving ground hit like a shockwave, all my senses still pitching and tossing.

'Sorry about that,' I heard Michael mutter as he took Leaf's hand to help her off the boat.

I unclasped the life jacket and slid it off, letting air flow down my back. I sat down with a thump on a bollard at the harbourside, the wind whipping my cagoule.

Last time hadn't been the last time then.

I thought back to the dark afternoon we saw the Sea House for the first time together.

We bought the house in a rush. I couldn't get time off from the lab work at such short notice so Michael had to go up and bid for the house at auction by himself. So on the day we landed at Tarbert harbour, I'd only ever seen the house in photographs.

It was twilight as we drove down towards the west coast, a cold half-light like a long eclipse. The view was of mile after mile of brown turf, matted and shrunk over the rocky landscape like a threadbare carpet; but mostly it was a view of rocks, shouldering their way out of the ground at every point. The sky was grey. The lochs were grey.

'Bit of an acquired taste, the land on this side, but wait till you see the view from the house,' Michael said after a long silence.

A mist was starting to come down, a sinking cloud sealing off the tops of the hills. By the time we got to the Sea House, it was almost dark. You could just about make out the shape of the building against the paler dark of the sea and the sand.

I got the torches from the car. Two little posts were standing in the middle of nowhere where there must once have been a gate. A rough path left us stumbling up and down hummocks in the faint torchlight.

I'd seen pictures of the house. I'd read the reports. I thought I knew what to expect. The windows were blank and boarded up. A strong, fusty smell came off the place. Inside, I shone my torch around. An old sideboard covered in plaster debris; rows of empty jars streaked with dirt along shelves; a sink hanging off one wall.

Michael flicked a light switch, but of course the electricity was off. I found myself trying not to breathe in the rotting stench.

'I know it's hard to picture it now,' Michael was saying, 'but...'

A scattering sound overhead. He ran the pale light of his torch over the cracked ceiling.

'Mice,' said Michael.

Scratchy nails were chasing back and forth after something. I could feel hairs rising on my scalp.

'Too big.'

The noise stopped.

'Bet it's rats squatting in the roof, cheeky things,' he said.

The noise started up again, louder, frantic this time.

But I was already struggling with the front door bolts. I burst out into the darkness. Stood breathing in the cold, damp air. We'd made a mistake. A horrible mistake. I heard Michael following. He moved in close and draped his long arm round my shoulders. My heart was starting to slow down, but my lungs felt raw and strained.

'Ruth, it'll be fine. We'll put down traps.'

'I can't believe I trusted you on this. We can't live here.'

'Come on, Ruth. I'll sort it out. I promise. At least finish looking round.'

I felt a slight pressure from his arm against my back, steering us back inside. Suddenly, I was struggling free of his hold, beating him off with a mad swimming movement, like someone going under for the last time. I felt the back of my hand hit his chin.

He put his hand to his mouth, his eyes wide with surprise. He touched his tongue, wincing. A patch of dark on his fingers. He'd bitten down on his tongue with the blow.

'I'm sorry. I'm sorry,' I said, hunting for a clean tissue. I couldn't believe what I'd done.

He held himself very still for a moment. Then he spoke very calmly, slowly. 'Okay. It's been too much. The journey and everything. We'll go to the bed and breakfast. Get something to eat and sort out what we're going to do about this tomorrow.'

We walked back to the car, following the jagged circles of torchlight sliding up and down the hummocks. Why couldn't I stay calm, discuss things like an adult instead of behaving like some kid throwing a tantrum? Fits of panic would flare up with a will of their own, out of nowhere. Each time I was sure I'd never be so stupid again.

But just now it had happened again. I was staring at the water, at the brown sea scum around a tangle of litter and a dead bird washed up against the An t'Obbe jetty. I was beginning to see something I didn't want to look at.

When we got back to the house, cold and exhausted by the boat trip, Michael and I carried on sitting in the van in silence.

I waited for Michael to speak, afraid of what he was going to say.

What do you have to do to make someone give up on you?

Michael shuffled in his seat and turned to face me.

'So what happened out there?'

'I'm sorry. I shouldn't have lost it like that, but I just knew. Something was going to happen. Michael, it wasn't safe.'

'But it was safe. What did you think was going to happen, for goodness' sake? Lachlan's been sailing for forty years.'

'Michael, I want you to cancel the boat.'

He didn't answer for a while.

He took my hand in his. His hand felt clammy, trembling and nervy. 'I know it can't be easy for you out on the water, with your mum and everything, but…'

I pulled away. 'It isn't that. It's just… I don't know what's happening. I get so scared by everything right now. Scared that something's going to happen to the baby. Scared that once the baby comes, I won't know what to do. I don't want to be like this, Michael. I can't even do a simple thing like take a boat trip. I don't know why I think I can bring up a kid. I just don't…'

'Shh.' He sighed and enveloped me in the familiar warmth of his Shetland jumper. 'It's okay to feel scared. Being parents, it's huge. I know I'm terrified.'

I could smell the anxious sweat from his armpit. I pulled back and looked at him. His face was white and shadowy with fatigue.

'If you talked to someone, Ruth. Maybe talked to a doctor?'

'No.'

He let his head fall back against the headrest. I heard a small thump.

I forced myself to say, 'Look, maybe you should go ahead with the boat. Run it with Jamie. It'll just be one of those things that we don't share. But promise me, promise, Michael, that you'll never ever take our kid out on that thing.'

'Ruth, I can't promise that.'

We stared through the windscreen at the blank side of the house.

'Why do you stay with me, Michael?'

'Oh, Ruth, do you honestly think that if there was any real risk, any chance that I could lose you, I'd have let you set foot on that boat today?'

I reached over, stroked back some strands of hair that were clinging stickily to his forehead, and he let his eyes close for a moment.

Back in the house, he went into the sea room to catch the end of the news. As I walked past with my mug of tea, I saw him through the doorway. He looked defeated, sprawled out on the sofa in front of the expanse of pine flooring, the new varnish still giving off its plasticky smell. I headed upstairs to finish off the last of the lizard drawings.

With so much going on, I was very behind and the publisher was starting to make polite enquiries about when he might be able to get hold of his illustrations.

The bedroom seemed diminished and underlit as I sat down at the desk. I couldn't concentrate, an unsettled feeling looming behind my shoulder, the faint but insistent sound of the TV downstairs.

I was working from textbooks now that the dissection drawings were finished. I spread the large reference book open on the desk with a slight thwack. There was an immediate scuffle from the lizard tank. I sighed. One lizard still remained in the tank, masquerading as a pet, scuttling away in nervous terror each time anyone approached the glass. I'd been hoping it would die.

I carried on with the drawing, my hand mapping out the skeletal structure, but my mind was elsewhere. Hot shame was creeping in as I thought about the boat trip again, how I'd lashed out at Michael.

The last time I'd hurt Michael hadn't been the last time then. But I'd promised myself. And what if it had been a child standing there?

The baby kicked, the small reverberations spreading and then stilling within its tightly bound world. This baby was getting bigger. Soon I'd have to buy some special maternity clothes instead of wearing Michael's trousers rolled up at the bottom, his big shirts and jumpers tenting over the bump.

I stared through the glass wall of the tank at the mess of droppings mixed in with the cotton wool and wood shavings. Something was bothering me at the back of my mind. I got up and peered down into the tank, the acrid smell of chrysalises and keratinised scales filling my nose. Poor, dry little lizard: a whole life lived in terror; his nose always flaring for the scent of a predator, toe pads alert to the vibrations of a footfall, perpetually tensed to flee.

I narrowed my eyes, reminded of all the things I'd learned about reptile biology. How there's a reptile brain still there at the base of the human cortex. Our history of evolution is all there in the body, patterned into the human blueprint: that useless appendix; the stub of a tail at the base of our spine; so many obsolete reminders of our ancestors.

But there's nothing obsolete about our lizard brain. We kept our lizard brain precisely because it's so successful, a tiny guardian barring the gateway to death; a knot of nerves wired directly into our sense of smell, ready in a split second to jerk the limbs into action and make sure we live through one more day. And mostly we don't hear from that little reptile. Mostly he sleeps, coiled up at the base of the cortex, only called up for grave and rare emergencies; stirred up by the sharp smell of death – by the smell of pond water, the oily sheen glinting on the canal, Mum's white body rising up, the water sliding off in planes of light, again and again.

But what if you were someone with death seared into your mind? What if you had got so close to death, its breath on your face, that the old lizard brain had woken up permanently? And what if it never stopped running around in your head, never slept, jerking your hands faster than thought, faster than reason?

It began to make horrible sense. I'd always been a nervy person, screaming at the smallest bang, jumping a mile at a slammed door, wakeful long into the night, but recently – perhaps because I knew I had another small life to take care of – it had all got so much worse. These days I was afraid of the dark, afraid of the water, afraid of the house I lived in; reptile-eyed and running around in a panic; and now lashing out at Michael.

It had been a point of pride for Michael that I had such quick reactions, ever since I'd reached out on a Tube train platform and pulled back a man who'd been going to jump; a flicker of movement in my peripheral vision, the limbic system kicked in and I grabbed him. I only realised what I'd done after I felt his weight swing round towards the platform like a dance partner, and understood then that I'd interrupted his trajectory towards the rails. Michael liked to tell the story of how I'd saved a man's life. But I always felt uneasy looking back on it. What if it hadn't been something good that I'd done that day?

I went over to the shelf where I kept the reference books and began to look up the limbic system, malfunctions of.

I still couldn't believe what I was piecing together. I definitely didn't like what I was seeing. With a feeling of mounting horror, I began to understand Mum's legacy, my history imprinted on my body like a personal mutation. Mum had been wrong. I wasn't part seal. I was the lizard girl, the girl with the claws and the panics and the stupid rages – a mess, a mess.

I sat down heavily on the bed, the book open on my knees.

Perhaps Michael was right. Couldn't you go and see a head doctor about this sort of thing, get help from a counsellor or therapist? A professional. The counsellor I'd seen on the list at the Tarbert practice, perhaps – Dr Montgomery.

I thought then of my social worker, how she used to turn up at whichever foster home, because once again, I'd caused mayhem. I'd have to get into the back of her car and we'd drive away.

And then my breath constricted. I pictured a social worker leaving the Sea House, in her arms a small bundle of blankets. She was stooping down, getting into the back of a car.

There was no way I could go and talk to people who wrote everything down in files: those blank, attentive faces, the rising panic I'd get in my chest as I tried to explain myself, palms wet with perspiration against the chair. Once you let them in, you never knew where it would end.

No, I couldn't do that. This was something I was going to have to work out by myself.

You left me.

You left me alone.

CHAPTER 16

Ruth

Mrs MacKay wasn't giving up on trying to get me to go and see Christine, the genealogist in Northton who traced family trees for American tourists. Mrs MacKay turned up one morning, just passing by, she said, and she happened to have Christine with her. I was stirring porridge at the stove.

'I already had my breakfast a couple of hours ago,' said Mrs MacKay when I offered her some porridge, 'but if you have some tea.'

They settled at the table. Christine was in her sixties but looked much younger with her boyish haircut and big roll-neck sweater, her eyes creased with concern and kindness. She accepted a bowl of porridge.

Leaf came in, the sleeves of her jumper down over her hands as it was still chilly.

'Look, five more this morning,' she said, showing us a clutch of chicken's eggs cradled in her wool-covered palms. There were wisps of down stuck to the polished brown shells.

Leaf had fallen in love with Angus John's chickens. She knew the name of each one, and exactly who was laying and who was broody. He had let her have six of her own to look after and she'd taken to getting up early each morning to go and feed them. Jamie was building a shed with a roost so that we could house the hens down by the house.

Leaf got out a pan and insisted that we all try some scrambled egg. It was yellow and buttery, on perfectly toasted home-made bread.

Before Christine left, I reluctantly handed over my birth certificate details and my handful of photos of Mum.

'But really, I don't think it's worth your time. I've sort of got used to having a blank when it comes to my relations.'

'They're there somewhere, Ruth, and I'm going to see what I can do for you,' said Christine.

After they went, Leaf gave my shoulders a hug. 'She'll find something, Ruth. I've got a good feeling about this.'

I shrugged. 'Thanks anyway.'

Of course, I began to get ridiculously excited about what Christine might find out. A week went by, two more weeks. Finally, she rang. 'When you're passing, pop by, any time this week.'

'I'm coming down that way today, if that suits.'

In fact, I had no plans to go down to Northton at all, but a tight feeling in the pit of my stomach meant I wasn't going to be able to rest until I'd found out what she had.

Christine's kitchen had a huge map covering its far wall. A starburst of black threads led out from Harris to little black flags pinned across the world, clustering heavily in America, Canada and Australia.

She put her fingertip on a pennant in Manitoba. 'My cousins, twice removed. They were among the last people to be cleared from this island, from the village over in Finsbay. My great-great-aunt, she went completely mad when she got there. Never recovered from having to commit two of her children to the sea after the smallpox went through the boat.'

'Oh. I'm so sorry.'

'It was a terrible time for the people then. There are more Scots in Canada now than there are in Scotland.'

The kettle whistled and she went to make the tea. Through the picture window, a vast plane of water, filled with sharp clouds and a deep blue sky. Between the houses and the sea, the land was a maze of bright green islets like a jigsaw puzzle.

Christine brought the mugs over to the table and cleared a space among her papers. 'I'm so sorry. I'm afraid I didn't have much luck, Ruth. I did trace your birth certificate back to where it was issued in Bethnal Green, but after that, nothing. And um…' She looked embarrassed. 'Of course, it's more difficult when there's no father registered.'

'Of course.'

'The main problem was, I couldn't find a woman called Macleod who matched your mother's details in any other records. It's very unusual. Ruth, do you think she gave her real name on your birth certificate? I'm so sorry to have nothing for you, dear.'

'Really,' I told her, 'don't worry about it. I'm used to my mystery family.'

Riding home on the bus from Northton, I wished I hadn't raked the whole thing up again. It was disturbing to no longer even be sure that my surname was correct. It made me wonder if Mum had been telling me the truth about coming from the islands. She'd never really told me anything useful about them.

I recalled watching the TV with her once, back in our flat in London. The weather came on and she got up and traced her finger over a scattering of islands at the top of the map of Britain.

'That's where we come from,' she said.

I wanted to see more, but the weatherman's head was in the way. Then the screen changed to adverts.

The next day, I got an atlas out of the school library. I opened it on the kitchen table while she was drying the dishes.

'Do we come from Skye?' I asked her.

'No, further out,' she said, putting the plates away in the cupboard.

I read out the names from a chain of islands that seemed to be floating away into the Atlantic: Lewis, Harris, Uist, Benbecula, Vatersay, Eriskay.

She said them back to me in a sing-song accent, the proper way.

'But which one do we come from?' I asked her.

'All of them and none of them. We come from the sea.' And that was all she would tell me. She'd lit a cigarette and stood looking out of the window over the jumble of city buildings for a long time, lost in her own thoughts.

Sometimes, I felt that if Mum were to walk through the door one day, I'd slap her, and not stop till she understood what it felt like, how little she'd left me with.

I couldn't bear to think that the islands weren't in some way my home now. I looked at the faint reflection in the bus window, a white face sliding over the hills – just the kind of face that you saw all around the islands, the straight black hair, the blue eyes. Surely Mum had been telling me something of the truth with her seal people stories: this was where we came from.

'Best view in the islands,' Angus John told us. 'Up behind the castle. Used to go up that way often, come home with a nice big salmon from the Avenbuidhe loch when I was a boy.'

So one Sunday afternoon, we set out to do a walk along the path marked on the Ordnance Survey map that led up behind Avenbuidhe Castle and into the mountains.

I'd managed to find out quite a lot about the castle's history. 'It was built by Lord Marstone in 1830,' I said, raising my voice against the Bedford's old engine. 'The one who made his money from opium.'

Jamie whistled. 'The Reverend Ferguson was in with the local drug lords, then.'

'Well, by that time, it was the second Lord Marstone living in the castle. He had married someone very wealthy from London, a Lady Erquart. But she wasn't too impressed with young Marstone and his castle. So she took herself and their daughter home to her father's mansion in London, and it must be that same daughter who was the Katriona mentioned in the Reverend Alexander's book. She returned to live at the castle after her mother's death, when she was about sixteen.'

'So the Reverend would have come visiting here, sweet-talking the lovely Katriona with his mermaid stories,' said Jamie. 'Wonder what Lord Marstone would have had to say about that.'

The main road to Hushinish went straight through the castle grounds, so we drove through the black iron gates and rattled over the cattle grid towards the turreted building and the little track up into the mountains. Amid the mineral blues of rock and water, Avenbuidhe Castle, with its red sandstone walls and bright green lawns, seemed to have been imported from somewhere else. We turned off along the small track behind the castle. The van had to pull hard up the steep incline. We rounded a bend and caught sight of the silent loch hidden away in a dip in the mountains, but at the same moment, we heard the swift crunch of another vehicle coming up behind us. A horn sounded several times.

Jamie slowed to a halt, pulled on the handbrake. A dark green Land Rover had parked its nose against a bank of moss. A man got out, and two dogs with sleek, polished coats spilled from the car. They hung close to his legs, their pink tongues the colour of cured ham, steaming in the cool air.

Leaf got out first, stretching her arms, the wind billowing out her dress. She knelt down to hug one of the dogs.

'I wouldn't do that, my dear.'

He was a broad man, wearing a boxy, bright mustard tweed jacket with a leather collar and a checked tweed cap. He had a very English accent and the authoritative bluster of a man used to being in charge.

'Sorry there, not a public road this way. You'll have to turn back.'

I felt something prickle in Michael. When he answered, he sounded ultra public school.

'Thing is, old chap, the right of way's marked on the map. We actually live on the island. Thought we'd go for a walk on the moor.'

'You can certainly walk up there if you'd like to hire the place for a few thousand, otherwise this land belongs to a consortium in the City. Not really safe for people to cross the moor when the shooting's on. Sorry, but you are trespassing.'

'Are you sure we can't take a very quick wander up to see the view?' Leaf said, her hair dancing in the wind like a hillside sprite's.

'Have to disappoint you, young lady. This is private land.'

We got back into the van, did a tight reverse, headed back down the hill and exited through the second set of iron gates. We decided to drive on towards Hushinish, a wild and lonely bay at the end of the island that felt like the edge of the world, where Ishbel had first seen her Selkie. We all agreed that Hushinish would be a much nicer walk but a feeling somewhere between disappointment and shame pervaded the quietly humming interior of the Bedford – which, now we thought about it, did seem awfully shabby compared to the solid new Land Rover. I thought of the way its dogs hung their heads from the windows, their eyes trained on us, watching us leave.

CHAPTER 17

Alexander

When I saw that Miss Marstone had returned homewards without coming to the manse to pay a visit, I was, I must say, rather surprised. But also somewhat relieved that I would be able to continue with my books for the rest of the day.

However, Miss Marstone had left a note with the maid saying I was enjoined by Lord Marstone to attend a late luncheon at the castle on Sunday. Miss Marstone would be at the morning service and I could thus travel back to the castle in her carriage. I mentioned the outing to Moira, and requested that she also accompany us, as to my mind it were best that Miss Marstone should be seen to be chaperoned. In one's role as spiritual counsellor, it is all too easy to reach misunderstandings with unmarried members of the fair sex. One cannot be too careful.

The following Sunday, I concluded the morning service and having installed Moira comfortably on the backboard of the carriage, Miss Marstone and I took our places inside.

His Lordship had sent a larger vehicle than the little governess carriage in which Miss Marstone usually liked to skip across the tracks. Our progress was therefore necessarily slow, but this was no hardship since it was a day of unparalleled brilliance, with the blue sea banded in turquoise and sapphire over the white sand of the vast beaches. The sky was open and equally startling in its blueness. The islands across the water and mountains of the north island were a vivid indigo. The air smelled pure as salt, clean and new as if it were the first day on earth. I pointed out and named the different birds as we rode along companionably, the curlews and plovers piping their nostalgic notes from the shoreline.

I was aware that this summons by Lord Marstone was something of an inspection, since I had taken the appointment without ever meeting the great man. It must have been this nervousness that made me more talkative and expansive than usual as I chatted on vainly, and I think this must have been why I was slow to undo the damage when Katriona slid her small hand under my arm and leaned in close against my side to better see the orchid flowers that I was describing to her.

I was slow, too slow in extricating myself, but after a polite pause, I gently returned her arm to its original place, placing her hand on her own knee, and giving a firm but forgiving small pat to the back of her hand. She looked all around her, laughed, and in the briefest trice, she kissed my cheek.

Lord Marstone was not at all as I had anticipated. I had modelled my expectations according to the refined men of quality in the city of Edinburgh, in their modern frock coats and spats, polished top hats and elegant cloaks. Lord Marstone was a man of considerable corpulence and wore the kilt. He favoured a tweed jacket, which showed the front of a shirt stained with gravy from previous meals. His large red face and heavy, bloodshot jowls appeared to be supported directly by his shoulders, and his hair, shiny with applied grease, was gathered back and tied like a nest of rodent tails. Most disconcerting were his eyes. During my entire stay in the castle, never once did he address me without looking either sideways or into the far distance, as if continually distracted by some unvoiced thought. He seemed, almost, to be spying around himself for a possible means of escape.

But it is an acknowledged truth that the truly great, isolated as they are by their position, often develop habits and characteristics which may not be construed as polite in more moderate society, so I was quite disposed to see such personal habits as mere quirks and to not take offence. I therefore set to entertaining His Lordship with an account of the morning's sermon, as we took a fortified beverage in the drawing room before the open fire. Above the fireplace, the head of a large stag with splendid antlers looked down in static judgement with glassy eyes.

His Lordship was rocking in front of the fire, and he had drawn his daughter to his side under one of his massive arms. As I was reaching my second point, he gave a grimace as if affected by some kind of toothache.

'So, missy here likes coming along to hear your sermonising. Tried to get her to stay and save herself, but it seems she prefers to gallivant about in the wind and rain, ruining her health, because she must hear the Reverend. It's a flighty little thing, isn't it?' He looked down at his daughter with something that might have been mistaken for disdain.

I opened my mouth to speak, but before I could think how I should reply, he downed the rest of his whisky and wheeled round with a swirl of his heavy kilt to lead his daughter away towards the aroma of roast dinner. I left my tumbler of whisky unfinished, and made to follow them.

CHAPTER 18

Moira

I watched Alexander go through the tall oak doors of the castle and stood there next to the carriage wondering what I should do. It was a beautiful little place His Lordship had picked for himself, with a clear burn making a waterfall into a sea loch, the water sparkling, and the hills all snug around the little castle with their pink granite shoulders soft in the sunlight. The only thing that spoiled the place, to my mind, was the sour block of dark brick pretending to be a castle, its new windows and sharp corners betraying that it had been all bought and paid for by a man who was no more from here than I am from the moon.

The driver was leading the horse out of the shafts and he gave me a sideways nod to say that I should go. So I made my way round the building, where the windows start up above your head to make sure no one can look in at the greatness of the Marstones, and I came to the back buildings, squashed in hard as they were against the mountain flank that rises steep above the castle back. I saw a maid throwing out a bucket of slops, and chickens running over and squabbling to get at the peelings scattered on the flagstones. She looked at me with suspicion.

'What's it you want?' she said, in a broad accent from Glasgow.

'I am the Reverend's maid.'

'Well, it's no good coming to look for work here if he's thrown you out. We don't want your sloppy ways. His Lordship never takes island girls; too dirty and heathen they are.'

I made myself as tall as I could, and even though she was stood up on the steps above me, I showed her that I was looking down on her.

'My master is dining with His Lordship, and Miss Katriona, to whom I am teaching the Gaelic, has requested that I be given Sunday lunch in your kitchens.'

I had made up the last bit, but I was terrible hungry, and felt sure that they did mean me to eat.

The maid was not so sure, but the calling up of her mistress's name had her, I could see. She looked worried for herself then and said, 'Well, it's as broad as it's lang for me if yers comes in.'

I took off my bonnet – Maggie had loaned me her straw bonnet, which, though a little bent, has a fine bunch of cherries – and I sat down at the end of a long wooden table that was being set for lunch, although the dirty bowls and vegetable scrapings from the meal's preparation were still strewn around on it. I looked around me and saw that His Lordship did not run a good kitchen and that the staff he had were slovenly and dirty. I could not understand how in such a great house the maids were joking and swearing at the sink and sloppily stirring pots of stew, and seeming to not care a bit about His Lordship's dinner. I had a plate slid across the table to me and then they all came in and began to eat. A tall woman dished out lumps of mutton and a dollop of turnip mash and potato. They each crouched over their plates like beasts afeared of someone stealing their meat.

I sat up very straight and cut dainty bits with my knife and fork and ate very neatly, dabbing my mouth with the back of my hand. I noticed a rack of knives above the draining boards by the sink – six of them in descending size.

The stable boys and the very young maids from Glasgow either sneered or looked ill and homesick. It must be a hard place here for a girl missing her home, I thought. So in the confusion of that kitchen, as stable boys sat with their muddy boots on the chairs and got slapped round the head, and while the smallest girl was left to scrub the pans and the older ones to smoke pipes by the back door, I slipped away to see if I could arrange myself a wee tour of the castle.

I made my way up the servants' back stairs and came out onto a long corridor with many doors. The carpet was thick, so no one heard me as I tried each heavy oak door and looked inside. It was a dark place with red carpets that snuffed out the noise, dark green silk on the walls, big furniture all varnished dark and very fancy. It wasn't a place that seemed anyone's home, but was very big and ugly, I thought.

When I got to the fifth door along on the seaward side and opened it, I saw a room that I knew must belong to His Lordship. There was no mirror but large paintings of himself in fancy kilts and military garb, looking much more slim and young than the old brute that I had seen taking Alexander in through his door. I noted the long drapes at the window and stood behind one to see if I was covered, and I measured how many paces to the bed. And then I did see if I could raise my arm high enough to get enough purchase, given that the bed was such a big and high old thing. I would need to stand on a stool, so I looked all around but saw nothing of the kind. I was beginning to feel a bit peculiar, with my heart going so very fast all the time, and a dread came down on me that I had been there too long. But then I saw a door half open leading off his bed chamber. So I went through to see what I might find in there.

Well, I was quite took aback. There was a great big white tub, longer than any man, with a big brass contraption at one end for where the water was to come out, and all round the walls were green tiles, like green seawater, with fish and hippopotamuses swimming under the glaze. And I thought, this is where His Lordship must thrash around in his bath like some old blubbery seal. And it was then that I heard the bed chamber door open, footsteps coming across the floor. I looked around me quickly, but there was nowhere for me to hide. Then all of a sudden the door was pushed open and a girl came in.

I don't know who was more frighted, her or me, but she screamed and dropped the pile of white towels she was carrying, and so I hurried to help her pick them up. It was this that made her take me for some new maid, because she began scolding me about how undermaids were not allowed up in the good bedrooms. She was only a little thing, but she acted very knowing about how everything was done. And she shooed me out of the bed chamber and marched me along the corridor to the back stairwell. But then she stopped and took me hard on the shoulder with her hand, pinched it really hard, I thought, and she stared at me. 'Don't come up here again. Don't. And if it ends up that you do have to, then don't let him trick you. If he calls for something, you never go in that bathroom place while he's in there. D'you hear me?'

So I promised solemnly that I would never go in there, and she left me to make my way back down.

I got on my bonnet and waited outside, sitting on the little wall that runs in front of the sea loch, letting the afternoon sun warm my bones, which felt very chilled from the cold inside that house, even though it was early summer.

After a long time, I saw them coming out. And when I was sat on the backboard ready to go home with the Reverend, I looked up to what must be Marstone's room and saw the little maid looking down from an upstairs window. When she saw me there and realised that I was but a visitor, she drew back from the window swiftly.

CHAPTER 19

Ruth

'It was ever the way with London men,' said Angus John when we told him about our visit to the castle. 'They come to catch the fish, drink the whisky and run over the sheep. Don't care who lives here.'

Angus John had appeared in the kitchen that evening and looked set to stay. He produced a whisky bottle – this time not filled with milk – and poured us all a dram. He tipped a slug into his own mug, saying he only took it in tea now and then to help his old bones, and settled back in the chair.

'See now, in the old days,' he began, 'it was our house that was the ceilidh house. It was none of your jigging around in the hall in An t'Obbe and having to pay for the pleasure. No, someone would tell a story and someone would pick up the fiddle or start a song, and the whisky was passed round.' He looked moved, his eyes glistening. He sniffed elaborately.

'We could do that now,' said Leaf. 'We could do a ceilidh here. She settled herself cross-legged on the old sofa and sang an old Cat Stevens song about moon shadows. There was a huskiness to her voice from the cigarettes that she and Jamie sometimes liked to smoke. The summer sun had brought out a faint rust of freckles across her face. Her second song was a folk song from America, a lullaby. 'For your baby,' she said, grinning at me and reaching over to pat the bump.

Jamie and Michael gave us a song by Bruce Springsteen, Jamie slapping his knee, their eyes shut and heads nodding in the groovy bits as if in pain. They did an encore.

'Ruth?' said Angus.

I wanted to. I had a memory of Mum singing something in Gaelic in her soft, slow voice. For a moment it was so clear that I felt some genetic memory might produce the words. Almost opened my mouth.

I shook my head, but it was no problem: Angus John was waiting for his turn so that the evening could start properly. He leaned forward and asked if we would like a story.

'A ghost story,' said Leaf.

'This,' he said sternly, 'is the true story of the haunted spoons, that happened to someone living not so far from here. And yes, it might be a ghost story or it might not, but you'll have to decide that. This is a story about a woman who was driven mad by twelve silver spoons.'

He nodded towards Leaf knowingly. 'The thing about the world of spirits,' he said, lifting his arm and letting it fall with an emphatic thump on the chair, 'is that you can't deny them. If you don't take into account the world of spirits, they'll come back and get you anyhow.

'Have you noticed how ordinary things around your own house can be haunted, how they will disappear, and then they'll appear again where they shouldn't be, trip you up even. A letter or a set of keys, say. And that's not the end of it. Beds will not let you get out of them when you need to, and then they'll throw you out in the early morning just when you are desperate for sleep. Cups will smash from your hand or sometimes they will fly across the room, when you had no intention of throwing them.

'I heard of one boy who was deafened by his own clock, but only when it spoke a certain time. Certain words can become unbearable to the mind. Ordinary words that people use every day, they can become so loud to some people that they can drive them mad for days on end.

'A lot of quarrels have been started by the spirits that settle in everyday objects, spirits that worm down into a silver candlestick, or slip inside an ugly teapot, or even slide themselves into a set of old spoons – ah yes, the spirits of quarrels that are not laid to rest for years. Sometimes these haunted things get hidden away in a cupboard, or the back of a drawer, but they can still have the power to cause disruption long after the person who put them there has died.

'That's how it was with the silver spoons, and this was a set of a dozen dessert spoons with fancy handles, the wedding dowry that Effie Macleod in Rodel brought to her husband Norman MacIver.

'Well, Effie has four bonny girls who grow up very handsome, and in time Effie gets old and she passes away. So the question is, who is to get these beautiful solid silver spoons, the like of which no one else on the island has? So while the sisters quarrel and quarrel, the youngest and quickest has a think. And before they can decide to do the sensible thing and keep three spoons each, she goes into the house while the wake is still on for her mother, takes the spoons and hides them away in the back of her bedroom drawer.

'And that was the last time that Effie's youngest daughter slept a whole night. Morag was woken night after night by the sound of rattling, though her husband swore he could hear nothing. On it went, every night, like the jangling of a hundred horses' bridles. Jangle rattle, rattle jangle till by the next month she was white as a sheet and thin as a stick.

'"It's dying I am," she told her husband. But she would not give those spoons up or confess that she had them, because she felt she was owed them, you see. She was sure in her heart that all her sisters looked down on her, and her mother had favoured the others more, and so she thought she must have those spoons to make up for all the years of slights. Which was an odd thing, because all her sisters had the same thoughts about themselves when it came to those spoons. They all felt they were owed those twelve silver spoons to make up for all the slights they had had to put up with from the other females in their family.

'So Effie's daughter, Morag, is now on her deathbed, and her own soon to be orphaned children are gathered round her bed, begging her to please get better now. And so she asks for the woman from Drinishader, the old woman with the second sight, who can see as far as the future, and deep, deep back into the heart's past. I knew her myself, when I was a child.

'The woman with the second sight comes and she sees straight away what the trouble is. She goes over to the chest of drawers and takes out the twelve spoons, all tied together with a piece of silk ribbon, and needing a shine with some polish since they've been hidden away that long. Now they don't look nice any more; they look black.

'But her sisters are there and they all know what she has found, and they start screaming and quarrelling like banshees till the old woman with the sight sends everyone out of the room but the sick sister, who can't get out of her bed anyway.

'"The problem here," she tells the dying woman – who has just the strength left to turn her head and see what the woman is holding – "is that you have put a spirit on these spoons, and it has changed their nature so that the silver is all agitated and in motion. We must first name the spirit so that we can order it to leave, and then we must call the spoons by their proper name again and eat from them. Only then can they return to the peace of being simple spoons."

'The woman shuts her eyes and sees that the trouble is a spirit of bitterness that is corrupting the metal. So Morag must sit up in bed and tell the spirit of bitterness to leave the spoons, and then she calls out their proper name three times, "Spoons, spoons, spoons." And at that very moment, as she finishes calling out their proper name, she puts her hands to her head and laughs, because for the first time in years, the jangling in her head has stopped, and she can hear some peace and quiet.

'Then the old woman summons in all the family and calls for a big pot of porridge. She hands round the spoons, since they must be used for their proper purpose, to make sure the bitter spirit does not come back. The youngest sister divides the spoons out fairly, and it comes back to everyone all the kindnesses they have been given by their sisters.

'Each sister left the house that day with their own three spoons, which they saw now were nothing but spoons. And each woman went home smiling, with the love of her sisters remembered in her heart.

'You see, that's what you have to do to send a haunting spirit back to the day it came from; you must call things by their true name. That is the easy part. Of course, the other part is harder – naming the spirit that was placed onto the spoons or the key or the letter. Many, many things can get a spirit put on them. But you always have to name a spirit to make it go back to its own time.'

'What a great story,' said Jamie as we gave Angus a round of applause.

'No need to clap,' he said. 'I am not making this story up, I am only telling you what is true.'

'A dram from the bottle of spirits,' said Jamie, unstoppering the bottle of Islay.

'Now here's haunted for you,' said Angus, holding his hand up as if to ward off some curse as he proffered his glass. He would have just one more small whisky with us, he decided. Then he had another. 'It's been a while,' he said.

After a couple more, and some songs in Gaelic, he straightened his cap, tightened the rope that was holding up his trousers, and went home still singing.

That night, as I crossed the hallway to go upstairs, I paused. I thought, Yes, they're just stairs. Stairs, stairs, stairs.

I was halfway up, thinking about Angus's whimsical story, wanting to smile and laugh it off, when I felt a chilly draught round my neck. Against all logic, I found myself thinking, 'But I need to name the spirit. She won't go away till I've named her.'

The next morning, Leaf went up to ask Angus John about one of the hens in the new roost that had stopped laying. Ten minutes later, she was back.

'He's not there. I think someone's burgled his house.'

As we reached the top of the slope, we saw Angus John making his way back along the road from Tarbert. He was taking shaky, exaggerated steps and working so hard at progressing along the road that it was just pitiful to see him. He was carrying a brown plastic shopping bag that clinked.

The door to his cottage stood open. The kitchen felt damp, as if the door had stood open all night and let in the mist. I was horrified to see every single one of his mother's cherished old plates had been taken down from the dresser and smashed: the willow pattern platters, the rose-covered jugs, the old cream bowls, all lay in pieces, scattered over the floor. Worst of all, someone had taken a poker to the old dresser – Angus always loved to point out how unique it was, how his mother had commissioned it especially from a carpenter in Skye. The wood was now scarred and splintered from repeated blows.

Two empty whisky bottles lay on the table.

Angus John sat down in his chair and immediately fell asleep.

'Oh, what have you done this time, Angus?' Mrs MacKay appeared at the door, a square, solid presence battened down in tweed skirt and nylon overall. She went and pulled his head up so she could see his face, then let it fall back onto his chest. 'You and that temper of yours,' she shouted, but he didn't stir.

'You can help me get him through to his bed, girls.'

Even in early summer, his bedroom was a cold little place. There were spots of black mould on the curtains and window; a wardrobe with an ancient suitcase on top; an elderly bed with a balding candle-wick bedspread. The matchboard walls had been painted in hard gloss. We got him laid out on the bed. I pulled off his boots. Leaf covered him with a blanket, and then we went through to clean up the kitchen.

'You've done enough now. I'll see to this. Goodness knows, I've been seeing to that man's disasters for enough years.'

Leaf was holding two halves of a blue-and-white plate, seeing if they would fit together. 'But I don't understand. He's always so sweet.'

'Not when he's drinking he's not.'

'Is that the reason his wife left him?' I said, a pulse high in my throat.

She looked at me in surprise.

'Oh, Katie. I haven't thought of Angus's Katie for years.' She sighed. 'It was the drink, and then the nightmares. He'd wake in the night of a sudden, lash out and hit her before he knew what he was about. She was afraid of him. That's why she took herself away, and their little boy.'

'He had a little boy?'

'Oh yes. Callum. It was very sad. The last day I saw Callum was the day his mother took him away.'

That afternoon, Dr Lawson visited Angus. Angus was taken over to the mainland for a stay in a psychiatric unit in Inverness.

'But isn't that a bit extreme?' I said to Dougal when he came by to tell us, after he'd helped Dr Lawson with getting Angus into his car.

'Angus did his bit in the war, but now he suffers from the shell-shock, and when he's addled with drink, things slip around in his head. He thought Dr Lawson and the nurse were German officers, taking him off for questioning. They had to go along with it to get him in the car.'

'Was it our fault?' I said. 'Letting him drink whisky?'

'You're not to blame for how Angus John is. We must keep him in our prayers, that with grace he may overcome.'

After Dougal left, I felt utterly drained. My arms and legs seemed so heavy. I went up to the bedroom, and told myself I was going to finish sewing the cover for a decrepit armchair – another old bit of furniture we'd collected that was going to be as good as new one day, with a bit of paint and hard work.

I sat down in the lumpy old chair, its arms shiny and frayed, and stared at the length of flowered cotton that was going to transform it. The light was growing faded and smoky, a sad hopelessness in the air. I stared at it until the light was almost all gone, then I took the scissors, and with tears running down my face, I sheared the new cloth into jagged, useless rips.

CHAPTER 20

Alexander

I awaited my departure for Edinburgh with some impatience, greatly pleased that Carfax, my old friend in the university museum, had offered me undisturbed access to the now vast collection of specimens in his care.

And of course, I could not think of being in Edinburgh without feeling the exhilaration of returning to those same streets Mr Darwin once walked as a medical student. I pictured him, then little more than a boy, standing white and sweating outside the medical buildings, unable to stomach another dismemberment of a human body.

I pictured him following his mentor Grant on cold and wet journeys along the coast to collect their sea specimens. Grant strides along, a little ahead of the stockier Darwin, all the while busily dropping his theories of species development into ears already attuned to transmology by Darwin's own grandfather, the radical Erasmus.

I almost felt a tingle in the soles of my feet as I anticipated following Darwin up the marble steps of the university museum, to perhaps make my own small contribution to our understanding of species.

At least, such was my hope.

Bad weather turned the crossing into an ordeal of twelve hours before we came near the harbour of Oban. I sat out on deck, shivering, since the wash of seasickness from suffering travellers made the interior of the cabin impossible. Sharing my end of the bench was an old man who belched and made other noises of an upset digestion for some hours. On my other side sat a fishwife who waved bread and pickled herring under my nose and declared them just the thing to settle the stomach.

Arriving at the large sandstone house that served Matthew and Fanny as a manse, I was once again encouraged to believe in civilisation. Edinburgh may have many alleys and wynds of unspeakable filth and degradation, but the New Town is a monument to progress and the rational mind.

I was as warmly greeted as ever by my hosts, but it was evident that Fanny had suffered from ill health since I had last seen her. She was a great deal thinner, with dark hollows round her eyes, and I wondered that Matthew had not thought to mention their troubles to me.

I had considered Fanny a somewhat silly girl, concerned only with puddings and purchasing furniture for their already well-appointed house, but the woman who greeted me in the hallway seemed to have passed through a sadness, now borne with silent dignity. She clasped my hand in both of hers and called me 'our dear friend'.

If Fanny was indeed convalescing from some grave illness, I decided that I should quietly enquire of Matthew whether my stay was inconveniencing them, and remove to lodgings nearby. But I soon discovered that they had my every waking moment mapped out. Indeed, my arrival must have been their main topic of conversation for some weeks, judging by the thought that they had given to my comfort.

Fanny told Matthew to show me straight away to my room, which she had readied for my arrival with great thoughtfulness. But as my eyes ranged around the walls and the tall windows overlooking the garden, I could not help recalling a previous visit when I had seen the same room, with a large rocking horse from Fanny's childhood; with sprigged wallpaper and lace curtains; and a strange chair with low legs and a high back. This, Fanny had termed a nursing chair – another family heirloom. A previous family had evidently used the room as a nursery and at that time the wooden rails across the window had been left untouched.

The bars had now been removed, the chair and the old toys cleared away. A writing desk was set beneath the window. A narrow, high bed took up one wall, with a marble washstand and dressing screen set nearby. I found a bookcase supplied with those books that Matthew clearly deemed might be of use in my studies.

After a pleasant luncheon taken on the terrace overlooking the lawn, Matthew and I set out through the avenues of the New Town. I was anxious to know if Matthew felt my visit a burden to his wife, when she seemed in delicate health. My question seemed to make him flinch. He walked on in silence and then said, 'We all but lost Fanny last winter, Alexander.'

'But why did you not tell me? If I could have helped in some way.'

'There was nothing you could have done. Fanny did not want me to tell anyone, other than those who must know about her troubles. We are fortunate indeed, living in a place where we have some of the most advanced hospitals and surgeons in the world. She lost the child she was carrying, but there were complications. She will never bear a child now.'

'I am so sorry, so deeply sorry. Is there nothing…?'

'It is quite final. She will never be a mother. She accepts it, although it has broken her heart. I am simply thankful that I did not lose her.'

He did not speak again for some while. I put my hand on his shoulder and we walked on until he rallied and regained the use of his voice. He left me at the steps of the museum, and I saw him hurry away, heading back in the direction of their house.

I found Carfax in an upper gallery, where a multitude of artefacts were being removed from their cases and packed into tea chests to be carried away by a procession of workmen in aprons. Robert the Bruce's dirk, the teacup from which Mary Queen of Scots once drank, and diverse curios from Africa were being put into storage as either surplus copies or items of dubious provenance. I stood aside while a large canoe went past in mid-air. One of the workmen stumbled as he turned the corner, dropping the boat on the floor with an unfortunate tearing sound. I helped him to regain his feet and studied the large rip along the bow. The fabric was ancient and varnished heavily. When I helped them lift the craft, I found it very light, being made not of paper as I had assumed, but a parchment-thin hide, with wooden struts inside to keep the long canoe shape. I turned over a label: 'Supposed Eskimo Canoe, found Sunderland, circa 1690'.

Carfax also came to assess the damage, but did not seem overly worried since the only place the craft would now be sailing was through the dusty museum attics. He apologised that he did not have time to show me to the rooms devoted to mammalian anatomy.

'Next year, you will see, I will have all our new acquisitions labelled and out on display, but since you cannot wait until then, I have asked my assistant Nicols to help you find whatever it is you want to see.'

I made my way up the stairs and found Nicols in one of the back rooms, engaged in cataloguing beetles. He was a research student, and several years younger than me, but he received me with a somewhat disrespectful, 'Ah, Ferguson. The mermaid man! Have you caught one yet?' He laughed to himself, and I realised with dismay that my quest had become widely known in Edinburgh's academic circles. From his tone, I also realised that I had become something of a joke.

He made me wait on a chair while he finished his work at his leisure. After some considerable while, I stood up to say that I would leave if it were inconvenient for him.

'What was it you wanted to see?'

'I was particularly interested in examining specimens of land mammals that have transmuted to adapt themselves to water: seals or dolphins, possibly the manatee.'

'We have a manatee skeleton,' he said doubtfully. 'Otherwise known as Columbus's mermaid, since the men on his ship mistook it for such a creature – just the thing to interest you. Although it would not help you very much, Reverend, because I believe it's a warm water creature. You are looking for a mermaid that can survive around the cold shores of the west coast of Scotland.'

'I am fully aware of that, thank you, Mr Nicols, though it is most kind of you to point it out.'

He gave a small mock bow, and led me into a maze of shelves. He waved his arm with largesse across the catacomb of bone collections in Manila boxes and the translucent walls of glass jars where strange, pickled creatures swam, pale and cramped.

'So many donations, and still they come – though oddly enough, not a single mermaid.' He turned to face me. 'I do admire you, Reverend. You're a man of great faith, in your mermaids, in your God, but truly, I am puzzled by you clerics. You do see, don't you, that once one has read Darwin, one can no longer believe in the account of Creation given to us in Genesis?'

'But to which account are you referring?' I said to him mildly. 'There are two accounts of Creation in Genesis, with quite evident differences, and neither is meant to be read as a scientific journal disclosing God's methods, my dear boy. St Anselm has long warned us against the heresy of taking such metaphorical accounts literally. They are truthful, but in the way that one sometimes requires a story to reveal to us the truth we cannot see; to answer where we come from, and thus know who we truly are.'

He scowled at me, a very black look, trying to locate a hole in the fabric of my argument so that he might make a larger tear and reveal to me the darkness beyond. Not a contented man, I thought.

'I only wish men like you would have the courage to wake up, see man for what he is, a most marvellous monkey, but with no immortal qualities, and quite alone in the universe except for his own kind. There you have the observed and scientific truth.'

'My dear boy,' I told him, 'we must never give in to despair. Simply because we have seen and even understood a little more of the processes of the Creator, we should not think we understand all the mysteries of grace.'

Nicols did not reply to that. He took a paper from his pocket, silently looked it over for a while. 'I saved this for you,' he said, 'to help you in your quest for truth.'

I thought he seemed quietly struck by my argument and I thanked him for his kindness.

After he had left me to my work, I unfolded the bill. It was for an impresario at a local fair who was displaying the 'Marvellous Feejee Mermaid'.

I spent an interesting afternoon studying bone formations in cetaceans. I was no further enlightened as darkness fell, but was particularly glad to find a good edition of Haeckel, and looked forward to spending the evening examining his illustrations of the morphology of the human foetus from fish to lizard to man.

On returning, I found that Fanny had gone to a great deal of trouble to arrange a supper whereby I could meet various suitable young ladies of her circle. All three of them seemed very happy to make the acquaintance of an unattached bachelor – even more so since my reputation had once again gone before me, and they wanted to hear stories about my mermaid. All three ladies declared themselves quite willing to believe in her, and on reading the notice about the Feejee mermaid, they became most excitable about the possibility of setting eyes upon such a phenomenon.

It became agreed Matthew and I should accompany Fanny's friends and visit the show the very next day.

I did not sleep soundly. I had hoped to quietly visit the Feejee mermaid by myself and ascertain whether this was a genuine specimen of something extraordinary or mere trickery. I had no wish to examine the specimen in front of an excitable and voluble audience in bonnets and lace. But I was also kept awake by my own impatience. What if this were to be my first concrete evidence? I tossed and turned, feeling exhausted and enervated. The rich food, along with so many feminine attentions – three soft kisses and three tender hands as the ladies left – had thoroughly undone the regime of quiet austerity I had followed until recently. It takes so little to awaken the appetites.

When I finally slept, flushed by wine and roast beef, those three soft hands woke me once again in the small hours with dreams that I hastily banished from my mind. It is indeed the work of Sisyphus to train the body into the ways of faith and chastity.

We did not buy tickets to go into the main tent for the matinee performance, but stayed in the side enclosure where exhibits of freaks and marvels were on display. A steam organ was gaily playing a military tune, the little wooden martinets banging cymbals and bells in time with the music. Smells of burned sugar and the dung of frightened animals pervaded the air. We passed a lion in a cage, too elderly and sick to frighten any creature, and an elephant chained to a post, moving to and fro on the spot as if in pain.

The Temple of Neptune was easily found, shrouded as it was in green silk drapes. At the entrance stood Neptune himself. He wore a crown and trident and the surly face of a man who has bare legs on a chilly morning. He called out in a thick Glasgow accent for us to come see the beautiful mermaid. I must admit that I hastened towards the entrance and promptly paid for all our tickets, anxious to understand the mystery of what lay inside.

The little creature was not alive. It was displayed in a glass case decorated with shells and paper sea plants. It had a grotesque little face, wizened by the preserving balm, wild, staring eyes and a mouth stretched in a permanent grimace. Skinny arms paddled the air as if frozen in the act of swimming, with the hair or mane artfully spread to resemble the motion of water. At the waist, the shrivelled creature was joined to what appeared to be the badly attached lower half of a large fish. It was clearly a trickery of taxidermy, nothing more than a small monkey with the appearance of a human goblin, joined at the mid section with a fish and painted in layers of brown varnish.

It was only then that I recalled Nicols's manner as he handed me the advertisement for the mermaid, and finally read the malice in his eye.

The ladies said nothing, but once they were sure that I was not taken in by this circus trick, they declared it as ugly as sin, and a perfect fright.

It had been foolish of me to expect anything else: from the depression that fell upon my mood like a sudden drop in the barometer, I realised that I had been expecting a great deal. So much had I longed to find proof of my elusive, postulated link, that I had hoped to find truth in a circus! I was ashamed to be so caught out in front of Matthew and Fanny's friends.

The ladies looked most discomfited and spared my feelings by declaring that they had a luncheon appointment that they must hurry to attend.

Matthew and I returned towards the house, neither of us inclined to talk, making our way through the press of crowds along the streets. Below, the steep valley and green park that run through the city gave a dizzying perspective on yet more people thirty feet below.

As I looked down into the park, I saw, walking along the path, a girl with long red hair and a slim green dress, and thought how like Moira she seemed. I found myself most unreasonably disappointed that it was not my Moira, and felt then an even greater longing to be back in my study overlooking a wide sea that was blue as stained glass, and with the peat's tarry, sweet smell in the fireplace.

Of course, she would soon have something to say about the varnished monkey fish. It was this thought that cheered me up most, quite what Moira would have to say about Mr Barnum.

When we got back to the house, the maid greeted us in a whisper: there was someone waiting to see the Master and the Reverend Ferguson in the drawing room. Fanny was asleep upstairs, and the maid had been left with strict instructions not to wake her, but the person had insisted upon coming in and sitting in the drawing room until the Master returned, and had been waiting there almost an hour.

I could not understand why Matthew's maid was speaking in such an overawed tone. Then Matthew showed me a calling card of the grandest kind, announcing a Lady Erquart of Grosvenor Square, London.

'What the deuce?' said Matthew. 'Must be some hospital charity looking for subscribers.'

In the drawing room, we found a lady wearing the type of elegant costume that speaks of great wealth, holding herself with a bearing that assumes an aristocratic standing in the world's eyes.

'Please forgive my intrusion,' she said, rising and coming towards us. 'You must wonder at my rudeness imposing upon your goodwill in this way, but I wanted to ask if I might speak with Reverend Ferguson.'

'I can only admire the soundness of your judgement in seeking the advice of my friend,' Matthew said, and indicated for us to sit, taking his accustomed place.

'I am embarrassed to have to ask a further kindness,' she added, not taking her seat, 'but it is essential that I speak to the minister in confidence.'

'Oh yes, indeed, indeed,' said Matthew, 'but of course.' Rising to give a quick nod, he hastened from the room.

She sat down and I saw that she was holding a small envelope.

'Reverend Ferguson, it may help if I introduce myself fully. I am the sister of Lady Marstone, now deceased, and the aunt of Katriona Marstone. I have come to ask of you a very great favour.'

She held out the letter.

'It is a great imposition, I know, but please would you give this to my niece, without Lord Marstone seeing or knowing anything about it. Since my sister passed away and my niece was called home to join her father, we have heard very little news from her. Of late there has been none at all. I am sure that Marstone is destroying my letters before they reach Katriona. She must think we have stopped caring.'

'There must be some misunderstanding. I am sure His Lordship…'

She continued to hold out the letter. 'Please,' was all she said.

Though she offered no further explanation, the urgency of her appeal was such that I said, 'I will be happy to convey your letter to her, with all discretion.'

'I am so very grateful. I heard through an acquaintance that you would be here during my visit to Edinburgh. You see, when Katriona last wrote, she mentioned you – that you have been kind to her; and so I hoped that if I found you, you might help us.'

From the heat in my cheeks, I felt I must have blushed a deep red.

Lady Erquart stood up as I took the letter. She leaned in very close and spoke in a low, emphatic voice.

'There is one more thing. If she ever needs me, will you tell her she can contact me through this address? The lady who lives there will make sure Katriona can come to me in London. I am embarrassed to be reduced to such subterfuge, but it is almost impossible to cross a man like Marstone.' She gave me a second note. This one had my name inscribed on the front. I began to open it and she nodded to me to continue. Inside she had written the name of a fishing family who lived down near Rodel harbour on the island.

'If Katriona ever wants me, the good people there will help her.'

'But surely Katriona can travel to visit you herself, when the season begins?' I began.

'He won't let her leave. He'll never willingly let her leave. It is a great comfort to me to know that she has a minister as a friend and counsellor, a man beyond reproach who will watch for her best interests.'

After she left, both Matthew and I agreed that she seemed very highly strung, and no doubt deeply affected by the death of her sister.

I returned over several days to continue my studies at the museum, taking care to show Nicols a calm and cheerful manner – and making no mention of his trick.

I had thought that it would be hard to leave Edinburgh and return to the meagre amusements of my isolated parish, but I found that the prospect of home gave a lift to my heart. Matthew made me a handsome present of two volumes – an account of Reverend Brand's visit to the Western Isles dated 1790, including further recorded sightings of merpeople, and a slim volume on the Nordic names common along the western seaboard. He had marked with a piece of paper a page that mentioned the name McOdrum.

'You must see inside,' he said with eagerness, 'for your mother's family name is quoted.'

McOdrum, from the Norse 'Son of Odrum, or son of the sea serpent'.
This family has attached to its lineage a Norse legend. The family are
reputedly descended from the King of Norway, who remarried with
a Sami witch. In a fit of jealousy she cursed his sons so that they
became seal men or 'sliochd nan ron'.

Descendants of this family are also reputed to be talented sailors
and fishermen, setting out with relish through the roughest of surf.

This made my heart skip a beat, for my own mother's family name, McOdrum, was indeed the same. I clasped Matthew affectionately. It meant a great deal to me that my faithful friend still held with me in my ill-omened quest.

'And keep to your theology of fish-men if you believe it to be true,' he said.

I left behind two of the dearest people that I know, my affection and admiration for them only increased by each renewal of friendship, and it was my heartfelt vow that on returning to my parish, I would prove myself as worthy a curator of the souls in my care as I knew Matthew to be of his.

On the morning that I returned home, I gave the letter directly into the hands of Callum the post, with instructions that it was to be handed to Katriona alone, or at the very least to her maid. I felt gratified to know that Katriona would receive the letter so promptly.

It was only much later, and far too late, that I discovered that the letter never did reach Katriona.

CHAPTER 21

Alexander

Over the following days the sea showed how mighty it could be. The waves resembled dark mountains from which streams of white spray levitated in the gale. Anything not fastened down was taken up by the wind and thrown around like a toy. The house trembled each time a blast hit the gable wall like a mighty fist.

When the storm finally abated and our ears were becoming accustomed to the return of less strident winds, Moira arrived with news that the gales had clawed away a vast part of the dunes and deposited the sand further inland towards the machair pastures. I put on my cap, buttoned up my stoutest jacket and walked out to see the changes to our shoreline.

The sky was filled with enormous canopies of dark cloud hurrying across to the west. Miles out beyond the headland, dark fingers of gigantic waterspouts reached down from the ragged clouds towards the sea. The wind was still forceful, and I had the strange sensation of having the air sucked from my chest even as I breathed in. The entire beach was covered by streams of sand levitated an inch or so above the ground, flowing towards a point on the horizon where a cold sun was a mere disc of brightness behind muted clouds. The veil of moving grains uncovered beneath it a history of fragmented shells, of broken sheep bone and dried claws of seaweed, embedded into the hard sand beneath.

Further down the beach, I could see where the wind had excavated the dunes. A small figure was bent over, examining the area. As I approached I saw that the man was investigating a pattern of rocks and boulders, newly uncovered by the wind.

It was Alan Carmichael, the schoolmaster from Finsbay. A small, grey-haired man in tweed jacket and plus fours, he was given to the independent opinions common among the people of the isolated fishing villages of the east coast, accessible as they are only by sea or by the rocky footpaths. He was an avid antiquarian and over a delicious meal in his homely schoolhouse, I had consulted him on more than one occasion while trying to better understand the history of the island.

We shook hands and shouted our greetings above the relentless booming of the wind.

As soon as he had heard reports that strange rocks had been uncovered by the wind, he had walked the eight miles across the island. He was quite sure now that we were looking at the remains of an Iron Age dwelling, constructed by people who had lived some three thousand years ago. He showed me a circle of blackened stones that had once served as their hearth, and a vast midden of bone-white limpet and cockle shells that protruded in layers from a mound of compacted sand – the accumulated remains of many meals eaten some thousands of years ago.

By now my hands had gone numb with the cold. I persuaded him to come back to the house for refreshment.

Out of the wind, and in front of a good fire in my study, I asked Moira to bring through hot water and the bottle of single malt from the dining room, since we were sorely in need of something to warm us through. I should really have trained Moira better: after she returned, she was soon leaning up against my desk with her arms folded and a cloth over her arm, joining in with our discussion on who these seashore dwellers might have been, and how they had come to the islands.

'Maggie Kintail always did say that there were fairies under those hillocks by the sea,' she said. I saw that Carmichael was more than a little impressed by how well Moira kept her part in our conversation, and I could not resist telling him that not only did she speak English fluently now, but she could also read it.

As Moira was holding out Carmichael's coat for him to leave, he said, 'By the way, we've yet more people moved into Finsbay – far too many for that barren piece of land to support. It can't go on. But aren't you a Gillies, now, Moira? We've an Anne Gillies moved in with her children. You're no related are ye?'

'Are they come from Pabbay Island?'

'Aye, it could be so.'

'Then it is my cousin and her bairns. I thought they were gone to Canada on the ship. Will you wait, Mr Carmichael, while I write a wee letter?'

This meant that Carmichael and I should take another small whisky by the fire and I insisted that Moira sit at my desk and take a sheet of paper and a pen to write her note. She blotted it, folded it and handed it to Carmichael with her good copperplate on the front: 'To my cousin Anne Gillies'.

'Moira,' he told her, 'if the Reverend here ever becomes too strict a master, then you can always come over to Finsbay and help me teach in the school.'

'But I should be quite lost without Moira to run the house,' I said.

And though she pretended not to mind me, I saw how pleased Moira was by this.

I sat up reading, until the candlelight made my eyes tired, following the journey of the Reverend Brand around the islands some fifty years before. I noted with great interest his reports on various sightings by islanders of mermaids, seal men and Finnmen. I was puzzled about this new mention of the Finnmen from Norway and wondered if this might have some significance to my research, but the only other reference I could find described the Finnmen as merely men dressed like Eskimos and so I discounted them.

Some days later, Katriona came for her lesson. Her attendance had been rather irregular of late. I had also had to cancel lessons during my visit to Edinburgh, and she seemed to have lost the small facility for Gaelic that she had previously gained; words that we had mastered some weeks ago had slipped away and she was very discouraged when I had to point out once again her small mistakes. She appeared deeply fatigued, and the more she tried, the less she was able to remember. As she struggled to recall simple household items in Gaelic, she pushed the reader from her lap and I saw tears begin to run down her cheeks.

'There surely can be no more stupid pupil than the one you see before you,' she said, so utterly dejected that I was unsure how best to help her.

I insisted that it was entirely my fault for having abandoned her lessons for two weeks.

'You are too exacting of yourself. Gaelic is the most difficult language on the earth for someone to master from its beginnings, and you have made excellent progress.' I attempted to distract her from her discouragement by telling her the news of the fairy house found beneath the sand hill.

'It must be,' I told her, 'that the islanders have kept some memory of a people who lived here long ago, before the great dunes crept over their ancient dwelling place, and their fireside tales have preserved the memory as a fairy story.'

She was very taken by this idea and so I proposed that we walk down to see the site, sure that a brisk turn in the open air would restore her spirits. It was not my habit to suggest such an outing with an unaccompanied young lady, but in the embarrassment of seeing her so distressed, I had thought only to make things better.

The fierce gales had died away but left behind turbulent winds that continued to put all the landscape in motion, the clouds speeding their shadows across the grasslands; the long marram grass shimmering and luxuriant, undulating across the dunes like a girl's hair blowing in the sun.

I let Miss Marstone lead the way along the sheep tracks, not an easy task, since those rough partings in the marram grass are apt to disappear of a sudden, leaving one to scramble up and down the sandy slopes. We arrived at the site and found that Carmichael must have returned at some point, for he had roped round the area with wooden posts and twine to denote the boundaries of the house. Miss Marstone was delighted with the fireplace of stones, and the smooth boulders arranged as seats. I showed her the prodigious layers of bone-white limpet shells that had been half uncovered by the storm, and explained how this was the midden of the household, and how one could clearly see their seasonal diet of shellfish, sea birds and the occasional mammal. Katriona must sit on the small boulders and try to imagine the family, and she was so animated and so like a child that I was in good spirits to see how my little expedition had done the trick.

I think she would have stayed there much longer, but taking her hand to help her up, I realised how very cold she had become, and so we made our way back through the dunes. As we went, we both called out above the wind our speculations about the people who had once walked these same beaches, fished in these seas, and gathered limpets from these very rocks, some thousands of years before us.

Katriona chose a longer route back as she wished to see where the wind had newly deposited the sand. It is a feature of these coasts that the gales can form dunes of great heights, some taller than a house, and

I went on ahead as the landscape became less familiar. Descending a slope into a hollow, each step became a slide through cool sand and I gave her my hand to guide her. But without warning, the slope began to move under our feet and I was able to save Katriona from a fall of considerable height only by catching her and holding her steady.

We made our careful way to the bottom and rested out of the wind in a hollow of sudden stillness and silence. I brushed quantities of sand from my jacket and my boots. Katriona, however, was standing motionless, and did nothing to sweep the damp patches of sand from her blue dress.

I felt rather than saw her move. She was suddenly hard against me, her face pressed to my face. I could feel the clink of her teeth against mine own. Taken completely off guard, a hot mood of surrendering poured over me, and I embraced her in a long kiss. I had no feeling of time, but the intensity seemed to last long minutes. Then, as I came back to myself and felt her limp and so easily led in my arms, I began to feel the wrongness of what I was doing, and my terrible abdication of responsibility. I pushed her away and turned from her, so bereft of any words to explain myself that I could not look at her.

But apologise I must. I turned back to speak, but saw that she had unbuttoned the front of her gown and had pushed it from her shoulders. She regarded me with an intent and bold look that shocked me to my core – an expression that could easily have been mistaken for knowing seduction by a woman of much experience. I was sure that she could have no real idea of what she was doing, or the effect she was provoking.

I moved towards her and hastily began to pull the material back up over her shoulders to cover her. As I did so, I noticed a long yellow bruise along her collarbone, but it was at this point that she took my hand and placed it on the cold softness of her breast, and then I felt my insides melt of all resolve.

CHAPTER 22

Moira

I do not know what got it into my head that I must follow the Reverend and the Miss on their little walk to see the fairy house.

It was Maggie Kintail who let the Miss into the house when she came for her lesson that day. The Reverend had said Maggie could help in the kitchen since I have so much to do to keep the house spick and span and his shirts clean and ironed, so I was out at the back seeing if the hens had laid when the Miss arrived.

When I came into the house with four eggs in my hands, Maggie looked very serious and frowning as she worked at making the bread. She said she thought the Miss looked ill, thin in the face, with dark shadows round her eyes, though when I went in to see if they wanted tea served, I thought she was pretty as ever in her blue, her cheeks very pink, and her hair gold and pinned up so elegant.

So I looked and looked and, yes, she did look tired and less in bloom maybe, but I could not see what Maggie had seen. And though I tried to get Maggie to tell me what was the sickness she had seen upon the Miss, she would not say. But I did know that Maggie had seen something bad, and that it was bad enough to not speak it to me.

The Miss looked very perky and well indeed as she put her bonnet back on to take a walk with the Reverend so as they could go and get some fresh air. And they was gone a long time, I thought. So, I did happen to take a little walk myself that way, since I needed some fresh air too, though I kept well back so they did not see me.

I knew they was going over to look at the fairy house that Maggie Kintail had always said was there under the hill. I walked out that way, but did not catch sight of them, and then I saw them walking back along the ridge of the high dunes, so I happened to take myself that way too.

I was cautious now, since I did not want to suddenly meet with them as if I was following them all along, and I lost them altogether. But something in my feet made me know the way, and as I came carefully to the ridge of a dune and looked over the top into the hollow below, I saw what I never did in my whole life expect to see.

There was the Miss, with her pretty gown pushed down around her shoulders and her breast as white and naked as a swan, and there was the Reverend with his hand resting upon her pale chest.

I fell down away from the ridge so they could not see me. Though I think I would have fallen down anyway – so great was the shock that my legs and my knees seemed to stop working. I lay panting in the grass and watched the clouds rolling across the sky, too heavy and thick and grey, and then I got up.

I ran like something was chasing me, and sometimes I stumbled because the wind made my eyes stream and I could not see. When I got back to the kitchen my chest was hurting and raw, and I saw I could not be in that house any more, so I told Maggie I was sick. She looked at my face and said nothing when I went back to the cottage that we share. I climbed into the box bed and pulled the curtain across the front and went to sleep and hoped I would never have to wake up again.

The next day, I decided that I would go away to the other side of the island. I had heard my cousin was now there. She had been cleared off the old island with us and gone to Uist, but now she had been cleared off that land also and sent on to the rocky coves over at Finsbay. I thought, I shall go and see her: if His Reverend Lordship can take a holiday, then so can I.

So he sat at his desk and said, 'Of course you must see your only family. Take two weeks,' he told me grandly. 'I am sure I can manage with Maggie well enough for the time being.'

I did not tell him I was thinking that I would never come back, and as he talked, I thought how I would soon be hearing of his engagement to that little witch. Yet as I looked upon the evenness of his brow, his graceful straight nose and his kind, beautiful eyes, my heart would not stop loving that face.

The thing that broke my heart was that the Reverend was still so young, and although he was the Reverend, he wasn't so very much older than me, with the face and the blush and the smooth cheek of a boy. And it was this that made my heart ache for him the most, for I knew that no other could love him as well or as earnestly, or care for him as I did.

I did not trust that Miss, but I saw that there was nothing I could say to warn him, since my voice would sound like nothing more than the scratching of a mouse or the flapping of washing in the wind. I did not count in the ways of the gentry. Everything was laid out for the taking for the likes of the Marstones, and it was she who could speak the language that counts in the ears of the Reverend, the hard English of the gentry.

I had a fierce longing then to be with my own people, to sit in a black house, where all are equal friends in a circle on the low stools, the hearth in the middle of a hard earth floor; where you can tap a foot to the beat of a song and where the supper may be only a wooden trencher of boiled potatoes, but each man is known and valued and has weight in this world.

At first light, I put on my heavy woollen skirts and my shawl around my old, rough blouse. I folded up my blue dress and my green dress that the Reverend had gotten the cloth for and left them on my bed. I put the tea and the sugar and the red jam that the Reverend did give me for my cousin Annie in a bag, and fastened it to my back like a creel. I set off for the pass to the other side of the island.

Setting out along the coast track, I was glad to get a lift on Callum the post's letter cart all the way to the bottom of the pass. He told me how things were bad where I was headed, due to the crowding, since more people had arrived after being cleared from Sollas, and so I might not be as welcome as I hoped.

The way through to the bays is along the coffin road. I was soon at the top of the climb, where the long track begins. The rocks of the bays are too hard to bury a body, so the people must carry their dead home to the soft machair of the west along this track. I stopped to get my breath and look back on the empty bay of Losgaintir all spread out under the pink of the early morning sun, the ribbons of the water streaming their bright turquoise over the fair sand. I was leaving the good lands and the great green pastures that were all the factor's now for his big sheep, and heading back to where those that had been cleared from their homes was now perched on the rocks of the Minch side, growing their bucketfuls of potatoes in the patches of soil gained from the runs of sour bogs between the rocks.

By noonday, I had crossed the island and walked the miles along the sea track. When I headed down the hill into Finsbay village, I saw for myself what a bad situation the people had come to now.

CHAPTER 23

Ruth

It was officially summer, but out of nowhere, a storm blew in off the Atlantic and the temperature dropped. We woke to see the hills in the distance white, every crevice delineated by blue shadows. The sheep had thin blankets of snow on their backs, melting away into the bedraggled wool as the sun warmed them. Huge clouds were speeding away: the culprits leaving the scene.

Snow is rare in the islands, and coming so unseasonably late, it would disappear quickly. Michael and I scrambled into our clothes like a couple of kids.

Outside, the air was still cold, the details of the houses in the distance sharp. We walked along the sand. The water of the sea was as brilliant as molten gemstones – turquoise, cobalt and purple.

In the distance, a curtain of filmy white was moving in off the Atlantic, huge veils of streaming snowflakes sweeping towards us. Within minutes we were surrounded by crystals that melted on our eyelashes, passed over us and away. We watched them trailing across the sand, gliding out to Toe Head, a veiled mirage leaving us.

'Beautiful,' we kept saying.

We were holding on to each other, crowding together for warmth. Michael said, 'Emily.'

We were having trouble settling on a girl's name. Somehow, I could never picture a girl. A little knot of anxiety each time.

'Emily.' I nodded. 'Could be. If it's a girl, then she should be Michaela, after you.'

'I knew a Michaela once. Not Michaela.'

'That bad?'

'That bad.'

We walked on for a few steps.

'Wonder what I'd have been called, if she'd named me after him, my father.'

'I can't believe she didn't tell you. Your mum never told you his name?'

'Well, not that I remember.'

'Perhaps you'll find out one day. Maybe Christine will find something?'

'I'm not that bothered.' I looked back at the house. 'Do you think she had a name, the child we found in there?'

He hugged my head against his chin. 'Yes. I think someone loved her.'

I reached up and kissed the side of his face. Drips fell from his hair as it curled down in dark fronds like the seaweed on the rocks.

The kitchen was warm, delicious with the aroma of brewing coffee and Jamie's freshly baked bread rolls. The clean, white walls and the new white dresser had transformed the room.

'Has somebody called by already?' There were three cups on the table, a plate of digestives.

'It was Christine,' said Jamie. 'She came by to talk to you, but she couldn't stay. Says she's still looking into your family tree and she might have a lead. She wants you to phone her, soon as you can.'

'Sure,' I said.

But I had no intention of calling Christine, not just to be disappointed all over again. And the incident on the boat, coming as it did so soon after thinking about Mum and all that sort of thing, had convinced me that dragging the past out into the open did nothing but raise up things that should stay in their own time, giving them a fresh energy to racket around and cause damage all over again.

I placed my hand on the dense half globe of my stomach. I was startled by an immediate responding movement, the hard tip of a tiny elbow, perhaps, or a heel, sliding smoothly under my hand.

We had enough real problems to concentrate on; so much to do still on the house before this little one arrived.

Michael took his coffee upstairs to start painting the small room next to ours. He had cut out a stencil of ducks and geese from thick card, to stipple a border round the walls. His mother had sent us an old rocking chair, with low arms that wouldn't bang against a baby's head when you were holding it. She said it was a nursing chair.

I went to follow him upstairs, to finish painting the chair. Taking the newel post in my hand, out of nowhere, I felt a sudden and unpleasant twinge of apprehension. I stopped, looked around the empty space, but then shook my head – ridiculous. I carried on up.

As I applied the final coat to the nursing chair, my thoughts turned to Ferguson again, as they did with increasing frequency. I wondered if the librarian in Stornoway might have finally come up with something. It had been a while since I'd asked her if she could look for anything that might help pin down the identity of the baby. She'd warned me that it would take some time, since they were halfway through putting the archives onto microfiche. If she found anything, she was going to send it down with the mobile library. The van was due to come by in the next few days. Maybe this time they'd have some news, and hopefully, something substantial

The few scraps of information we had seemed to have done nothing but let indistinct shapes loose in the house, free to whisper their secrets round corners and behind doors; half-heard murmurs that left me more confused and frustrated than ever.

I'd also asked her if she had any books on the Selkie myth. That odd little fable that linked me to Mum and took me back to when she would sit on the side of the bed and begin the story that changed a little with every telling.

CHAPTER 24

Alexander

Early in the morning, Maggie brought one of the MacAllister boys through to the study with a message from his mother. He had the red, wind-chafed cheeks of a child that spends the summer out of doors, and a wide pair of shorts thriftily cropped down from a man's trousers. He stood on the Turkey rug shedding sand from his bare feet.

'Please, sir, we was picking up the seaware to burn, and there's a beast down there they says you will want to see.'

'Thank you, Robert. I will be with you directly. Why don't you run and ask Maggie if she has something for you in the kitchen?'

I hurriedly packed my notebooks along with several cases for specimens and went outside to where the child was waiting, a fold of Maggie's bread and bacon in his hand.

My young companion set off with alacrity on a zigzag route across the dunes. I followed, trying to keep him in my sights as he disappeared and reappeared among the undulating slopes of grass. I saw him skirting the very place where I had so recently caught Katriona. The memories of all that had transpired between us that day made my stomach lurch with regret.

As the boy reached the final rise of sand, I finally re-joined him. He was pointing to the far end of the beach where a stream flowed down from the mountain, its waters stained a reddish purple, changing to viridian as fresh water joined with salt. Beyond the stream, a group of figures were gathered around a prostrate creature that I estimated to be the size of a large dolphin or a small whale.

The boy plunged swiftly down the steep slope and I did likewise, though with more caution.

On arriving at the beast's side I consulted my reference volume. Noting the animal's long beak, the white skin, the sharp and almost wolfish jaw line, I was able to confirm that the creature was indeed from the cetacean family, but of a rare genus: *Lagenorhynchus albirostris*, a breed of Arctic dolphin seldom seen this far south and noted for its ability to conserve its breath below the freezing surfaces of the Arctic Ocean for several days.

Among the party gathering kelp was the venerable Mr MacAllister. A sailor for over fifty years, he was now of an age too great to endure the rigours of life at sea, and was lately returned to live with his granddaughter on the glebe farm. I found him stood very close to my elbow, and most interested in the facts and diagrams contained within my book. It soon became clear to me that any information that might be missing from that volume, old Mr MacAllister would be happy and willing to supply. Leaning on his stick, he began a lecture drawn from his own wisdom and travels. He spoke a fair English, but with the slow, almost Nordic intonation of the long Gaelic vowels, whistling over the sibilants. He shifted his position on the sand when I moved so that he might stand closer to me again.

'So have you ever seen such a beast before, Your Reverend? Have they got it there in your book?'

'Indeed they have, but it is so rare that only two specimens have been discovered, both along the coasts of Norway, and never before this far south of its Arctic home.'

'Aye, well you see, Reverend, there's always been a good sea road between here and the coasts of Norway. It's the currents and the winds; they bring down all manner of things from up where it's too cold for Christian men and beasts. We think the Norway peoples as all churchgoing, but there's many things go on up there past all Christian understanding – little savage men, who never heard of the Bible and who eat raw meat for breakfast. I was anchored at Bergen one time, and the Eskimo witches came on board to sell us winds, and forgive me, Reverend, but I bought one. When my ship was becalmed off the shores of Canada, I did remember that string in my top pocket and true as I am standing here, when I loosened the knot, a wind sprang straight up off the sea from nowhere. True as I am standing here.'

The truth was, I rather wished that the old seaman might stand elsewhere, since I was trying to pace out the length of the dolphin, and found the old fellow to be impeding my passage.

Then, without warning, MacAllister raised his stick and began to chant, 'Huishival, Cleisheval, Bleaval, Chaipaval,' pointing in turn to each of the tallest mountains around us. '*Val*, you see! Every one of them! The Viking's word for mountain! 'Twas the Vikings named these peaks when they used them to navigate down the sea road. Oh aye, a lot of people from hereabouts have a Viking ancestor or two. Take this nose now, Reverend…' He turned in profile so that I might gain a sideways view of the noble prominence. 'A Viking nose.'

I congratulated him on the appendage, but I had to excuse myself from further conversation. The incoming tide was now rapidly approaching and I had precious little opportunity left to record the dolphin in the detail I required. I was sure the specimen would be of interest to Carfax for his collection at the museum, so I resolved upon a plan whereby I would ask the crofters to dig a long, sandy pit at the top of the headland while I arranged to have the beast dragged up there and buried. The bones would then be cleaned by nature's work and leave a skeletal specimen ready for exhumation and removal to Edinburgh.

Ropes and a horse were duly fetched from the glebe farm, and we followed in the beast's sandy wake as it made its slow way up the beach, old MacAllister hobbling alongside me and still garrulous concerning his travels as a young man.

'Oh aye,' he continued, 'there's a lot more stranger things in God's Creation than we give credit for. These, now, have seen many a strange thing,' and he indicated his own prominent orbs. 'They've seen flying fishes off the shores of Venezuela; and great clouds of light down in the night seas of Patagonia; and off the shores of Orkney, a Finnman who sank his little boat in a flash, swam beneath the sea and then came up again where least expected. The Finnmen get their powers from those Norway witches, you see.'

With so much demanding my attention, I found it difficult to properly follow his tale, but I asked him, 'I hear that there have been sightings of mermaids or seal men along these coasts. Have you ever seen such a thing, Mr MacAllister?'

'Not with these eyes, Your Reverend, not with these eyes, but I wouldn't be surprised if I were to.' He gave a nod to the Arctic dolphin now leaving a sandy furrow behind it. 'We think we know everything,' he said. 'We think we know.' He tapped the side of his nose.

After supervising the dolphin's burial, I returned to the manse, this time taking the longer route round the machair fields. I went straight to my desk to jot down my notes, paying particular attention to those anatomical features of the mammal that might throw light upon the physiological adaptations of my sea people. Then I added a brief note on the old sailor's stories, for my small collection of folklore.

But as I closed my notebook, I was left with an inexplicable feeling of disappointment, and it took me some moments' reflection to locate the source of this low mood; it occurred to me that without Moira's bright intelligence there to share in it, my discovery seemed unfinished and uncelebrated.

I stayed up late, searching out references to old MacAllister's Finnmen, puzzled by his claim that their boats were able to pass beneath the waters for some distance. I did not see how this could occur without the vessel sinking, and felt that there might be something to be gained by understanding this account of a boat with the properties of a seal. I found no further articles to enlighten me on this point, but did establish that the Finnmen of his story were most probably members of an ancient aboriginal tribe living to the north of Norway and Finland.

I read until the small hours, hoping to cheat sleep into its blessed arrival, since the incidents of the previous few days had left me troubled and wakeful. Miss Marstone had failed to attend church on the Sunday following our visit to the fairy house. My cheeks had burned with a fiery heat that morning as I gave a sermon admonishing my little congregation to greater striving, all the while only too keenly aware that it was I, the minister charged with her soul's welfare, who had driven Miss Marstone from her place of worship.

I had tried to resolve upon a satisfactory course of action, but either to call at the castle uninvited or to write a letter of apology that might fall into the wrong hands seemed unconscionable.

It was a relief to let my thoughts wander among my sea people, to almost hear their distant voices calling to me as they sat rocking upon the deeps – the half-glimpsed flick of a muscular tail as I turned my head and then nothing more than a ripple on the empty sea.

CHAPTER 25

Ruth

I was sewing curtains in the kitchen one morning, the rickety table shaking with the motion of the machine, when a horn sounded. Looking out, I saw the mobile library parked at the bottom of the track. The librarian waved from the window.

'It did take me a while to find the sort of things you asked for, Ruth, but I think you're going to be very interested in these. Now, this one on the top is old, so you will have to take great care of it. It's a report on the islands by Vicar Brand for the Church Missionary Society in 1709. I've put a marker in where he records people's tales of seeing Selkies and mermaids. Then all of these books here are collections of folk stories – lots of stories of sea people in those.'

I took the stack of books from her. 'You've gone to such a lot of trouble. Thank you so much. I'll bring them back in four weeks,' I said, turning to go.

'But wait, I haven't given you the photocopy. I was so excited for you when I came across this.'

I shuffled the books under one arm as she handed me a photostat. Most of the page was taken up with a long list of names written out in Victorian copperplate. Several of the names were grouped in families, many with large numbers of children.

'It's Lord Marstone's eviction order for the people of Finsbay, for all the men, women and children in the village.'

'What a horrible man.' I glanced down at two signatures at the bottom. One was for a Mr Stewart, bailiff and tacksman for Marstone.

But it was the second signature that stopped me dead in my tracks. 'What's this?'

She nodded. 'It's the only information on your Reverend Ferguson that I turned up. Disappointing really, isn't it, that he should sign the order for eviction? You'd think he'd have had more heart.'

I stared down at the scratchy and jagged signature – writing done by the hand of Alexander Ferguson. I couldn't believe it.

'I always thought that if I met Alexander, I'd rather like him. But now I'm beginning to wonder.'

I carried the books into the sea room, where I was collecting anything to do with Ferguson's time in a box file. I knelt down on the rug in front of the fireplace and opened the file. I leafed through the photostats of the mermaid baby that Professor Carter had sent. Under them was 'The Story of Ishbel and the Seal Man', along with several other diary-type extracts that I'd copied from Alexander's notebook, as well as a copy of the letter to *The Times* and a tracing of his clumsy mermaid skeletons.

I'd also got hold of a rather dark photocopy of the picture of Alexander and his servants from the museum. Now I added in the photocopy of the eviction order.

I felt frustrated that I still couldn't get a clear picture of just what had happened during Ferguson's years in our house; I still had no real idea as to why the little mermaid baby had been buried beneath the floorboards. I took down the writing set and the brass lion paperweight from the mantelpiece and then I knelt back and surveyed my collection.

Michael came in. He was wiping his hands on a cloth, bringing the smell of turps. He shoved the cloth in his pocket and knelt down by me.

'Quite a collection now. What's the verdict?'

I gave him the copy of the eviction order to read.

'Ferguson signed this?'

'I know. Makes you wonder what he was like.'

Michael left a thumbprint on the paper when I took it from his hands, a trace of the linseed smell of cleaned paintbrushes.

'Well, it's certainly a lot more than I've got for my own history.' I'd left a slim envelope on the desk with its six photographs inside. I kept it in the same drawer as my Ferguson notes.

'When we first got here, I had a mad hope that someone was going to come up to me in the street one day and say, "Aren't you Ellie's daughter? We've been looking for you. Come on home." Silly really, but there you are.'

'You are home, Ruth.'

He leaned over and kissed the top of my head like a blessing.

It had been twenty days since I'd lost it with Michael on the boat. I thought, Come on, I can do this; I just need to keep vigilant, make sure I don't get into a flap like that again; just stay sensible and reasonable; think about things before I react.

Twenty days of watching how I behaved behind me, a whole lifetime of vigilance in front, but I was determined not to slip up again, determined – and I was so, so tired.

We'd spent weeks wearing paint-encrusted shirts and grubby jeans, so it was fun to make a real effort for the ceilidh in An t'Obbe. Leaf and I dug out long dresses and pooled make-up.

We got there a bit late, but even so, the ceilidh didn't seem to have started. No men visible, just girls and women. As we sat down by a poster of crofting regulations and a notice for a talk by the Temperance Society, it struck me how nearly all the girls chatting around the empty expanse of floorboards had that same straight black hair and white skin as Mum – and me.

For a moment, I had a mad impulse to go round the room and ask if any of the older women there might have lost a daughter, a girl who left for London one day, never returned, had a daughter of her own.

Michael and Jamie went to get drinks. Most of the men were still out in the lobby, gathered in a siege around the temporary bar; a couple had ventured halfway through the door. They wore white shirts, hair plastered flat and shiny – CalMac men straight from the ferry.

A man and a woman I hadn't seen before came into the hall. He looked very much like a teacher, in rust-coloured cords and a green jumper. She was petite, with long, dark hair and sloping cheekbones; her hands were thrust into the back pockets of her jeans in that confident way some women display as they near forty. She stood looking around, quizzical and interested.

'That's the Montgomerys. She's the new doctor at the surgery,' I heard the lady on the next table tell her neighbour in English. 'Not a real doctor though.'

'Oh? What sort of doctor is she then?'

'For people with problems up here.' She tapped her forehead.

'Well, she'll have her work cut out in these parts then.' The woman nodded over at old Harry, a grey-haired man in a grimy denim jacket who was clutching a carrier bag of beer cans and cheerfully dancing alone in the middle of the floor to the taped music.

'Oh, but it's a shame. My niece had the depression. It was bad. She had to have tablets for it.'

'Yes, it's a shame when people get like that. Of course, we never called it depression. Hadn't been invented.'

'We had hard work. That was our cure. And I hear that she's an American, the new lady doctor.'

'Fancy that. From America.' They shook their heads.

I saw Mrs MacKay come out of the kitchen with a tea towel on her shoulder. She chatted with the Montgomerys for a while and then found them some chairs at one of the tables.

A tall man in a red waistcoat and jeans was walking across the floor towards us, tawny hair brushed and shining. For a moment, I didn't recognise him, but it was Michael, all spruced up for the evening. I wanted to tell him how I'd just fallen in love with him all over again, but someone on the stage was running their fingers down the buttons of an accordion. Michael put down the drinks. He held out his hand, bowed, and we joined the ladies slowly waltzing in pairs around the hall.

'I'd forgotten that dress.'

It was a long muslin thing that I hadn't worn for ages, but it was gathered above the waist and so still fitted in spite of the bump.

'I got the material caught in a bicycle wheel. I don't think the mend shows.'

'You look just beautiful.'

It felt tender and sweet dancing together again, like remembering a lost art. The dances began to get faster and more complicated. As we sat down for a break, I saw Christine MacAulay heading over towards us.

She sat down at our table and pulled her chair closer to mine.

'Did you not get my message from Jamie the other day? Why don't you drop by the house and see me tomorrow now? There's something I want to run by you.'

I nodded. 'I'll try.'

Privately, I resolved to forget her invitation, not wanting to go through yet more unsettling speculation.

I was relieved when a ceilidh group from Skye crowded onto the stage. A boy began a thin, nostalgic tune on a tin whistle, and a guitar and violin joined with the melody. A drummer ramped up the beat, then a man in a kilt swung a fan of pipes on his hip and suddenly added a piercing wail to the mix.

As if on cue, the hall erupted, the dancing fast and manic. I watched a grey-haired fisherman, his eyes shut, leaping up and down like a salmon in the middle of a reel of dancers. And those pairs of lovely island girls, with their white arms and pretty faces, were getting wilder and cheekier at pulling the boys onto the floor, sometimes capturing Michael. I didn't mind. Soon we would go home together. I would light candles along the windowsills in our room, leave the window open to the stars.

We left the hall towards one in the morning. The moon was so bright, it seemed plugged into its own source of electricity. Jamie threw the van into gear and we set out for Scarista, the tarmac in front of us nothing but a sinking ribbon of dark through sheened air. It was chilly now and I leaned into Michael's warmth.

Michael was in bed and asleep in minutes. I went down to make a drink – couldn't resist looking through the work schedules again. We needed a new delivery of lining paper; the order for curtain material in the guest bedrooms needed decisions. Since everything had to be shipped over from the mainland, it was important to get the orders right if there weren't to be delays. As I sat working, I became aware that the baby had gone very quiet, no little thumps or judders; it was something that happened if I got too tired – less oxygen available for the baby. I needed to go to bed.

As I pinned the list back up, I wondered for a moment what it was that Christine MacAulay had wanted to tell me. I snapped out the kitchen light.

Crossing the hall in the darkness, I felt a knot of apprehension, even though I knew now that what had bothered me so much before had been some kind of internal panic and not some otherworldly manifestation. I paused at the foot of the stairs; nothing in the shadowy air but a dull sadness.

A rustle. Something made me look round, eyes travelling quickly over the empty space. And suddenly the horrible fear was flooding in again, my heart thudding faster, air constricted, my palms sticky and hot.

It was starting again.

Just the amygdala overreacting, I told myself. Something had triggered it – the dark, my imagination. I simply needed to stay still, wait for the nerve pathways to stop firing, wait till I calmed down.

But the back of my neck was prickling, my lungs were tight. There was an awful pressure in the air, a will that was refusing to let me pass in the shadowy darkness.

She was there. I could feel her malevolence, how she wanted to bring me overwhelming unhappiness, to drown me in her grief.

'Tell me who you are,' I said to the dark.

Almost like a reply, I had an odd feeling, like a half-forgotten word, there on my tongue, waiting to be spoken.

Surely there'd been another time when I'd stood in a hallway like this, waiting and alone, with my hand on the cold paint of the newel post....

I gasped, put my hand to my mouth. I saw her; I saw that solitary child, waiting, always waiting, in the hallway of a stranger's house.

It always started with a stranger's hallway, another foster home, the blank walls opening onto unknown rooms. The uncomfortable smells of someone else's home. She was small and distressed and she was seared by grief, every nerve end raw and vulnerable.

Not everyone was kind in those places. Things I couldn't bear to recall. The last and the worst placement was the home. The dawning realisation that you didn't matter, that no one was going to care if you slipped off the world.

I learned to keep away from the so-called house father, Terry, and the mates he'd ask round to his flat.

The day I finally walked out of the children's home, I walked away from that small, lonely figure. I left her and all her swirling sadness behind, left her standing alone in that last, cavernous hall.

That's what I'd believed; but now I saw how she'd waited for me, standing her ground close by. All that time, she'd waited for me to turn and see her. And ever since the baby had started to grow inside me, the wall I'd so carefully constructed between me and her had started to fade. Finally, it had allowed her to put her hands out and pull me back to her, her every moment crowding back in, live with fear and distress.

I reached out and pressed my hand hard against the cold paintwork, needing to make sure I was there in the present and not scattered through time. My heart was still racing horribly fast as unbearable feelings swarmed in. I was so afraid of her, and so ashamed for her, that refugee child with her stink of poverty, of stale fat and rancid onion from her poor refugee meals; the sort of child that nobody wants around.

All those years, I'd worked so hard not to see her, that girl from the home; to forget her, deformed somehow by what she'd seen and done and been.

And yet she was just a child. Not even grown. All that had happened to a child.

Something cracked in my chest and pity began to seep out. She hadn't done anything wrong. And she was so, so lonely.

I stood very still. For the first time, I let her come to me. And she brought with her all her heavy load of fear and grief. I sank slowly down on the step, my bones broken, the pain and the sorrow of being so unwanted rushing in on a dark tide.

You left me.

And I wanted it to stop. I was sobbing now. I banged my head back against the wall, kept on doing it. One pain to drive out another. As I fought for air, I saw how Mum could do what she did, how she could slip away beneath the water; all I wanted was that peaceful place, the peacefulness of a body rolling in oblivion.

I made myself stand up, sliding my back up against the wall, staggering upright. I was holding onto my swelling stomach, clinging on.

I waited till she faded, waited till I could breathe again, then I went through to the cupboard where we kept the bottle of Laphroaig, poured a glass, and let the hot liquid burn my throat.

CHAPTER 26

Alexander

I slept that night with my head on my books and awoke in the morning to the sound of Maggie Kintail banging on the study door and calling out in urgent Gaelic that His Lordship's factor was here to see me. I brushed down my clothes and thought to straighten my books and papers, strewn as they were across the floor, but the factor gave himself entry into my study directly. I greeted him, very conscious of my personal disarray, and from thereon the day went from bad to worse.

The factor for Lord Marstone was on his way to the extensive tracts of farmland that he had bought for himself around Borve. I did not find Mr Stewart good company at the best of times, so I was dismayed to see him move about the room, taking his time, examining the bookshelves and my pictures with bemused attention, as if he must see if there might be something of value – something he might wish to acquire. Satisfied that this was not the case, he settled himself comfortably in my chair as a man who will leave only when he has completed his business to his liking.

Mr Stewart possessed the flat vowels formed in the lower jaw and the progressive ideas about farming that come from the vast estates along the east coast of Aberdeenshire, where a landlord may own a thousand acres put to wheat or beef cattle. It was open knowledge that Mr Stewart had done very well for himself as His Lordship's factor, building a house that ranked second only to the castle. Solid in person, with the broad shoulders of a man of considerable physical strength, he was some twenty years older than I, and apt to labour the point.

'So the farm's doing well here, Alexander?' he said, leaning over to take a slurp from his tea, which he held from the top in a fist of fingers, as if the handle were too fragile for his particular needs.

'I believe so. I must confess that I leave the running of it to the MacAllisters, who have far more experience in these things, and who will no doubt continue to run things just as smoothly for the next incumbent.'

'That's probably a wise attitude,' he said, draining his tea and raking through the plate of baking for something he liked. He broke a scone and threw half in his mouth. 'But this is a lot of land to care for. His Lordship's left a generous piece for the clergy. Are ye aware, Alexander, that the church land runs from here right to the other side of the island?'

'I have seen the deeds, but not given it much thought.'

'Oh aye, from here all the way to the village of Finsbay on the other side. You could say that it's you who owns Finsbay.'

I gave a laugh. 'Well, I hardly think of it like that.'

'Being a landlord, it comes with benefits and it comes with duties, Alexander. Have ye heard that there's a whole influx of squatters there right now who've been cleared from Uist, turning the place to squalor and ruining the land? His Lordship's no pleased, Alexander.'

I felt my face grow hot.

'I have been considering how best I might help them and I see now, it is truly remiss of me not to have begun sooner. As it is my responsibility, then I can assure His Lordship that, with his permission, I have some schemes that might improve their lot. I shall set off tomorrow and—'

'I haven't finished relating to you the wishes of His Lordship. Just hold on there now. There's no place for the squatters over there in Finsbay, and it's your duty, Alexander, to tell them they canna' stay. The boat will come for them on Friday, and my secretary will come along with us to keep accounts of how each man may pay for his passage.'

'But where will the people go?'

'They'll leave for Stornoway for a ship that goes to Canada. I hear it's a very nice place, Canada. Plenty of land over there. They are fortunate that we have arranged this for them. The men will come by in the morning and we will go with you to Finsbay.'

He handed me a letter.

'As soon as we arrive, you will call the villagers out and read it to them. Then my men can set to work.'

I heard him leaving the house as I unfolded the paper and began to read it through. It was an order for eviction, pertaining to every person recently arrived in Finsbay, signed by Stewart.

I ran out. Stewart was climbing up into his dogcart, his broad back to me.

'I cannot read this to the people,' I called out.

He did not turn but seated himself and took the reins. The horse moved a step or two to the side, nervous.

'As the incumbent in Lord Marstone's gift, Reverend, it's your legal duty to do so – that's if you wish to remain the incumbent. You'll be adding your own signature there.' And he rattled away towards his farms at Borve.

After much praying, I resolved that I must speak with Marstone about the injustice being meted out upon this unfortunate refugee class. It was now late afternoon and would soon be dark, but I saddled up the horse and rode out to Avenbuidhe Castle, determined to convince His Lordship of a more humane course of action.

It was against my every inclination to make that journey, so anxious was I as to how Miss Marstone might construe the visit, but as my horse's hooves echoed around the shouldering hills that hemmed in the castle, I slid down from the beast resolved to accept whatever she should say to me. I pulled on the bell at the great oak door. Even though they must have been aware of my arrival, it was a long time before a man answered. From his dress I saw that he was far below the usual rank of servant who attended the door of such a house.

'Lord Marstone,' he told me, 'is no receiving visitors.'

'But this is a matter of great urgency. It is imperative that I speak with His Lordship immediately.'

'Well, that's as may be, but you canna' come in and he will not see you. The Miss is sick and we're to let no one over the threshold. The doctor's gone and put her in the quarantine. Half the staff have left already, and the other half is wanting to leave. I'm leaving here for the boats, soon as I can.'

'But will she recover?' I asked, stunned by this news of poor Katriona. 'What is the matter with the good lady?'

He shrugged his shoulders, went to close the door.

'But wait, at least you must let His Lordship know about this urgent matter. I will write a note.' I searched for a stub of pencil in my pocket, tore a page from my pocketbook and began to scribble. 'And please, please will you convey my sincere best wishes and my prayers to Miss Marstone for her well-being and full recovery to health. May I not come in and see her?'

The man drew back, shook his head.

'That you can't. And I can't take your message or your paper. He'll no want to know. There's no one but the Miss's own maid and the Glasgow doctor allowed up there to speak with him. And there's no one here that will dare to go up there and cross him.'

As I stood stupefied by this information, he suddenly closed the door. I remained motionless under the portico for some time, but there was nothing more for me to do but return by the way I had come.

As darkness fell, it was only the instincts of my horse picking its way over the stony track that prevented a laming. I hardly noticed where I was going, so perturbed was I in my thoughts, my mind returning to that quiet hollow in the sand dunes. I was now convinced that it was surely the turmoil of those moments that had caused her to fall prey to some illness. How had it happened, that I had let matters slide so disastrously into chaos?

My thoughts returned to that day.

So swiftly she had loosened her dress at the front, slid it from her shoulder, a marble bust of ideal form emerging from the folds of blue silk.

She took my hand, placed it on the cold whiteness of her skin and in the next moment we stood closely embracing in that sheltered place, no sound reaching our ears but her faint breath. Once or twice a soft, damp pattering of sandfalls from the great cliffs of sand dunes around us.

But gradually, effortfully, I began to return to my senses, and with a struggle against my very nature, I pushed her away, using more force than I intended, so that she staggered a little. She moved to approach me again, but I held her away at arm's length. Her face stared into mine, startled, confused.

I turned my own face away. 'You must cover yourself.'

'But we shall be married, Alexander. We can be married tomorrow. I shall come here and live with you.'

She moved towards me again.

'Katriona, you are young and impressionable and you cannot understand what you are saying or what you are doing. I am to blame, for letting this happen. I must resign from your father's parish, and then you can go about your life in peace. One day, you will be of age to marry, someone your father will approve of, when you can understand more of what love is.'

She gave me a look of such pinched bitterness and began to pull up her dress, but she was weeping so much that she stopped and abandoned herself, unmoving, half dressed. I had to help her with her buttons, smooth her hair with my fingers and try to attach it in its net. All the while she did nothing to resist, like a person turned to water, broken of all resolve.

'Don't go,' she said quietly, her eyes cast to the ground, tears falling. 'Let me at least know that you are still here. Promise me you won't resign. I won't ask you such questions again.'

She gave a long, tired sigh, wiped her face with her hands and began to walk towards the manse. I followed.

'Will you think very badly of me?' she said into the wind.

'Katriona, the fault was all mine. Never yours.'

But her head remained bowed, and it took us a long time to regain the house, so fatigued was she. As soon as we arrived, she stepped up into the trap and let the pony walk on, not turning her head or saying goodbye.

As my horse now made its way through the drizzle of rain precipitating from the darkness, my heart constricted with guilt to think of how she must have returned home, already in the first throes of her sickness, and fallen into her mortal fever the very next day.

Then it began to dawn on me, that surely this fever must already have been acting upon her person, must surely have been the cause of her strange and sudden behaviour; the incipient fever weighing down her fragile limbs as she let circumstances buffet her about, falling into my arms with the streams of sand, jolted by the stones in the path as she rode home in her little wooden carriage.

No other cause, I reasoned, no other cause could explain her sudden moods.

As soon as I was home, I went to my study and fetched the whisky from the cupboard. I stoked up the peats to get some warmth into the chill air and sat at my desk, trying and failing over and over again to formulate some plan for the affair in Finsbay the next day. And all the time I was never completely able to escape the din of my anxiety for Miss Marstone.

CHAPTER 27

Moira

My cousin had heard that I had died along with my parents and brothers and sisters, so my letter to her came as a great surprise. She had to ask the schoolmaster, Mr Carmichael, to read it out to her twice over.

When she saw me in her doorway, she fell upon me as if I were back from death itself, but though she sat me down and gave me a hot cup of water and was heartily glad of the gifts of tea and jam and a fresh whey cheese I had made, I could see that she was hard pressed to want that I should stay.

She and her husband had thrown together a small house made from rocks taken from the shore, but the only bit of earth left for the new squatters was boggy and raw land. The children's feet did sink into it, down at the end of their house where the cattle should be kept – not that Annie had herself a cow. They never had time to let the floor harden before they must live in there, and no one had the heart or the strength to get up a ceilidh to dance the floor hard and pack down the earth in the old way. The bairns were playing a jumping game to see how far they could sink down in the mud until Annie gave the boys a slap – something I had never seen her do before.

I told Annie of my life so far, of the days of the coughing disease that carried off my dear ones. She said she had heard of the place and that no one will touch the rocks of our walls now lest they catch the disease. I told her how I worked at the manse, but I did not tell her I was not going back, since she cried and said it were a great good fortune that I should eat so well each day, and I did then promise to send her more provisions with my pay. I helped her with preparing a pot of limpets taken from the rocks for our supper, a meal of salt and gristle that no man will choose to eat except when he be starving.

On the morrow, we must all get up early, for Norman Paul, the travelling evangelist, had come to preach on the hill behind the village. He gave a sermon full of great hellfire which was mostly directed to the oppressors of the people. And though he did term them the Egyptians who oppressed the Israelites to wander the desert, we all did know who he was referring to as we looked about the poor lands and the great rocks pushing through the rough moor like some beast waking up from their sleep. Indeed, this land my people have to live on, at first the eye thinks it is all rock and desolate of any life, till you begin to see rags of land, a little moss and rushes, some patches of crops no bigger than a blanket. And every last inch must be drained and fed with endless baskets of seaware brought up from the shore if it is to grow stubby rigs of potatoes.

The people who had been moved here a while back had accustomed themselves to the harshness, and by plucking a living from the sea, and by the women weaving all night, they might survive. But the fifty new people come from the cleared islands like mine own – who had been first cleared to Uist and Sollas and then cleared again to here – they had nothing but their chains to hang a pot over the fire, and their peat tongs and their bowls and their pots. How they were to get food to put in their pots with no boats and no line and no land was a cruel question. They had no choice but to take loans from His Lordship's factor to buy meal that came from his stores, so they were now entirely in His Lordship's hands, in debt to him for every last mouthful they supped – and with no means at all to pay.

I stayed with Annie through that week, helping to dig out some of the moor peat into banks to let the soil drain, going down to the foreshore where the bay is ringed with rocks covered in brown seaweed like heads covered in long hair; the great heads of old gods about to rise up from under the water, it felt to me, as I filled my creel, the water lap, lapping against the rocks, the oyster catchers piping their sad and lonely notes. Then we must climb the hill with baskets of weed to turn the soil less sour. It was a marvel to see how those that had long lived there had crofted a farmland from barrenness, and heartbreaking to see how small the plots.

But it was this improvement in the soil and grazings, so hard won out of necessity, that had got the factor's eye on the place to put more of his big sheep and disallow the incomers from staying. On the wall inside the schoolroom porch, the factor had put up a notice in English. Annie took me up to read it to her, to know if the people had understood it correctly. It was an advertisement for a ship leaving to Canada. All those who could not pay back their debts for the winter meal they had took from His Lordship were to be evicted, and must sail on the ship.

'If they make you go, Annie,' I told her, 'then I will come with you and we will make a life in Manitoba.'

That night, I dreamed again of the dogs barking, back in my home on our island. It was the dogs that first smelled the rot in the fields, and by morning we could all catch the bad smell in the air. My father walked up to the rigs, and the stench there was worse than the rotted seaware, having a smell like something burned and then left to wetly rot. He turned over one of the plants, and all the roots that should have had little white fists of potatoes came away in a black, stinking mush.

I woke up and realised I was in Annie's house, but I heard the dogs barking still, all around the bay. I wrapped my shawl round my shoulders and found Annie up too, alarmed by the din. We went to the door, and picking our way along the track in the white mist lying on the ground, we saw three mounted men silhouetted on a rise against the half-awake sky. They were moving down the track to our village, and behind them, on the hill brow, we saw men walking with rifles on their shoulders: the guard that Lord Marstone kept down at Rodel.

Carmichael was out too, in his nightshirt with his coat thrown over it, and he was running over to them. The people were coming out from their houses.

Out in the bay, I saw that there was a boat waiting, a dark shape floating on a white sea, and big enough it was to ship out the whole village to Stornoway where the ship to Canada was anchored. A pink stain was spreading into the water beyond, all the way towards the mainland, but it was no good looking over there for I knew that no one would be coming to help us, no one to see that His Lordship dealt fairly with us. I saw that my people, harassed from bad place to worse place had nowhere left to go now but choose to go upon the sea.

I walked fast up to the men on horses, so filled with anger that I felt sure I had the strength to stop every one of His Lordship's rotten soldiers. Carmichael was already trying to reason with the factor, and appealing with gestures to the man sat alongside him. I reached where they were gathered, and I had the shock of my life, for the man sat next to the factor and come to evict us was none other than my own Reverend Alexander.

The Reverend did look as if he were half kidnapped, and I saw plain he had been up all night, riding out with them and no doubt sneaking round the coast with the factor to collect the men at the garrison at the Rodel customs house before they set out here.

'Reverend, if you will,' the factor said. Alexander took out a paper and looked at it as if he did not comprehend what he saw there, but then he made a little speech about how he was obliged to do his sad duty, and I heard him read out the order of eviction for every last soul, every man and woman and child who was in debts of arrears to the Marstones.

I could not think, as my breast filled up with anger, how it had come to be that our people, who was born of this land and had lived in these islands for generations before time was remembered, were now gypsies to be chased away as worthless paupers.

There was a silence, and then an old *cailleach* screamed that the Reverend would die young, that his gravestone would never stand upright for the wickedness he had brought with him that day. I saw Alexander go very white and Carmichael looked away from him.

The factor set up a table in the village, and his men began to turn out the houses, making a list of the things he would keep to pay for the people's removal, and saying what they could take on the boat.

I saw Alexander wandering up and down among the scattered *cas-chroms* and pieces of broken looms, the upturned stools, and someone's precious bothy blanket trodden into the mud. He was thinking to speak to the people to give comfort, but no one would stay to speak with him. I hung back and would not go near him, though he walked towards me. I turned and I walked quickly away from him.

I was determined to get in the boat that was filling up with those good, strong men trembling and shaking with the shock of that day, their wives and children crying so that the wailing carried across the water and haunted the land all that long day. And not one man there fought back, since there was nothing more to be done.

The factor's men began to carry an old *cailleach* out from the poor bothy she had on the shore. The old woman was too sick to get up and leave her bed, but the soldiers were pulling the canvas sail that was her poor roof from off the walls. Then Alexander did go and remonstrate with the soldiers but was pushed away hard. I saw how he staggered and, falling, he hit his head upon a rock.

I was set to go with Annie. I was carrying her youngest bairn, and my heart was set hard against ever coming back to that place, but when I saw that no one was going to look to the Reverend as he lay there with his head against a rock and with the blood running into his eye, then I gave the bairn to his sister. Even as I ran to help him, I knew I was not going on that boat, because though I hated him now along with the Marstones for such cruelty, I could not leave him any more than I could leave myself and go.

I sat with his head in my lap while the boat filled and I held my shawl to his head until the bleeding began to stop, his face so sunk into sleep and unguarded. The crying and the loading of the boat went on around us for many hours, and even after the boat was gone from sight, the sound of the people wailing their grief could be heard across the water for a long time.

By the end of that terrible day he was stirring back to life, the bay quiet now, the boat with the people of Finsbay gone from that place.

The soldiers were still there, loading what they would take onto a cart, firing the roofs of the hovels so no one would come back, stopping to make a joke or light up their smokes, a boot on a broken table.

They got the Reverend up on his horse. He was awake now, but slumped and not yet right at all. When I told them I worked at the manse, the soldiers let me walk by his horse and watch that he did not slide off, and they must make coarse comments behind my back as I walked, which I heard clear enough, so I did turn and spit at them.

CHAPTER 28

Moira

The journey on the horse across the rough paths jolted his sick head so that his condition worsened. The Reverend had stopped speaking and his eyelids had fallen shut by the time we arrived back at the manse. I had to get two of the farm boys to help me fetch him down from off the horse's back, and still he could not move his feet to walk, even when they took one arm each over their shoulders. So they carried him up, and none too careful; I saw them bump his head against the newel post.

They did take off his clothes for me and get him in his nightshirt, and then they left. It was just me and the silent Reverend in that big house then. His breath was so quiet and shallow that I had to keep stooping over to see he was still alive.

I had not thought to pray very much before, but I prayed hard those days. He lay fallen into a sleep so sound that the doctor began to say how the Reverend might never open his eyes.

At least there was one blessing. She did not come back to the house. Not once, as he lay sick and near to death.

Then on the fifteenth morning, he opened his eyes, and from then on each day brought a small improvement. He was able to sit up, come down to his study, and in time, walk outside and look at the sea and the weather.

One month after the Sollas people and my cousin Annie were cleared from Finsbay, he was saying how he must start to give the sermon on Sunday, anxious to relieve the cleric from Tarbert who travelled down to do his duties.

The doctor told him this was too soon. He examined the Reverend's skull and told him the fracture was healing, but that he was in need of a great deal of rest and sleep if he was not to suffer in some permanent way. The doctor pulled me aside after, to say that I must make sure the Reverend did not read more than two hours a day, and that he slept of a night for at least nine hours.

This near scared me to death, since I knew that what the Reverend did was read for nine hours, and sleep scarcely two. When I came in of a morning to do his study, I would see yet more books open, the notes growing in piles on his desk. I could fair work out how he had spent the night and follow his feverish thinking, just by looking at the passages he had read.

And each morning he told me outrageous fibs about how refreshed he felt after staying tucked up in bed all night – forgetting that I had eyes in my head to see how his own eyes hung like faint lamps in the cloud of darkness round them. I saw the tight lips he pressed together from his headaches that left him feeling sick to the stomach so that he pushed away his plate. And I was afeared to see how he had become but skin over a skeleton, and every precious ounce of him too dear to lose.

Now his fevered studies were not just for his mermaids and seal men, but he must also find out all he can about the Finnmen, a savage kind of body that lives in the northern snows. So I must look at pictures of the Finnman's tents all made from skins, and their sledges and their spears and the Finnpeople's strange clothes sewn from animal furs.

'Sit down, Moira,' he says one morning. I see his tea has gone cold on his desk, his hair standing up on end from where he has passed a hand through it, and I would like to smooth it back down. I first fetch hot tea before I will agree to sit with him a moment.

He reads me the story of the Selkie again, but this time it is a story from Orkney Islands, far in the north, and this time it is the story of a seal that takes off his seal skin with the express purpose of becoming a Finnman.

'So, what do you think of that?' he asks me. 'The seal becomes a Finnman.'

'That's what they say up in the Orkney Isles, sir. We only have seals and mermaids down here and are not so mixed up in our stories.'

'I agree that it is all very confusing. I am at a loss myself to understand why we have these three variations on a similar story of a seaman: the mermaid, the Selkie and the Finnman.'

'But where do the Finnmen come from, sir? Do they come from Finland?'

'Well, yes and no. The Finnmen are nomads who inhabit the polar regions of Europe – a tribe who wrap themselves in animal skins like Eskimos or Red Indians, but who, to my knowledge, have no attributes of fish or seal. So I cannot, at the moment, understand why these Orkney tales include Finnmen. But it is very interesting, because it seems to me, Moira, that what is called a mermaid in Benbecula, and a Selkie or seal man in Lewis, and a Finnman in Orkney could all be ways to attempt to describe the same thing: a creature, with human attributes, yes, but also with the bodily adaptations of a seal or fish. You see, I'm sure that the Finnman reported in the stories cannot be a mere man, since he is able to dive below the sea for some time and exist in intolerable marine conditions. So don't you see, Moira, if I can find what these old stories mean by terming the creature a Finnman, then I might finally have my link in the transmutation of species; perhaps a man with gills, or perhaps where others have legs, a man with some fin-like adaptation?'

'He sounds like something you would dream up in a night of bad sleep.'

His face fell. 'Ah, bad sleep is all I have now.'

Then I say my piece. 'Sir, what if the seal stories are truly just stories? Would it not be for the best to give your brain some rest from all its striving?'

He sighed and sat quiet; seemingly trying out how it might feel to sit in peaceful slumber in his silk armchair by the fire, untroubled by the seal man calling out to him day and night.

'Moira, I know you are concerned for me, having as you do such a good heart, and I see the good sense in what you are saying, but have you considered this? If my seal man is real, if he is here, living and breathing and walking on the earth, then how foolish to fail to do everything in one's power to understand and perhaps even see such a marvellous being.'

I decided that I should make up my old sleeping place on the settle in the kitchen, since the doctor had told me Alexander's head was so weak in its bones and I should not be surprised were he to fall down in a fit of a sudden. I was worried this might happen as he paced around at night.

I found that though I slept passably well on the bench near the smoored fire, I never did sleep entirely fast, but kept an ear tuned to the sounds of the house. So I knew when he was turning over and over in his sheets, and I knew when he was padding around the house in bare feet, letting the cold flagstones draw all the heat from his body till his feet were numb and icy. I knew when he was in his study in the small hours, searching his bookshelves by the candlelight that guttered around the walls. I could tell when he was seated quiet in his armchair, the blanket wrapped round his legs, reading again about the sea people.

It must have been that I did sleep deeply one night, for just as the light began to spread across the window, I was startled awake by his voice close to me in the kitchen.

'Moira! What are you doing here?'

'I've been here each night since you got back, Reverend. The doctor said it was for the best that I listen out.'

'Really, there is no need. You must regain your own bed.'

'You are up mighty early, sir. What time is it?'

'I am not sure. Oh, yes, it is just after four o'clock.'

'Are you going for a walk, sir?'

'I am going to call on old Mr MacAllister, since I need to urgently question him about the boats of the Finnmen.'

I screwed up my eyes against the bright light, sharp and clear in the window, and saw how he had a blanket wrapped round his nightshirt, a pair of breeches pulled up with the nightshirt tucked in.

'I don't think he will thank you, sir, for such an early visit. Why don't you rest a while till they may be up and dressed? I will heat you up some milk while you wait for a more Christian hour for calling on folk.'

He was forced to agree to the sense in this, and I busied myself warming a cup of milk. While he waited on the settle, he outlined his newest discoveries as to the indisputable similarities between the legends of his mermaid and the Selkie and the Finnmen.

So listen I must, but I was heartily sick of the sea lady and the Finnman and wished them both away at the bottom of the sea so that they might leave my Alexander alone; leave his poor head with a moment's peace to get better.

At least, I said to myself, they have driven all thoughts of her away. At least she has become too grand to bother us any more, and is keeping herself away in her castle where she may no more harm us.

The milk all drunk, I think he was overcome then with tiredness, his stomach recalling what it was to be warm and full. He did not get up off the bench to go, but he leaned back and pulled the blanket round his shoulders.

'Did you hear from your cousin, Moira?'

'No, sir, and I don't expect to until she gets there.'

'If I could have done anything… If I had the power…'

I did not know how to rightly reply, not without the bitterness showing in my speaking.

'I dream of Finsbay. I keep hearing that old woman's voice. Her words go through my head again and again. In my dreams, I see that headstone in the graveyard with my name on it, and I see how it will never stand upright now.'

'I'll thank you, sir, to talk no such nonsense. She's a simple-minded and spiteful old woman, Norma Macleod.'

'Even when I'm awake, Moira, I hear that dreadful keening of the people, in the wind, in the silence.'

He leaned his head against the wall and I saw a tear come out from under his closed eyelids and go down his cheek. A small thing, but to me it felt like I was watching the ground in front of the house start to move about.

'I did try,' he said. 'I did try, Moira, to be a good man. To be the man I meant to be. If I could have stopped them from throwing the people into the boats, sending them off to God knows where.'

I knew not what to say. I had only ever seen a man cry one time before, my father as we must leave our island, and it was something to tear a heart, to see the Reverend so broken up like that of all his hopes, so I pretended not to have noticed his tears and got all bright and busy at the sink.

'Is that rain coming in?' I said. 'Might be as well to go see old MacAllister later, after you have done your devotions.'

'Ah yes, MacAllister,' he said. 'Was I going there? Perhaps I will go to my study first, do you think?'

'Or catch a nap upstairs? The doctor would be pleased by that.'

'D'you think so? Perhaps I will.'

Off he wandered in his blanket, and I listened out for his steps going up the stairs slowly. I heard the creak of the bedsprings as he lay down, and at last the house went quiet again.

Six weeks more, and the Reverend decides he must begin to give sermons again. So I ironed his surplus and he fretted away with prayers and concordances, scratching out words, starting over again, crumpling up pages that would not do. I had never before seen him so nervous; it was as if those weeks had driven from his head how it was he used to go about doing those things. And he was back to his old tricks with the fasting and night prayers and the early devotions, chasing after holiness like a tired fisherman who must rise early while it is dark, stay on the sea till evening and yet still come home exhausted and with the nets empty.

His nerves must have been catching, because as I sat on the wooden pew next to Maggie that Sunday, I was wringing my hands like it was me who was about to get up and address the people – which I felt all but ready to do, since for the past two weeks I had listened to him over and over, rehearsing his good advice concerning the hope of grace in us who are but sinners.

I felt my heart jump like a cart going over a bump in the path as I saw the Reverend rise up and climb to his pulpit. But then the precentor got up at the same time, and he also went down to the front to open the psalm singing. I saw then with dismay that the Reverend had misremembered the office, got up too soon; he must stand in the pulpit, holding onto the sides like it was a boat tossing at sea, and with us all examining him while we sang through the whole of Psalm 84.

In churches hereabouts, we do not sing hymns that are fancy and rhyming like the popish do down in Uist, but we sing only psalms, straight from the Bible. So the precentor stood himself at the front, looking humbly like someone standing in for a better man. He wailed out the first line of Psalm 84, telling us the true confession of pain in his heart – though we did see him all week tending his sheep or working his croft, a quiet and plain man. Then the whole congregation decided that they too must truly sing their woes to God, and there was a wailing sound of all our voices replying with the same line of scripture, each man making up the tune as he remembered, or inventing how he felt it should be sung so that it was not so much a song as a roomful of laments. On it went, line by line throughout the entire scripture, till we all sat down spent and wrung of our sorrows. And all this time, the Reverend must hang onto the rail of his pulpit above and join in the lament, and must compose his mind ready for his sermon.

The church went quiet. All eyes turned up to the Reverend, all ears ready for his words. With a white face and a sticky shine of sweat across his brow, he read out his text.

'Jeremiah, Chapter Eight: "The harvest is past, the summer is ended, and we are not saved!"'

A long pause; eyes closed, he seemed to be meditating in his heart. Then he continued.

'"Is there no balm in Gilead, no physician there? Why then is there no recovery? Oh, that my head were waters, and my eyes a fountain of tears, that I might weep—"'

There was a sliding noise of papers. A book fell from the lectern shelf and thudded onto the wooden floor. We watched the Reverend sink down behind the front of the pulpit. Then there was no more of him to be seen. We waited for him to gather his papers together and continue, but we must sit a long time in silence and must listen to the crack from time to time of Maggie Kintail's peppermint which she always sucks through a sermon to guard against the tedium of so much good teaching.

Then there was another noise, the sound of someone gulping air, a shuddering of the wood of the pulpit. Clear across the church, as the sun shone down through the windows, we heard the sound of a grown man sobbing. The steward and his wife turned their heads and looked at each other above their daughters' bonnets. Then they quickly stood and did hurry from the church, walking in a line.

As if a sign had been given, each man and woman did stand up and walk away, as if hurriedly called to be elsewhere, until only Maggie and I were sitting there in that empty place, with the sound of crying. Then I too stood up. I walked down to the front of the church and up the steps of the pulpit.

There was the Reverend in his white surplus, like a gannet crashed on the ground with its wings broken. He looked up at me, his face a mess of crying. He looked ashamed and lost and horrified.

'Shall we go back to the manse now, sir?'

He looked about him and got himself up slowly. Maggie was waiting at the foot of the pulpit and we took his arm each side and walked him back home.

Halfway there he stopped. 'I've lost the words, Moira. My grave-stone will never stand upright now.'

'Oh hush now, sir. You're talking old foolishness.'

While Maggie got him settled in a chair in his study, I went for one of the farm boys to tell them to ride up and ask for the doctor to come. Although in my heart I knew that the sickness the Reverend had was nothing that could be cured by some bottle from the doctor's bag.

CHAPTER 29

Ruth

I didn't sleep much that night, disorientated by meeting that lost child from another time. Getting the shopping in Tarbert the next morning, I opened the van door ready to drive back home. I glanced over at Dr Lawson's surgery, a white house half hidden under dripping trees. I hesitated, gripping the van door, then dumped the carrier bags on the front seat, slammed the door and walked across the car park.

The receptionist looked through her appointment book.

'I could squeeze you in at two thirty, if you'd like to wait. It'll only be half an hour, unless Dr Lawson gets held up with a patient.'

I sat down and picked up a magazine. The pages felt soft and crazed from being turned so many times. A drooping spider plant sat in the window beneath a venetian blind that was caught on one side and sloped down at an angle. A little boy with bright red cheeks was pulling toys from a box while his mother shut her eyes and tipped her head back against the wall, coughing every so often.

It was hot in there. The chair was hard. The backs of my legs were sticking to the plastic through my thin skirt.

How many times had I sat on a chair exactly like this one? Waiting in a corridor, the edge of the plastic cutting into the backs of my legs, waiting to see the social worker with that falling feeling in my stomach?

I made a complaint once, about a foster father and his wandering hands. It went with the territory: kids like me were easy game. And he was mean to the other kids.

I was so angry, I decided to tell them; already knew it was going to end badly.

When the social worker was out of the room, I got up and looked at my files to find out what she'd written.

She fabricates incidents for attention and seems to have difficulty telling fact from fiction. We do not recommend a further placement in a family home until this is resolved. Under the circumstances, placing Ruth in the girls' home would be advisable.

The little boy with a cough threw a metal car at his mum's leg. She woke and spoke to him in Gaelic, pulled him up onto her lap. A buzzer sounded and the receptionist called out her name. The woman gathered up her things, took the child's hand, and went through to the doctor's room.

I felt breathless in the dry air. What exactly was I going to say to Dr Lawson? Blurt out something about how I wanted to see Dr Montgomery, the head doctor? The old familiar panic, a feeling that things were about to get worse, trying to explain myself to the person who was writing everything down in a Manila folder, their expression closed and attentive.

I took off my jumper. I felt too restless to keep still. I shut my eyes, tried breathing slowly.

I mumbled a 'Sorry' to the receptionist as I walked past her, dropping my bag and then my jacket, bending down to bundle them under my arm.

'I didn't realise you were in such a hurry, Ruth,' she called after me as I pushed through the heavy fire door. Standing outside, I breathed in the relief of cooler air.

I walked down to the sea loch over the road, dumped everything on a bench and sank down beside it. I sat waiting for my heart to slow down. I pulled at my T-shirt to dry the slick of sweat. I could feel the cold patches under my arms.

What a fool. If I was going to be the sort of grown-up you'd hand a baby to, I should have gone in, asked for help.

But I knew only too well, once you let them in, once they took over, you never knew where it was going to end. Things written in a folder that you could never change.

I saw a woman in a suit as she bent down to get into the back of a car, my baby in her arms.

The back of my hand was burning. I looked down and realised that I had scraped three long welts across the skin, a trail of watery blood seeping up through the flesh, stinging as it met the air.

CHAPTER 30

Alexander, 1861

I recall that Fanny had left the house, as she did each afternoon on her errands, to help oversee a small school in one of the poorer parts of town, or perhaps to meet with her ladies and plot to raise subscriptions for a new school in the Great Glen, cut off as it was at that time from any education.

I had come to greatly admire Fanny, for her strength of character. It seemed to me that she had turned all her disappointment not to self-pity but to a great desire to see an improvement in the lives of other people's children. I had made her promise, that as soon as my headaches abated, she would allow me to see what help I might offer in teaching her children.

My enforced idleness, as prescribed by the doctor, left me with a great deal of time, and Matthew advised me to take up again the project of researching the sea lady. However, my capacity to concentrate remained poor, and a morning studying in my room left me with a pounding head and a consequent habit of sleeping too much. It was thus late when I woke and realised that I must hurry if I were to keep my appointment that morning at the Bishop's residence in Morningside – a meeting that I anticipated with some dread. I had written to the Bishop some days before, tending my resignation from the ministry.

I took breakfast with Matthew and Fanny in the morning room, uncomfortably aware from their cheerfulness that they were under the impression my meeting with His Grace was to confirm a promotion in the ministry. I thought to drop some hint of my intentions, but before I could say anything, Matthew shook his paper straight to better read some article. 'There's news here, Alexander, of a ship that left Stornoway some weeks back, heading to Canada. Dreadful business.'

'What has happened?' I asked him, my heart beginning to beat hard with some premonition. 'Did she founder?'

'Almost as bad,' he replied as he read the print with close attention. 'Some poor devil boarded the ship with a case of smallpox. The ship was packed with emigrants. By the time they reached port in Canada, the disease had raged right through it. Only half the passengers and crew survived, the rest had to be committed to the sea.'

'Conditions are so dreadful on those ships,' said Fanny. 'What hope did they have? Alexander, are you well?'

I had gone to read the report over Matthew's shoulder. Saw the name of the ship, *The Caledonia*. The very same ship that had taken the Finsbay people.

I regained my chair and all but collapsed upon the seat. I saw the linen-wrapped bodies sliding down into the dark water, and knew them to be the same men, women and children – yes, children, there would be children – from the Finsbay village where I had stood and read out the eviction notice, and where, a moment later, all hell had broken loose across the bay.

'Would you like Matthew to send word to the Bishop that you are unwell? Perhaps you should delay your appointment with him?' Fanny said.

I gulped some cold water and stood up, feeling shaky but determined.

'More than ever, more than ever, it is imperative that I speak with the Bishop. I cannot continue. I must go through with my resignation.'

From the look that Fanny and Matthew exchanged, I saw how sorely disappointed they were to hear such news.

'I am sorry. I am sorry,' I told them.

I left Matthew gazing down at the mess of his boiled egg, the broken shell trailing across the white cloth.

I waited in the Bishop's study, but he did not appear. It was some time before a maid came to say that I would find him in the garden. She indicated the French windows that led out onto lawns. I followed steps down a grassy bank, and saw no one but an elderly gardener in a hessian apron hoeing the weeds along a bed of gillic flowers. I walked over to ask of him directions as to where I might find the Bishop, but before I could speak, the man dusted down his hand and held it out to shake.

'How are ye, Alexander? I can't say how unhappy I am that you feel we must lose you.'

The intelligence of the gaze with which he fixed me, with its unstudied authority, left me in no doubt that I was addressing His Grace.

He indicated a stone bench set in an alcove in a wall, saying, 'Sit ye down,' and settled alongside me.

I found myself stumbling through my answers in a way that even to my own ears seemed most unsatisfactory. I had failed my parishioners by my lack of progress in spiritual disciplines. I had become entangled in the affections of a lady. I had failed to support the needy when they were driven from their homes – had helped to drive them from their homes. I had come to the realisation that I was, in truth, unable to reach that state of Godliness that one may expect from the clergy.

I could not speak of the news from the ship, of those that had perished. No words would describe such an awful matter.

He paused for a moment, sighed and leaned forward.

'How old are you now, Alexander?'

'Almost thirty, Your Grace.'

'Are you indeed? And this is your first parish since you were a curate?'

I nodded.

'And it's how long that you've been out there on the island, with no one to whom you may confide your worries?'

'A year, a year and a half now, Your Grace.'

He got up, stood in front of me and peered into my face. He tapped on my chest with his finger, and pulled down my bottom eyelid and frowned.

'And you've no' been looking after yourself too well, I would say. Too much pruning and not enough feeding. You can't go on like that. I know, I've been down that road.'

He went and sat back down, heavily now.

'You have failed, Alexander. A broken man, yes, but it is only as broken men that we are ready to come to truth and grace, to walk beyond ourselves to where faith begins. If ye'll only consider biding in your post as a curate for a while, then you will serve a parish well. Will ye no return and bide one more month there?'

Out of obedience, I agreed to his request, but I knew already as I walked from his garden, that even if I returned to my parish, it would not change the knowledge of my own failed nature. I would return and serve out my time at Scarista, but at the end of the promised month, I knew that I must pack up my effects and remove myself to some occupation on the mainland whereby I might usefully gain a living.

I cannot say what grieved me most, the thought that the God I loved and so longed to serve was hidden from me, or the thought that I would no longer walk in a landscape that now seemed to me a home, or the loss of those simple people I had come to love.

CHAPTER 31

Ruth

At three o'clock on a glorious afternoon, we walked across to Scarista church for the burial of the mermaid baby, her remains having been finally released to the island.

The MacKays and the MacDonalds were already seated in the pews. Most of the local people had turned out, the women wearing those black straw hats that they seemed to keep specifically for church each Sunday. Two men in dark suits sat near the front – policemen from Tarbert. Shortly after the service had begun, the door creaked open again. Lachlan slipped in and sat down at the back.

The congregation sang Gaelic psalms, a kind of wailing that makes your hair stand on end. In the pauses you could hear the competing, tuneless sound of a corncrake outside, rasping its one-idea song.

We filed out of the church in silence and followed the small box down to the graveyard turf. All around, the island was shimmering, blue sea and green machair, the corncrake creaking away from somewhere in the silverweed. Two men slowly lowered the tiny box into a hole at the end of the row of headstones. Dougal read prayers, a couple of skylarks winding higher and higher over the sea pastures, a warm wind lifting my hair. I took Michael's hand; it felt warm. I realised how cold my own was.

There was no name on the stumpy little headstone, simply: 'A child known to God'. Well, if he knew about that child, he might at least have taken better care of it.

We were invited back to Dougal's manse in An t'Obbe, a neat bungalow with beige, pebbledash walls. The ladies from church had sandwiches ready, and the essential nip of whisky came out. Lachlan was evidently Mr Popular with the old ladies. They rushed to stow his coat and get him a well-stocked plate of home-baking.

Someone caught my elbow. It was Christine. 'You didn't come and see me, Ruth.'

'Sorry. I've been so busy. Oh, and here's Lachlan.'

Lachlan had managed to escape the fan club and was on his way over, bringing Dougal with him.

'Come by, tomorrow, Ruth. Don't forget now. It may all be nothing, but there's someone I think you should speak with.'

I was relieved to see her move away to catch someone else.

'Sorry to have arrived so late,' said Lachlan as he joined us. 'But I was determined to get here for the burial.'

'I hope you had a good trip to Edinburgh anyway,' said Dougal.

'Yes, very good. And I spent quite a lot of time in the library at the Historical Society.' He glanced in my direction, looking very pleased with himself.

'You found out some more about Ferguson?'

'I did. The archivist there was very helpful. Apparently there's an entry for a manuscript written by a Reverend Ferguson in the library catalogue. She can't put her hands on it as yet, but she thinks it must be in the archives somewhere, since there's no record of anyone taking it out, and so she's trying to locate it for me.'

'That's great news.'

'Right now though, Ruth, the reason I rushed back today is that I wanted to hand over this.'

Looking somewhat apprehensive, he fetched an envelope from the inside of his jacket. It was a brown, slim envelope, like a bill. He'd promised to give Michael a final costing out for the boat, but I couldn't understand why he was giving it to us now, at a funeral. He held it out for me to take.

'I think you should give that to Michael.'

But as Michael unfolded the paper inside, I could see it didn't look anything like a bill. The paper was old, so thin that it was almost transparent, the pages sharply creased as if they'd been lying folded up for a long time.

'What is this?' said Michael.

'The Reverend's wife bequeathed her husband's manuscript to the library after he passed away, and she must have slipped that letter inside. The letter was left unopened, but stored separately with other small documents. When the archivist came across it yesterday, she called me immediately.'

'D'you mean it's a letter from Alexander?'

'Not from Alexander, Ruth. It's from his wife. That's her signature at the end of the letter.'

'What was she called?'

'I'm afraid she signed herself as Mrs Alexander Ferguson, as was the way then. Her writing's quite shaky, so the letter must have been written when she was very old. Anyway, once I read it, I asked the archivist if I might bring it with me, on account of the circumstances today.' He turned to the vicar. 'Dougal, the baby you buried today, she does have a name, and her name is in that letter.'

Michael had already started reading. 'This is dreadful. Have you read this, Lachlan?'

'But I still don't understand. Why put a letter in with the manuscript?' I said.

'I think the details were simply too shocking to make public at that time and this must have been his wife's way of leaving a record of the poor wee child we buried today at Scarista. I have to warn you, it's not a nice story in that letter.'

CHAPTER 32

Moira, 1861

I kept the house dusted and aired, ready for the Reverend, but the weeks went by and no letter came to say when he would be back from Edinburgh.

And no letter came from my cousin Annie, though it were still early to expect one to arrive all the way from Canada, but I did heartily long for a word from someone who knew me.

The grasslands of Scarista seemed more empty in all their beauty than ever. I began to see how very strange it was to have but one or two children running about the open machair, which was now coming into full bloom, and heavy with the scent of flowers and honey. It had not rained for days. The sea was such a holy, deep blue, and the sky so innocent, with the green of the grass as cheerful as the beginning of Creation, and yet it was an empty place, with the people gone.

I walked down along the white foam and saw the seals bobbing up with their dark heads, the oyster catchers with their beaks dipping in the sea, skittering in the foam with their quick feet. Surely, I thought, men may have stolen the land, and yet the land remains itself, and has always greeted me like a friend.

But for all the crashing of the great surf on the beach and the thrumming of the wind from the Atlantic across my ears, I stood there alone on that shore. I stood bitter with the knowledge that no one would be coming to put right all the wrongs done to my people. No one on this earth would ever come and restore to me all that I had lost.

At night I was still sleeping on the settle bench in the manse – some foolish notion that I should be there lest the Reverend return unexpected. Being so alone in that house got my thoughts wandering bitter and lonely, back along the thick carpets of the corridors of Avenbuidhe Castle, waiting behind the drapes for him to come out from his bathroom with the green-glazed crocodile tiles, waiting silently with the knife in my hand raised and ready. But still I did not go. I waited on, hoping for the Reverend's return.

Finally, the letter came one morning. The Reverend was due back in a week. I set to around the manse, opening windows, beating rugs, baking bread and getting Maggie to help me move the furniture so we could clean proper.

The date of his arrival came and went. He did not appear. No further letter to explain his delay, though the days kept coming and going till it was some two weeks after he was due.

I knew then that what the doctor had said was the truth. My Alexander would not be returning to the island; he would go back to his old life in Edinburgh and not think of us again – of me.

The next day, I was more than surprised to have a knock on the door again and get a letter with my name writ large. The postman did say it was from Canada and with great joy I saw that it was from my cousin.

But the news inside was heartbreaking. Poor Annie's husband had had a letter scribed to say that they had to throw their three children in the sea when they died from the smallpox on the boat. He did not think that Annie would ever be right again. I sat and wept for those bairns then, and I decided that if the Reverend was not come home by the end of the week, then I would do it. I would set out for Avenbuidhe Castle and justly settle my accounts.

*

It was a couple of nights before I was to set out. Though I had got used to my hard bed, it was close to midnight before I slept, my thoughts so anxious and distracted. And as soon as I was asleep, something woke me. Straight out of a deep sleep, I was sat up wide awake and listening. I knew in my bones that something was very wrong, though I could say not what.

I listened hard, and though it does not concern me much that we do live next to a graveyard, that night I was afraid to get up and look about.

Then I heard it, the thing that had woken me, a noise outside like the sound of a horse's hoof on stone, and I laughed, because I thought, it is the Reverend. He has come back to his house.

But I hesitated still to go to the door, for all was silent again; no noise of bridle or of horse stirrups as someone dismounts. So I went quietly to the side window, nervous now, and looked out. A moon was up over the hills, and when the moon is clear in these parts then it is clear as day, everything the colour of a steel knife. Big black streaks of cloud were climbing up to the moon, making the dark go thick.

I went then to the back door and opened it. The dark and the wind made me very wary, since I was now sure something was out there, and I could not say what. The byre was black against the sky, the clouds sliding by fast, a sheet of white cloud with a red stain passing fast over the moon. And then I saw something white move, over near the byre, and it almost stopped my heart – for it was the gliding, white shape of a person.

I was froze there with fear, trying not to see what I could plainly see, a faint white shape floating above the grass. Then it called out, 'Moira, please help me,' and I knew from that voice that this was no ghost.

I went out to her in the wind, and there she was, standing in nothing but the thinnest white nightgown all stuck to her with the wet of the night chill.

That is when I saw what her trouble was, for Miss Marstone, all wild and half naked as she was, was as round in the belly as I have ever seen such a thing, and I saw that the Miss was with child.

'You'd better come in, Miss,' I told her, though I had to pull at her arm to get her to follow me, since she seemed of a mind to just stand there in the dark and the cold, till all the world could see her in the plain light of day. My Lord, she was cold. She was icy to touch. I got her into the kitchen and wrapped her in the blanket from my settle. I lit the lamp and saw her lips were a strange blue and her eyes had gone sunk in with inky shadows all round them. And her hair, her lovely fair hair, was matted like weed and I know not when it had last been washed or combed.

But while I tried to get her to drink something warm, I had one thought filling up my mind, and then my chest, till I felt I might burst open with tears. I thought, It is that day. It is because of that day when I saw them in the dunes and left them.

I would have hated her very much then, but there was surely nothing much left to hate but her troubles, and she was greatly in pains and crying out, so I lay her down on the bench and found her feet all cut up. I sat by and held her hand, as she did not want me to leave her but kept telling me to make sure the candle was still burning.

'But Miss,' I said, 'shall I get word to the castle for them to come and get you?'

This got her very agitated and shouting at me not to tell them where she was. I said, 'But they will surely come looking for you.'

Then she was more in pain and it began to dawn on me from the calves I have helped watch into birth that the Miss's time was very near. So I told her to keep looking hard at the candle and I would get help.

I came back with Maggie Kintail, who has watched half the island into this world, and she did not seem so very surprised when she saw the Miss there in the Reverend's kitchen in all her trouble and pain.

Maggie said then that we should take her to the bed in the cottage, but I said no, we shall take her upstairs.

Maggie looked shocked. 'What if the Reverend comes back? What shall we say then?'

'We shall tell him it is his Christian duty to help this poor girl,' I said, though I was more sure of his not returning that night, or any night, than I was of how I would explain my reasons as to where the Miss should birth her baby.

Half of me was hoping that he would come back, and see what he had done.

When we helped the Miss upstairs to the small bedroom, the moon was on the rise over the back hills. That moon would be sinking down into the sea in front of the house before the Miss had stopped screaming all night; for once a girl has a child within her, then it must come out or they must both perish. There is no way out of such a long night.

Her nightdress that she came in was wet as a sheet on the line and so Maggie found a nightshirt that was the Reverend's from out of his own chest, and would not listen when I said that was surely wrong. So we peeled off the Miss's wet things, and she was all bones like an old lady, knock-kneed, and her hips all sharp as stones, but with a stomach bigger than I had ever thought to see, hard and dark and round as the globe of the world that sits in the Reverend's study, veined over with blue lines and silvery rivers where the skin had stretched apart. She held out her broomstick arms, covered as they was in fine rabbit's down, and as we pulled the clean nightshirt over her bony little face and thin scrapes of fair hair, then I felt my feet wet and saw her waters had broke down her legs.

I knew my world was ending that night as we waited for the Reverend's child, but I had to put that thought aside, as it must surely be easier to die than to go through the travails the Miss went through. Waiting all night while a child is being born is much like waiting through a night vigil as a soul leaves this world in agonies.

With a last great groan to tear the world apart, the babe was delivered and Maggie had a tiny scrap of a child in her arms. As we heard its thin cry, I looked up and was surprised to see that the morning had come in at the windows.

Maggie told me to take the babe, all covered in mess as it was, for there was work still to be done. As I know from helping my own mother with my sister, you must deliver all that is left or the mother will bleed to death.

But Maggie said, 'For the love of God,' and the Miss began to groan again like a creature possessed of the Devil. A few minutes later, Maggie delivered to the world a second babe, which I also took from her as she then turned to finish the last of the birthings.

I had washed the first little girl, wrapped her in a cloth, and set her in a drawer padded out with a blanket. I took this second child in a dry cloth to wash it in the warm water that we had got ready, but I almost dropped it as I carried it across the room. Its tiny face was as round as a soft little mushroom, and its long, swollen eyes were closed, but the poor wee thing had no legs where the legs should be. Instead, it had a long, tapering body, like a seal or a fish, with two bony flippers that twitched as it mewed.

I washed that poor babe. I took some linen from the pile, a damask hand cloth with lace around it. I wrapped up the child, and laid it next to its sister. The second child had its eyes closed in the way of a new kitten. And then I saw this smaller child had become very still and the child did not move any more, though I picked it up and rocked it.

The Miss was asking for her babies, so Maggie carried over the little girl that was alive, and she laid it in the crook of the Miss's arm and told her how to give suck, which she did well.

And then the Miss said, but you must bring me her sister, when she is awake.

So I told the Miss that I did not think the child would ever wake up again. And the Miss bowed her head and cried, and told me I must let her hold the babe.

So I took it over, and the Miss unwrapped the child, and saw how it was, and she was happy in her tears. She said that it was a blessing for a girl child to be a mermaid.

And I was crying too, and I said, 'Miss, I will never forgive the Reverend for all that has happened to you.'

And she looked up at me puzzled. Then she said, 'Moira, you are very mistaken. Alexander is not their father.'

'Then who is their father, Miss?' I blurted out.

'Marstone,' she said.

'No, Lord Marstone is *your* father, Miss.'

'That man was never my father.'

And I looked up at Maggie, because I could not understand what the Miss was saying. Maggie looked like she had seen a sight that was horrible, and shocked out of her wits.

So I tried again to get the Miss to talk sense. 'I think you are mishearing me, Your Ladyship. Who is the father of your bairns, Miss, that he should come help you now?'

'I told you this, Moira. Marstone only brought me back here to want me dead. He is the father.'

Maggie pulled on my arm and she shook her head at me to ask no more. Then she turned to gathering up the bloody linen, her face grim and set.

The awfulness of what the Miss was saying worked slowly into my mind, though I resisted it hard, and I could not think that I had worked it out right.

The Miss was getting sleepy now. The babe had finished its feed and was sleeping already, so Maggie took it to lay it down.

'But who shall we ask to help you, Miss? Where shall you go?' Maggie asked her.

'I may sleep here now,' she answered. 'No one shall hurt me now. I have killed him, Maggie.'

'Killed who, Miss?'

'Killed him as he slept, with the knife he used for the stags. It is over,' she told us calmly, and she moved slowly down her pillows and turned her face into a sleep.

We cleaned up the bed as best we could while she slept and I carried the bloody linen down to soak. Then we made tea with sugar and we sat and drank something hot at last, waiting in her room lest she wake or the baby stir. We sat a long time, with faces wide eyed and stunned, and sometimes I thought, Surely it was me who was there who killed Marstone, so long had I seen myself doing just such a thing. But no, it was she that had done it, who lay sleeping in front of us, grey hued and blue lipped.

Maggie said, 'They will come for her, Moira. The poor girl will hang for this.'

'But we shall not let them have her,' I said.

And it was then that we heard what I had been longing for, for so many nights – that could not have come at a worse time – the sound of a horse's hooves in the yard outside. We looked around at the room; so many, many things wrong in that room, and who was to explain what we were doing there? Maggie was white as a sheet, the Miss hardly stirring in her sleep.

'But the Reverend will tell them,' she said. 'After all, he is a man of justice and right.'

I looked around madly as if I was looking for somewhere to hide the Miss, but saw there was nothing to do but that I must go down the stairs and say things to the Reverend that ought never be said. I heard the front door open and the stamp of his boots on the mat. I looked at Maggie and she nodded, so I got up and went downstairs.

I had longed and longed for the sound of the Reverend coming home. Now as I walked down the stairs I saw that I was beyond all feelings. I looked down at my arms and saw there were many new freckles, but they were not freckles, but spots of dried blood, and the front of my dress was bloody and stained.

I spoke with the Reverend, who was looking in horror at the state of me as he listened, and then he followed quickly upstairs. He stood in the room and looked around. The Miss was sleeping, the child by her side, the mermaid baby wrapped up and at peace.

Maggie took the Reverend aside; she told him those things that should not be. He shook his head and then he must get up and walk about the room.

'I should have seen. I should have understood,' he was saying. 'But who should we tell?' he said. 'There are laws…'

'If you tell them, then they will take her away and she will hang,' Maggie said.

I thought he would fall over, he looked so spun around and desperate. He stood with his eyes closed for a long time.

'No, no. The Church preaches the forgiveness of the cross. I have preached it often, but I see now, I see, it was for this moment. Don't you see, Maggie, we can't let them take her, because she is forgiven by the blood of the Lamb.'

Maggie made the sign of the cross, and then so did I.

'Praise be,' said Maggie. 'So shall we get her away from here before they come, sir?'

He looked around again, as if all his thoughts were exhausted. Then his face cleared. He began to stride around the room as if leaving already. 'But of course, I have the note that her aunt gave me. Wait.'

He went then, and fetched a letter from his study. He said there was a name in it, of a family on the island whom he could ask for help. And then the Reverend rode away to try to make some arrangements to get Katriona away by boat to the mainland.

I took up the letter to read it, telling Maggie what was said: how Lady Erquart had feared for the Miss, and she had wrote down the name of a good family on the island who could be depended upon for help.

And Maggie said she thought that the Miss's real father must have been some soft sweetheart of the Lady Marstone, somebody she fell for in London after she had fled away from His Lordship, back to her sister. But after Lady Marstone died, then Marstone had been able to use the law to call the child back to him as his own.

The following night, under dark, we lay the Miss and the baby in a bed of blankets in the back of a cart, covered them over with more blankets and a tarpaulin. Then I watched the Reverend lead the horse off towards a village by Rodel, where it was arranged that the people named would meet them with a boat. I stood and watched the cart until the dark had taken them completely, waited until I could hear no more the sound of them going.

I knew that I might never see the Miss no more, so sick was she, but I never thought, as the white face of the Reverend faded into the dark, that it would also be the last sight of my Alexander on the island.

Maggie and I turned back to the manse.

The Miss had refused to go unless she could take her mermaid baby along with her also. Alexander had had to be very firm with her, that she must loose hold of the poor bundle of blankets now, for the child was with God and must stay here to be lain in peace.

'But I know how it will be,' said the Miss. 'She did not get baptised. She will have to lie all on her own, away from the good people. Will you promise me, if you take her, that my Clare will lie with all the other good people, in holy ground?'

Maggie stepped forward and she promised that she would bury the baby in holy ground, in a place that was blessed by holy prayers.

And so the Miss let her take the mermaid baby.

'But Maggie,' I said as we took the little body back into the house, 'we cannot bury the child in the churchyard. The turf is so smooth; they will all see at once, even a tiny new grave.'

'We shall bury her in another holy place, where the Reverend says his prayers each day,' she said.

'In the church?'

'Not in the church,' she said.

She took the babe into the Reverend's study, and I had to help her take up the nails and pull up the boards under the Turkey rug, and dig down in the soft sandy soil under the house. Then I found a small red trunk that was used to send over books, and we made the little mite a bed. We wrapped her well in my best shawl, and laid her to rest, covering the box over with the soil, patting it down like a blanket.

Maggie and I found the Reverend's prayer book and I read out some prayers for those that have passed away. Maggie sang a psalm, and we must hammer the nails back down, and then we must close up the house and go.

CHAPTER 33

Ruth

I'd thought that finding out about the child buried under our house would solve things, but all I'd discovered was the precise amount of cruelty that one person can inflict on another.

Katriona and her poor, stunted mermaid baby, what chance had they ever had? And as for the sister who'd survived, what had happened to her?

Nobody seemed to know or care.

'But how could that other little girl simply vanish off the face of the earth?' I said, pushing away a half-eaten plate of bean casserole. It tasted bitter and burnt, though no one else thought so. 'It's as if no one cared one bit about her, as if she didn't matter.'

'Most probably she passed away with Katriona,' Michael suggested. 'In those days, an illegitimate child could have been buried with the mother and left unrecorded.'

He helped Jamie and Leaf wash up the dishes. I sat on at the table, the same thoughts going round and round in my head; getting nothing done. After a while I realised they had finished and had gone through to catch the evening news, leaving the kitchen silent and empty. A few weeks till the baby arrived, and here I was, part ghost girl, part lizard, trying to make it add up to a grown-up capable of raising a tiny child; and too tired, too tired to keep on holding it all together.

When you left me so alone, did you have any idea what it

would be like, the miles of rubble you left me to walk through?

The next morning, I woke up too early, the dawn white and blank.
I knew straight away it had come in again, like rain, that same old
blank depression. A white-out. No energy to rise and invent someone.

After Michael had got up, it was a long time before I made myself
sit up. Pulled yesterday's jeans and shirt from the back of the chair. They
felt heavy and cold, as if they had taken in moisture during the night.

I heard Michael downstairs, whistling. He was very upbeat about
how much progress we were making on the house. But by the end
of the morning my coldness had begun to seep into him.

'Not feeling so good again?' he said.

I shrugged.

I couldn't think of anything to say for the rest of the day. Nor for
the following few days, and then the days seemed to merge together.
A heavy feeling of moving through water, slowly travelling to some
inevitable conclusion.

Finally, I realised I was sleepwalking to a place I didn't want to
think about. I went up to bed early, and woke in the dark some time
later to find Michael's side of the bed still flat and cold. It was two
in the morning.

I could hear muffled voices. They seemed to be coming up through
the dormer window from the garden.

Downstairs, I went out into the garden, the dark warm and soft.
I found Michael and Leaf sitting together on the bench at the side
of the house. A huge canopy of stars in a vast sky hung above them.

Leaf uncurled her legs, and stretched. 'Night then. And Ruth,
sweetie, it's going to get better. This depression, it will pass. I promise.'

She hugged me. Held me for a beat or two. Then she blew a kiss
to Michael. We listened to the soft pad, pad of her feet round the side
of the house, her patchouli scent sweetening the night air.

'What were you doing?'

'Nothing. Talking. We should get you back into bed. You need your sleep.'

The summer was suddenly brilliant over the island. I'd hardly noticed it arrive. I needed to wake up.

I said to Michael, why don't we go down to Losgaintir, take a picnic to the dunes – a kind of last-chance date before the baby appeared.

I packed a basket with a bottle of our home-made beer, a slab of cheese and some oatcakes, and we took some old beach towels and books.

By the time we set out, it was late afternoon: the warmth was starting to go out of the air. At seven months, the bump made me heavy and slow as we walked in silence through the dunes. Down on the beach, we found an amphitheatre of dunes as shelter from the wind. In front of us, the mountains hunkered together over the glassy water; amethyst reflections streaked across the white sands where the waves left a sheen of water. Michael stripped off to his bathing trunks, ran down to the icy breakers in a moment of madness and plunged in.

He came running back minutes later, shivering in the bright sun. 'Grief,' he said. 'That water never warms up, does it?' I rubbed him down with a towel. He swayed as I rubbed him hard, but he didn't seem to notice, looking out at the water in a dreamy and distant way as if the cold had made him sleepy. The sand caught in the blond hairs on his arms, like minute lights. Cold drops of seawater fell from his hair onto my skin. I licked one from my forearm, kissed his lips with a salty kiss. I sat alongside him, trying to warm him up, looking out at the sea, but my eyes soon got dazzled and felt weary from the brightness and the wind.

As the sun got lower, it started to draw out long shadows across the slopes of the dunes; the sand there felt chilly when you stepped into it. No one else was on the beach, nothing but miles of flat sand and the sea glare.

'What were you talking to Leaf about, the other night?'

Michael stared at the sand as if it had the answer written on it. He took his time in answering. I folded the towel, fiddled with the material so that it was exactly even over my lap.

'We were talking about you.'

'Oh?'

'She was saying how it can really help, to talk to someone. Leaf's aunt's a psychologist and she says—'

'Wait. So you've been discussing me with Leaf? You and Leaf have been talking about me? That's so disloyal, Michael. Thanks.'

'But listen. If we asked the doctor, like Leaf said; got some counselling.'

'Like Angus John in his loony bin.'

'It's not like that.'

'Isn't it? Thanks for the vote of confidence. Why can't you just talk to me, Michael?'

'Because everything I say is wrong these days. Because you get so angry.'

'Well of course I'm angry now.'

'Ruth, you're always angry, and I get so tired of being your punch bag.'

'It's not like that.'

He got up and shook the sand from the towel, and started packing everything away.

With a sick feeling in my stomach, I followed after him. He looked so slender and lopsided, weighted down on one side with the blanket and the basket. Then I stopped walking, stood and watched him growing smaller against the miles of empty beach.

After our child was born, wouldn't it be better for them, better for us all, if I got up one morning and slipped away?

How do you know when something is ending? I started after him heavily. Slowly walking towards something inevitable.

Once we were back in the house, Michael disappeared. I went through and sat in the sea room, and stared out at the blue of the thickening twilight.

I could see the sense in what Michael wanted me to do, but I simply couldn't afford to do it. There's a reason for forgetting some things – all the things I'd never told even Michael about those lost years.

I felt so tired, so weary. I looked out at the vast plains of sea, the water opaque under the horizontal light, a dazzle of clouds and shards of setting sun. How peaceful it must be to walk there, gradually let yourself sink down; the burn and cold of rolling in oblivious waters. I think for the first time I understood how Mum felt, before she stepped off the edge, let herself slip away into the dark canal water.

I carried on sitting in the half dark for a long time. No sound but the breaths of the waves coming in, the beat of them falling onto the beach.

I saw the brown bottle of pills on Mum's dressing table with its typed label. Pills for clinical depression; the evidence that swung the coroner in favour of a suicide verdict.

A Selkie goes back to the sea.

And it was a comfort to me, knowing that Michael would be a good father; that he would take good care of our child.

A Selkie always goes back to the sea.

CHAPTER 34

Ruth

'There's a light in Angus John's house,' Jamie said when he came back in after filling up the basket of peats late one evening. 'He must be back from the loony bin.'

First thing next morning, I went up to see how Angus John was, in case he needed something.

The sun was already long up, everything quiet, the grasslands sharp in the early light. A sheep was lying at the side of the road on a cushion of grass. With its black forefoot extended like an evening glove and its yellow eyes rimmed in black, it looked like an old debutante collapsed after a heavy night out.

I found Angus John sitting at the kitchen table, the teapot on the stove nearby. Someone had washed the tea cosy – turned out it was blue. In fact the whole kitchen looked as if it had been combed down and tidied up, all the surfaces bare. Mrs MacKay had evidently made the most of her opportunity to get the place in order. Angus John seemed diminished by such tidiness, his face gaunt, his nose with a bloom of red veins beneath the thick glasses propped there to read a letter.

'It's you,' he said, going back to his letter. 'How are things in the commune?'

'Fine. And how are you, Angus John?'

'I get by,' he said. 'Aye, I'm taking it one day at a time, as they say.

Being away doesn't stop the gas and the electric sending bills.'

He shook his head and then reached for a mug. Pushed it in my direction and pointed at the teapot. I noticed his hand had developed a slight tremor. There were patches of grey stubble in the empty folds of skin under his chin, silver when he turned his head to the light.

'A day at a time,' he repeated, watching the stream of tea thoughtfully as I poured it. 'You see, I'm not drinking any more now, Ruth. Not again.'

'That's really good.'

'And it's not that I like a drink, to tell the truth. It doesn't suit me, in fact.'

I nodded.

'Good tea,' I said. 'You seem so much better.'

He gave a shuddering sigh. The effort involved made me feel quite worried for him.

'I walked away from that war, you see, and came home, and all the time, I didn't know I had come home with my pockets all full of it, like so many grenades ready to go off.'

'You mean you had shellshock?'

'Oh yes. Except, they don't call it by that now.' He lifted up his tea and took a loud sip, stared towards the window. We sat and watched his shirt on the washing line, flapping and punching madly in the wind. I felt so sorry for him, as he sat in his battered chair, so decrepit and broken down. Something boyish lingered on in Angus John's face, but it was worked over by folds of creased skin, altered by the slippage of the years. I tried to see him as the young man in the photo before the war, a smooth face that someone had loved once, a woman and a child at his table, but all I could see was the worn jacket, the long, knobbly wrists, the bony hands with swollen knuckles.

'Can I do something to help, Angus? Can we fetch some shopping for you?'

'Mrs MacDonald has already filled up the cupboard. I'll never eat all of what she has put in there. All Bran. What is that now? And Donny is fetching me back the cow, so I will be bringing you some milk down soon. And the sisters are saying they are going to be visiting more often.' Another deep sigh. 'But I've got a lady, here in Tarbert.' He sounded brighter now. 'Any time I need to, I can go and talk with her.'

I thought for a moment he might be telling me he had a girlfriend, but realised he was talking about a counsellor, someone probably recommend by the Inverness centre.

'She's called Dr Montgomery, come to live here for a couple of years on account of her husband's job in the fisheries.' He leaned in and lowered his voice. 'And she's half Red Indian. She and her husband are renting the old schoolhouse there down on Strond, not so far from Rodel. Oh yes, she's just lovely. I only wish that I had met her thirty years ago, then, perhaps, my boy would have stayed.'

He fell silent; he looked suddenly drawn in on himself, as if he might fall asleep. I stood up to go.

'You'll tell us if we can do something?'

He didn't reply. With the greasy tweed cap he always wore shading his eyes, it was hard to know if he was gazing out of the window or sleeping. I slipped out of the door, paused on the threshold.

For a moment, I had an impulse to go back in, wake him up urgently and ask him for the number of his American doctor. Then I felt a blur of shame: was I really in the same category as an old drunk? And anyway, what exactly was I going to say to her? It was never going to help.

Mrs MacDonald had evidently been watching from her place by the post office window. As I left the cottage, she came out and waved, hurried towards the path.

'How is he?'

'Sleeping.'

'I'll be there later to take his lunch over. But I was going to say, don't forget now, you're all to come over for Charlie's birthday this afternoon. He's going to be five. Doesn't seem possible.'

We went over that afternoon and found her house given over to a small riot of jelly and crisps.

She said it was to be a double celebration, since Jamie had just been told that he'd got a job as a teacher at the school in Seilebost. He and Leaf were going to move out from the Sea House and they were looking for a cottage to rent down by the estuary.

The other seven children from Charlie's nursery came along with their mums, women who were mostly about our age.

The mums were all slightly in awe of Jamie since he'd become something official, but when it came to those island women, it was me who was in awe of them. They were so at ease as they handled their kids: a word in a child's ear while handing them juice, hoisting a toddler onto a hip while chatting and drinking cups of tea, everything so instinctive and natural.

Possibly a bit too relaxed, I thought, as I watched two little boys sword-fighting with the butter knives. I disarmed them and they ran off outside. They found some sticks and carried on with their war. Their mums watched serenely through the window.

One of the kids popped a balloon with a bang. I jumped a mile, let out a loud scream.

'You're silly,' said Charlie.

Mrs MacKay called everyone in to light the candles. I took Michael's hand as we crowded round the kitchen table and sang 'Happy Birthday' twice, once in English for our benefit, and then in Gaelic, the sheepdog outside barking hysterically.

Shona started handing round the cake. She completed every movement while balancing the sleeping baby in the crook of her arm like a gift on a platter.

'This one's a tinker,' she admitted, catching me watching her. 'The moment I put her down, she wakes up and cries.'

'Do they all do that?'

'New babies do, but this one's the queen of "Don't leave me now". You wouldn't hold her for me a moment, Ruth? Here's me bursting to go to the loo.'

I found a small weight filling my arms, compact and soft as plums. A warmth radiated through the cotton blanket into my skin. The baby turned its cheek to rest against my arm.

I was mesmerised, the minute face drawing the eyes like a candle flame at Christmas. For a moment I thought I could scent pine and juniper and candle wax.

I knew I was having a baby. Of course I knew that. And yet it remained an idea, a problem, never a person. Now it struck me with breathtaking force that my child was real. I would hold it like this, its hot weight tiny and real, a being so, so vulnerable, so utterly dependent on me and Michael.

How did you do it? How did you care for a baby? How could you know what it needed, even when you loved your child as fiercely as I did mine? Because surely even love was no proof you would care for it properly in the end.

I felt Shona's arms sliding under mine to take the baby back. I watched her lift the little girl and turn her body in the air to place the child against her shoulder, a hand cradling the back of the head; a fluid gesture, simple and caring and right.

But that was how you did it. I couldn't take my eyes off her. You just did it. I was going to have a tiny baby, and I could do it – if I wanted to. I could learn all the little things a child like that needed.

Down to me now. Time to grow up.

I knew what I had to do.

Michael seemed glum as we left, as if the noise of the party had worn him out. He fetched my coat, held it out wordlessly for me to put my arms in the sleeves, looking away as if he had no expectation that we'd speak.

So much I had to tell him, soon.

I slept very little. I was awake and dressed at first light, sitting down in the kitchen with a mug of coffee, waiting for the light to gather itself, nervous about the day ahead.

By seven o'clock, I was parked a little way down from the old schoolhouse in Strond, watching the house for any signs of life. The early morning's glassy blue light threw the sea and the flat shapes of the Uists into a blur of legends and glare that made my eyes sore.

A woman in red cargo trousers and a pink top came out. She held back a rope of long, straight hair with one hand and put something in a bin at the side of the house, shutting the lid with a scraping sound.

I slammed the car door and was by her side as she opened the back door to go in.

'Dr Montgomery?'

She turned, looked puzzled.

'Yes.'

'Can you help me?'

CHAPTER 35

Alexander, 1862

It can sometimes happen that in the course of a day everything we
believe is turned upside down, and we understand for the first time
what it is that we have been looking at for so long. So it was for me,
one dark autumnal day in Edinburgh.

I had taken rooms near to where Fanny and Matthew had once
lived. For reasons I perfectly understood, they had quit Edinburgh
some months earlier to return to Cambridgeshire. Without my old
friends – and with most of my acquaintances embarrassed by my sudden
demotion to an apprentice teacher – it was necessarily a lonely life,
though my working days were full enough since I had started teaching in
a school set up by Fanny's circle to serve the poorer parts of Edinburgh.

I was, however, greatly troubled by fatigue, since nothing could
prevent the night's dreams from resurrecting the hours when I had
last seen Katriona alive. My sleep shattered, I would then lie awake,
and my mind would try to fathom the strange transmutation that
had resulted in Katriona's mermaid child. None of my enquiries
to Edinburgh or Glasgow had yet returned any news of a similarly
mutant specimen in their collections, and yet, in the answer to this
conundrum, beyond a veil of darkness, I was sure that the seal man
waited for me. When I slept, I saw him, a shadowy being on a glimmer
of water.

I spent that Saturday marking exercise books, then remembered to run out to the market before the stalls closed to buy bread and apples and a cold pie. I could not afford a maid on my wages and had learnt to greatly appreciate the efforts involved in all the tasks that Moira had once undertaken on my behalf.

My errands finished, it was thus late afternoon before I lit a lamp and took up the morning's paper, and found therein an article that captured my curiosity.

It was a notice for a lecture to be given that same day at the Edinburgh Historical Society. Dr Gordon MacIntyre was to speak on 'A study of folk tales as oral history. A discussion of fairies, Finns and Selkies and their place in the history of the Gaelic peoples.'

I was not interested in Dr MacIntyre's theories on fairies, but I was very keen to hear his ideas concerning the Selkies. That is not to say that I expected any enlightenment on possible transmutational links between man and seal, yet the topic was such that I was determined to attend the lecture.

Two papers were to be presented that evening and I arrived at the university buildings as the first talk was beginning. I made as discreet an entrance as I could, walking gingerly up the high wooden steps and sliding in along one of the banks of seats near the back.

The first lecture concerned the archaeological evidence for the supposed site of a battle in the Jacobite uprising. A purposeful young man had laid out his exhibits before him: a sword that was disintegrating away into rust, and a parcel of yellow bones with various cuts and chops. Rubbing his glasses and checking that his notes were in order, he proceeded to hold the audience with a winning exposition of his argument. At his conclusion, the room echoed with measured applause. The company looked satisfied, intellects and curiosity well exercised.

As Dr MacIntyre got up and went to the lectern, a noise of shuffling feet and coughing echoed around the panelled room, the audience become seemingly more aware of the cramped nature of the stalls rising in close tiers around the lecture pit. I could well appreciate, that to those of an academic mind, MacIntyre's line of enquiry must have appeared somewhat fanciful.

He was a short, elderly man, ruddy-faced and with white hair. MacIntyre had no exhibits displayed before him, but giving a broad smile around the room, he launched into his discussion.

MacIntyre's proposal was this: that certain folk tales of the Highlands preserve within them unique historic information predating any written accounts. He cited as evidence the tombs and dwellings recently uncovered at sites that had long been considered as enchanted by the local population. MacIntyre's claim was that such stories of underground fairy houses were in fact the folk memories of ancient Neolithic peoples who had once lived in subterranean dwellings alongside the incoming farming communities.

A tall red-faced man rose to his feet and interrupted.

'And where, sir, is the evidence that these unearthed dwellings have always been connected to local fairy tales?'

'From the local crofters, naturally.'

'Well, naturally, your average crofter is going to tell you anything you wish to hear. Especially if they can turn a penny for themselves by taking gullible visitors on tours of fairy mounds – no doubt making their stories up as they go. This supposition and make believe is surely entirely superfluous to modern history or archaeology.'

'I beg to differ with the good gentleman,' Dr MacIntyre replied evenly, but his face flushed a worryingly deep red for a man of his age. He cleared his throat, found his place and ploughed on.

'I would like now to turn to the legend of the Selkie, the story of a seal man who is able to remove his seal skin on land and so transform into a human – a folk tale common along the entire western seaboard, from Ireland to Orkney.'

Again, more coughing and shuffling from the audience. Two men stood up and left the room. People were losing patience with MacIntyre's whimsy.

MacIntyre paused and bent to reach into a box placed on the floor by the lectern. He took from it a small native artefact: a model of a boat or canoe, approximately ten inches long. He placed this upon the lectern and looked around the room, waiting for complete quiet.

There was a low buzz of voices and I sat forward in my seat to hear better. I for one found his theory of ancient dwellings remembered as fairy houses to be of great merit. I recalled the ancient hearth uncovered beneath the dunes that Maggie had always declared to be haunted by underground sprites.

But as to what MacIntyre could have to say about my seal people, there my imagination failed me.

CHAPTER 36

Ruth

With Susan Montgomery, I learned so much, so fast. That old lizard, for all that he was strong enough to make sure a body kept alive, he was actually quite stupid. With her charts and her tips and techniques, Susan showed me how to start to tame him. Just understanding how those survival reflexes worked helped me to see what was going on and showed me that I could choose how I reacted to a situation.

She helped me tell the story of how such close knowledge of death had carried out a subtle transmology on my body, and she helped me tell the story of the parts of my soul that I had tried to abandon.

And when I told Susan about the little refugee girl in the hallway, she helped me to tell that child's story from the first night I spent in the first foster home; to let her become part of my own history once more.

All those strangers' homes. I got so much wrong, so many misunderstandings. Meeting the woman in her hairnet in the middle of the night when I tried to creep downstairs and put my wet sheets in the washing machine. The bowl of Bird's instant trifle, its hundreds and thousands melting into the fake cream, fairground lights drowned in rain. He said, 'Eat it, we're not made of money.' He held the spoon to my chin. I bit his hand.

The social worker took me to the girls' home, after that last foster home failed to work out. Terry, the house father, showed us round. The social worker kept saying, 'This is nice, isn't it?' We stood in a bedroom. It was crammed with old beds. Every piece of ramshackle furniture had been painted over with white gloss: the wooden headboards, the iron bedsteads like hospital beds; the rickety side cupboards. There were gritty bits in the paint. All the usual bedroom clutter was there – hairbrushes, blouses hanging over the backs of chairs, posters on the walls – but there were too many beds, too much of everything.

We stopped by a bed pushed into a bay window. 'You've got a bed with your own window,' said Carole, the house mother. I sat on the bed with my coat and my bag on my knee and waited while they talked, ran my hands over the thin cotton cover. It looked pale and washed-out. I heard the crackling of gravel in the driveway outside, and saw a van drive up. With the slamming of doors, girls started to jump out.

'They're back,' said Terry.

The grown-ups drifted to the door, talking.

'Well, come on then,' said Terry.

In the kitchen I met the other girls. They were all about two years older than me and wore dishevelled school uniforms. I thought their faces were closed or sort of slapped-looking, like something bad had just happened and they had to rush off and sort it out. They grabbed at the biscuits, took the mugs of tea and left.

I went out into the gardens and walked around. There was no one else out there. I went right up to the top lawns, and found a stone birdbath in the middle of a flowerbed covered over by creeping grass. You could see it would have been a grand garden once, but now it was rubbed away by the thick blanket of dead grass. It was getting cold, my breath like smoke in the air, a glimmer of frost hardening in the shadows.

In the kitchen, Carole was ripping open packets of fish fingers and lining them up under the biggest grill pan I'd ever seen.

'Here,' she said, and I began helping her to open the cold boxes and lay out the rows of frozen sticks. They were covered in knobbly orange breadcrumbs and dusted with frost. She got out a red washing-up bowl from a cupboard, poured in four pints of milk and began ripping open packets of Butterscotch Instant Whip. She let me hold the mixer and I watched the streams of yellow dust make a milkshake, then thicken into a bubbly froth. She stuck in a finger, licked it and made a naughty face, then nodded at the bowl. So I did the same.

Two girls came in and began laying the table with metal beakers and plates, slinging them down with a clattering noise, but Carole didn't seem to notice or mind. She stood at the grill turning the fish fingers and watching a huge pot of frozen peas. She was tall with a long face and long hands, and so calm. A faraway smile as if she was half in a dream. I practised saying 'Mum' to her in my head.

After a few days, I noticed that no one ever did say 'Mum' and 'Dad' to them. Carole was so serene and gliding, loving her was a bit like trying to love a tree, or a huge cloud passing by in the sky. Terry was more straightforward: he didn't like kids — except for the older girls. He let them steal cigarettes from him, giggled with them while they smoked, but mostly he was irritated about something, especially if you knocked on the door of their flat in the evening. Then you'd get a blast of the TV, a vinegary smell of beer on his breath, his arm holding the door ready to shut it.

One chair, one bed, one side cupboard. A heavy stone on my chest as I waited for sleep in the dark, listening to the noises of so many girls coughing, their snores.

A year or so later, Terry began to tease me, pay me attention, bring me little treats. He'd ask me round to the flat when Carole was out. We'd have crisps in front of a video. I couldn't believe my luck. Somebody really liked me, really understood me.

If you ever told, he said, he'd make you disappear. He'd done it before, he said. The girls who had run away, not all of them had gone to London. He knew where they were, he told me, as he stopped the car next to a wood, putting out his cigarette.

Where do you go when you're the sort of person anything can happen to and no one cares? The sort of person where just thinking about her makes you melt with shame.

Sometimes, as I talked to Susan, it made me so angry, the loneliness that child had lived through, and sometimes the sadness she carried was all but unbearable, but I told her story. I told all of it. There were some things that went on at the girls' home that, even as I spoke them, I still couldn't believe they had really happened. And as I sat recounting those days to Susan, I could have stood up and gone out and killed Terry — for the things he did, for all that he stole.

It was hard, really hard, but gathering up all that had happened to that angry teenage girl was a way of giving her back her dignity.

One night, I dreamt about a girl. She was waiting outside on the machair grass, the wind blowing her hair. I went outside and took the child's hand. She looked up at me, hesitated, and then we came home together, walking into the hallway.

When I woke, the sun was bright through the curtains, the sound outside of Michael up and digging the garden, the crunch of a spade turning the soil. I remembered, this was how it used to be, before, to wake up and feel this excitement at the start of a new day.

It was time to start talking to Michael. From the first moment I met Michael in the warm damp of the laundromat, I'd feared that once he really knew me, he'd walk away. For him, I'd worked and vowed, daily, to be a better person.

I made my confession to Michael. I told him who I really was, the story of the lizard girl with the claws and rages. I told him about that small ghost, wandering lost in the hallway of our home like a refugee; how she'd stood her ground, made me listen to her story. I told him about the years in the home.

He listened. Then he was angry and upset. I watched the hurt of those years go out and claim another victim, thought how wrong I had been to tell him everything. And then, he didn't turn away.

'But I think I see now, what you're saying, what it must be like,' he told me, nodding. And then, fierce now, 'We're going to get through this, Ruth; together.'

He responded with such love, with so many small kindnesses. By then I was severely weighed down by the rounded bulge of my middle. The skin of my belly was silvery with rivers of stretch marks, my ankles like pale dough. During those weeks while I was working with Dr Montgomery, while we were waiting for the baby to arrive, Michael did a hundred kind things, and then a hundred more: bringing me cups of tea in bed; cooking meals; getting the baby's room ready; listening; talking. I don't think I'd ever really understood who Michael was till those weeks, his kindness and tenderness.

It wasn't a perfect cure, talking to Susan. She was keen to work on what she called a 'spirit of bitterness'. I found it hard to understand what she wanted me to do. Yes, I was angry with Mum, for the mess she left behind, for the way she had chosen to abandon me. But I didn't see how it could help to pretend I wasn't angry with her.

'But why not try and think about how your mum did care about you? She must have done really,' Michael said when we talked about the impasse I'd reached with Susan. He got into bed beside me, leaned his cheek against my belly. I sighed and moved him away with my hand.

'She didn't care enough to stick around though, did she? I can see it, Michael. I can see what Susan is asking. You know, look on the bright side, but if I let go of that anger, then she's won. I don't count.

How can I live like that?' I switched off my bedside lamp and rolled over, wrapped in the duvet.

I thought of the yellowing scrap of paper that was still on the dressing table. It was the telephone number that I'd finally got round to collecting from Christine MacAulay. I hadn't managed to call whoever it was. I think it was part of how angry I was with Mum that I couldn't bear to take a step forward towards finding something out, not when she'd chosen to take herself away. I crumpled up that slip of paper. Dropped it in the bin. It would be a dead end anyway.

Later, I found that Michael had fished it out again. He'd tried to flatten it out and had left it lying in front of the mirror like a crumpled reproach.

We got back from Tarbert Co-op late one morning to find a brown paper parcel on the chair in the hall. The handwriting looked like Lachlan's. The postman must have been and left it with Leaf, while Michael and I were out getting things ready for our first actual guests in a few days' time.

'But what if this baby arrives the same time as the guests do?' I'd asked Michael as we all sat at breakfast wondering if we should say yes to their enquiry.

'Don't worry, me and Leaf will be fine holding the fort if the sproggit arrives early,' Jamie chipped in.

I'd rung the people back and accepted their booking, hoping the sound of someone knocking a stepladder over upstairs wasn't going to alert them too much to their status as our first guests.

I carried the parcel through to the sea room and carefully undid the tape. Inside, a ream of yellowed paper tied together by a green cotton ribbon. The title on the front was written in brown copperplate: 'The True History of the Selkie'.

Lachlan had been promising that the book was going to arrive for a couple of weeks now, but you never knew with the ferry mail.

'You'll see, Ruth,' he said over the phone when he called to tell me he'd posted the manuscript, the line from Edinburgh crackly with static as our words travelled along a phone cable deep on the seabed. 'Your Selkie people lived and breathed, as real as you and me.'

So why not, I thought, why not? I was ridiculously excited. I turned the front page, my fingers tingling.

CHAPTER 37

Alexander

Holding on to the sides of his lectern, MacIntyre continued with his lecture, working against a current of murmurs.

'I would like to propose to you this evening, gentlemen, a second example of oral history passed down to us in the form of a legend. I would like to suggest that the Selkie fable, particular to the shores of northern Scotland, in fact holds within it a historical memory of an ancient polar race, a race that travelled in sealskin canoes and from time to time visited our western seaboard.'

He now held up the small skin canoe, no bigger than a toy. In the centre a small wooden figure, his painted eyes eternally patrolling the seas.

'Consider the kayak of Eskimo design. Long and slender, light in the water, and with the superlative seamanship of the polar sailors, it may put to sea in the roughest of weather. But most tellingly, the vessel is made from seal skin; the occupant wears a hooded jacket made from seal skin, so that with the jacket tied fast at the wrists, and the waist securely tied round the opening of the kayak, the seated kayaker is in a completely waterproof condition. It is important to also understand that with long exposure to the water, the skin of the kayak becomes waterlogged and heavy, lying just below the surface of the sea until the boat is dried out again.

'Now imagine how this boatman must appear to a man standing on the shore, a man who has never seen such a craft before. Our observer sees a creature covered from head to waist in seal skin, but with the face of a man. And our observer on the shore sees not legs, but lying slightly beneath the water's surface, a long, tail-shaped appendage appearing to move with the refraction of light on water. Based on all previous knowledge, our shore dweller is observing a seal with a man's face. Or perhaps, as he gazes at the human torso, the long tail-like appendage moving beneath the water, our observer believes that he is seeing a mermaid.'

As MacIntyre spoke, the kayak model continued its journey up and down the rows of benches, and finally came into my hands. I saw then what Ishbel must have seen: her seal skin kayaker, his water-logged craft lying just beneath the shine of the water as they stood and gazed at each other with equal curiosity. I continued to examine the taut seal skin stretched over the tiny wooden frame, the small figure seated within, and I saw her Selkie man, smooth-skinned and with the Asiatic features of the Eskimo tribes, as he lay half drowned on the beach until Ishbel found him. Ishbel would never before have seen such a face, and as she peeled off his waterlogged seal skins, she would have assumed that she was looking on one of the *sliochd nan ron* – the seal people. But the talk was not yet finished, and I returned my attention to the speaker.

MacIntyre continued. 'So watertight is his apparel, the kayaker is able to submerge beneath the waves, and thus travel some distance before re-emerging. He can, and must, haul his light craft onto a rock from time to time and dry out the skin and so prevent it becoming waterlogged to the point of sinking. He must then launch the vessel back into the water while still seated within it. So as our observer watches the kayaker dive beneath the surf, or rest on rocks inaccessible to man, then slide back into the sea, he must conclude that he is watching the specific antics of seals or of legendary mermaids. And what could be more natural than that the female kayaker, pausing to dry out her canoe on a sea-bound rock, would pull down her hood, shake out her hair and comb it through, the very picture of a mermaid?'

As he spoke, it was as if I were watching all the diverse fragments of my research come together like the pieces of a puzzle. I held the boat before me, staring into the pinprick eyes of the tiny wooden kayaker's face, the figure like some token passed down through generations, and given into my hand so that I might understand my own history.

And yet I was also appalled, because, in the space of a moment, all my theories of a fish man, so publicly researched amid the university halls, had become entirely redundant. I had a strange impulse to cover the item with my coat, deny that I had ever seen it and continue with building my own hypothesis. I heard applause ringing and saw myself stand up to speak at the Linnean Society on my theories of transmutation. But here, in my hands, was the truth I had sought, more humbling and commonplace than I had hoped – and yet how infinitely fascinating, to finally gaze into the face of my own people.

'But our polar kayaker does not always remain upon the sea,' continued MacIntyre, raising his voice above a background of murmuring voices. 'We may well imagine the astonishment of the land population on seeing a seal man arrive on shore, divest himself of his garments, and appear before the observer entirely as a human. And it is always the case, in the Selkie tales, that once the seal man's skin or belt is stolen, then he is helpless to return to his seal state, just as a kayaker whose kayak and seal skin jacket have been confiscated would be unable to return to the sea.'

MacIntyre's voice had risen to a pitch of indignation, appearing to feel greatly for the poor kayaker whose boat and jacket had been stolen. He tugged at the high-knotted cravat round his neck as if it were impeding him. One longed for him to remove the jacket with its overlarge collar and great buttons, which he must have chosen to wear as an item of impressive tailoring, forgetting the likely warmth of the room. He picked up the end of his now unknotted cravat and wiped at his perspiring brow in a way that did not entirely serve his delivery.

'It is a matter of speculation as to when the first kayakers reached our shores. Perhaps some ten thousand years ago, when the ice sheets extended this far south. But such sightings of kayakers believed to be mermaids have been reported even within our own century. Sirs, I give to you this evening the proposition that within our native fireside fairy tales we may find essential historical evidence that is unavailable to us elsewhere. And I give to you, sirs, that in the legend of the Selkie we are hearing an account of a meeting between two cultures; between the Celtic farmers who arrived from the south, and the polar tribes who visited our shores from the north. And I propose, sirs, that in this hall tonight, we may well have among us men descended from such polar ancestors. Yes, the Selkie tale is a folk tale, a mere fairy story, but held within that fable we may find historical truths, about the diverse tribes that make up our great nation.'

MacIntyre ended his lecture, but there was scant applause. The room bristled with hands ready to quiz him.

MacIntyre removed his heavy jacket and in limply rolled shirtsleeves and exposed braces, he began to take questions from the floor, grasping the lectern like some workman to the task.

A belligerent student caught his attention and stood up to speak.

'You say a kayak can stay in the water for three days?'

'Yes, until the skin becomes waterlogged.'

'And how many days then would you estimate that it takes for such a kayak to cross from the nearest polar landmass inhabited by Eskimo tribes, which is, I believe, Greenland?'

'It would take approximately eight days from Greenland to the Faeroes.'

'Eight days. And would there be rocks or islands where an Eskimo could dry out his kayak?'

'Not before the Faeroes.'

'I see. So by your own account, such a journey from the Arctic Circle must be impossible.'

'I agree with you that the feat is an impossibility, for a kayaker travelling from Iceland or Greenland,' replied MacIntyre.

'Then you must admit that your theory of polar kayakers reaching the north of Scotland is unfounded,' the student concluded triumphantly.

'Let me make a further suggestion,' said MacIntyre, 'if you will bear with me for a few minutes longer. It is my belief that our fair and tall Viking ancestors were not the only people to travel down from Norway. The far north of that land is also home to a native polar people of Eskimo type, shorter and dark-haired, who continue with their Stone Age customs of following reindeer herds, building skin tents and wearing skin clothes. They are known as the Sami tribe, sometimes called Finns or Lapps. I would like to postulate that among these Arctic aboriginals there once existed a seafaring branch, who lived on the inaccessible islands along Norway's coast and travelled the seas in seal skin kayaks. It is highly likely, sir, that it was these Sami kayakers who visited our coasts in seal skin canoes, following the same route taken by the Viking longships.'

A second young student stood up, his thumb in his lapel, anxious to make his mark.

'This is a fascinating hypothesis, and one would wish it to be fact, the idea is so appealing, but we must look for empirical evidence. Have any remains been found to prove this race of Sea Sami?'

'Regretfully, none. It is the case that their fragile culture seems to have become extinct, and with it any artefacts. There were continued sightings over the turn of the last century, but sadly, in modern times, such reports have dwindled to one mermaid sighting in Benbecula.'

'Then has anyone produced an example of a skin kayak, as used specifically by a member of the Norwegian races?'

'To this date, no. There remains to us only the anecdotal evidence taken from the folk tales of seal men and mermaids.'

'Then where is the archaeological evidence for your theory, sir? The empirical methodology? What you offer, though very entertaining, is no more than a patchwork of suppositions – a fairy story.'

Laughter around the room.

'It is my prediction that we may yet find a kayak where the struts are constructed, not from the whalebone used by Eskimo craftsmen, but from northern pinewood. But, yes, you are right: at present, my only proof comes from the legends themselves, and from the descendants of the *sliochd nan ron*, who unshakeably believe themselves to be the people of the sea.'

There were no more questions. MacIntyre gathered his papers, visibly upset by such a hostile response. As the audience began to disperse, I left my seat and took the little kayak model back to its owner.

'Thank you for your most interesting talk.'

Dr MacIntyre looked up. He seemed exhausted by the evening, more like a man who has run a race and pained to keep up than a man engaged in academic debate. He shook my hand, seemingly glad to hear a friendly note in what must have been a horrible evening. He had a large wet patch down the back of his shirt and I feared that he might have over-exerted himself given his advanced years.

'My name is Alexander Ferguson. I found your talk fascinating. My grandmother was a McOdrum and always claimed to be a descendant of one of the seal people.'

MacIntyre kept shaking my hand, staring into my face with narrowed eyes. 'Well, I can see it in the set of your eyes and your cheekbones. Have you ever thought about that when you've looked at yourself in a mirror?'

'Now you mention it, I suppose there was a cast to my mother's face that some praised as an exotic type of beauty. Although she always bemoaned her looks, despairing because her hair would never keep its curls.'

'Ah, well, the Eskimo and Asiatic have a different kind of hair, and the children are never born with hair that curls. I must say, I am delighted to make your acquaintance. It's a nice change to meet a believer.'

'Sir, I must tell you that I have been searching for the creature that lies behind the Selkie and mermaid myths for some time. I cannot thank you enough for your most enlightening lecture. The only smart for me is that I did not arrive at this revelation by myself.'

'We all progress on the theories of others, my friend; no one does these things alone. But sadly for me, I can go no further without finding some kind of archaeological evidence.'

He shook his head and began to pack the kayak model away in its box.

'Dr MacIntyre, forgive me if I am mistaken in a way that may cause you to hope unduly, but I think I might know where one can find just the proof that you are seeking, right here in Edinburgh.'

I did, I am ashamed to admit it, hesitate a moment before making this offer; for doing so was to hammer in the final nail in my now discredited hopes of discovering some fresh link in the transmutation of species. It was a sore blow to my pride, to watch the intricate scaffold of my theories of men adapted to the sea, all collapsed in a moment. I prickled to think of the hours spent, the notebooks filled, the volumes purchased and read – and then to be given the answer without the least sweat from my brow, in MacIntyre's lecture.

At Dr MacIntyre's insistence, I agreed to continue our discussion and accompanied him back to his lodgings. We made our way to a tenement in a cobbled wynd that ran under a bridge supporting a row of shops near to Princes Street. I saw little of comfortable living in his narrow rooms, piled as they were with documents and books, and removed a plate with the remains of sardine bones from a pile of papers, and then removed the papers before I might sit down on a chair.

We passed a convivial evening sharing our discoveries, and it was very late when we found his half bottle of Talisker empty.

As I left down the winding staircase of MacIntyre's tenement, my heart contracted to reflect on the narrowing down of a life; the intransigent obsessions, the neglected career, the block of cheese wrapped in greaseproof paper, a lonely supper in a meagre room.

And I saw mapped before me, the small parameters of my own life to come.

I must confess that I pressed Carfax to allow us to view the museum storerooms most urgently. He was nonplussed by my gabbled stories of historical facts enfolded within folk tales, but conceded that we might visit his museum attics that same afternoon.

My intention was to locate the canoe that I had seen removed for storage some months before, for I recalled – though it had seemed to me nothing unusual at the time – that when the kayak was dropped, the tear to its skin had revealed an inner strut made not from white whalebone but from a type of dark-stained wood.

The workmen sent to aid us in searching through the dusty mansards were all for discouraging us from ever setting eyes on the object, but with a donation towards their evening beer, they gained courage. After an hour or so displacing boxes, we found, hidden behind a wall of trunks and covered over by dustsheets, the very article.

It was a remarkably shallow craft, truly no more than the height of a man's pelvis, a long, flattened sheath tapering upwards to a point at each end. It was covered over in thin hide darkened to the colour of ancient parchment. In the centre was a hooped opening with a series of holes in the rim where one might lash the seaman's jacket tight to the boat. MacIntyre paused and then knelt down in front of the craft like a hungry man presented with a good dinner and ran his hands along the smooth wooden laths inside the craft. After what seemed a considerable time, he sprang up again, dusting off his hands and looking delighted.

'It is as you said, a kayak that is supported not with whalebone, but with struts made from some type of wood.'

We carried it into the dusty light of the attic windows to better examine it.

'I'd say that's pine, from the way the wood knots and the leak of resin there,' he continued, tipping the craft to let the light reach inside, 'but it is hard to find pine that's hard and dense enough to cut into such lathe-thin pieces. This wood has surely been taken from a tree that grew slowly, in a cold climate, high up in the mountains – exactly the type of tree you would find along the mountainous coasts of Norway. Alexander, my sharp-eyed friend, I do believe that this is the evidence I have been seeking for our Sami kayaker.'

'There's a box here,' called out the young lad apprenticed to the workmen. 'The label says it goes with the little boat. Shall I drag it over?'

'No, we don't drag priceless relics about the floor,' remonstrated his elder. 'We lift it carefully, two of us together, and we carry it over, respectfully, like this.'

The box contained several artefacts of Eskimo origin, not connected to the boat, but demonstrating how a man might survive in the cold of the northern seas. We found luxurious seal skin jackets and mittens, cream-coloured carvings of seals made to fit round a spear and so support the weight of it in the hand, a leather bag for water.

Wrapped in layers of tissue paper was another Eskimo jacket, made of a material so light and flimsy that I doubted it had ever been worn at sea.

On seeing it, MacIntyre let out a delighted gasp.

'A ghost jacket!' he cried out. 'I have heard of such a thing, but never seen one.'

He came over and took it from my hands, holding it up to the window. It was a garment made more of light than of material; thin as tissue paper, yellowed by time, it seemed the empty chrysalis of the man who once inhabited it.

I rubbed the silky stuff a little. The garment was constructed in narrow bands, held together by rows of minute stitches.

'But surely the water would have penetrated the stitching?'

'It may appear so,' MacIntyre replied, 'but once the garment is damp, the thread expands and becomes fully watertight. And you see, this delicate hide is in fact seal gut, the most impermeable material known to man. Once the string round the base of the jacket is secured to the kayak opening, the man inside becomes impervious to the sea. Your own ancestor would have arrived wearing a jacket very like this, Alexander.'

'There's another piece here, sir,' called out the younger man, who was now investigating the contents of a second box.

'You get out of there,' the older workman scolded him, as the boy held up a long silk funnel with its tapered end sewed shut.

I followed MacIntyre to investigate the article. This garment was also constructed from transparent strips of seal gut and sewn together with the neatest of stitches.

'Did you not tell me, Alexander, that you longed to have seen the little mermaid at Benbecula, to understand what it was the people there so earnestly believed was a woman that was half fish? See here, my friend, this is the companion to the jacket, worn inside the craft to keep the damp off the legs. Your poor wee mermaid, parted from her canoe, was most probably found on the beach with her legs encased in just such a cover. To the crofters, it must have appeared exactly like a smooth fish tail.'

'So my mermaid was a little kayaker, a very long way from her northern home. I never considered it before, but there must surely have been people who waited for her return. How sad to think that they would never have known what became of her.'

The light was beginning to fade and we were forced to watch reluctantly as the artefacts were packed away. It had been a long afternoon and I was beginning to feel fatigued by that airless and dusty place, my head pounding. We went outside to rejoin the cold autumn air.

'You do realise, MacIntyre, what a sore blow this is to my pride, to have all my theories swept off the table so thoroughly. I had dreamed of how I would stand as you did and astonish my audience with my demonstration of man evolving back into a fish, but it is clear to me now that I shall not be receiving any congratulatory letter from Mr Darwin.'

'I am sorry to have caused you some discomfort.'

'No, you have given me what I sought: you have given me the truth about who I am, and an entire family of ancestors. I am truly happy to have met you.'

'You have done a great deal of research into sightings of the sea people and the folk myths around them. I have come to it from the other direction, from my theories of kayaks and Arctic customs. Why don't we put it all together into one paper, or even a book perhaps? It seems to me that you know the right people, Alexander, when it comes to getting the university to publish.'

'If I have a few friends in the university, then I am happy to put them at your service. Let us see what we may achieve together in this matter.'

CHAPTER 38

Ruth

Three weeks till the baby was due. I was filled with a surge of energy and a mania for cleaning – a nesting instinct, Shona called it when she came by to drop off some good-as-new baby clothes.

I took the tiny nighties and knitted jackets up to the bedroom chest. Next to it, a Moses basket was set up on a table near the bed. I'd cleaned the room from top to bottom, but the scrap of paper was somehow still there, weighted down on the windowsill by a collection of shells: a white limpet scoured down to bone, a worn mussel shell with wintery lines of blue like a pale sky.

'But I thought you would have contacted her weeks ago,' Christine had said when I bumped into her in the Co-op in Tarbert earlier in the week. 'You remember her, the lady who's been trying to trace a cousin that moved to London and suddenly stopped writing – a lady who had a little girl who'd be about your age now. She so wants to meet you, Ruth. Call her, why don't you?'

I was taking a pile of washing downstairs anyway, so I picked up the paper and took it with me, down to the phone in the hallway. I dialled the number more in a spirit of tidiness than any hope that I was going to trace some relatives. I listened to the phone ringing somewhere across the water in Uist. It rang for a long time. I was on the point of replacing the receiver when a soft and tentative voice answered.

She was called Sally, Sally Nicolson. For some reason – to put an end to any false hopes she might have – I agreed to meet her at the Harris Hotel in Tarbert.

It was past five o'clock, the agreed time, but she hadn't arrived. The shadows were getting long in the garden outside, a low dazzle from the sun beginning its descent towards Loch Tarbert. I ordered a tray of tea and a plate of rock-hard scones and sat waiting in the chilly conservatory of the Harris Hotel – not the most appealing place, but at least it was quiet. Through the window, a view of overgrown flowerbeds, the valiant fuchsia bushes making mounds of red flowers, everything else killed off by the wind, as is often the case so far north.

A short, heavy-set woman came into the conservatory. I saw a cheerful face, a perm tousled by the wind as if she might well have come up on the ferry from Lochboisdale. I noted the island way of plain dressing: tan stockings and a wool skirt with a forgettable cardy.

She came straight over and asked if I was Ruth, took my hand in both of hers.

She pressed my hands so intently that I realised that she'd already decided she recognised something in my face. I was worried how I was going to put her off if she was wrong, or, worse, if she was a bit of a crackpot. She organised the tea things in a way that made me feel uncomfortable – motherly, intrusive.

After some stilted conversation, rather guarded on my part, she opened the clasp of her large handbag and pulled out a frayed envelope. She produced a jumbled handful of black and white snaps.

The first one showed two young women in front of a low, white-washed cottage: one plump with curly hair tipped up by the wind, the other a little taller. That girl was my height, slim, her long black hair held back by a scarf. I felt tears sliding down my face. I brushed them flat. I'd never seen a picture of Mum looking so young.

'Where was the picture taken?' I asked. Sally produced an ironed handkerchief and I dried my cheeks. The fabric had the faded smell of clothes in a drawer.

'In front of Gran's cottage. Your mum told you that she was brought up by Gran?'

I don't remember.

'Oh. Well, her dad passed away when she was twelve, and her mum passed soon after, so that's where your mum lived. It was a lovely old place, quite dark inside, but cosy with a big fire. Your mum had her own little wooden room built in one end, with one of those old-fashioned box beds with curtains you could pull at night. She loved that house.'

'Where was it?'

'Up at Point of Ness, in Lewis. And here, see, this one is your mum with Gran.' Mum looked about eighteen in that one. She was standing outside the door of a cottage, next to an elderly lady seated at a spinning wheel.

'She liked to sit out in summer, Gran. The light was better. She was a weaver. You could hear the loom clacking away as you went up the path. You know she taught your mum?'

I shook my head again.

She sighed. 'That face, Ruth. You look so like your mother.'

I swallowed, determined not to cry again, keep a clear head.

'This is me and your mum, the first day we started work in Stornoway at the department store. Oh, it was a big deal, moving to the town like that. We had lodgings in the main street, and we had money to spend. We were the bees knees, went to all the dances in the church hall, and that's where she met your father.'

'You knew my father, Sally?'

'Oh yes, of course. He was one of the Stornoway fishermen, very handsome, and charming with it. More than he'd any business to be. And she fell so in love, you see.'

'So why did they split up?'

'He was married. They always knew there could be no future in it; there was no such thing as divorce on the islands then. When she realised you were on the way, she knew she was on her own.'

'He wouldn't help her?'

'She didn't tell him. If she'd told him, he'd have left his wife, and then he'd have had to leave the island. And he was an island man to his bones, worked on the trawlers going out from Stornoway. She knew he'd never be happy anywhere else. But she was desperate to keep you, Ruth, not to go to the girls' home in Inverness and have to give you away. So that's why she took herself off to Oban and worked as a maid in one of the big hotels, for as long as she could, and that's where you were born, in Oban.'

'You were still in touch with her then?'

'Oh yes. I went down to help her when you arrived. I worked in the same hotel as your mother, taking it in turns to look after you. When she got a job in London, in an office, to make a life for you, I came to the station and got you both on the milk train down to Euston at two in the morning – the cheapest ticket, you see.'

Sally stopped and took a moment, swallowing, her eyes swimming and watery.

'I remember seeing you sleeping, seeing you through the window in the dark. Never thought that I wouldn't see you again – till now.'

She reached over and crushed my hand in hers.

'Ruth, if I'd known… if I had known you were on your own, you know I would have come to get you.'

A whole other life flashed by, growing up in the islands, living with Sally.

'I appreciate that. It means a lot. But Sally, there's something about Mum you ought to know. Has Christine told you? The police said that Mum took her own life. I mean, after what she went through, you can understand.'

Sally squeezed my hand tighter in her own large grip.

'Ruth, she loved you. She would never, never have willingly left you.'

'Maybe. But you see, she was on anti-depressants. That's how they came to the suicide verdict.'

'There's no possible way that the woman I knew would take her own life. She must have had some kind of accident, taking a short cut in the dark. Your mother turned her whole life upside down to keep you with her: she would never, never have left you while there was breath in her body.'

'I want to believe you, I do, but...' Something cracked inside my chest then. Sally's handkerchief became a cold and crumpled ball of wetness before I finally stopped blubbing.

'Sally, I haven't asked you this, but do you think my father might still be alive?'

'I'm so sorry, my dear; he passed away. He drowned in a winter storm out in the Atlantic. You would have been only two or three at the time.'

I couldn't speak, trying to unknot the ball of disappointment in my throat.

'But he has a brother, your uncle. He lives in Finsbay still. Alone now since his wife passed on, years back. He builds boats. His name's Lachlan Macleod.'

'Lachlan! Lachlan Macleod? Are you sure, Sally?'

'Absolutely.'

'But we're buying a boat from him. I know him really well.'

'Would you like me to ring him? I'd like to tell him if that would help.'

'No. I think I'd like to tell him, Sally. Though I'm not sure where to start.'

'Ruth, just tell him you're Ellie's daughter. Tell him you've come home. But look, here's me needing to get on the ferry back to Uist. I wish I could stay, but I've got work tomorrow. Will you call me once you've spoken to Lachlan, yes?'

We hugged, a bit clumsily, because she was still a stranger really, and, well, she was a sizeable woman. Not a tall person but plump, a soft face. Insisting again that I keep the pictures of Mum, she gathered up her bags and left for the ferry.

I went to the ladies' and splashed my face with cold water. In the mirror, roadkill, a face red and shiny from crying. I couldn't stop shaking.

I couldn't get it together to drive home. I called Michael. Felt so grateful when he said he'd be there really soon.

I sat down, trying to take it all in. I knew who my father was. I had a sort of cousin, and an uncle – an uncle who was a really nice man.

What would he say when I told him?

I stared out of the window, over towards the shine of the sea loch. I thought of Mum trying to work out what to do, younger than me, expecting a baby and no one but Sally to help her. She must have been so strong to decide to not tell my father; she must have loved him to try and protect him like that. And she must have been so determined to keep me, working so hard to make a life for us together.

I though of Sally's indignant conviction that Mum would never have chosen to take her own life. A stirring of hope: Mum had been on her way home to me, hurrying; that unerring impulse that drove her, to protect the child she loved.

As I looked out at the bay, it came back to me how I used to stare through the window of our flat in London, watching the smoke and the sun rising over the cityscape as Mum brushed my hair in the morning. She used a soft hairbrush and she was very gentle. I shut my eyes. I could almost feel her cool hand, smoothing my hair back from my forehead. She would sing in time to the brushstrokes while my head rocked back a little with each stroke. I didn't know what the words meant exactly, but she sang the same song to me so often, I could reproduce the sounds. I hummed the first notes, tried out that old tune again. And then an odd thing happened in that cold and empty hotel conservatory; I started quietly singing, under my breath, the words coming from some deep place.

I let the coolness of her hand sooth my forehead. I felt the song travel through my lungs and diaphragm, felt it travel down into a tight little world of amniotic fluid and mingled heartbeats, and I placed my hand on the brow of the little hill where my baby was sleeping.

PART TWO

CHAPTER 39

Alexander, 1879

As inspector for Board schools I was allotted a low, whitewashed building at Kilmaluag on the Trotternish peninsula of Skye. One end of the building served as the parish schoolroom, the smaller portion containing my simple accommodation. An elderly lady came early each morning to cook and clean, but so shy was old Jesse that she would slip out and go to her cottage as soon as I came down to eat my breakfast, only returning to finish the housework and set a meal on the stove while I was away teaching the afternoon lessons.

So it was that my meals were necessarily silent and solitary affairs, interrupted only by the rustle of book pages turning, or the crack and spit of an ancient root embedded in a peat brick on the fire. Such was the sparsely provisioned but calm life that I had established. And though remembrance of the hopes and the failures of my earlier days sometimes pierced my heart, I counted myself fortunate to have found an occupation that would meet my daily needs and also allow me to be useful to others.

There were moments however, many moments, when the solitude of that place weighed heavily upon me. Isolated as I was, between the Quiraing mountains that loomed up behind the house, and the grey ocean before, I often felt entirely cut off from mankind. For once the children and the assistants left for their homes on Friday, then scarcely a soul passed on the track before the schoolhouse. I saw company only when I walked down to the morning service at the chapel in Trotternish.

I had lost none of my love for the divine, though I now attended the services more in the spirit of a novice or a supplicant – in spite of my advancing years. For it seemed to me that I now gazed as through a dim glass at my past self, that man so sure and so precise, so confident of the eternal prize, sitting secure in the study that looked out over the machair with its carpets of flowers and the bright sea continuously renewing the white sands.

I saw often, in dreams, that dear place, and dear little Moira; how she would bring in tea, her cap askew, chattering away on every subject as she read her way through the books on my shelves. And it was clear to me, on reflection, that given a different start in life, Moira could have been the equal and more of any of the fine ladies that Fanny once paraded in Edinburgh as a good catch.

Standing in front of the glass propped up on the washstand, it seemed to me that, now, I would be considered a great catch by no one. I saw before me as I fastened my collar, a man approaching the middle of his fifth decade, hair turned to a steely grey, a tightness, perhaps even a bitter twist, to the lips, a weary narrowing of the eyes, the face of a man set in its disappointments. A face, it was true, that did not encourage the children to misbehave, and of this I was glad, since I had lately removed the leather tawse so beloved of small-minded disciplinarians – entirely unneeded among the docile boys and girls who often walked the long miles to school across moor and heathland in bare feet.

I busied myself with preparations for the day ahead, a tour of inspection to three schools on the Knoydart peninsula on the mainland. As I fetched down the ledgers and record books from the shelves, my hand paused for a moment in front of a manuscript wrapped in brown paper, the title in now faded ink: 'A study of the folk stories of the Western Isles: of mermaids, seal men and Finnmen kayakers, by Dr G. MacIntyre and Rev. A. Ferguson'.

Not a single publisher in Edinburgh had wished to take it, not a single academic in the university had been willing to be associated with such a work. Carfax did me the courtesy of being quite candid when I asked him if he might help us in procuring an introduction to the university publishers.

'We would have gone along with you, Alexander, with an open mind, so long as you were examining the physicality of species. But you must see, can you not, that after all the support you have been publicly given, with access to the zoology collection and libraries, for you to be seen branching off into superstitions and fairy tales, well it is only going to cause confusion and harm those supporters of Mr Darwin's theories. You do see that, don't you?'

One by one, my social connections among the eminent scientists of the university fell away, for while it is perfectly acceptable for their wives to know the clergy and invite them to dine, it is not acceptable to know a schoolmaster, except perhaps to nod at him from across the street.

Thus it was that my enquiries into the transmutation of species had lately become a much less grand affair. I found various species of seabirds along the shore, and mice and other small creatures in the heather, and buried the small carcasses in the soil behind my dwelling. After some two or three months, I was able to dig them up, cleaned as they were by small insects, and wash the skeletons in the stream. I thus began to amass a number of items for the children to study and draw. They in turn delighted in bringing me soft-bodied moles, and insects and bones found on the island. Even gruff fathers were known to present me with such prizes as an entire deer backbone, or an antler set scoured to white by the winter weather. I took great solace in the beauty of such structures, and in the collections of bird feathers and butterflies that I stored in trays in my loft. Once a year, I brought them down to the schoolroom and held open house for the crofters, letting them examine the specimens and giving a somewhat simplistic lecture, in which they took a great interest.

Pride of place was always given to the fossils, of which there was an abundant supply from the basalt rocks of Skye. It was a matter of astonishment to the populace that the black toe ends that they picked up on the beach were not, as they termed them, the Devil's toenails, but rather seashells dating back millions of years, now mineralised by their long encasement in rock.

Following a journey of two days, by steam ferry and then on foot, I arrived at the first establishment to be inspected – a small Knoydart school isolated in a remarkably green glen. A storm had recently blown over, and the day was of some brilliance as I neared the village, the sea to my right a vivid gentian, bright as a rolled-out bolt of satin; the hills above, the glowing rust of autumn heather.

The teacher in charge of the school was recorded as a Miss Gallies. During my travels, I had met many such women, plain but unarguably good spinster women, dedicated to their pupils, or, as in many cases, saddened widows in middle age, only too glad to take on teaching duties in return for accommodation and the means to support their offspring.

Arriving at the schoolhouse a little earlier than expected, I found the lady not at home however. I was invited by the servant girl to come in and wait, as her mistress was due to return directly.

I entered a porch lined with bookshelves and was led through to a neat parlour stocked with many more books. Here was a person, I thought, as enamoured with the solace of reading as I was. A well-tended fire burned in the grate, and a white cloth covered a side table set with scones and sandwiches in preparation for my visit. The room afforded all the comforts of a well-run household, the brass fender before the fire shining and a red rug covering polished floorboards.

On the walls were several watercolours of the islands, including a view from my old island that I knew well. From their slightly rudimentary execution, I deemed them to be by the hand of the schoolmistress. There was, inevitably, a desk with a stack of school exercise books, a blotter and inkwell. I stepped over to the desk and could not help noticing with some interest that she appeared to be gathering a collection of island stories.

As there was still no sign of the lady's return, I placed myself by the window to enjoy the landscape, and after a brief time, espied a figure walking along the track towards the house, a slim person in green who walked with elastic agility. As she made her rapid approach towards the house, the lady took off her bonnet, and I saw generously furnished red hair, unsuccessfully tamed by a net, the weight of curls already losing its battle with the wind.

How like Moira she is, I thought, turning from the window, feeling once more the sadness that I had grown accustomed to over the years. I heard the front door open, and stood by the armchair that had been earlier indicated to me by the maid. I heard voices in the hallway, and then the woman appeared in the doorway, and I thought my heart would surely stop beating.

It was Moira! Changed, yes; a woman of some thirty years now, her face sculpted by maturity, but unmistakably and irrevocably my same Moira. The name 'Gallies' on the inspection register had been incorrect by one letter. Moira Gillies stood before me. And I saw from the look of horror on her face that she knew it was me.

'I saw the name on the letter sent to me,' she said, 'but I didn't know. I never thought that it truly might be you. I thought you had taken a parish in Edinburgh. But why are you not a minister any more?'

Yes, the same dear Moira, I thought, as she scolded me. And then

I watched her face cloud, for she, more than anyone, knew why I had left my calling.

'Oh,' was all she said.

For since that terrible day, I had never had occasion to speak to her about what had happened. The last time I saw Moira was the night I rode away from the manse in the farm trap, Katriona sick and covered by blankets, and no one to help care for my suffering burden as we drove down to the bay near Rodel.

My last view of Moira had been her white and tear-marked face, the stained frock she wore and the sweat-braided hair. Maggie Kintail by her side, silent and grim, as I left them to their task and the dark swallowed them up.

I had never asked how they disposed of the earthly remains of that poor infant, and now as Moira walked to the table and turned her back to me to pour the tea, I understood that I would never find the courage to ask.

Moira held out a teacup and I took it from her, the delicate china needing both my hands to prevent it from rattling – my nerves had started to cause a tremor in my hand, oft troublesome of late. She placed a plate furnished with several items beside me, but I had lost my appetite.

She sat down.

'I think you will find all the registers in order for you to inspect,' she told me. 'We begin lessons in the morning at eight thirty.'

'I will come to the school then.'

And I searched for a way into some conversation with some easier topic than my role as purveyor of judgement. She drank her tea. After a brief silence we talked of my lodgings nearby, quite satisfactory, the weather, the beauty of the situation.

There seemed no more to say. We sat listening to the wind play over the chimney, both watched the glow of the peat fire. No words to speak of poor Katriona, who had passed away some three days after she came to her aunt's house. No words to recall all the children, her own flesh and blood, who had slipped from this life and slid into the sea as the Finsbay people crossed the Atlantic to Canada.

Finally, I rose and bade her goodbye.

I walked away from that house with an impression of having left behind me something rare and precious, the very essence of my Moira. In a different time, I thought, if circumstances had been otherwise… And I felt the bitter pulling of my lips into their now familiar set. Not a man I would care to spend time with, I thought, as I saw myself climb the hill to my lodgings; the creased boots that had already done many miles, the tweed jacket and plus fours that served well in all weathers and still had wear remaining in the cloth, but which had worn into the resigned and stretched outline of a man in middle age.

On the morrow I made myself ready and walked down to the schoolhouse before lessons were due to begin. I entered the quiet classroom, which was already warmed by the stove next to the chalk-board. She was at the far end of the schoolroom, standing at some shelves, reaching down a book. She wore a grey and simple dress, a red and grey shawl that added to the brightness of her hair.

All through the morning I watched her, the children eager to please and show off their teacher, sitting up straight, raising their hands en masse in the damp warmth of the parish schoolroom when I questioned them on their maths and scripture. At the end of the morning, the children gone out to play, she stood by her desk, waiting for my verdict.

'Excellent,' I told her. 'You run an admirable and happy school.'

'After the manse was closed up, I walked over to Carmichael's school. He gave me work there. It was he who put me forward for the certificate. I gained top mark that year. So you see, you taught me well.'

I wanted with all my heart to talk more. But I said, 'There is truly nothing to improve here.'

'When will you return?'

'In three years.'

Her face fell.

'That is the normal rate of inspection, but where everything is running so smoothly, I will not need to trouble you again for at least four or five years.'

'I see. Then I have taught them too well.'

'No, it is all as it should be. Goodbye then, Miss Gillies,' I said and we shook hands.

I set off down the track towards my rendezvous with the ferry and then a long walk to the next isolated village. But as I walked on I became aware of what was pressing inside my breast: I had thought that it was my home in the island that I missed so painfully, the white house by the shore, but as I walked further and further away from Moira's cottage I understood that for me, my home was and always would be where my Moira was.

The rain came in off the sea two miles outside the village and I arrived at the next lodging with raw, cold lungs and aching limbs. The bed sheets that night seemed to freeze my skin, and in the morning my throat had swollen to a constricted mass where only the smallest sips of water could pass. By the time of my return to my own dwelling in Kilmaluag, I was barely able to walk into the house. I collapsed upon my bed until old Jesse found me there the next day, and sent for the doctor.

It was a long illness, and the end of it left me low in my solitude. It was at this time that I began my habit of writing letters to Moira. I did not post these letters, or intend to ever post them, but it was a great release to my soul to pour out my every last thought and feeling to her. Each letter I sealed and addressed, and placed in a growing stack upon the desk. Knowing that my missives would never be seen by her eyes, I did not spare my own sad history. It was my confessional, to spell out all my failings in those pages.

I stayed up late, writing, one night, until the fire burned out, allowing the chill to take hold again. I recall that I lay in bed in fever and despair for a long time, and as I lay there alone for such long hours in the dark, I finally gave up all hope, let every last thing fall from my hands and let the dark universe chill me with its senseless winds. I thought, I will let it come now, I will do the thing that I have feared to do for so long, I will say to myself that there is no God in this world, no divine love that will hold us in the dark. For if there is a God, nothing I can do can reach him.

I waited. Only the darkness answered me.

I think I woke at three, perhaps four, into a cold blackness, listening to the wind rising bleakly over the Quiraing mountains. I opened my eyes on a void without a heart.

It came then, without warning. It came without reason, the room suffused with such comfort and companionship.

You are not alone.

It was some days before I came out of my fevers, but even when my mind returned to clarity, that sudden, intense moment of tryst stayed in my soul. A seed of metal remained, taken from the fire after all had burned away, small to the eye, but solid and dense and true, for a sweetness had kept vigil by me, would not leave me.

And what also became clear to me, as I got up and started to wash, was that the room had been cared for and tidied while I lay sick – the work of dear old Jesse. I sat in the chair by the fire, experiencing a strange sensation of peacefulness, of the limbs relaxing after a long time running.

And then I saw that all the letters were gone from my desk.

'Oh, don't you worry,' Jesse told me when I asked her. 'I put those in the post for you, sir, and there's no hurry to pay me for the stamps.'

My dismay at this information may well be imagined. I burned with shame for several long minutes as I recalled all I had written in those pages, a confessional never meant for any human eyes.

In the last of my letters I had asked Moira if she would ever consent to be my wife. I stood rooted to the spot, unable to move or speak, knowing that this letter would now be in Moira's hands.

I had a reckless moment of hope then, a moment of madness, hoping that she would respond favourably to my letter, but it came as no surprise to me when Moira did not reply.

CHAPTER 40

Alexander

I did not regain full health for some time. Moving from the bed to the chair next to the fire exhausted me. I was only thankful that Moira had had the kindness to ignore my letters. I shuddered with embarrassment to think how she must have felt as she read through my uncensored outpourings and confessions, and how she must have viewed my entreaties that she agree to be my wife. My only consolation was that she was spared from seeing a man so finished in body and mind.

Jesse was persistent in making me her good broth, and my body decided to proceed with its business of healing itself; in time, therefore, I was once more walking along the beach under an expansive blue sky. At the line of surf I espied a glistening black head rise up out of the water and then disappear. It was a small seal. It was hard to keep in sight, as the creature slipped behind a roll of white wave, then reappeared yards away. I wondered that the seal stayed so close to the shore and did not flee. It was the size of a small child, its head sideways, one black flipper cutting the rolling waves, enjoying the play of the surf. I followed the pup for half a mile as it swam along the shoreline, and when I could follow it no more, I stood exhilarated by this encounter.

I turned back up the long and empty beach, the sky stretching out to the horizon, and breathed deeply and easily in the healing air.

Then I saw that the landscape was not empty. Someone was walking up by the machair above the dunes in the distance, a shawl billowing up round her shoulders. For a moment, I was annoyed that the purity of the land should have to be shared with another person, and then I stood very still. There was something familiar about the gait of that figure, a sense of purpose about her walk as she moved towards me. I laughed at myself, alone and so prone to no end of fanciful imaginings, my head still weak from the fevers.

The figure continued to walk towards me and then raised an arm and waved. I strained my eyes to see if it were perhaps old Jesse, come to get me out of the breeze. But this was a slight and nimble figure, and no one I recognised from the island. The sun caught the woman's shawl, a rich amber colour. Her hair, the same hue, was gathered up on top of her head but beginning to stream out in the wind. My heart started to race; I walked slowly forward and saw Moira walking towards me.

I surely could not have been more surprised if I had seen the Lord Jesus Christ walk across the beach and take my hands, nor more overjoyed. Her own small hands were cold but alive and her thumbs worked against the skin of my hands as if chaffing them back into life. Tendrils of hair were streaming across her eyes that she must brush away with her fine-boned hand. I saw her freckled cheeks, the kind concern in her eyes.

I found myself smiling at her in great joy, she smiling back with those grey eyes and their lights of amber. I took the shawl that was wrapped round her and pulled her close against my coat and held her. She put her head against my chest and sighed, stayed there, quietly. The wind sang across my ears as I looked down at that dear head.

'Dear Moira,' I said. The wisps of her hair tickled around my face. She looked up directly into my eyes.

'I have come to answer your letter. I wanted to be here with you when I told you that when I say I will be your wife, then I mean it. You have written such sad and despairing letters.'

'You would marry me?'

I looked at her steady eyes, the fine lines at their corners as she smiled at me.

'Yes. Of course.' She took my hand, put it against her cheek. 'But you must come into the warm. You're quite frozen. Let's walk back to the house.'

We walked up the beach. She put her arm through mine, leaning in against the wind. But I stopped, moved to stand in front of her, still holding her hand.

'Are you sure, Moira? So much has happened. I am no longer the man you remember, the boy you remember.'

'You are the man I love,' she said. 'That is how it is.'

We walked on in silence and great happiness. How strange it was to unfasten the front door and have Moira enter there, watch her walk round the table and the chairs by the fire, pick up my shells from the shore along the mantelpiece, and smile at everything and examine it as if she were reading the story of my life in the intervening years. She ran her hand along the book spines on the shelves, stopping to greet an old friend as she took it down to read a little.

I watched her and shook my head, for it seemed to me so very right and comfortable to have Moira there in the room.

'I cannot think how it is that I should be so blessed, that you should decide you could love me.'

She shut the book. 'Alexander, I have loved you from the moment I saw you.' She walked over to me and put her slim hands each side of my face, stood on tiptoe, and that was the first time that Moira kissed me.

CHAPTER 41

Ruth, 1996

I am standing in the shower, still half asleep, letting the water run over my body. The morning light is white and peaceful through the silvery drops on the shower screen, and the faint outlines of older drops visible beneath them. I am standing and letting the last of the soap run off, relaxed with that feeling of well-being that you get from water, from swimming or from standing in a long, hot shower.

I watch my hands turning off the taps. They are pale and new-looking hands, solid and capable. I watch them carry on getting the towel almost as if they have their own agenda, their own good sense.

And it strikes me, but of course, they always did have their own agenda. My hands and my body always remembered. They were living my real life, getting on with what was really happening, while I was trying to live the life I thought I had. They remembered all the days I forgot, when I couldn't see how I had died and come back again, a body and a soul for ever changed by fear.

I look at those poor white dumb things and I think, It's okay now. I know you. I know our story. I wrap the towel round my shoulders, open the shower door and emerge into the chilly room. I balance on one leg, then the other, getting dry, rubbing down my skin.

I am thirty-three years old and I am slightly overweight for a smallish person. I have long black hair, a few grey hairs on one side at the front. I love chocolate almonds and I hate the taste of nougat. I have post-traumatic stress disorder and my body can go from nought to sixty in panic for no good reason; when my palms sweat and my heart begins to gallop, when I feel like I have to run or fight, then I know I must stand and slowly let it all stop. I wait for the fear to finish drowning me, and then I start to breathe, start to think again.

And I say, Poor old hands and brain, it's okay now. We are safe. Then we remember our story, how we came to be here, and we are tired, but we are okay. I can choose how my days will turn out now – and my days are good.

I pull on my clothes, twist my hair into a pleat, pin it up still damp.

In the kitchen Michael is in his shorts and T-shirt, not showered yet, his fair hair tousled by sleep. Euan at four has that same mop of curls, only much fairer after a summer spent outdoors in the sun.

Euan has three tractors lined up in front of his porridge, multi-tasking, eating while making tractor noises and re-parking them round the bowl.

Emily – our little surprise arrival sixth months ago – is in her highchair. She is sitting with her tiny hands one each side of a bowl of baby porridge, clenching and unclenching her fists. Michael is spooning it slowly into her mouth, shaving it off as they go.

I take over from Michael. He puts a mug of coffee beside me as he goes to shower. Emily keeps her mouth open while we change shifts and gives a shudder of happiness when she sees me carry on with the gloop. As the spoon travels towards her, she fastens on it and her eyes turn up and look at me, centre on my face.

The porridge finally all gone, I clean her cheeks and chin and undo the highchair strap, lift her small, heavy weight and balance her against my shoulder. She smells of damp skin and oatmeal and gently bangs her cheek against my chin as she wobbles.

She sees a bird go past the window and lifts her arm. I carry her over and we stand at the back door, looking at the sparrows fussing and hopping in the fuchsia bushes outside. I balance and rock her as we watch them, and think, I can do this. I can do this because I changed.

My body grew and swelled and tore and I became a new creature, a mother. And I saw that all my old life stopped then. It was up to me, to choose to let go, because me and my hands, we had to stop asking and we had to start giving; we had to stop fighting and start holding instead.

I am thirty-three years old. I have black hair. I am slightly overweight and I had a grotty childhood. I like chocolate and I know no one is coming back from those days to say sorry for what happened. But I believe there's a sweetness and a kindness in this world that infuses the morning with yellow sunlight, and I am married to a man who is kind and loving. And I don't know how I got so lucky. I am thirty-three years old and I am the mother of Emily and Euan and I am so, so lucky.

The door goes. Leaf arrives, comes into the kitchen and grabs an apron from the back of the door. 'Hi, sweetie,' she says, blowing a kiss at Emily. She grabs a hug from Euan and goes through to the main kitchen to begin cooking the breakfasts. Leaf has become the chef for the guesthouse and the evening restaurant we now run together, her lentil soups and home-made bread and cheese soufflés always bringing the Sea House guests back for more. I hear her moving quickly around the kitchen, sliding a CD into the player, cracking eggs, swooshing them into the pan of hot oil in time to a fiddle and a bodhran beat. She sings along in a phonetic approximation of Gaelic that Angus John tells me is actually rather good.

I hear guests moving around upstairs, water running in the showers. At the moment, we've got a group of sixteen teenagers from Lanarkshire.

A toot from a car outside and Euan jumps off his chair. Maire, Donald Allan's wife, drops by every other morning to take Euan to the little school, a two-room building on a spit of blond dunes and sandy machair that stretches halfway out into the Seilebost estuary – land that looks far too fragile to withstand the winter storms, but it does, year after year. I put his snack in his backpack. Euan adds a tractor. We go out to the car and he climbs in the back, chatting away in Gaelic to his best friend, Kirsty. I kiss him, fasten his seatbelt and wave to him until they are out of sight.

The thing that has taken longest for me to cope with has been letting the kids take those small daily risks, letting them out of my sight. But I am working on it, working out the difference between a real risk and a feeling of panic. The car is gone and I turn and go into the house.

Michael has the back carrier ready for Emily. She's going with him and eight of the kids for a hike to Hushinish. She loves sailing along on Daddy's back with the tassel on her hat swinging from her little head.

I hurriedly finish my coffee, kiss Emily and Michael, and head out to get ready for the morning.

Down at the new shed that we built at the bottom of Angus John's croft, on a piece of land he sold to us, I unbolt the doors and open them up onto the sand. Ten kayaks in blues and reds sit on a rack under the roof, paddles fixed up against the wall, and beneath them, the larger dinghy. Donald Allan arrives and we start to pull the dinghy out. Once the kids are down, I get them to help me unload the kayaks, check they all know what to do, a little talk on safety, and then we go down to the water. They've had a good two weeks to get used to the kayaks, so today we are going to do a slightly longer trip.

I lead on the way out, as we start to glide round the peninsula between the shore and the island of Taransay across the sound. Nothing but the slap of the paddles dipping, the rocking waves like a dance partner as we measure the pull and swing of the water. Beneath us, the intense glassy turquoise and purples of the sea as we cross over white sand and dark rocks, heading out to deeper water. Donald Allan cuts the motor on the dinghy, lets it track in the currents, and we travel along in silence, the kids awed to be afloat on the sea, the surface of light melting into a view of deep water and caves of shadow.

I think of Michael. He'll be walking out towards Hushinish Point in the distance in front of us, above the beaches where Ishbel first saw her man gliding along the surface of the sea.

And I think of my mother's Selkie ancestor now as I paddle, pulling her skin boat up the sands, pulling off her seal skin jacket, and shaking out her long black hair. The Selkie woman walks up the beach, and as she does, a woman in a yellow dress with long sleeves and a floaty skirt waits for her, wind fanning out the long black hair that is tied off her face with a chiffon band. I see how they talk together as they go. Sometimes they stop, shade their eyes and wave at me, just to check I'm all right.

Before we turn round to go back, Donald Allan cuts the motor again while the kayaks make a detour into a cave beneath the cliffs, a silent space that belongs only to the clip-clopping of the sea. A mineral light, blue and vivid green, shines up from the water, throwing bright nets over the roof. Blooms of red seaweed and bunches of purple mussel beds, hushed by the quiet echo.

'It's beautiful,' they say.

A tall boy with a stud through his lip, shaved eyebrows and scars on his wrists, his face thin and hungry, hangs there on the water, rocking. 'Wow,' he says, 'you'd never believe it, would you?'

At seven we are due in Stornoway at the An Lanntair Arts Centre. The Hebridean summer festival is quite a big thing now, and this year the centre is holding a multi-media presentation: 'The Selkie, based on a book by Rev. Alexander Ferguson and Dr Gordon MacIntyre'.

When my uncle, Lachlan Macleod, tracked down Alexander Ferguson's manuscript, it seemed incredible that the book had never been published so I approached Edinburgh University to see if they could suggest what we might do with it. They seized on the pages immediately and were very keen to publish it under the university's name.

A few months after that, the director of the summer festival approached us. He'd seen the manuscript and wanted to present the story of the Selkie and the mermaid. The Glasgow schools of music and art were going to take part, and there would be dancers and an audio-visual presentation with a huge screen at the back of the stage.

The An Lanntair Arts Centre is a lovely modern building with a large glass atrium. Sally and Lachlan are already there, Lachlan dapper in a tweed overcoat as he looks at one of the photos in the exhibition. Euan runs up to him and grabs his knees and Lachlan swings him up in the air. Lachlan kisses my cheek, shakes Michael's hand and then gives us a tour of the exhibition as if he personally organised it, Sally following behind and unwrapping a toffee for Euan.

It's a small exhibition about Alexander and his co-author Mac-Intyre's work on Selkies and Samis. The manuscript is open in a glass case, with beautiful illustrations of the Ishbel story, done by Alexander's wife, Moira.

Euan runs over to a tall glass case containing a delicate ghost jacket on loan from the Edinburgh museum, and presses his hands and face to the glass. Back lit, arms spread out, the jacket is made of material so fine it seems transparent.

The bell for the performance sounds.

The theatre auditorium is packed, everyone we know and everyone we don't know from the island seems to have turned out. Angus John, unrecognisable in a dark suit, flashes us a smile; he has put his teeth in for the occasion.

The auditorium goes dark. The screen across the back of the stage lights up, a grey seascape of moving waves. A booming low note fills the hall, and a single voice starts to sing above it in Gaelic, the song of the Sula Skerrie seal man.

Emily grasps my hair in one of her fists and tests if it is well attached. By the watery light of the seascape, I untangle her fingers, kiss the top of her head and smile as I think of the last little secret that Christine MacAulay managed to uncover in her sleuthing through census lists.

CHAPTER 42

Edinburgh, 1862

Every so often the gaslights in the wall sconces gave an almost imper-
ceptible flutter, minute winds troubling the gas flame as if each globe
contained its own climate. Fanny looked up from her sewing. She was
used to the fluctuations in Edinburgh's gas supply, but this evening she
was alert to any small change in the room, any movement outside in
the street; she was listening for footsteps that might approach along
the paving stones, turn in at the garden gate.

Matthew was sitting cross-legged in the wing chair by the fire,
a large foot in its leather slipper tapping out a silent beat. He had in
his hands a concordance, but Fanny noticed that he turned the pages
slowly. His head turned to the window when footsteps ran past the
building and continued up the street with a slapping sound.

At eleven, the clocks in the house began to chime, first the feminine
notes of the mantel clock, then the deeper sounds of the hall clock in
its oak casement, and then, a little late as always, the notes from the
dining room grandfather followed, wheezy with age. As the music
died away, spreading behind it the accustomed, well-ordered silence,
they heard, at last, the tread of feet along the garden path. A pause,
and then a hand took the knocker, let it slip with a crash, started again
with a series of heavy knocks.

Fanny immediately dropped her sewing, stood as if about to answer,
but Matthew motioned for her to wait while he went instead. She

moved quickly to the drawing room doorway, paused halfway out into the hall where she could see.

A woman in a thick tweed shawl stood on the doorstep, a white frill under a black bonnet, a full skirt of some plain heavy material, of the type worn by most working women – old-fashioned clothes, although she was not old. A young woman from the islands, come over perhaps to work at a post in one of the city's households.

In her arms, a small bundle of blankets.

She spoke in Gaelic, a low sing-song voice, clear and completely unintelligible. Then she tried again. 'Please, it is for the Missis.'

But Fanny was already there. She took the well-wrapped bundle into her arms, watched as a tiny arm appeared from between the folds, made a circling motion. She parted the rough cloth, a softer woollen shawl inside, and uncovered the face of a baby, wide awake but quiet, eyes that were more the colour of shadows in water than the blue they were to become one day; a tiny, perfectly proportioned face with a soft down of fair hair. The child turned her head to one side and attempted to suck the blanket. She made a small puzzled sound, and Fanny's face distorted into a crumple of amazement and love.

'Thank you,' she whispered. 'Tell them thank you.'

Fanny took the child upstairs while Matthew spoke some more with the woman, his eyes still on Fanny as she went.

Fanny sat on the nursing chair that had been placed ready by the lamp, slowly feeding the baby with warm milk from a teaspoon.

Soon she would hear Matthew running up the stairs.

'Anna Katriona,' Fanny whispered to the baby. 'Welcome home.'

ACKNOWLEDGEMENTS

I would like to thank John MacAulay whose book, *Sliochd nan Ron: Seal-Folk and Ocean Paddlers*, furnished much of the information used in this novel, with his kind permission. He introduced me to the work of David MacRitchie, upon whom I have based the fictional character of Gordon MacIntyre, and also to the letter in *The Times* newspaper of 1809, reporting a mermaid sighting in Western Scotland. Bill and Christine Lawson at the Seallam genealogy centre in Harris, are wonderful curators of the history of the islands. Enormous thanks to renowned artists Willie and Moira Fulton at the Ardbuidhe Cottage Gallery, Drinishader, where I began working on the book in earnest. Their generously shared memories were invaluable for understanding life on the islands. Thank you to Rev. Murdo Smith, Hamish Taylor, and the congregations at Manish and Scarista. And thank you to Hamish for trips on his boat.

Thank you to William and Helen Watson who first introduced us to the Hebrides; and to Jane Knight for her hospitality; also to the many wonderful people on Harris who have let their cottages to us over the years.

I owe a great debt to Patricia Law, Margaret Leroy and Nicola and Rhidian Brook-Sulman for reading the early and later drafts and for their encouragement to keep going. Many thanks to the tutors on the Oxford creative writing diploma, especially Antonia Logue-Bose who helped in finding a voice for the story; also to John Bahan, Kate Clanchy, Jane Draycott, Frank Egerton and Clare Morgan. Very many thanks to fellow writers on the course: Marianne Allen, Neville Beal, Alastair Beck, Sarah-Jane de Brito Martin, Sue Cox, Stephanie van Driel, Suellen Dainty, Pauline Fiennes, Nick Harries, Brian Harrison, James McDermott, Karen Pomerantz, Margaret Keeping, Peter Saxby, Nageena Shaheen and Fred Volans.

I would like to thank the tutors on the Royal Holloway University of London creative writing MA: Susanna Jones, Jo Shapcott and Andrew Motion. Very warm thanks for long-standing support from the tutor group: Emma Chapman, Tom Feltham, Carolina Gonzalez Carvajal, Kat Gordon, Lucy Hounsom, Liza Klaussmann and Rebecca Lloyd Jones.

Thanks to Marion Urch and Isabel Collins for help with editing and sorting out my bizarre spelling.

I am indebted to Jenny Hewson at the RCW agency who has taken on and championed the book to publication. Maddie West and Sara O'Keeffe at Corvus have been enormously encouraging and wise editors. Thanks to Lucy Ridout for copy-editing and to Melissa Marshall for proof-reading.

Many thanks to my husband, Josh, scientific illustrator and cartoonist, whose interest in evolution helped inform this book. Thank you to my wonderful parents, Joan and Frank, for raising us always in sight of a churchyard. Thank you to my amazing children, Hugh, Kirsty and George, who have lived with the Selkie story for a long time and who know the island well.

BIBLIOGRAPHY

CALDER, Jenni, *Scots in Canada*, Edinburgh: Luath, 2003

CAMERON, A. D., *Go Listen to the Crofters: The Napier Commission and Crofting a Century Ago*, Stornoway: Acair, 1997

CRAIG, David, *On The Crofters' Trail*, Edinburgh: Birlinn, 2007

DESMOND, Adrian and MOORE James, *Darwin*, London: Penguin, 2009

FAY SHAW, Margaret, *From the Alleghenies to the Hebrides*, Edinburgh: Birlinn, 2008

HALL, Christina, *Tales from an Island*, Edinburgh: Birlinn, 2008

JOHNSON, Alison, *A House by the Shore*, London: Warner Books, 1995

KOHN, Marek, *A Reason for Everything: Natural Selection and the English Imagination*, London: Faber and Faber, 2004

LAWSON, Bill, *Harris in History and Legend*, Edinburgh: Birlinn, 2008

MACAULAY, John M., *Sliochd nan Ron: Seal-Folk and Ocean Paddlers*, Cambridge: The White Horse Press, 1998

MACLEAN, Charles, *Island on the Edge of the World*, Edinburgh: Canongate, 2006

MACDONALD, Finlay J., *Crowdie and Cream and other stories: Memoirs of a Hebridean Childhood*, England: Time Warner, 2005

MACDONALD ROBERTSON, R., *Highland Folktales*, Colonsay: House of Lochar, 1998

MACLEOID, Fionnlagh, *Sgaile is Solas: Lasting Traces – Mingulay to Scarp: Robert M. Adam photographs,* Stornoway: Acair, 2007

MACNEICE, Louis, *I Crossed the Minch*, Edinburgh: Birlinn, 2007

MACRITCHIE, David, *Testimony of Tradition* 1890 (Project Gutenberg)

NICOLSON, Adam, *Sea Room*, London: HarperCollins, 2002

REA, F.G., *A School in South Uist, Reminiscences of a Hebridean Schoolmaster, 1890–1913, Edinburgh*: Birlinn, 2007

STEEL, Tom, *The Life and Death of St. Kilda*, London: HarperCollins, 1988

THOMPSON, David, *The People of the Sea: Celtic Tales of the Seal Folk*, Edinburgh: Canongate, 2001

WILLIS, Douglas, *Crofting*, Edinburgh: John Donald, 2001